MOONRAKER'S
BRIDE

By Madeleine Brent:

MOONRAKER'S BRIDE

TREGARON'S DAUGHTER

Madeleine Brent

Moonraker's Bride

DOUBLEDAY & COMPANY, INC.
GARDEN CITY, NEW YORK

MOONRAKER'S
BRIDE

« O N E »

ON THE morning of that day in March, in the Year of the Boar, when the ugly stranger came to Tsin Kai-feng, I opened my eyes at dawn and felt a pang of despair to find nothing had changed. I suppose this was foolish of me, for I had learned long ago that troubles rarely just disappear during the night. Mine were most unlikely to do so.

I had fifteen girl children and Miss Prothero to feed, and the small cellar we used for a larder was empty but for some potatoes and a few pounds of millet. There was only one answer to the problem. Today I would once again have to make the journey into the town of Chengfu and steal some money.

I shivered, pulling the worn blanket up about my shoulders and huddling down on the lumpy straw mattress which lay between me and the scrubbed floorboards. I knew from experience that it was useless for me to go begging in the streets of Chengfu. The people were generous and considered begging an honorable occupation because it gave them the opportunity to show charity, but the Beggars' Guild was very strict. They would never permit a young female person to engage in casual begging, especially one like me, for they counted me among the *yang kuei-tzu*—the foreign devils.

I had tried begging a year before, when I was sixteen, soon after Miss Prothero was first taken ill, but three men of the guild caught me. I spoke Mandarin Chinese as readily as they did, for I had been speaking it all my life, and luckily I managed to say something which made them laugh, otherwise they might have cut off my ears. As it was, they only gave me a good beating with canes. I remembered now how stiff my shoulders had been, and how I had told Miss Prothero lies when I got back to the Mission, pretending I had fallen in a ditch and hurt my back.

I was going to have to tell her more lies today, I thought gloomily.

Through the shutters I could hear the dawn chorus of birds in the courtyard, and knew that I was already late getting up. It was past six o'clock. No doubt I was unwilling to leave my bed because I was afraid of the day ahead, but it had to be faced. The walk to Chengfu would take me two hours each way, and there was much to be done before I could leave. From beyond the rag of curtain which separated me from the rest of the long room I could hear some of the children stirring. Kimi, the baby, had woken and was whimpering, but I could hear the voice of Yu-lan soothing her.

I threw back the blanket, got up, and quickly sponged myself down with water from the bowl I had filled before going to bed, then put on my jacket and trousers and slipped my feet into the thongs of my sandals. The thin quilting of my clothes was not very warm, but I knew that when I started to work I would be warm enough.

The only mirror in the whole Mission now was on the dressing table in Miss Prothero's room. Over the past winter I had sold almost everything that was not a necessity. But on the wall of my little cubicle was a long bronze shield, not hanging but set in the plaster of the wall, and I kept this polished to use as a mirror. Before Miss Prothero and her sister began their work in the village forty years earlier, the Mission had been a partly ruined and abandoned Chinese temple. The ancient bronze shield was the only relic of that time, for all the effigies of ferocious Chinese gods had been removed by the Misses Prothero when they restored the temple for use as a Mission School, long before I was born, even long before my mother and father had been sent out by the Christian China Mission to help them in their work.

I had no memory of my parents. They had both died in a cholera outbreak a year after I was born, and so had Miss Adelaide Prothero, leaving only her sister, Victoria.

I liked my strange mirror. The curve of the surface distorted everything, taking away the ugliness of my big round eyes and huge feet. The bronze disguised the freakish white color of my skin, especially in winter when there was no tanning from the sun to help me look a little more normal. When I looked in my mirror shield I could pretend that I was quite pretty, with smooth yellow skin, nice narrow eyes and tiny bound feet. I was glad Miss Prothero had never allowed the children's feet to be bound, because it made me look less strange among them.

I gave my hair a quick brush with a bundle of pine needles set in baked clay, then pulled back the curtain and walked between the two rows of mattresses, calling to the children to wake up. The baby lay well wrapped in a drawer I had taken from one of the desks in the schoolroom. Beside her squatted Yu-lan, who at fourteen was the oldest girl we had left at the Mission. She looked up with a smile as I knelt beside her.

"The little one has a new tooth, Lu-tsi. She will feel better now it has come." None of the children could pronounce my name properly. Lu-tsi was the nearest they could get to Lucy. By speaking in Chinese before midday, Yu-lan was breaking a rule. All the girls were supposed to speak in English throughout the morning, or at least try to, but with Miss Prothero ill in bed for months now I had been so busy that I simply could not spare time to help the girls with their English. In any case, I could not see that it mattered. Once they left the Mission it was unlikely they would ever speak it again.

I unwrapped the baby and was pleased to see that she seemed to be growing nicely, with good firm flesh, though that would not last long unless I could fill the empty shelves in our larder soon.

"Change her napkin, then feed her," I said to Yu-lan in Chinese.

"There is some milk left, Lu-tsi?"

"Just a little. I'll try to get some more in the village today. There's a scrap of dried fish, too. Mash it up with a knob of soybean cake, and add a little warm milk to help her swallow it easily."

I stood up and looked along the room. The children were pulling on their padded jackets and trousers, chattering like birds. Some of the little ones wanted to romp and play, but the older ones quickly restrained them. There was too much work to be done. Three of the girls were between ten and twelve, and I had put each of them in charge of a few smaller ones.

I called, "Pay attention, children. Chu-yi's band cleans the sleeping room, Mei-lin's band cleans the school, Mai-chai's band cleans the dining room and the corridors. When you've finished, the big girls must fetch water from the river for all children to wash clean—" There were wails of protest. They wanted pails of warm water heated in the kitchen, for this was our winter custom. "From the river," I repeated sternly. "Don't be such babies, the snow has been gone for days now, and I've no time for heating water today, I have to go into Chengfu. When everybody and everything is clean, we'll have the morning hymn in the schoolroom, and then breakfast."

Another burst of chatter broke out as the older girls began

[4]

to organize their little bands. I did not mind breaking Miss Prothero's rule about speaking English in the mornings, but her rules of cleanliness were so deeply ingrained in me that I would never think of breaking them. Besides, I knew how important they were. They had saved us from a great deal of infection and disease over the years. "Cleanliness is next to godliness, Lucy dear," I had heard her say a thousand times, and to be honest I think she placed cleanliness a little higher of the two.

I lingered for a moment to watch Yu-lan change the napkin. She was a very pretty girl and had a kind nature. Not for the first time I thought what a pity it was that Miss Prothero would not let me sell Yu-lan as a laborer or a concubine. She would become one or the other anyway, when she left the Mission, and we could not keep her much longer now. The money would have solved many problems for months to come, and I knew that old Mr. Chuan, who lived in the big house across the river, would gladly have bought her for a good price, for he had told me so.

But Miss Prothero always angrily refused such offers. "It's barbaric!" she would cry, her cheeks flushed with indignation. "Do they think we save their unwanted girl babies and bring them up only to sell them into concubinage or slavery?" Yet that is what happened to them when they left us, even though Miss Prothero always believed she had placed them in service with "a nice family." After spending more than half her life among the Chinese she still did not understand many of the ways they had followed for thousands of years. To me these ways seemed natural and inevitable, even if I did not like some of them very much, but perhaps I accepted them more easily because I had been born here. Where the girls were concerned, as the result was bound to be the same it seemed to me a pity that we gave them away for nothing when we could have got money for them. There were always new young mouths to feed.

I looked at the baby, and felt an ache in my heart at the

thought that if her mother had not brought her to the Mission she would have been left out in the cold at birth, to die of exposure, or perhaps been thrown into the river. I understood the Chinese far better than Miss Prothero, in fact most of the time I thought of myself as Chinese, but this was one custom I could not bear to dwell on. Strong sons would look after their parents when old age came, but girl children were useless, and so they were often allowed to die as soon as they were born. I would never understand it.

Yu-lan looked up and said, "What is for breakfast, Lu-tsi?"

"Today we have a change," I said, and smiled. "Instead of soybean milk and porridge we shall have porridge and soybean milk."

She gave a trill of laughter. I could always count on the girls to laugh with real merriment at the simplest joke repeated for the tenth time. "And for dinner, Lu-tsi?" she asked expectantly.

"Potatoes," I said, and gave a little shrug. There had been nothing but potatoes for dinner for a week now, and I had no heart to joke about it.

Yu-lan stood up, holding the baby, watching me with troubled eyes. "What will you do, Lu-tsi? The small ones are always hungry."

"Not hungry. Greedy." I tried to smile, but this time Yu-lan did not respond.

"Soon they will be hungry. We shall all be hungry."

"Don't be silly," I said impatiently. "None of you has gone hungry so far. At least, not very hungry. And there's enough food for two days."

"Where will you get food after that, Lu-tsi?"

I gave the only answer I could think of, the answer Miss Prothero had always given me whenever I asked such a question. "The Lord will provide," I said confidently, and turned away to go down to the kitchen, thinking of what I would have to do that day in Chengfu, and hoping that at least the Lord

[6]

would make sure I did not get caught while I was busy providing.

Ten minutes later I took Miss Prothero's breakfast to her in her little room overlooking the courtyard. As she sat propped up in bed she looked so gray and shrunken that it was hard to recognize her as the brisk, plump, warm hearted woman who had been a mother to me almost since I was born. She and her sister Adelaide had come to China forty years ago to set up one of the centers of the Christian China Mission. They must have been very remarkable women, for they had been through flood and pestilence, famine and wars, yet nothing had ever turned them from their task. Other helpers sent out by the C.C.M. had come and gone, but the Misses Prothero had remained.

In 1882 my parents, Charles and Mary Waring, were sent out. Miss Prothero had often told me that they were the finest helpers she ever had. By this time she and her sister were over fifty, and it was a great relief to them to feel that some of the work would now be lifted from their shoulders. But within eighteen months the cholera took them both, and Adelaide Prothero as well. At the same time the C.C.M. was beset by squabbles with missionary bodies of other sects, and withdrew from Northern China.

But Miss Victoria Prothero remained. I sometimes tried to imagine how it must have been for her at that time. She had twenty-two girls at the Mission, ten of them under five. She had Lucy Waring, a baby of six months. Her helpers and her sister were dead. There would be no more money or support from the C.C.M. And all this at a time when she had hoped to shed some of the burdens she had carried for so long. Somehow she had risen above sorrow and weariness, and braced herself to the task all over again. There was a legacy left by her father, untouched till now by either of the sisters. They had planned to use it to ease their old age, which they hoped to spend in England. She had transferred the money to a bank in

[7]

Chengfu, and eked it out over many years to keep the Mission going.

Often I did not understand Miss Prothero. She had many funny ways and strange ideas. But for all that she had done I loved and admired her more than any human being I had ever known.

She had been unable to leave her bed for six months, and I knew that she had little time to live now. Dr. Langdon, the American doctor I had brought from Chengfu to see her, had told me so. I cried that night, a strange sensation, for it was the first time I had cried since I was very small, but when I had dried my tears I realized that the only thing left for me to do was to protect Miss Prothero from all worry and difficulties during the time that remained to her.

Beyond that time I could not think at all. I remembered once asking Miss Prothero how she had ever managed to meet all the terrible troubles which had fallen upon her within a few weeks at the time of the cholera, and I had never forgotten her answer. "Whenever you can't think what to do, Lucy dear, just do whatever comes next and carry on from there."

What came next for me now was to go into Chengfu and steal some money, but I did not dare to tell Miss Prothero that. She gave me a vague little smile as I plumped up the lifeless old pillows at her back and set the tray on her lap. There was a cup of tea, with the last of the milk, and a bowl of food which was just the same as the food Yu-lan was now giving Kimi the baby, except that I had cooked and chopped up very small a sheep's liver I had got from a farmer for clearing a ditch yesterday.

"Thank you, Lucy dear, that looks very nice." Her voice was feeble but steady. She looked at me and frowned. "I do wish you would wear your nice dress, child."

She was speaking of a dress she had made for me when I was six, a dress of pale green cotton with a pleated skirt. It was the only English dress I had ever had, and I could still remem-

[8]

ber how I hated it because it made me look like the foreign devil I was instead of like the rest of the children.

"It's being washed, Miss Prothero," I said, and thought sadly that there was today's first lie for the Recording Angel to write down on Lucy Waring's page of his book. I think Miss Prothero had been too busy keeping us all alive and well over the years to do as much preaching as she would have wished, but she had always read to us from the Bible once a day and given us a little talk, so I knew about the Recording Angel.

I always imagined him sitting at a big school desk, writing in his ledger with a golden pen. For some strange reason his body was like the body of a bee, striped yellow and black, and he wore glasses. I never dared to think how many pages he had used up on me. Apart from four trips to Chengfu for stealing, I had been telling lies to Miss Prothero for months now.

Almost a year ago her memory had begun to fail. She did not know that all her money had gone at last, even though the manager of the bank had told her so and written letters about it. Soon after this she became too weak to make the journey into Chengfu, and so she wrote a note authorizing me to draw money on her behalf. Mr. Wei, the manager, was very polite to me considering I was just a girl, but explained that there was no money left. That was when I had to start stealing. I could think of nothing else to do. Almost every winter since I could remember, I had seen starvation, and I could not bear the thought of it coming to our children.

Miss Prothero said, "Do wear your pretty dress tomorrow, Lucy. I don't like to see you in trousers all the time. You must always remember that you are an *English* child, dear. That does not make you *better* than a Chinese child, of course, but it is right to take pride in your own country. I don't like to see you going native, you know."

"Yes, Miss Prothero." I sat down on the chair beside the bed. "Eat up your breakfast before it gets cold."

"Breakfast?" She looked down at the tray. "Oh, yes. I'm afraid I'm not very hungry, Lucy."

[9]

"But you must eat your breakfast. Dr. Langdon said the medicine he gave me is to be taken after meals."

She nodded, her eyes wandering vaguely. "It does help to take the pain away. Will you be able to get some more, dear?"

"Yes, he told me to come again before the bottle was empty."

She picked up the fork and began to eat slowly. After a moment or two her expression became more alert and a touch of her usual brisk manner returned. She said, "Are you keeping everywhere clean and shining, Lucy? And the children, too?"

"Yes, Miss Prothero. All the Daily Duties are being done, just the same as ever."

"And the baby? What did we call her . . . ?"

"Kimi. She's very well. All the children are well at the moment."

"I haven't heard the morning hymn yet, dear."

"That comes later, Miss Prothero. After cleaning and before breakfast."

"Of course. How silly of me." I saw her go rigid for a moment as she suppressed a wince of pain. "Now it's time for your reading, Lucy. What shall it be? A chapter from Mr. Borrow or Mr. Trollope, or perhaps some pages from Lord Tennyson's *In Memoriam* . . . ? No dear, I think after all it would be nice to read from one of the lady novelists. We'll have something from Miss Austen."

This was a daily custom, and had been so ever since I could read. Miss Prothero had always been determined that I should never forget the proper use of my mother tongue, and so for half an hour each morning I would sit and read to her, and for an hour each evening we would indulge in what she called the art of conversation.

I enjoyed the books, though often I could scarcely understand them. I knew what the words meant, but the stories took place in the strange world of the foreign devils and were quite baffling to me. The world I knew daily was made up of the Mission and the little village of Tsin Kai-feng at the foot of the hill, a village which held two or three hundred souls within the bounds of its ancient mud-brick walls. I knew every person in the village by name, knew their customs and the way they thought. The world that Miss Prothero knew best, the world in which she had spent the first thirty years of her life and now tried to teach me about, had no more reality for me than a land described in a fairy tale.

Still, I did not find the daily reading a waste of time. I had read Miss Prothero's collection of books several times over, and no longer had to concentrate while reading aloud. This gave me a quiet half hour every day in which I could think about the problems facing me and try to make plans.

Sometimes it was very disheartening to find how seldom my plans succeeded. Last year I had tried to make use of the small patch of ground behind the Mission for growing vegetables to store for the winter. It was very barren ground, and because it lay on top of the hill it became parched during the hot weeks of summer. With the older children I had carried buckets of water from the river for two or three hours every morning, but we could never seem to satisfy the thirsty earth.

Miss Prothero had been full of enthusiasm for the work, and held special prayers for our little patch of crops, but when the time came for Harvest Festival we had only a few sacks of beans and some rather spongy potatoes to show for all the months of hard work.

As I sat reading to Miss Prothero now I decided that I would have to try harder with growing our own food this year. It was a pity the Mission had not been set up in the south, where it was easy to grow rice. Here in the north we could only grow small rice, as it was called, which was really a kind of millet, and anyway our patch of ground was unsuitable.

I thought that if I worked for a few days without payment for Mr. Hsun the farmer, who was quite a kindly man, he might help by telling me what crops to grow and how best to raise them. I also had in mind that we might try to rear silk-worms and sell the cocoons to a merchant in Chengfu. We had no mulberry trees, on which the silkworms feed, but I thought that if I could get some tasar worm eggs we might hatch them in the kitchen, if we could keep it warm enough, and then feed the worms on oak leaves until they spun their cocoons.

These cocoons would only give wild silk, not true silk, which meant that the merchant would pay less for them, but if everything went right and we could raise enough cocoons I would be able to keep us all fed for a few weeks at least. I wished I knew more about it, but I was ready to try anything that might save me from going on stealing expeditions, for every time I was more frightened than the last.

When I finished reading the chapter from *Pride and Prejudice* I saw that Miss Prothero had eaten only half her breakfast and was lying back against the pillows with her eyes closed. I thought she had fallen asleep, but as I put the book back on the shelf she said, "Have you planned the day's work, Lucy? I hope you're being methodical, dear. Always remember that a little careful forethought saves time and labor in the long run."

"Yes, Miss Prothero, I've worked everything out for today. After breakfast I'll give the children lessons, and in the afternoon, when it's not so cold, I'll see if Mr. Hsun can find half a day's work for the older ones. Mei-lin can supervise the little girls while they do some patching and mending." I hesitated, then went on, "I have to go into Chengfu myself this afternoon."

"Whatever for, Lucy?"

"To go to the bank for some money." That was another lie, and there were more to come, I thought unhappily.

"Money?" Miss Prothero opened her eyes and looked surprised. "But you went in for money only a month or two ago, dear. Surely you can't have spent two whole sovereigns since then?"

I felt suddenly very shaky and agitated inside. Miss Prothero always seemed to remember the few things I didn't want her to remember. On my last expedition to Chengfu I had managed to steal a few silver tael from a man who had come into town to sell some donkeys and had got so drunk in one of the wine houses that he could scarcely stand up. When Miss Prothero asked me about my trip, I told her I had drawn two sovereigns from the bank—and this of all things had remained in her feeble memory.

"I'm sorry, but the money's all gone," I said, feeling a little desperate.

"Two whole sovereigns." She shook her head sadly. "Really, dear, you must try to be more thrifty."

"I haven't wasted any of it, truly, Miss Prothero."

"I should hope not, child. But when you go to the village market you must shop more *carefully*. The stall-keepers always ask far more than they expect to get. Really, you used to be very good at beating them down to the lowest price. I can't think what's come over you."

"I'm sorry, Miss Prothero. I'll try to do better."

"Very well, Lucy. Now run along. It must be nearly time for the morning hymn, and you have to get breakfast ready for the children first."

"It won't take me long. I'll come and see you after breakfast, when I've heated some water to wash you."

"Thank you, dear. You're a very good girl. Just do try not to be careless with the money. It doesn't grow on trees, you know."

"I'll remember, Miss Prothero." I took the tray and went out of the bedroom. In the hall I had to stand still for a little while because it seemed that everything was shaking about inside my chest and trying to come out. I don't know what made it happen to me just then, but I managed not to cry and I was very glad of that. I felt that if ever the children saw me in tears they would think the world had come to an end. With Miss Prothero so ill, I was the only one they had to care for them, and I could not let them see how worried I was. If Lu-tsi cried, they would be very frightened.

Down in the kitchen the millet gruel was boiling and so was

another saucepan of water for making tea. We had managed to grow a little patch of tea last year, and had made bricks by pressing the damp leaves in a mold. I counted the bricks of tea in the jar, and found there were enough left for three days.

Above I could hear Yu-lan's voice as she called the children to assembly in the school hall. I went up to join them and watched them settle into their seats, picking up the cards with the day's hymn written out on them. Sitting down at the creaky old harmonium, I looked at the hymn Yu-lan had chosen. It was *Bread of Heaven*. I could read no music, but I had learned to play four hymn tunes automatically. I struck a chord and turned to the children.

"All stand up," I said in English, "and sing very loudly so Miss Prothero will hear. Yu-lan, I think you'd better take Kimi outside in case the noise frightens her." I had to say that twice in English, and use the Chinese word for "frighten," before Yu-lan understood.

"Ready, children? One, two, three . . . *now!*"

The hymn began. One way in which I knew I was a foreign devil was that I could follow and understand a tune in the same way as Miss Prothero. To the Chinese children the melody meant nothing, and neither did the time. They simply shrieked out the words, all on the same note and as fast as possible. There was no pause between the verses, and I had to play faster and faster to keep up.

Chu-yi finished first, but I was very close behind, and then came the older ones who happened to be a little slow, followed finally by the small ones who were slower still. When everybody had finished we said the Lord's Prayer, and this time Mei-lin won.

"All right, children, breakfast now. Go and get your spoons and wait quietly at table."

They all marched out, each one showing me her hands as I stood at the door to make sure they were clean, then I called Chu-yi to the kitchen to help me share out the food in fifteen bowls.

The morning passed quickly, all too quickly for me. I dreaded the moment when I would have to set off for Chengfu. While I was giving a lesson on how to use the abacus I sent Yu-lan to see Mr. Hsun at his farm a mile along the road and to ask if he could offer any work. He kept her waiting for nearly an hour to mark her insignificance, but then said that although he had no work for us today he would be making mud bricks for a new wall next day, and would pay a few cash for four of the big girls to come and trample the mud and straw together, ready for molding into bricks. I was very pleased, because a few cash would at least buy some milk for Kimi.

At midday we ate hot mashed potatoes, and then I went to my cubicle to change for the journey. I pulled on my warm felt boots and the coat I had made from an old blanket, then settled a conical straw hat on my head. I liked the hat because it helped me to look more like everybody else, but there was a hood attached to my coat in case the wind became cold. My hands were trembling already, not with cold but with fear. I rubbed them hard and pushed them up my sleeves. Then, ashamed of my cowardice, I told myself that it would not matter if I delayed just for five minutes, and I went to the box which stood at the head of my rolled mattress.

It was a small box made of rough wood, but it was important to me because it contained everything I treasured. There was nothing of real value, for I had sold my father's watch and my mother's silver bracelet long ago, before I began stealing, but there was a rather blurred photograph of my parents, a prayer book, some embroidery samplers my mother had made, and a piece of fading blue ribbon which I had been keeping for my hair, to be used on a special occasion, though I could never imagine what that special occasion might be. There were also my summer sandals, which had been made for me as a present by two of the ten-year-old girls, a thin pile of yellowing photographs and illustrations, cut from magazines and newspapers which had occasionally found their way to the Mission over past years, and . . . the picture.

The picture had held and haunted me ever since I had first discovered it three years ago under a thick layer of dust in a recess of the larger cellar where we kept logs for our winter fires. It was drawn in black ink, or some black substance, on very coarse canvas that was light brown in color. There was no frame, and the edges of the canvas were irregular, as if it had been roughly hacked out from a larger piece. I thought the canvas might be useful for patching, and it was only when I had cleaned away all the dust that I discovered the drawing. It covered an area about twenty inches long and rather more than half as deep. At first the picture seemed distorted, but when I stretched it over a piece of board it sprang to life.

There was a fine house, standing on a ridge or hill with a line of trees to one side. Tall chimneys rose from a steeply pitched roof. The gables were straight, not incurving and with upturning eaves as we had in China. There were two rows of elegantly proportioned rectangular windows, and a handsome entrance. Just beneath the line of the roof, in the center, was a single semicircular window. In front of the end gables were two parapets, with stone balls set on short pillars. The walls were partly covered by some sort of climbing plant which I imagined to be ivy. The drawing was bold and confident, almost casual, as if it had been dashed off quickly by the hand of a skilled artist. Beneath the picture and to one side was a single word: Moonrakers.

Miss Prothero had no idea where the drawing might have come from. "It must have been here before *my* time, Lucy," she said. "What a strange thing to be sure. It's an English house, of course."

"Who was here before you, Miss Prothero?"

"Why nobody, dear, except some temple priests, I suppose. But the whole place was badly damaged during the Opium Wars, and was left deserted for years before Adelaide and I came."

[16]

"Is Moonrakers the name of the artist, do you think?"

"Good heavens no, child. Whoever heard of anybody called that?"

"I don't know, Miss Prothero. I don't know much about English names. They all sound strange to me."

"Yes, of course, dear. How silly of me." She gave a little sigh. "I do wish you didn't think so much like a Chinese child, but I can scarcely blame you. It's my own fault. I should have found some way to send you home to England long ago."

She had said this many times before, and I had stopped worrying about it now. "Is Moonrakers the name of the house, then?" I asked.

"Yes, I should think so, dear."

"What does it mean? It sounds like something very tall, to rake the moon, but the house isn't as tall as some of the pagodas in Chengfu."

"No, there's another meaning, and I've come across it somewhere, but that was years ago and I can't remember now."

Miss Prothero did not seem to find the picture or the circumstances surrounding it particularly interesting, and she scarcely mentioned it again. But I was fascinated, not only by the picture itself but also by the mystery behind it, and often I would try to make up a story to account for that strange piece of canvas, on which an unknown hand had drawn, lying lost in an abandoned Chinese temple all down the years.

The house itself held an uncanny attraction for me. From the first moment, my heart seemed to reach out toward it, and that sense of yearning had not faded since, though I could not even begin to understand it in myself.

It was a fine house, but that meant little to me, and there were no doubt many far more splendid even than this. Perhaps the attraction lay in the fact that it was an English house. I had never known my parents, never had the chance to absorb any love of England from them, but it may be that the blood carries memories unknown to the mind, and that the longing I felt was for my own kind rather than for the house itself.

I was certain that an English hand had made the sketch, and I felt that it had been drawn lovingly. Perhaps this was why the picture restored me when I was troubled. I could sit and gaze at it, imagining the rooms within, or how the surroundings would look as the seasons changed, and when I put the picture away to set about whatever problem came next, there was a new quietness and hope in me. It was not a feeling which lasted for very long, but at least it was enough to help me take the initial plunge into whatever fresh difficulty had to be faced.

Sometimes I felt ashamed of being so babyish, for I realized that I was using the picture as a kind of comforter, in the same way that the little children used rag dolls when they were tucked up in their blankets for the night.

On this occasion the magic did not work very well. Although I stood looking at the picture, I hardly saw it. My mind was busy with what I would have to do in Chengfu that day. It was as I put the picture away in my box that I heard Yu-lan calling: "Lu-tsi! The husband of Liu has come for you. He says the time of her baby is near."

A great wave of relief swept me. Now I could not go to Chengfu. By the time Liu's baby was delivered it would be too late for me to make the journey. Of course, it meant that we would be another day nearer to having no food at all, and I would have to go on a stealing expedition tomorrow, come what might, but I was still glad of the reprieve.

Five minutes later, with Miss Prothero's big leather case weighing me down, I was on my way to the village with Liu's husband beside me. His name was Lok, and he did not attempt to help me carry the case. Miss Prothero would have given him a good telling-off, but I knew that he was not really behaving badly, he simply felt that it was a woman's work. Miss Prothero had trained as a midwife in London before coming to China, and I had helped her deliver babies from the time I was fourteen, as well as stitching, splinting, and bandaging for villagers who had hurt themselves in their daily work. Since Miss Prothero had been confined to her bed I had delivered more than twenty babies on my own.

Some of the village women would not let us have anything to do with them at such times, because we were foreign devils and they were afraid the gods might be displeased, but there were now many women, and their men too, who were glad to call in Miss Prothero because they found that babies she delivered were more likely to survive, and so were the mothers. Now this mantle of success had fallen upon me, because I was her helper. I had been very lucky, and felt enormously grateful that I had lost only two babies out of the twenty or more, and I think even Miss Prothero could not have saved them. The village folk could never grasp that the secret of our great magic was mainly a matter of keeping everything as clean and antiseptic as possible.

This was Liu's third baby, and was more difficult than the first two had been because it was the wrong way round, but luckily Lok had come for me in good time, so I hoped I would be able to put things right. I would have been frightened if there had been time to think. As it was, I just wished fleetingly but desperately that Miss Prothero had been there to take charge, and then there was no time to spare even for wishing. After ten minutes of strenuous effort I was soaked with sweat, and so was poor Liu after such a mauling, but I had managed the all-important task of turning the baby.

Now I took off my clothes and put on one of the special smocks from the suitcase. This smock, like the sheets we kept specially for childbirth, had been boiled in water containing carbolic. I scarcely had time to prepare Liu and to go through all the cleansing and antiseptic precautions Miss Prothero had taught me when the birth began. Liu always had her babies quickly once they started, and in less than two hours it was all over. I was truly happy to find the baby was a boy, for Liu and

[19]

Lok already had one girl child and had kept her instead of leaving her to die or handing her over to us at the Mission. They were good people, and I was glad for them to have another son.

When I had done all that I could to see that Liu and her baby were comfortable I called Lok to see his new son, then went into the fodder store to wash once again and change back into my clothes. As I repacked the case, feeling glad that I had not had to use the forceps or do any stitching, I heard a chatter of excited voices from a little way off. The moment I appeared in the narrow street a dozen people began to call me.

"Lu-tsi! Come and speak!"

"Here is a new foreign devil, with gold hair!"

"Will his eye bring evil if he looks upon us, Lu-tsi?" Then I saw him. Some of the bolder villagers were standing near the pony on which he sat, others were hanging back fearfully. They had long ago become used to Miss Prothero and to me, but this was a new foreign devil, much stranger than either of us, and even more ugly. His hair was the color of pale gold, his eyes blue as a summer sky. His face was neither yellow nor white, but weathered to a light bronze. The blue eyes were round, as unpleasantly round as my own except that he kept them narrowed as he looked about him. He wore breeches, a short topcoat the color of sand, and no hat. A long bundle wrapped in a mackintosh sheet was strapped across the crupper of his pony. He looked like a man who had traveled for many days, or perhaps even weeks, and had often slept by the roadside in his clothes, but in spite of this he had the air of a man more accustomed to command than to obey.

He sat at ease, just inside the south gate of the village, gazing with a detached manner at the crowd gathered about him. As I drew near he lifted a hand to quieten the chatter, consulted a slip of paper in his other hand, then pronounced a few words which were meant to be Chinese, though I would never have guessed it if I had not been used to hearing Miss Prothero speak Chinese. Even after so many years in the country she had a very strong foreign accent. The ugly stranger repeated the words, and I just managed to understand something of what he was trying to say: "I look . . . place . . . big man . . . knife bent."

He paused and looked up. When he saw the uncomprehending faces all about him he shrugged, and his lips tightened with annoyance. The crowd pushed me toward him, the fearful ones no doubt hoping I could placate this foreign devil. I said, "Good afternoon, sir. Can I help you?"

He leaned forward to peer at my face, but evidently it was shadowed by the straw coolie hat I wore, for he said, "Take your hat off, girl." As I obeyed he straightened up in the saddle and said, "I'll be damned. You're English. What are you doing here?"

"I just came down to the village to deliver a baby, sir."

The brows over his cold eyes rose slowly. "Did you now? And how old are you?"

"Seventeen, sir."

"And you came down from where?"

"The Mission School." I pointed. "Up there on the hill."

"What do you do at the Mission School up there on the hill?"

"I've always been there, sir. I look after the children."

The villagers were nodding to one another, pleased. They could not understand a word, but they felt proud to have produced somebody who could talk to this foreign devil in his own tongue. It gave them much face.

The ugly stranger said, "What's your name, girl?"

"Lucy Waring, sir." Automatically I bobbed a little curtsy, as Miss Prothero had taught me. Then suddenly, for a moment or two, I forgot all about the Chinese ways and customs which made me so polite and submissive to any male person. It must have been something in my English blood which sparked off a wave of anger and dislike toward this man for the brusqueness of his manner. I felt color rush to my cheeks, and I tried to think how the young ladies in *Pride and Preju-*

dice would have acted. This was exceptionally foolish, even for me, for those young ladies were rich and lived in big houses with many servants, while I was Lucy Waring with an empty larder and fifteen mouths to feed. However, I said in a very cool voice, "Pray do not trouble to introduce yourself if it embarrasses you to do so."

I felt immensely proud of that, for it seemed to me to be quite crushing, but the ugly stranger was not at all crushed. He looked at me appraisingly for several seconds, then said, "Falcon. Robert Falcon. Is the baby all right?"

The unexpected question threw me into confusion. "Baby?" I echoed, almost stammering. "Oh . . . yes. I mean, yes, thank you. I had to turn him in the womb, but he's all right and so is the mother."

To my surprise the ugly stranger grinned. It was a hard, sour grin, but I caught a brief glint of genuine amusement in his eyes. "By God, I'd enjoy turning you loose in a few English drawing rooms, Lucy Waring. Your brand of conversation would set the good ladies back on their heels, I fancy—if they had such things. But English ladies don't exist below the waist, of course."

I had no idea what he meant, but I found that my moment of indignation had passed. I now felt shy instead. The Europeans I had known in all my life could be counted on the fingers of one hand, and all of them had been quite old. This was the first young Englishman I had ever seen, and though I naturally thought him ugly he stirred peculiar feelings inside me. I put my hat on again, so my face was partly hidden, and said, "I must go back to the Mission. Is there anything I can do for you first, Mr. Falcon?"

I thought perhaps he might want to buy food in the village, or a night's lodging, but he said, "I'll walk up the hill with you." He swung down from the saddle, took my case from me, then walked beside me through the south gate, leading his pony. I could hear the villagers exclaiming in astonishment to see him carrying the case for an unimportant female person, but I tried to look as if this was exactly what I had expected.

As we followed the track leading up the hill he said, "Do you know of a temple near here? An old one?"

It was hard not to smile at such a question. "There are hundreds of them, sir, and most of them are old. There are big ones and small ones, some in use and some abandoned. You can see them near every village and all the way along the road to Chengfu, though quite a lot are hidden in groves of trees off the road."

He said, "I'm looking for a particular one."

"Is it a temple of Buddha, or Confucius, or one of the old Chinese gods?"

"You have all kinds to offer?"

"Oh yes, Mr. Falcon. You see—"

"Never mind," he broke in impatiently. We had reached the top of. the hill now. He halted by the Mission wall, putting down my case and opening his coat. From an inner pocket he took a flat leather wallet and drew out a folded piece of parchment. Spreading this against the saddle of the pony, he gestured for me to look at it. The map was hand-drawn in black ink. There was no scale, but I saw one or two hills marked, a river, a few groves of trees, and a walled town or village. No names were lettered on the map.

"Some of the features are missing," said Mr. Falcon. "There's a second map showing the other features, and they can't be read properly until they're put together. But this is the area where the temple is supposed to be, and perhaps there's enough here for you to recognize the place."

After only a moment or two I shook my head. "It could be one of a hundred places, sir. Small villages in China are much alike. I only know it's not here, because the course of the river is wrong."

He shrugged, folded the parchment and put it away, then said, "Are you good at riddles?"

"I don't think so. I haven't had much practice, Mr. Falcon.

Was that a riddle you were trying to ask the people down in Tsin Kai-feng?"

"Yes. A phonetic translation I got from an English merchant in Tientsin who claimed he spoke Chinese well. A false claim, I fancy. Did you understand a word of it?"

"Not very much, sir. In Chinese the same word can have different meanings according to the tone that's used, so it's rather difficult for a foreign dev—I mean, a foreign person." I went on hastily, "But I think there was something about a big man and a bent knife."

"My God, was that how it came out?" He shook his head and gave a bleak smile. "Well, listen to it in full, in English:

> *"Above the twisted giant's knife*
> *Where the wind-blown blossom flies*
> *Stands the temple where fortune lies.*
> *Beyond the golden world reversed*
> *Marked by the bear-cub of the skies*
> *Rest the sightless tiger's eyes."*

I wondered if Mr. Falcon was making a joke, but he looked at me with a raised eyebrow and there was no humor in his face.

"I'm sorry," I said apologetically. "I don't understand. Does it mean a twisted giant or a giant with a twisted knife?"

He shrugged again. "That's the first of many questions you could ask, but I have no answers. I wondered if the villagers have a legend about a giant, preferably with a sword or knife. Perhaps he cut a pass through a mountain, or dug a valley for a river—you know the sort of thing."

"The people in Tsin Kai-feng have their legends, but nothing to fit your riddle, sir."

"Listen to it once again." He repeated the two verses slowly. "Does nothing strike you? Nothing at all?"

"No, sir. Only that it seems very bad poetry."

[24]

"You're an expert?"

I flushed. "No, but I've read Miss Prothero's volumes of Tennyson and Wordsworth."

"I see. Well, this was written by my grandfather."

Now I felt the blood drain from my cheeks, for I knew that I had insulted Mr. Falcon's ancestor. It was scarcely possible to imagine a worse offense.

He went on, "This wasn't meant to be a poem, or even verse. It's just doggerel."

I stammered, "Yes, sir. I'm very sorry."

"Don't look so stricken, girl. I doubt if he could have written a decent line of poetry to save his life—which was somewhat short in any event. The young fool got himself killed in a duel when he was my age."

I heaved an inward sigh of relief. I had been thinking as a Chinese, knowing that they revered and worshiped their ancestors. Evidently Mr. Falcon had no such feelings toward his forebears, and was not offended. He stood with a hand resting on the saddle, his cold eyes thoughtful. He was gazing past me, and it almost seemed that he had forgotten my presence. After a few moments he left the pony and strolled on a few paces to where the ground was scarred by a black circle. This was the place where the ashes from the big range in the kitchen were put when we cleaned it out each week. Most of the fine wood ash soon blew away or was washed into the ground, but there were several heavily charred sticks lying there. The ugly stranger picked up one of them and stood facing the outer wall which surrounded the Mission, then he reached out and made a bold black stroke on the wall.

For a moment I could not imagine what he was doing, and then I caught my breath with astonishment. As the blackened stick scraped on the stone, a face began to appear on the wall. I would never have believed that such a clear picture could be made with so few strokes. The face, drawn several times larger than life-size, was a man's face, lean-jawed and wide-mouthed. The hair was thick and curly, reaching well down the cheeks.

The nose was long, and one corner of the mouth was upcurved in a half smile. Then I saw magic performed, as with a quick scribble the ugly stranger put in the eyes; they were just charcoal marks on rough stone, yet they were eyes which lived, sparkling with a kind of wicked laughter.

Mr. Falcon tossed the stick aside and brushed his hands. With a jerk of his head toward the face on the wall he said, "Do you know him?"

I was too astonished to speak, and could only shake my head. Mr. Falcon walked back to the pony. "It's quite possible you'll see something of him one fine day," he said. "If so, he'll ask the same questions I've asked, and recite the same riddle. I advise you not to mention that you've met me."

"But where's the harm in it, sir?" I asked, feeling more puzzled every second.

"The harm? I'll tell you." His eyes were grim. "He may well think you've helped me with the riddle and that I've paid you not to help *him* in the same way. Then you wouldn't be safe, Lucy Waring, for that one's dangerous. He has a devious mind, and he's the most ruthless devil you're ever likely to meet."

When I looked at the bold, startling portrait on the wall I could believe it, for there were demons in his eyes. Yet quite without reason or logic I felt that if ever I met this man he would not be dangerous to me. In any case, I thought it very unlikely that another foreign devil would come visiting Tsin Kai-feng and asking riddles.

Mr. Falcon was tightening the pony's girth now, and as I watched him a thought stole into my mind. He was an Englishman, and even though he was traveling in rough fashion he was bound to have some money. If I could beg a little from him, perhaps I would not have to go stealing in Chengfu for a week or more. I would be grateful even for a day's delay.

I had seen beggars at work, both in the village and in Chengfu, so I knew how to do it. I hunched my shoulders, drawing down the corners of my mouth and letting my head loll to one side, at the same time rubbing my hands feebly together and adopting a limp as I moved toward him, dragging one foot.

"Please, sir," I said in a whining voice, "please give me money. The Mission lady is very ill, and I have fifteen children to feed. We have no food, sir. Please help . . ." My voice faltered genuinely then, for to my surprise I was suddenly swept by a feeling of bitter shame. There was no cause for shame, I was only begging, which was better than stealing, but the words stuck in my throat as I tried to go on whining and pleading.

Next moment an open hand struck me so sharply across the face that my hat flew off and I staggered.

"How *dare* you?" His voice was low but hard. "You're not some starving peasant. You're a girl with advantages—it's in your voice, your face, the way you move. How dare you degrade yourself by begging?"

He put a foot in the stirrup and swung up into the saddle. Evidently he expected no answer to his question, and for the moment I had none to give. I was too confused. As I stood with a hand to my aching cheek, some corner of my mind was absorbing the fact that the ugly stranger and I lived in two different worlds. In his world it was shameful to beg. In mine it was no dishonor. But I partly belonged in his world also, for it was a heritage in my blood. I had felt the shame myself, so deep that I could well use it to measure his contempt.

He sat his horse, looking down at me with empty blue eyes, and said, "It dawns on me that you're a liar. I'll not believe you have charge of children or that you'd be trusted to deliver babies. Perhaps the riddle meant something to you and you lied about that, too? Well, so be it. I'll find what I'm seeking in my own way." He jerked a thumb at the picture he had drawn on the wall. "But by God, be careful how you lie to *him* if he comes your way, girl."

I found my voice, shaky though it was. I wanted to apologize for begging. I wanted to say that I had told him no lies.

And I wanted to make him come and look in our larder and then ask him what advantages he thought I had.

"Mr. Falcon," I began, "I'm very sorry—"

Even as I spoke he turned the pony, patted its neck, dug in his heels and said, "Go, Moonraker." Then they were away, going down the hill at a good canter. I watched them skirt the village and turn south along the road which led away from Chengfu.

Moonraker.

The name echoed in my mind. He had called his pony Moonraker. And in my box of treasures was that mysterious picture of a great house called Moonrakers drawn on coarse canvas long ago by a hand as bold and skillful as Robert Falcon's had been as he slashed that quick likeness on the wall with a charred stick.

A shiver ran through me. I had the eerie impression that I had unwittingly roused some nameless ghost which would haunt me until I had done whatever was needed to bring it peace again.

«TWO»

I PICKED UP the case and trudged along the wall to where the Mission gate was set. The sun was going down. I felt tired and angry and ashamed, all at the same time, and my head ached.

That evening I was bad-tempered with the children, and during the night I had troubled dreams in which I was pursued by a huge Chinese giant carrying a twisted knife. As I fled, the ugly stranger galloped by on Moonraker. I called to him for help, but he only turned his head and cried, "How *dare* you beg, girl?" then galloped on, chanting the strange riddle he had asked me. When I looked over my shoulder the giant was almost upon me, but his face was no longer Chinese, it had changed to the face of the dangerous foreign devil Robert Falcon had drawn in order to warn me.

Then I woke, and lay gazing up through the narrow window as the stars faded and dawn crept across the sky. At first I felt the overwhelming relief that comes with waking from a nightmare, but that feeling was short-lived, for I knew that to-day there could be no further reprieve. I would have to go into Chengfu and steal, for today the last scraps of food would be gone.

That morning I went through all the usual routine of work, trying to keep my mind blank. Miss Prothero seemed in less pain and was very sleepy, too sleepy to ask any awkward questions, and I was thankful for that. After an early dinner I put on my coat and felt boots, and spent a few minutes giving instructions to Yu-lan, as she would be in charge while I was away.

"At what hour will you come home, Lu-tsi?" she asked as she followed me to the door, carrying Kimi.

"I won't be home until well after dark," I said, "so you'll have to get supper for the children. Just give them whatever's left." I hesitated, then went on, "And just in case I'm delayed or—or something happens to prevent me getting home to-night, you'd better have this."

Stitched into the hem of my jacket was a silver tael. It had been there for weeks, and it was my precious reserve. Miss Prothero had always said how important it was to have something tucked away for a rainy day, and I had kept this for an emergency. If I was caught stealing in Chengfu there would be a real emergency, so I picked at the stitches with my fingernail, squeezed the coin out and gave it to Yu-lan. She stared at me in alarm and said, "But you *will* come back, Lu-tsi?"

"Yes, of course. But you're very grown-up now, so if something unexpected happens you'll be able to manage somehow. That money will be enough to feed everybody for a few days, as long as you're careful. And after that . . ."

My voice trailed away. After that, I could not begin to think what Yu-lan would do. She was still looking at me hopefully so I said, "After that, you'll just have to do whatever comes next." Without waiting for an answer I opened the door and set off down the broad pathway which led to the gate.

[30]

The village of Tsin Kai-feng stood in a broad loop of the river which ran at the foot of the hill. It was too small to have any government official in charge of it, even a magistrate, which was the lowest rank of official, and so it came under the Mandarin of Chengfu, who ignored it except when the time came to send the tax-gatherers.

When I reached the bridge over the river I turned and looked back. There on the hillcrest was the Mission, the only home I had ever known, a place of gray brick, two stories high, built around three sides of a courtyard, with the long double-tiered roof curving up at the eaves, and a small marble pagoda, part of the original temple, rising from the western corner.

On one side was a big old cedar, and on the other some clumps of oleander and two plum trees which I looked out upon from my bedroom window. The plum trees were very ancient, and there had once been more of them, so Miss Prothero said, but it was years since the remaining two had borne fruit. The patch of ground I called our farm was on the far side and hidden from me.

As I turned and stepped out quickly along the road I tried to thrust anxiety out of my mind, but it kept returning. I must not be caught stealing. I *must* not. Chengfu was governed by a very important person, a three-button mandarin whose name was Huang Kung, and he was the terror of all wrongdoers. Over the years I had often crossed the square outside the House of Justice, where punishments were carried out. Many people would gather there for the entertainment when a whipping or an execution took place. Once, by chance, I had glimpsed the executioner myself, a grim figure clad in a black leather jerkin and carrying his big curved sword. That was enough for me. I had not lingered to watch.

I knew that even under Mandarin Huang Kung's judgment I would not lose my head just for stealing, at least not the first time. In these modern days, with a new century about to dawn, punishments were much lighter than in the past. Even so, I would be beaten severely if I was lucky but would more probably lose a hand if the mandarin was in a bad temper when my case was tried, particularly when he saw that I was a foreign devil. Huang Kung was renowned as a hater of foreign devils, and considered them all barbarians.

To stop myself thinking about what lay ahead I began to recite to myself all the pieces I knew from a book of plays by a man called William Shakespeare. This was one of Miss Prothero's favorite books for my morning reading. The plays were rather stupid, for the people in them behaved in such strange ways that I felt they must be quite mad most of the time, or at best simple-minded. But the words were beautiful. Even when I could not completely understand them they still seemed like the most glorious music.

After a while the sick feeling of fear in my stomach faded away and I was able to chew some of the millet kernels I had brought with me for the journey. Beyond the valley where the village lay, the road wound between stony hills and then across a plain where the wind blew keenly. There were few people on the road so early in the year. I was glad of this, because the carts had not broken the frozen surface and churned it to mud. With spring, the journey would take me almost twice as long because of the mud.

After an hour I had good luck. Near one of the small red-walled temples along the road I came upon a young woman I knew from the village. She was driving a little donkey cart to Chengfu and had stopped for a while to let the two donkeys graze. When I greeted her, she invited me to ride in the cart. She was the number two woman of the sandal-maker, so her action was very charitable.

We talked politely during the journey, each of us being very careful to claim how unworthy and insignificant she was, and how gracious and important the other was. The woman said how good it was of me to condescend to ride in her cart, and I said how honored I was that she had condescended to be accompanied by one so unimportant as myself. All this was second nature to me, for it was part of the age-old ways of the Chinese, and it seemed much more normal to me than my evening talks with Miss Prothero, when I practised the art of conversation in the way of the foreign devils.

At last we saw the walls of Chengfu ahead of us. I always thought of it as a huge city, but Miss Prothero had told me that it would be lost in Peking or Tientsin. We entered by the northern gate and made our way slowly along the narrow street leading to the House of Justice Square. The streets were crowded with carts, rickshaws, people on foot, people on donkeys, and the occasional sedan chair in which bearers were carrying some important person.

Hardly anybody was emptyhanded. Men, women, and carts were laden with food or wares they were taking to the market or carrying away from it. Just ahead of us was a woman driving a few geese, and behind us another woman carried a huge load of logs on her back, held in a blanket which was brought forward in a band across her forehead, so that she leaned forward against the weight of her burden. I always used this way myself, and it was surprising how much weight I could carry.

Not all the people were peasants and laborers. Mingling with them in the streets or sitting in the open-fronted tea houses were the more important gentlemen, the merchants and scholars and landowners. They wore warm, beautifully embroidered gowns reaching to their feet, with high collars and very wide sleeves. Their nails were long, sometimes half as long as a finger, to show that they were rich and did not have to work with their hands. One or two of them carried a cicada, a chirping winged insect, in a tiny wicker cage on the end of a stick. They made a continual screeching sound which the Chinese thought very musical.

When we reached the square I parted company with the woman from the village, but only after the necessary long exchange of compliments in flowery phrases.

I had decided to do my stealing in the street of the goldsmiths. It was no use stealing food, which would be much too bulky for me to carry. Money, or something very small that I could sell elsewhere, was what I needed. In any case, the goldsmiths were rich and it seemed better to steal from them than from poorer people. The goldsmiths were also very careful, so I knew my task would be dangerous and I felt my stomach shrink within me at the thought of it.

I suppose it was cowardice, but I suddenly decided that I would first go to see Dr. Langdon. If he would make up a bottle of the pain-killing medicine for Miss Prothero today, it would save me another journey into Chengfu later in the week. There were no more than half a dozen foreign devils in the whole of Chengfu, and Dr. Langdon was one of them, an American with gray hair and tired eyes who had come to China before I was born. It was said that he had once done something bad in his own country when he was young, and that he was not allowed to be a doctor there. When I asked Miss Prothero about it she told me not to gossip, and said Dr. Langdon was giving his services to people who needed them perhaps more than any other people in the world, and that though he was not a Christian and not even religious, he should be respected for what he had done for so long.

I made my way to the *kungyu* where he lived. This was a large room divided into two, which had once been part of a big mansion now made into a number of small apartments. The apartments all looked out upon a courtyard, and the latticed paper windows were set in brightly lacquered frames.

Dr. Langdon had just finished seeing a patient when I arrived, the boy child of a Chinese woman. He looked surprised to see me at first, then gave me a friendly smile and said, "Hello, young Lucy. Like some tea?"

I had not met Dr. Langdon very often, perhaps three or four times a year, when he came out to the Mission to see a sick child, or Miss Prothero, and I thought it very kind of him to remember my name. I had to stop myself protesting in Chinese fashion that an insignificant person like myself would not dream of putting a greatly honorable elder-born to such trouble, and I just said, "Thank you, Dr. Langdon. I'd like some tea very much."

"And perhaps a few cookies, eh?"

"I don't know what they are, Dr. Langdon."

"Cookies. What do you call them in English? Biscuits, isn't it? I've got some *shaoping* here somewhere." He looked me up and down shrewdly. "You look as if you could do with something in your tummy. Take your coat off and sit down."

My mouth watered at the thought of the salted sesemumseed pastries called *shaoping*. I sat in one of the creaky chairs while Dr. Langdon made the tea, and asked him if I could have another bottle of medicine for Miss Prothero. He nodded a little wearily. "Yes, I'll make one up for you, Lucy. I wish I could do more, but to be honest there's nothing more anyone can do for her except keep the pain down until . . ." He glanced at me. "Well, until she dies. You know it can't be much longer now?"

"Yes. I know, Dr. Langdon. It makes me very sad, but I've become used to the thought of it happening."

"Lord, the child's grown up with real Chinese fatalism," he muttered and shook his gray head uneasily. I did not quite understand, but he seemed to be talking more to himself than to me, so I thought it would be impolite to ask what he meant.

It was strange to see a man making tea, even though I knew Dr. Langdon had no woman to do these things for him. Miss Prothero had told me that in England the men allowed their wives to eat and drink with them at the same table, and that they had only one wife and no concubines. I knew all these things must be true, but they seemed quite unreal to me and more like fairy tales than facts. Dr. Langdon poured the tea into cups with handles, but I had been used to this kind of cup at the Mission until the last of them was broken, so I had no difficulty. He put down a little plate with three *shaoping*, told me to eat them all, then settled himself in a cane chair and stretched out his legs.

[35]

"How are you getting along at the Mission?" he asked.

"All the children are well, thank you, Doctor."

"That's something. But you have quite a few to take care of."

"Well, it's difficult sometimes, but I've managed all right so far."

He frowned almost angrily. "You shouldn't have the burden of it, child. Why the devil haven't some of your English missionary people taken over?"

"We haven't been connected with any of the missionary societies for years, Doctor. Miss Prothero wrote several letters to a society in Soochow a few months ago, asking for help, but nothing has happened."

He sat sipping his tea and gazing into space for a long time. There seemed to be a deep sadness in him. When at last he spoke it was as if he were thinking aloud. "China . . . always teeming with life and death. She breeds by millions and her children die by millions, and they accept this because it's never been otherwise. A few foolish souls come here and try to help." He looked at me with a tired smile. "I suppose I've saved a few hundred lives. A drop in the ocean. I suppose Miss Prothero has saved a few hundred girl children. Perhaps the big missionary societies do a little better, but they're mainly concerned with making converts. Most of their converts are just rice Christians anyway, ready to join up for food in their bellies, and I don't blame them. But everything we do, all of it put together, is still just a drop in the ocean. Do you think it's worth it, Lucy?"

This was almost like a conversation practice with Miss Prothero, except that it was much more interesting. I found I was having to think about things I had never really considered before. It was fascinating to decide what I felt and then to express those feelings in words.

I said, "I don't know whether it's worth while, Dr. Langdon. I can't really grasp things on a big scale like that. I mean, I never see these millions of people you speak of, I just see the children at the Mission most of the time. They need taking care of, and there's only me to do it now. I'm sure they don't feel like a drop in the ocean. I don't suppose the people you cure feel like that either."

Dr. Langdon was looking at me curiously. Then he got to his feet and began to pace across the little room. "It's not good enough," he said, frowning. "I'm in China by my own wish, and Miss Prothero by hers." He turned. "But what about you, Lucy? You've had no choice and you've been taken for granted. Much as I respect Miss Prothero, I'm afraid she's mainly to blame, but I should have seen it for myself long ago. I've been a fool." He shook his head impatiently. "You're an English girl, and you should be home in England, living a decent life and being properly educated, not working like a slave to keep a few Chinese kids alive."

I must have looked startled for he went on, "Oh, they should be kept alive all right, but it's not *your* job, Lucy. If the British Government would only give the missions as much as they spent on the Opium Wars here, or if the United States Government would only—"

He broke off with a shrug. "No, that's hardly fair. The Chinese themselves wouldn't have it. The Empress and the Manchu Court would never let hordes of us barbarians come in to clean up the country for them, and maybe I don't blame them. But that's another thing, Lucy . . . there's trouble coming, maybe this year, maybe next. But it's coming all right, as sure as God made little apples. One day soon the Chinese are going to decide they don't want foreign devils in their country any longer. And they'll do something about it. They'll start chopping off heads."

He stopped pacing and stood in front of me, but I said nothing because I was busy eating the last of the little pastries, and Miss Prothero had always forbidden me ever to speak with my mouth full.

"You must go home, Lucy," he said slowly. "I've been very

much at fault in not thinking about this before. You *must* go home, child."

"It's very kind of you to worry about me, Doctor," I said as soon as I had swallowed, "but this is my home, and I haven't any other home to go to. Besides, who would look after the children?"

He rubbed his eyes with a finger and thumb. "Yes, I know it's all very difficult. Most of the time we're so busy living from day to day that there's no chance to think ahead. But this is important, Lucy. When trouble breaks, it's going to be bad. I know this country. I know Chengfu. And I know Mandarin Huang Kung. He's just itching for the day when he can send soldiers against the foreign devils. I'm going to write to your Ambassador in Peking myself. And I'll write to one of the American missionary groups. *Somebody* must take care of the children, so that you can go home."

I said, "Yes, Dr. Langdon," because it would have been bad manners to argue with an older person, particularly a man, but the things he had been saying were quite impossible. Sometimes I had a very great longing to see this strange country called England, to which I belonged and which Miss Prothero had so often described to me. But I knew it could never happen, and it was no use to say that somebody else must take care of the children. There *was* nobody but me.

I had eaten the *shaoping* slowly, to make the enjoyment of them last, and now I felt much less nervous about my stealing expedition. Perhaps I had been hungry before, and that had made me more anxious.

"Do you think you can manage for another month or so, until I can arrange something?" Dr. Langdon was saying now as he mixed some medicine from the array of bottles on a table in the corner of his room.

"Yes, I'm sure I can manage, thank you."

He looked round at me and made a little smiling grimace. "Wish I could help with a few dollars, but I've just paid for a new consignment of medical supplies and I'm what Americans

[38]

call broke. You won't learn that word from Miss Prothero, I guess. It means I'm out of money." He stirred the mixture with a long glass rod. "Most of my patients are too poor to pay me."

"I'm sorry. Don't you have any rich ones, Dr. Langdon?"

He gave a grin, which made him look younger and less tired. "Not enough. Mainly I get poor people who can't afford a Chinese doctor. That's just as well for them, because if you go to a Chinese doctor he sticks needles into your arms to cure a stomach ache, or maybe if you've got a nasty gash he writes a magic charm on a piece of paper and binds it over the wound to drive out the bad demons in the blood."

He poured the mixture into two bottles and corked them. "Well, there you are, young lady. I've made up a double quantity, and that ought to see you through."

I felt a little shiver of alarm. "You mean Miss Prothero won't . . . won't be needing any more?"

"It's very unlikely." He put a hand on my shoulder. "As the pain gets worse, increase the dose. You'll find she'll sleep most of the time then, but that doesn't matter. All we can do now is make things easier for her. I'll come out to the Mission next week if I don't hear from you before then."

"Yes, Doctor." Even though I had known Miss Prothero was dying it was a shock to realize that her time was so near. I said, "I have an errand to do, so would you mind if I called back for the medicine on my way home, please?"

"Any time. If I'm called out, I'll leave it with the washing lady next door. She's very reliable."

I put on my coat and hat, thanked Dr. Langdon for the tea and pastries, and was about to bow when I remembered my English manners, so I held out my hand and dropped a little curtsy as he took it. He held my hand gently, looking at me with a strange expression, then said, "I wonder if you know how pretty you are, Lucy?"

For a moment I went hot with shame, for I thought he was making a joke about me, but then I saw he was quite serious and realized that foreign devils must like girls with round eyes and big feet and white skins, because they were all made that way, as I was.

"It's a funny world," he went on slowly. "All over England and America right now there must be a million girls your age whose biggest problem is getting their hair to curl just right." He smiled suddenly. "If I was thirty years younger I'd trade the whole damn million of them for a girl like you, Lucy."

I didn't quite know what he meant about girls curling their hair, or about "trading" them for me, but I understood that he was paying me a compliment, and that made me sad, because if he had known what I was about to do he would have had no respect for me and certainly would not have paid me any compliments.

Twenty minutes later I was walking along the line of shops and booths where the goldsmiths worked. There were silversmiths too, and dealers in precious stones, but I had decided on gold. First I walked along the front of the shops, trying to decide which of them offered most hope for me. Small boys, apprentices, pumped the bellows of the little brick furnaces in which the crucibles rested. The smiths peered down at the molten gold, watching its color, or sat at their benches working with leather-covered hammers, fine chisels, molds, and strangely shaped pincers. Nowhere was there any money or gold object left carelessly in view.

I turned and walked along the narrow alley which ran behind the shops. If I could enter one of them unseen from the back, I might find myself in a little store room where there would be something to steal. Only six of the shops had doors at the back, and when I tested these gently I found only one unlocked. It was the shop at the end of the row.

My heart was pounding faster and faster, and the sickness of fear was growing steadily within me, mingling with shame and gnawing like acid in my stomach. After my first stealing expedition I had thought I would grow used to it and be less terrified, but instead I felt worse every time. At that moment I would have given anything to turn away and start the journey home. But it was impossible, I could not go back to the children empty handed.

Suddenly I almost jumped out of my skin as something cold and wet touched my hand. I looked down and saw a big dog, one of the many strays that roamed Chengfu, its coat filthy and its ribs showing plainly under the skin. I let out a sigh of relief, gave him the few millet kernels I had left, and shooed him silently away. For a few moments I clasped my hands tightly together, trying to prevent them trembling, then very carefully eased the flimsy door open.

Beyond lay a room scarcely bigger than a large cupboard. There were tools hanging on the walls, and the floor was covered with all kinds of rubbish, empty sacks, pieces of rope, earthenware pots, and pieces of rusty iron, but there was nothing worth taking. Through a partly open door on the far side I could hear the tapping of the smith's hammer.

I pulled the back door to, and walked round into the street again. There was no apprentice in the shop. The goldsmith was a big man with a drooping mustache, wearing a leather apron. He was making a filigree brooch, and as I stood among the passers-by to watch him I saw him fix it gently in the jaws of a wooden vise and pick up a slim steel tool. It was just as he started to use the tool that I felt my cheeks prickle as if the blood had drained from them, for an idea had suddenly come to me.

I knew that if I waited, or thought too long about it, my courage would fail, so I hurried round the side of the shop and into the alley again. The stray dog was still there. I clicked my fingers and whispered to him quietly. He came to me at once, no doubt hoping for some more millet kernels. I coaxed him to the back door of the shop, opened it cautiously, and reached inside to pick up a piece of rope from the dusty floor. Soothing the dog in whispers, I tied one end of the rope round his neck in a loop that would not slip, then pushed him inside the cupboard-like room and closed the door so that it jammed tightly on the free end of the rope.

I ran quickly round the corner to the front of the shop, slowing to a halt as I passed by, and lingering by the next shop, pretending to study the silver combs and hairpins laid out on a little tray beside the silversmith's bench. But from the corner of my eye I was watching the goldsmith with the drooping mustache, and straining my ears for the sound I expected. I was sure that before long the dog I had tethered just inside the back room would become frightened and start to bark.

The next moment it happened. There came a sudden whining and barking from the room beyond where the goldsmith sat. His head came up with a startled expression, he jumped to his feet and ran into the back room, thrusting the door open so hard that it banged back behind him.

In three quick paces I was beside his bench. I twisted the lever of the vise down and snatched up the gold brooch as it came free. I could hear the smith shouting as he tried to get the back door open and send the stray dog on its way. With the brooch clutched in my hand I turned to run. Nobody was passing the booth at that moment, nobody had seen me. I would turn right, away from the Street of Goldsmiths, and be hidden in a maze of alleys in a few seconds.

It was as I reached the front of the shop that the boy appeared suddenly in front of me, a rather fat boy wearing a leather apron and carrying a bowl of soup or stew in both hands. The smith's apprentice, sent to fetch his master's dinner, had returned at just the wrong moment. I barely had time to see the startled look on his face before we collided. The bowl flew from his hands, but he scarcely staggered. I bounced back, lost my balance and went sprawling on the floor of the shop. My elbow hit a leg of the bench, and the brooch dropped from my hand.

The fat boy's eyes widened and he began to shout. "Master! Master! A thief!" I snatched up the brooch, scrambled to my feet and ran straight at the fat boy, swerving at the last moment and ducking as he flung out a clumsy arm to stop me. In another moment I would have been away, but one foot came down on the mess of stew and skidded from beneath me.

I heard myself grunt as the breath was knocked from me. Still clutching the brooch I was coming shakily to my feet again when a big hand clamped down on my shoulder. I was wrenched round, and saw the furious face of the goldsmith glaring down at me. The fat boy was quivering with excitement and crying, "She took the brooch, master! She has it in her hand!"

Still gripping my shoulder so hard that I almost cried out with pain, the smith snatched at my hand and squeezed it open. The fat boy caught the brooch as it fell.

"Thief!" the smith said fiercely. "Foreign devil thief!" Then he swung his fist in a great buffet to the side of my head. I went reeling across the shop, hit my head on the wall, and felt myself slithering down to the floor as my mind blurred and spun dizzily. There seemed to be pain everywhere, but it was small compared with the huge fear that possessed me. I did not completely lose consciousness, but there was a time when I thought that the chattering voices I could distantly hear and the fear and the despair were all part of a bad dream, from which I could wake if only I made a big enough effort.

Then cold water was dashed in my face, a rough hand dragged me to my feet and shook me. I opened my eyes, saw one of Huang Kung's policemen standing over me, and knew that all was real. I had been caught stealing. The smith was jabbering excitedly, and I think he must have been repeating his story, for the policeman silenced him with a quick, impatient word. Several shopkeepers and passers-by had gathered to watch, and the fat boy was gleefully telling them how he had caught me in the act.

The policeman asked me a question, but my mind was

[43]

still fuzzy and faraway. I could only shake my head dumbly, trying to tell him that I did not understand. Some time later I found myself being marched through the streets with the policeman's hand on my shoulder. As we walked he lectured me in an angry voice about my wickedness, and said that Mandarin Huang Kung would know how to deal with foreign barbarians who stole from the People of Heaven.

My head ached and I was shaking with fright. I realized dimly that what Dr. Langdon had said to me only an hour ago was true. There was a growing hatred toward all foreigners here in the city. It was a strange fact that the poorest Chinese always considered himself superior to any barbarian from another country. They thought of themselves as the children of Heaven and the only civilized people in the world. Now this feeling was turning toward hatred. I did not think of myself as a foreign devil, but that was how the Chinese saw me, except perhaps in my own little village, and the policeman seemed very glad to be taking me to prison.

We passed through the winding streets and came at last to the prison building behind the House of Justice. A clerk was called to write down the details of my crime, and then I was handed over to the jailer, a squat, round-faced man with enormous shoulders. He wore a broad leather belt with metal studs in it. On one hip hung a bunch of big keys which clanked as he walked, and on the other hip was a broad, curving sword in a leather sheath.

When he saw that I was a girl he spent some minutes in a grumbling argument with the clerk, saying that as the west wall was being repaired there was no more room in the women's section of the prison. In the end I was taken from the room where the clerk sat and led down some steps to a broad stone corridor. The lamps were unlit and it was very gloomy. Along one side were heavy grille doors. There were men in this part of the prison. I glimpsed them through the bars as we passed along the corridor, sometimes several to one cell. One or two of them were wailing with grief, some were silent,

and some were busy playing a makeshift gambling game together, using straws or threads of cotton. I was not surprised.
Though they might be going to die next day, the Chinese
would always gamble. It seemed to be in their blood.

The cells were in pairs, with stone walls between. Iron bars
running from floor to ceiling divided each pair into separate
cells. Some of the men were gambling through the bars between them. I wondered vaguely what they could be gambling for, then heard the chink of coin and realized that a
prisoner's money would not be taken from him when he
was locked up. Of course not. It would be left with him so
that he could offer bribes for better treatment—if he could
afford it. The practice of bribery was an ancient and very
deep-rooted Chinese custom.

At the end of the corridor was a rather small pair of cells.
The jailer opened the door of the second cell, pushed me inside and locked the door behind me, then walked away down
the corridor muttering to himself in annoyance. No doubt I
was an unsatisfactory prisoner. He would have preferred a
man with a few coins who might bribe him to bring in food
and perhaps a cup of wine.

There was nothing in the cell but a stool, a dirty mattress
and a bucket. I sat on the stool and tried not to think of anything, but despair kept thrusting into my mind. How would
Yu-lan manage at the Mission? Would she remember all my
instructions? What would she do when Miss Prothero's medicine ran out? It might be several days before the mandarin
decided to try my case. I would be found guilty, of course.
Then I would be beaten. Or much worse . . .

I shuddered. He might sentence me to lose a hand. There
was an old man in our village who had been crippled in this
way. Panic rose up like sickness in my throat. Even after it
was over, how would I ever do all that had to be done at the
Mission? I had been at my wit's end before. With only one
hand it would be ten times more difficult.

A voice spoke in bad Chinese, just a few clumsy words. I

looked up and saw that a man now stood by the bars separating his cell from mine. In the narrow beam of daylight which angled down from a small window set high in the wall I saw his face, and my whole body seemed to jump with shock. I had never seen the man before, but in spite of the two-day growth of bristle on his chin I recognized him. This was the face Robert Falcon had sketched in charcoal on the Mission wall with a few bold and brilliant strokes. This was the dangerous man he had warned me to beware of.

He was an inch or two taller than Mr. Falcon, but a little slighter in build. His hair was black and curly. His expression was different from that in the drawing, for he was unsmiling, but there was no mistaking the set of his eyes, the long jaw and the shape of the chin. He wore slim riding trousers tucked into leather boots, and a warm sheepskin jacket.

I rose and moved to the bars, taking off my hat as I said in a rather shaky voice, "Good afternoon, sir."

He was surprised, and it was as if surprise was a pleasure he relished, for at once the eyes laughed and one corner of the mouth curved up in a half smile, so that for a moment he matched the drawing completely.

"Good Lord, a girl—and English!" he said. His voice was deep and lazy. "What the devil are you doing dressed up like that and in jail?"

"I'm always dressed this way, sir. I live here. I mean, I live in a village not far away." My cheeks grew hot. "And I'm in prison because I tried to steal a gold brooch and the man caught me."

He gave a little chuckle. "Hard luck. Though I wouldn't have thought you were a girl who went in for wearing much jewelry."

"I'm not. I didn't steal it to wear, sir."

"No?" His eyes and the tone of his voice mocked me. "What's your story, then?"

I felt confused. "What story do you mean, sir?"

[46]

"I mean why did you steal the brooch?"

"Oh, because I have to take care of some children at the Mission, and we have no food or money left. The guild gave me a beating when I tried to beg, so there was nothing else I could do but steal."

He reached between the bars, and for a moment I was so petrified that I could not move. But he only cupped my chin in his hand, holding me quite gently, and tilted my head so that the light caught my face. I could have counted slowly to thirty in the time that he studied me. After the first moment of surprise I no longer felt afraid, and was able to look back at him.

At last he said cheerfully, "I know a fellow rogue when I see one, and you're not. Will you accept an apology, ma'am?" It was so strange to have an apology from an older male person, and to be called madam, that I could only nod, too embarrassed to answer. He let me go and said, "Yours is the first English voice I've heard for some time, and it's a tonic. Bring your stool up to the bars and talk to me for a while. Do you mind?"

"No, of course not, sir. But I'm not very good at the art of conversation, so Miss Prothero says."

"I don't suppose Miss Prothero, whoever she may be, would think me a great hand at the gentle art myself," he said solemnly. "So we'll make a good pair." He turned and brought his stool close to the bars. I did the same with my own stool and we sat side by side in the gathering gloom. Everything seemed completely unreal to me, and I wanted it to remain so, for this dreamlike sensation was less frightening than reality.

"We'd better introduce ourselves," he said. "I'm Nicholas Sabine, of many occupations and no fixed abode."

"I'm Lucy Waring and I live at the Mission by Tsin Kaifeng."

"How do you do, Miss Waring."

"How do you do, Mr. Sabine."

We shook hands politely through the bars, and I said, "What subject would you like to talk about, sir?"

"Now let me see." He fingered his chin thoughtfully. "Perhaps we could start with you, Lucy. May I call you Lucy?"

"Oh . . . yes, of course. Please do."

"Thank you. Very well, then. You tell me all about yourself, Lucy, and about Miss Prothero and the Mission."

That made everything very much easier for me. I had been afraid that he might want to discuss William Shakespeare's plays or Miss Austen's books. I started to tell him my story briefly, but he kept asking questions, and it went on for almost an hour before I had finished. At the end of it all he sat with his chin resting on his hand, gazing down at the flagstones for a long time in silence. I wished he would speak, because in the silence I began to think once more about Yulan and the children, and poor Miss Prothero, and about what might happen to me.

I said, "I hope I'm not being impolite to ask, Mr. Sabine, but why have you been put in prison?"

"H'mm?" His thoughts seemed to be elsewhere. "Oh, I came to China to find something, and in trying to find it I made a bad mistake. Mandarin Huang Kung is gravely offended. But never mind about that." He turned his head to look at me, though the gloom had deepened so that we could only see each other dimly now. "Your Miss Prothero is dying. The children will soon be starving. And you're here in jail. What will happen now?"

"I hope I'll be tried tomorrow and that I'll just be whipped. But . . ." I could hear my voice beginning to falter, though I tried hard to keep it steady. "I'm afraid they may cut off a hand."

Even in the semidarkness I saw the sudden flare in his eyes, and it was frightening. The laughter was gone, leaving only the devil that hid behind it. I felt the back of my neck creep as if the hairs were bristling. Mr. Falcon had said this man was dangerous. Now I knew it to be true. Even locked within stone walls and steel bars he was dangerous. It seemed to radiate from him.

When he spoke his voice was quiet. "Have you friends here? Anyone who would help you?"

"There's Dr. Langdon, but he can't help. He has no money. Broke, he called it."

"Suppose he had money, what then?"

"Well . . . then he could go to the goldsmith and pay him twice what the brooch was worth to say it was all a mistake and he wanted to withdraw his accusation. The clerk would have to be paid to destroy the paper, and the jailer to forget he'd ever seen me. Oh, and the policeman. I can't think of anybody else."

Mr. Sabine seemed to relax. "Is that how things are done here, by bribery?"

"Oh yes, sir. Except at the Mission. Miss Prothero always said it was bad for the character. But we never had enough money to bribe people anyway."

"How much would your friend Dr. Langdon need to get you out of here?"

I thought for a while. "I expect he'd need three sovereigns for the goldsmith, one for the policeman, one for the clerk, and half a sovereign for the jailer." I closed my eyes, suddenly feeling drained of all strength. It was foolish to talk in this way, as if there were any spark of hope that somebody would come along with the huge sum of money needed to save me.

Mr. Sabine said, "Let's call it six."

I opened my eyes and saw that he was reaching down inside one of his boots. He drew out something that looked like a short round stick. Then I saw it was not a stick but a cylinder of leather as thick as a man's thumb. He twisted off a cap at one end, tilted the cylinder, and next moment there was the glitter of gold in his palm.

I gasped, and my eyes must have been rounder and uglier than ever as I watched him count out several sovereigns before tipping the rest back into the strange purse. It seemed to be full of them, stacked one upon another, and if so there must surely have been a hundred there.

"That allows an extra half sovereign to persuade the jailer to send for your friend Dr. Langdon," he said.

I stared at the six gold coins in his hand. "But you *can't!*" I whispered shakily. "I—I don't know why you're in prison, Mr. Sabine, but if you've offended the mandarin it's very serious, and you'll need all your money for yourself."

"If I had ten times as much it wouldn't be enough to change Huang Kung's mind." He grinned suddenly. "He has very special plans for me. He told me so when I was taken to be examined by him a couple of days ago. Come on now, Lucy. Call the jailer and start bargaining."

Before I could reply there came the sound of feet in the stone-flagged corridor and a circle of yellow light began to throw back the gloom. The clanking of keys told us that it was the jailer coming. Mr. Sabine put one of the sovereigns in my hand and said softly, "Use that to start with. I'll keep the rest for now in case he searches you."

The sound of feet grew louder, and the jailer appeared carrying an oil lamp. He was not alone. Dr. Langdon followed close behind him, a strained look on his face. The jailer hung the lamp on a hook and said, "There she is. You can talk for a few minutes." He tossed a small coin on the palm of his hand, spat contemptuously, and trudged away.

Dr. Landgon came to the bars of the door. He was breathless, as if he had been running. "Oh my God, so it *was* true!" he said in an unsteady voice. "I went out looking for you when you didn't come for the medicine . . ." He wiped sweat from his forehead. "Some people told me a foreign-devil girl had been caught stealing in the Street of Goldsmiths. Oh, Lucy . . . what have you done, child?"

I was too ashamed to speak. He rested his head against the bars, closed his eyes for a moment and said again, "Oh, my God." His voice was a groan of despair, and I knew he was thinking about what might happen to me. From the cell beside me Mr. Sabine said, "We've saved half a sovereign and a lot of time, Lucy. Introduce me to your friend."

I think Dr. Langdon was too worried about me to show much surprise at finding an Englishman in the next cell, but the look on his face when Mr. Sabine put the sovereigns in his hand was one that remained in my memory for a long time. In the weeks and months that lay ahead, a new and unimaginable future was in store for me, a future most people would have thought a miracle of good fortune for me, but which I found harder and stranger and more frightening than all the difficulties of my past. Throughout that time I was often to think of Dr. Langdon, and it was always this moment I remembered, when his weary, anxious face was suddenly lit with relief because he had been given the gold that would save me.

He looked at the Englishman and said, "I've no words to thank you."

"To hell with your thanks." Mr. Sabine's voice was low and hard. "You're supposed to be her friend. Why didn't you help her before she was driven to steal? What about the other Europeans here? What about your Ambassador, or mine? This scrawny little monkey's alone in the world with a pack of kids and a dying woman totally dependent on her. She risks losing a hand—a *hand*, damn your eyes—just to keep them fed for a few more days, and nobody cares!"

"I care, Mr. Sabine," said Dr. Langdon in a tired voice that held no resentment. "To my shame I didn't know the full situation, but I care very much."

"If you care, why didn't you know the situation?"

I said hastily, "I didn't tell Dr. Langdon. I didn't tell anybody, sir."

Dr. Langdon shook his head and gave a wry smile. "Don't defend me, Lucy." He looked at Mr. Sabine. "You're a young man and you don't know China. You don't know what she does to people. When a million or so die of starvation every year, it tends to dull your senses. It shouldn't, but it

[51]

does. I've been at fault regarding Lucy, but that's all past. I'm going to get her out of this country and send her home to England. I don't know how yet, but I'll do it if it's the last thing I ever do."

"Just get her out of this prison first," Mr. Sabine said curtly. "She tells me that if you go to the goldsmith——"

Dr. Langdon lifted a hand to silence him and said with a touch of impatience, "You needn't tell *me,* young man. I've lived here since long before Lucy was born, and I know whose palms have to be greased."

"Good." Mr. Sabine turned and glanced up at the tiny window. In the patch of sky beyond, the first stars were beginning to show. "It's getting on," he said. "Can you do everything tonight?"

"Don't worry." Dr. Langdon patted the pocket where he had put the sovereigns. "When money's talking, the Chinese are never sleepy." He turned to go, then paused and looked back, glancing from one to the other of us as we stood at the doors of our cells. "I'm sure Lucy will thank you for herself, but I'm grateful on my own account, Mr. Sabine. I gave my last half dollar to the jailer to let me in, so if it wasn't for your generosity in providing the palm oil I'd have to turn to stealing myself. And I don't think I'd be very clever at it."

He went away down the corridor, walking briskly, and I heard him calling to the jailer with the authority of a man who can pay for what he wants. I moved to the bars between the two cells and said, "I only wish I could thank you properly, Mr. Sabine. I just don't think there are any words big enough."

Quite without warning I began to cry. I bit my lip to stifle the noise, but he must have heard something for he came across and reached between the bars to hold my hand. "Most young ladies cry when things are bad," he said. "But you're crying now that everything's going to be all right."

"I—I'm terribly sorry, Mr. Sabine," I stammered. "I don't usually cry at all."

"That's little wonder, if you only shed tears for good fortune," he said dryly, "for not much has come your way. Here, my handkerchief's bigger than yours, and I've a spare one."

"Thank you, Mr. Sabine." I took the square of linen he passed between the bars. "Do you—do you really think I'm like a scrawny monkey?"

For a moment there was silence, then he looked at me with his eyes very wide. "A what?"

"A scrawny monkey."

"Who called you that?"

"You did, sir. Just now."

"I did? Good Lord, what on earth can have made me say anything so ridiculous?"

"I don't know, sir."

"Well, I must have been confused when I said it. I was thinking of . . . of Huang Kung. Now there's a scrawny monkey for you, if ever I saw one. That's not what made you cry, was it, Lucy?"

"Oh no, Mr. Sabine. At least, I don't think so . . . but now that you ask, I'm not quite sure."

He laughed. "Lucy, you're as transparent as a pane of glass, and there's not a speck of guile to be seen in you. Yet in a way you're a mystery to me. A puzzle. A riddle I'd like to solve."

"I don't feel mysterious, Mr. Sabine."

"No, you wouldn't." He thought for a moment or two, then looked at me with a half-smile. "As a matter of fact I came here to solve a riddle. Listen now, Lucy." I think I must have been too dazed with all the shocks of the day to show any surprise. I just stood looking stupidly at him through the bars as he recited the lines I expected.

> *"Above the twisted giant's knife*
> *Where the wind-blown blossom flies.*
> *Stands the temple where fortune lies.*

Beyond the golden world reversed
Marked by the bear-cub of the skies
Rest the sightless tiger's eyes."

As he was speaking I tried to think whether or not I should speak of my meeting with Robert Falcon the day before, and say that I had already heard this strange riddle. I did not so much make any decision as simply remain silent because I was too weary to launch into explanations.

"Well, does it all sound like nonsense to you?" he said.

When I nodded he gave a shrug and ran a hand through his hair. "And that's probably just what it is, nonsense and no more. Ah well, whichever way it is, Nick Sabine's gambled once too often." He let go of my hand and glanced at the sky through the slit of a window. "It'll take your friend Dr. Langdon a while to arrange matters, so try to sleep for an hour or so, Lucy. I don't want to talk any more. I've some thinking to do."

He turned away and lay down on his mattress. I went to my own mattress, knowing that in spite of my weariness I would never sleep. I was much too anxious for Dr. Langdon's return. As I lay there I wondered what Mr. Sabine meant by saying that he had gambled once too often. Now that I thought about it, the words had an ominous ring. I still did not know exactly why he was in prison, but if he had offended Mandarin Huang Kung in some way then he was in serious trouble, even more serious than my own had been. With a shock I realized my selfishness. I had scarcely given a thought to what might lie ahead for Nicholas Sabine, yet his very life might be in danger.

A feeling of shame came over me, and in the same moment I must have fallen asleep, for I remember nothing more until, as if in a dream, I heard a voice calling, "Lucy . . . Lucy." Not Lu-tsi, but Lucy, the foreign-devil way of saying my name. I lifted my head, puzzled, wondering where I was.

[54]

Then memory returned as I came up from the depths to see the long shadows of the bars falling across the cell.

Mr. Sabine was crouched by the bars, calling to me in a soft but penetrating whisper. I went across to squat down facing him, and rubbed my eyes.

"Are you awake, Lucy?" he said. "Really awake?"

"Yes, Mr. Sabine."

"All right, now listen. What's your religion?"

"Church of England. Like Miss Prothero."

"Of course. And is there a Church of England clergyman in Chengfu?"

"No, not since the Mission here was closed years ago. Oh, wait though. There's old Mr. Tattersall. He stayed on, and I think he's still alive. He had a little church here and it was burned down during a riot years ago, but he wouldn't leave. He just stayed on. Dr. Langdon would be sure to know him."

"All right. Now, how old are you, Lucy?"

"Seventeen and a half."

"Is Miss Prothero your legal guardian?"

"No, I haven't really got anybody like that, Mr. Sabine."

He rubbed a thumb across his bristly chin and I saw the wicked laughter that glinted and sparkled deep in his eyes as he said, "Lucy, will you do something for me?"

"Yes, Mr. Sabine. I don't suppose I can ever repay what you've done for me, but I'll do anything I can."

He reached through the bars and took my hands gently. "Well now . . . don't be shocked and don't be afraid, because there's no need for either, Lucy. But what I'm going to ask you to do for me, if it can be arranged, is to marry me. I want us to be married tonight."

« THREE »

I FELT DAZED, and although I was chilled by the cold of the cell my cheeks burned, for I thought he was mocking me, but then I saw that there was no hint of mockery in his gaze, and my mind seemed to splinter in confusion. There were a dozen questions all mixed up in my head and wanting to be asked. I chose the most stupid, and stammered, "But . . . *can* people get married in prison?"

Crouched on the other side of the bars, and still holding my hands, Nicholas Sabine gave a wry grin. "I know it's not usual, Lucy, but there's no law against it."

My head was still spinning. I said, "But *why,* Mr. Sabine? I mean, why would an English gentleman like you want to marry a young girl he's met in prison and doesn't know anything about?"

"I think I've learned quite a lot about you in a short time, Lucy Waring," he said thoughtfully. "But that isn't really

[56]

the point. There's something that belongs to me, and if I have a wife she'll inherit it. Otherwise it might go to somebody who's my enemy, and I'd do anything to prevent that."

It was hard to collect my thoughts. I said, "But your wife would only inherit when you die. And even if . . . even if I agreed, I'm sure Mr. Tattersall wouldn't just come here and marry us tonight. There are banns to be read, and . . . and things," I ended lamely.

"In a country like this he'll have a dispensation for acting at his discretion in an emergency, Lucy. He can marry us by special license."

"But I don't think he would consider this an emergency, Mr. Sabine. He'd say you must wait until you come out of prison."

Nicholas Sabine hesitated, then said almost apologetically: "The fact is, Lucy, I won't be coming out. This marriage will only last for about twenty-four hours at most."

I jumped, and horror flooded through me as his meaning dawned. "Is that why you want a wife to inherit whatever it is?" I whispered. "Because you're going to . . . *to be executed?*"

"Steady, Lucy." He tightened his hold on my hands as if trying to stop them trembling. "It's true, I'm afraid. You see, a few days ago I made a bad mistake, though I didn't know it at the time. I was trying to find something that was hidden long ago, and I searched what I thought was a small temple, but it was a tomb."

I stared at him and felt the blood draining away from my face. "But that's worse than almost *anything,* Mr. Sabine! It's desecration. The Chinese worship their ancestors, and their tombs are sacred."

"So I gather. The soldiers made that very clear."

"Soldiers?"

"This tomb stands in a grove on top of a hill just south of the town, and some soldiers caught me there."

"Was it the tomb of a poor family?" I asked quickly. "If

[57]

they were very poor, and if you gave enough money to Mandarin Huang Kung—"

"Well now, that's the trouble," he broke in with a smile and a self-mocking shake of his head. "This turned out to be Huang Kung's family tomb. How's that for bad luck?"

I shivered, wondering if he was mad to speak so lightly of what had happened, but then I remembered Miss Prothero telling me that Englishmen were sometimes very strange. They would do the most reckless things just for sport or for a wager, and considered it bad manners to be too serious about danger. When I could think clearly I said, "You must send a message to your Ambassador in Peking, Mr. Sabine. He can petition the Empress, and if she forbids Mandarin Huang Kung to harm you then you'll be safe."

"No good, Lucy. He's not going to risk trouble by having a foreign devil publicly executed. He told me so. Officially I'm to be killed by bandits." Nicholas Sabine spoke absently, as if his mind was on other matters. Before I could say anything more there came the sound of footsteps in the corridor, and as we stood up Dr. Langdon appeared. He looked drawn he was smiling. The jailer clanked along beside him, no longer surly but chatting politely. A piece of gold had changed his manner very quickly.

"All's well," Dr. Langdon said with a sigh of relief. "You're free, Lucy." He peered through the bars. "I don't know how to thank you, young man."

"I've suggested a way Lucy can repay me," Nicholas Sabine said briskly. "Can you spare a moment to discuss it, Doctor?"

Dr. Langdon looked puzzled, then shrugged and said, "Well, sure." The jailer unlocked my door, and as I came out I said to him in Chinese, "It would be a great kindness if you permitted us to talk with the foreign-devil prisoner for a few minutes, honored sir."

I think he must have received a whole sovereign, for he grinned and said, "As long as you please. But talking will not help him. All the gold in Chengfu will not help that one.

[58]

He has offended against the noble ancestors of Huang Kung." He drew a hand across his throat and guffawed, then walked away down the corridor.

Dr. Langdon said, "What's this all about, Lucy?"

I moved to where he stood outside the door of Nicholas Sabine's cell and rubbed my brow, trying to find words for a simple explanation. I was beginning to feel very tired now, and everything seemed dreamlike. "This gentleman wants me to marry him tonight," I said.

Dr. Langdon blinked, then looked through the bars at Nicholas Sabine. "Are you crazy?"

"No, Doctor. It's really quite simple. I have about twenty-four hours to live and I have pressing personal reasons for wishing to be legally married before I die. Lucy seems to be the only candidate, but I'm open to other ideas if you have any."

"Twenty-four hours to live?" Dr. Langdon said slowly. "You'd better explain a little more."

In a few sentences Nicholas Sabine repeated the story I had just heard. When he told how he had desecrated the tomb of Huang Kung's ancestors I saw Dr. Langdon wince and give a despairing shake of his head.

"My God, boy," he said at last, "you couldn't have made a worse enemy in all China. Huang Kung hates us."

"He made that clear enough, and dwelt on the details of my departure with great relish," Nicholas Sabine said calmly. "There's nothing anyone can do about that, so let's not waste time. I want to marry Lucy tonight. Can you help arrange it?"

Dr. Langdon took out a handkerchief and wiped his face. "I don't like it," he said abruptly. "Dammit, Sabine, she's only seventeen."

"What the devil does that matter? She'll be widowed soon enough. It'll make no difference to her except that she'll be my heir, which is all I'm concerned with. Oh, and there's something else. I've got about a hundred and twenty sovereigns left. Maybe you'll need some to get the marriage arranged, but there should be a hundred left at least. That's my wedding present to her. It ought to help her keep those poor little brats at the Mission alive for a while."

At any other time I would have felt excited beyond words at the thought of such a huge fortune. It was enough to keep the Mission going for as far ahead as I could imagine. But I did not feel any excitement. I felt cold and sick, and close to that strange sensation of weeping which usually came to me only when I was very happy. Dr. Langdon stood rubbing his chin, a harassed look on his face. At last he said, "Well, Lucy?"

I was silent for a long time, but neither man spoke. They seemed to understand that I was trying to work things out in my mind, and they waited for me. It was hard to think clearly, especially when I looked at Nicholas Sabine with the horrifying knowledge that soon he would be cruelly destroyed by Huang Kung. An unbearable sadness pressed down upon me. I closed my eyes and tried to order my thoughts. I owed this man an enormous debt. He had shown me the one way in which I could repay him, and it would cost me nothing. On the contrary, it would give me a great deal. For a long time to come, perhaps for five whole years and more, I would be free from the dread of waking each morning and wondering how to feed the children.

I had read the Marriage Service in Miss Prothero's prayer book, and I thought of the vows I would have to make, promising to love and honor Nicholas Sabine until we were parted by death. It would be a lie, but a short-lived one. I shivered again, and said, "If you want me to marry you, Mr. Sabine, then I will."

"Thank you, Lucy," he said politely. "I'm very grateful." He looked at Dr. Langdon. "Can it be arranged? Lucy mentioned a minister called Tattersall."

"Yes. I'm his doctor, and I'd say he's your only hope, mainly because he's become very vague in his old age. I doubt if he'll understand much of what's going on, and why."

"But will he do it?"

"I think I can persuade him to."

"It has to be done legally and in due form, Doctor. A license. A certificate. All the necessary documents."

"I don't know about these things, but you may be lucky. I had to sort through his desk for something when he was ill a few months ago, and he seemed to have forms and certificates for all emergencies."

"Nice to be lucky for a change," Nicholas Sabine said gravely. "Perhaps you'll pay the clerk to let me have paper and pen before you go. I want to make a will."

I remember very little of the next two hours. We took a rickshaw to Mr. Tattersall's house. He had gone to bed, but did not seem to mind being roused, in fact he asked us to have tea with him, for he was under the impression that this was a dark afternoon in early winter. With his mind wandering so, I thought it would take hours to make him understand why we had come, but I was wrong. When Dr. Langdon had carefully explained the situation the white-haired old minister said, "Ah, yes. Yes, I had a similar case back in . . . when was it now? In 1872, I think. No, perhaps it was '73. Young naval officer who found himself caught up in a battle between two war lords on his way south. Mortally injured. Married the girl who nursed him at the Mission we had here then. Or was it '74? I'll look it up. I keep all my diaries, you know."

He started to get to his feet, but Dr. Langdon gently persuaded him that looking up his old diaries could wait for another day. Although I was sitting upright I must have half-dozed in my chair then, for I was only vaguely conscious of their voices as they talked. It went on for quite a little while, and several times I heard Mr. Tattersall say, "Well, if *you* say so, Doctor . . ."

Then Dr. Langdon shook me gently to wakefulness and I had to confirm that I had no parents or guardian and that I agreed to the marriage. It was another half hour before we left the house, for it took Mr. Tattersall some time to find all the papers he needed, but at last we made our way in rickshaws through the now dark and silent city to the jail.

"And Huang Kung is going to have this poor young man executed?" Mr. Tattersall said dreamily, leaning on Dr. Langdon's arm as we entered. "Very sad, very sad. I can't pretend it surprises me, though." He wagged his head. "Nothing that happens in China can surprise me now."

The men in the other cells were asleep, but Nicholas Sabine was at the door of his cell as we came down the corridor. In return for a small bribe, the jailer brought a chair for Mr. Tattersall to sit on and a little table. It was an eerie, unreal scene. Part of my mind seemed to have fallen asleep. I suppose the weariness, fear and horror of the long day had taken their toll. Dr. Langdon introduced Nicholas Sabine to the minister and the three men talked for a while, but I barely took in what was said. For what seemed a long time Mr. Tattersall asked questions and wrote on some of the papers he had brought with him. At last he was satisfied and ready to perform the ceremony.

The jailer had refused to unlock the door, even for another whole sovereign. It was more than his life was worth, he said, to give the foreign devil any chance of escape. Mandarin Huang Kung had made that very clear. So my marriage ceremony was performed through the bars of the cell door.

When the time came, I repeated my vows after Mr. Tattersall automatically. My voice sounded strange to me, like the voice of one of the children at the Mission chanting English words without understanding them.

"Oh dear," Mr. Tattersall said suddenly. "The ring. We forgot about a ring."

"This will do," said Nicholas Sabine, and drew a gold signet ring from his finger. He reached between the bars and took my left hand, repeating the words after Mr. Tattersall as he slipped the ring on my finger. It was much too big, and I had to curl my finger to keep it on. In the flickering yellow light of

[62]

the lamp I saw that he was smiling at me as he spoke, a gentle and reassuring smile. I tried to respond, but I was empty, numb with the knowledge that this man I was marrying would soon be killed. The smile was in his eyes, too, yet beyond it I could still see a lingering echo of that wicked laughter I had seen before, first in the sketch Robert Falcon had drawn as a warning to me, and again in reality only a few hours ago when we had first talked together. In a corner of my mind an image of Robert Falcon's face appeared, and a quiver of shock ran through me as I remembered his words. *A devious mind . . . dangerous . . . the most ruthless devil you're ever likely to meet.*

I thrust the memory from me. The words spoken of Nicholas Sabine were untrue. I would not believe them, for he had shown me nothing but kindness. And even if they were true, it no longer mattered now. The man I was marrying would never be a danger to anybody again.

I came to myself just as Mr. Tattersall spoke the final words, ". . . that ye may please Him both in body and soul, and live together in holy love unto your lives' end. Amen."

There was a silence, then Nicholas Sabine said, "Thank you, Lucy. Now I'd like to kiss the bride." He drew my hand between the bars and touched it to his lips. His stubble of beard was prickly against my skin. He felt the loose ring on my finger and said, "You'd better take it off if you don't want to lose it." He looked at Dr. Langdon. "Are all the papers in order?"

"Yes, so Mr. Tattersall assures me."

"I'm greatly obliged to you both." He released my hand and took a sheet of paper from his pocket. "This is my will, leaving everything I possess to Lucy as my wife. My signature needs witnessing if you'll be so kind."

Dr. Langdon took the will, and he and Mr. Tattersall signed it at the table. I was watching Nicholas Sabine—my husband, I realized with a dazed sense of unbelief. He was looking toward the two men at the table, and now there was no mistaking the laughing devils that dwelt in his eyes. It was as if he had achieved some triumph of mischief. He said, "Will you keep that safely for Lucy until you've arranged for her to go home to England, please, Doctor? She must have the marriage papers as well, of course." He reached down and drew the long, slim purse from his boot. "I think you'd better take charge of her wedding present, too. Safer than keeping it at the Mission. She can ask you for whatever money she wants for as long as she's here."

As he passed the purse of sovereigns through the bars I thought how mistaken he was to believe that I would soon be going to England. I knew that Dr. Langdon would do his best to arrange it, but I simply believed it was quite impossible. Nobody would ever come to take care of the children at Tsin Kaifeng, and I would never leave them.

Dr. Langdon said in a low, unhappy voice, "Is there anybody . . . I mean, who's to be informed?"

"About my death? There's no need for you to do anything. On the back of the will I've written the address of the firm of solicitors who handle my affairs in England. All Lucy has to do is go to them, tell her story, produce the papers and claim her rights. Now will you take her away with you, please, Doctor? The poor child's as white as a sheet and nearly asleep on her feet. Perhaps you could provide somewhere for her to sleep tonight, and then see her on her way first thing in the morning. I want her well clear of Chengfu tomorrow, so there's no chance of her seeing me brought in after I've been officially killed by some imaginary bandits." He shrugged, half smiling. "That's no way to start married life."

My stomach seemed to shrink until it felt like a little ball of ice within me, and I had to clench my jaws to stop my teeth chattering. I heard Mr. Tattersall say vaguely, "I'm sure it was in '73. That other young man, I mean."

Nicholas Sabine reached through the bars and put a hand on my shoulder. I wanted to speak, to thank him for saving me and for the money, and to say how sorry I was that he was to die, but no words could have told what I felt, and besides, my throat seemed frozen and would not respond. I think he understood, for he shook his head and said, "Don't try to say anything, Lucy. Don't even think about me after you've walked out of here. Try not to think about any of this again until you're back in England. It's just a dream, really. Good-bye, Lucy."

He smiled once more, then turned away. The last I saw of him was as he stretched himself out on the mattress and put his hands behind his head. Then I was walking down the corridor, with Dr. Langdon holding my arm and Mr. Tattersall following behind.

For what was left of that night I slept on a couch in Dr. Langdon's surgery. By the time the sun had been risen an hour I was at the northern gate with him, sitting on a small cart laden with provisions bought in the market, a sturdy mule between the shafts. I had paid a few cash for a bale of hay and spread it over the top of my provisions, for I did not want anyone to see how rich a load I was carrying. I had two sovereigns tucked away in the lining of my coat, the rest were safely hidden in Dr. Langdon's house.

He stood beside the cart, looking along the road beyond the gate a little anxiously, and said, "Are you sure you'll be all right, Lucy? There are sometimes robbers on the road, even in daylight."

"Please don't worry, Dr. Langdon. I've met robbers twice before and they've never stopped me. They know I'm too poor to be worth stealing from."

He ran a hand through his gray hair and sighed. "It's not only being robbed that you have to think about, Lucy. There's yourself. You're well grown-up now by Chinese standards, and . . . do you understand what I'm trying to say?"

"Yes, Dr. Langdon, you mean they might use me for themselves by force. It happened to a young woman from our village last summer. But I don't have to worry, I'm much too ugly for them."

He gave a half-laugh, an angry sound, and grunted, "For

them, perhaps. I suppose it's just as well." He patted my hand as I held the reins. "Off you go, then. I'll come and see you as soon as I can."

I said, "Will you do one more thing for me, Doctor? I'm trying not to think about, well, about what will happen to Mr. Sabine today . . ." I had to wait for a few moments because my throat began to close up again and I could not speak properly. He waited patiently, and at last I said in a rush, "He told me they were going to pretend he'd been killed by bandits. I don't know what they'll do with him when . . . I mean, after it's all over. But please, will you try to get his—his body, and take what money you need from the sovereigns and see that he's . . . buried properly? There's that little English cemetery in the grove south of the town, where the church used to be. Perhaps you could ask Mr. Tattersall to . . ."

My voice failed again. Dr. Langdon said, "Leave everything to me, Lucy. I'll do the best I can. Look, there's a man and woman in a cart just going through the gate. You follow along and stay close to them on the road."

I nodded, still unable to speak, and set the mule to a steady plod. When I looked back, Dr. Langdon was standing against the big gray wall to one side of the gate, watching me. He raised a hand. I waved back, then settled to the task of reaching an understanding with this new mule I was driving for the first time.

If I had known the day before that this morning I would be driving home to the Mission with more food and stores than we had seen all at once for years, and a great fortune in money in Dr. Langdon's safe keeping, I would have found the excitement and joy almost too much to bear. But now there was a great heaviness inside me, and a bitter taste in my mouth. I tried to imagine seeing our larder full, and waking in the mornings without worry or fear, but other pictures kept darting into my mind. The ring, my wedding ring, now hung round my neck on a piece of twine under my tunic. I kept feeling it press against me with the movement of the cart, and this would bring to my mind a swift picture of the mandarin's soldiers coming to the jail to take Nicholas Sabine away for whatever cruel plans Huang Kung had made for him.

It seemed a very long journey, yet the sun was still low in the sky when we came over the crest of the hill and I saw the walls of the village in the valley below, with the Mission standing on the slope beyond. Several of the village women called a greeting to me as I drove slowly through and out of the gate on the far side. "Ah, you have a mule and cart, Lu-tsi!" said one. "Did you meet a magician on the road?"

"A truly illustrious magician," I answered, echoing her tittering laugh. "But not on the road. He sat in the bank of the foreign-devils in Chengfu, where the Donkey-Leg-Lady keeps her money." The villagers had always called Miss Prothero the Donkey-Leg-Lady because of the way she walked. There were more giggles and titters, and I could hear the woman repeating my silly joke about the magician in the bank as I went on my way.

Yu-lan must have set one of the children to watch from a window, for I was only halfway up the hill when I saw them come pouring through the gate in the outer wall, chirruping and calling to me in great excitement. "Keep them away from the cart!" I cried to Yu-lan, shaking my whip threateningly at the children. "Don't let them touch anything until we're inside the walls." I did not want the villagers even to glimpse the rich store I had brought home, for if they knew I had money they would charge higher prices for everything.

I drove in through the gate and turned right. As I got down from the cart, all the little children swarmed around me, tugging at my coat and trousers, twittering with joy.

"How is Miss Prothero?" I said to Yu-lan. "Is the baby all right?" I gave her no chance to answer, but hurried on. "I'm sorry, I couldn't come home last night, I was delayed, but I've brought lots and lots of food. Take the little ones away and keep them quiet while the big ones help me unload."

Twenty minutes later, when everything was stored safely

away, I gathered all the children in the schoolroom and set them to copying out a hymn on new pieces of card, then went to the kitchen where Yu-lan had just changed Kimi and was putting her into her crib. As soon as I entered I saw another baby, only a few days old, wrapped in a piece of blanket and lying in a straw-filled box on the table.

"The woman Lan Ping from the village brought the baby last night," Yu-lan said with a shrug. "It is a girl child, of course, and the husband wished to throw it into the river."

"Have we to feed her?" I said anxiously. This was always the problem when a newborn baby was left with us. Many could not keep down the watered milk which was all we could give them, and sometimes they died.

"I spoke sternly to the mother," Yu-lan said, "as I have heard you speak, Lu-tsi. She will come three times each day to feed the baby. Before she goes to work in the fields in the morning, and when she finishes work at dusk, and in the time of rest between. Her husband has given permission."

I sighed with relief. "Good. We must make her give extra milk for us to keep in a scalded basin, so we can feed the baby at other times and at night. If her milk is plentiful, perhaps there will be some to spare for little Kimi, too." I unwrapped the baby to look at her. She was tiny, but her crying was lusty and she seemed quite strong. I went to fetch one of the new blankets I had bought, wrapped her more warmly, and put her in her box near the kitchen range. Almost at once her crying stopped and she slept.

"Now," I said, "is Miss Prothero all right? Did she eat her breakfast? What did you say when she asked where I was?"

Yu-lan looked at me sorrowfully from her beautiful almond eyes. "I could not speak to her, Lu-tsi," she whispered. "When I took breakfast to her this morning, I found that she had died. I think it happened in her sleep, for she had not moved from the way I left her when I saw to her at bedtime last night."

Everything seemed to be rushing away from me, and I heard Yu-lan's voice as if from a great distance. "I have not told any of the children, Lu-tsi. Without you, I did not know what to do. I have been so frightened, and praying for you to come home."

With a great effort I brought the world into focus again, and saw that tears were rolling slowly down Yu-lan's cheeks. I could imagine the terror she had felt, thinking I might never come back, with Miss Prothero dead and all the responsibility for the children resting upon her young shoulders.

"You're a good girl, Yu-lan," I said. "You've done well."

She smiled through her tears for a moment. "I made the children sing the morning hymn, even though she was dead. I thought she would want that."

"She'll be very proud of you," I said. "And the Recording Angel will write it down in big letters on the good side of his book. Now stay here and look after the babies. I have a lot of things to do." I went to Miss Prothero's room with a small, foolish hope that Yu-lan had been mistaken. But, like me, she had seen death too often to make any mistake. I tidied Miss Prothero's hair and put a clean nightdress on her. She was no longer stiff, and from this I was sure she must have died early the night before. She had wasted away so much that she was very light and it was easy to wrap her neatly in a blanket with only her face showing. Then I went down to speak to Yu-lan again.

"We'll get the children out of the way and use a plank to carry her down into the chapel." This was a tiny place at the back of the old temple building. "I'll have a coffin made in the village today, and tomorrow I'll leave early and take her into Chengfu on the cart. Dr. Langdon and Mr. Tattersall will help me arrange about the burial. But we'll say nothing to the children until it's all over."

Yu-lan nodded. "They will not wonder about her. They have not seen her for a long time now."

"That's true. And today we'll set them to work spring-cleaning the whole Mission. There won't be time for us to give them any lessons."

[69]

It was a blessing to be so busy, for this helped to ease my grief over Miss Prothero. It also helped to distract me from something not only sad but terrible, for all day long I had to struggle against the horror of imagining what might be happening to Nicholas Sabine now, at this moment, whatever I might be doing.

That evening I was so tired that I told Yu-lan to see the children to bed, which was always an exhausting business. Down in the kitchen I gave the new baby a bath, fed her, and had just put her down to sleep in her box when I heard the unmistakable sound of the big wooden Mission gate creaking loudly as it was opened. I ran from the kitchen and peered through the little peep-hole in the stout front door.

An ox-drawn wagon, one of the biggest I had ever seen, was moving in through the gateway. The team of two oxen were thrusting against the traces, urged on by a man beside them mounted on a pony. He wore a thick cloak and a round hat of black fur. In the clear moonlight I could see every detail, and his face was the face of a foreign devil I had never seen before. The man driving the oxen was Chinese, but on the seat beside him was another foreign devil, a tall woman, heavily wrapped against the cold and wearing a big hat of a kind I had seen only in photographs, in the newspapers and magazines which at one time came regularly to Miss Prothero from England.

As I opened the door the horseman called out in Chinese with a bad accent, "Don't be afraid. We are friends." I moved forward, and as he rode to meet me he must have seen my face clearly, for he said in English, "It's all right. We're from the Anglican Mission in Tientsin. My name is Stanley Fenshaw."

I said in what must have been a startled voice, "Oh! Good evening, Mr. Fenshaw."

He turned and called, "This is the place, Margaret," then swung down from the saddle and came toward me. His movements were vigorous, as if he had so much energy that he found it hard to move slowly. When he pushed back his fur cap I saw that he was about forty years old, with a square brown face creased with deep lines around the eyes. It would have been a stern face but for the eyes, which were very bright and smiling.

"You must be Lucy Waring," he said.

"Yes, sir. I'm Lucy Waring."

He pulled off a glove and put a hand on my shoulder. "Well, Lucy, I believe Miss Prothero has been having a very difficult time, but her troubles are over now, and so are yours. She's had to wait a long while for help, I'm afraid, but we're here now."

I did not know whether to laugh or cry, whether I felt glad or sorry. After all the years of struggle, help had come at last, less than a day after Miss Prothero's death and at a time when we needed it less than ever before in my memory. I opened the door wide and said, "Please come in, sir. You and your friends must be cold. I'll make some tea for you."

The tall lady had got down from the wagon unaided. As she strode toward us I saw that she was English and had red hair. The Chinese driver moved to the back of the wagon and helped two young Chinese women to descend. In the hall, the red-haired lady threw back the cloak from her shoulders, rested her hands on her hips and stared about her with a fierce gaze. I had never seen red hair before, and now I was fascinated to see that her eyes were green. When she spoke I had to listen carefully, for her accent was strange to me.

"A cluster of bairns in this auld ruin, and with only a spinster in her seventies to see after them. There's good wurrk for us here, Stanley."

"Yes indeed." Mr. Fenshaw looked at me with a smile. "Perhaps you'll tell Miss Prothero that we've arrived, Lucy."

I said, "I'm sorry, sir. Miss Prothero . . . she's been ill in bed for months now, and she died last night."

There was a long silence. Mr. Fenshaw and the red-haired lady looked at one another and then looked back at me. "Ill for months?" Mr. Fenshaw said. "Do you mean you've been managing on your own?"

"Yes, sir. There isn't anybody else."

The red-haired lady moved toward me and put her arm around my shoulders. Her voice was softer and seemed much less fierce as she said, "There's somebody else now, lassie."

* * *

An hour later I sat with the two of them in Miss Prothero's room. Though I still felt confused, I now knew much more about my unexpected visitors. The Reverend Stanley Fenshaw and his wife had been working for the last five years at the Mission in Tientsin. She was Scottish, and I suppose that explained her strange accent and some of the words she used. The wagon driver was a convert and so were the two Chinese young women, who had been trained in nursing. The amount of clothes, blankets, medicines, and provisions in the big wagon made the precious supply of stores I had brought in on the mule cart that morning seem very unimportant.

During the past hour I had shown Mr. Fenshaw and his wife over the whole Mission, each of us carrying a splendid oil lamp from their stores. The lamps burned so clearly that they made the rooms seem almost as bright as day. Mrs. Fenshaw had as much energy as her husband. She spoke quite good Chinese, and had talked to all the children in the dormitory. She had examined both the babies, asked a hundred questions, and given a whole list of instructions to the two young Chinese nurses. Before the tour of the Mission I had taken them first to the little chapel where Miss Prothero lay, and Mr. Fenshaw had said some prayers for her.

"Clean as a pin," Mrs. Fenshaw was saying now as she sat with her hands on her knees, gazing at me with an air of surprise. "The whole place as clean as a pin, and all the bairns with some flesh covering their ribs at least. You're a bonnie girl, Lucy Waring."

[72]

I did not know what bonnie meant, so I smiled politely and said nothing. I was beginning to feel afraid—not of these people, for it was clear that they wished me nothing but good, and I knew already that they would be able to manage the work of the Mission far better than I could ever do it. But that was the trouble. I was no longer needed, and I felt lost.

Mr. Fenshaw looked up from the papers he was sorting through on Miss Prothero's desk. "I see that her bank account was exhausted long ago, Lucy. How have you been managing?"

I said, "We grew a little food ourselves, and whenever I can find work in the fields I take some of the bigger girls with me to earn a few cash." I could not bring myself to tell of my stealing expeditions, or of what had happened to me only the day before, so I said no more. Mr. Fenshaw jumped to his feet and began to pace up and down, his hands clasped behind his back. "It chills me to think of such responsibility falling upon your young shoulders, my dear," he said almost angrily. "But that's all over now, and perhaps I should explain how all this has come about. Over the past two years Miss Prothero wrote several times to the Anglican Mission appealing for help. Unfortunately they could not respond." He grimaced. "Lack of funds. There's never enough money to do all that needs to be done."

He stopped pacing and stood in front of me. "However, an event has occurred which I now regard as something of a miracle. An English gentleman, living in the county of Kent, approached our people at headquarters in London with a most unusual request. His name is Mr. Charles Gresham and he said that he was interested in receiving into his family a young English-speaking Chinese girl from North China. It appears that he has for many years made a scholarly study of the region in much detail, historically and geographically. He promised that if we could recommend a suitable young person he would make a substantial donation to our work. Well, at first it seemed quite impossible to meet his wishes. As you know, there are very few English-speaking Chinese, and even fewer who would wish to go to a land of foreign devils."

As Mr. Fenshaw spoke the last words he gave me a twinkling smile. "I'm sure you know how they feel about us, Lucy. However, our director at Tientsin remembered Miss Prothero's letters, in which she had spoken of you at some length. He therefore cabled London, asking if Mr. Gresham would accept an English girl, but one who had lived all her life here. And Mr. Gresham was delighted."

I sat with growing fear. My face felt stiff. Whenever I was afraid, my face became stiff and lost all expression. I knew because I had seen it once, when Miss Prothero was first taken ill and I saw myself in the mirror on her dressing table.

"I may say," Mr. Fenshaw went on, "that our people at home made full inquiries about Mr. Gresham and found no blemish on his reputation. He is married, with a family, and held in high respect. So now everything will be splendid for you, Lucy. You'll go to England, live with a good family, and be well cared for." He smiled down at me, expecting me to show delight.

"That's . . . very kind," I said. My voice was shaking. "But I—I don't want to go, Mr. Fenshaw. I'd rather stay here."

Mrs. Fenshaw leaned forward and stared at me. "Don't look sullen, lassie," she said briskly. "I'd never have thought it of you."

"I'm sorry. I didn't mean to look sullen, Mrs. Fenshaw," I said automatically, but my face still felt stiff and I could not change it. "Please don't think I'm ungrateful, but couldn't I stay here and help? Please? I'm sure I could be useful to you."

It was Mr. Fenshaw who answered. He looked a little sad at my response, but there was a note of sympathy in his voice. "I'm afraid not, my dear. You see, Mr. Gresham is providing the initial funds necessary for our Mission to take over Miss Prothero's work here, but his generosity depends upon your going to England to live as one of his family. That was the ar-

[74]

rangement. Now, would you have us go away and leave the children with only you to care for them through the years to come? Surely not, if you love them. And we've seen enough to be certain of that."

Hope died within me as I realized that it was cowardly of me even to ask if I might stay. I had always believed that Miss Prothero was mistaken in refusing to sell our girls as concubines or laborers when they were too big to keep at the Mission any longer. It simply meant that we gave them away for the same result. Only two days ago I had been thinking what a pity it was that I could not sell Yu-lan. Now I was the one to be sold, and I could scarcely complain, for I gathered that the price would provide for the Mission over several years at least. I wondered briefly what Mr. Gresham was like, and then hurriedly closed my mind against any further thought of him.

I tried to smile, and said, "Yes. I understand, sir. When must I go?"

"In a few days. I shall take you to the railway station at Yang-su myself. The Mission will send somebody to meet you there and take you back on the train to Tientsin." He smiled at me encouragingly. "Have you ever seen the sea?" I shook my head. "Well, that will be a great adventure for you, Lucy. You will be going home by ship, of course. It will be a year or two before this wonderful Trans-Siberian Railway is completed. Two of our people who are retiring to England will accompany you, and I'm sure you will have a splendid time."

I said, "Thank you, sir," and stood up. My head felt very strange, as if my mind had curled up inside it and gone to sleep so that it could forget everything for a little while, and be at peace. With an effort I remembered my manners and said, "You and your friends will need places to sleep. There's Miss Prothero's bedroom, I've changed the bedclothes there. I'm afraid they're very worn and patched, but they're clean. And there are several other rooms, with no mattresses or bedclothes, but I know you've brought some with you. Shall I show you the rooms now?"

"No need, lassie," Mrs. Fenshaw said firmly. "I've seen the whole place and you can leave me to arrange everything now."

"Very well, Mrs. Fenshaw. I'll take the new baby with me. She'll need feeding in the night, and I have some of the mother's milk in the kitchen."

"You'll do no such thing, Lucy," she said, not unkindly. "One of the Chinese girls will see to that. Now off to bed with you, child, you must be tired."

I slept deeply that night, but not well, for my dreams were so troubled that I was glad to wake in the morning. They were muddled, frightening dreams, in which Miss Prothero rose from her coffin to play madly on the harmonium; in which Robert Falcon, on horseback and with his golden hair glowing like a halo about his head, pursued me through endless woods with a long sword until I ran for safety into a great tomb of red stone, only to find a mandarin in a shining blue silken robe barring my way. He held a mask to his face, and I thought this must be Mandarin Huang Kung, but when he lowered the mask I saw the face of Nicholas Sabine, the man I had married and who was surely dead now. He laughed, and the demons danced in his eyes as he said, "You were warned, Lucy! You were warned!" I turned and ran again, but now there was mist everywhere, and somewhere a bodiless voice was chanting in a thin wail: *"Beyond the golden world reversed, Marked by the bear-cub of the skies . . ."* The voice faded, the mist cleared, and I was in Dr. Langdon's surgery, watching him dissolve gold sovereigns in a glass jar of green liquid. In the jumble of my dreams I saw the house that I knew only from the mysterious drawing I had found long ago, the house called Moonrakers. I entered, and I moved among English foreign devils who could not see or hear me, and who walked through me as if I were a ghost.

In the morning I took out the piece of coarse canvas with the sketch of Moonrakers on it. Often before it had given me a sense of comfort, though I could never say why. Today it made me feel uneasy, almost afraid. I told myself that this was because it reminded me of the strange land where I would soon have to face a new life, and I put the sketch away.

For the next two days I felt almost as much like a ghost as I had felt in my dreams, for suddenly there was nothing for me to do, nothing for me to worry about. Under Mrs. Fenshaw the Mission began to run so easily and well that I felt miserable on realizing how poorly I had been managing all this time. On the second day, Miss Prothero was buried under the old plum tree near the Mission wall. Mr. Fenshaw conducted the service and a wooden cross was set on the grave until he could arrange for a proper headstone with words on it to be set up. Again I saw that I had failed when I planned to take Miss Prothero into Chengfu. It was much better that she should be buried here, in the place where she had worked for so long and saved so many lives.

On the third day I rose early and set off for Chengfu on foot. I could have taken the mule cart, but now I felt I had no right to do so. Two hours later I was at Dr. Langdon's house. When he opened the door to me I saw that his face was drawn and there were dark hollows under his eyes. He looked startled on first seeing me, then took my hand and drew me inside. "Come in, Lucy. I didn't expect to see you so soon. I was planning to come out to the Mission in a day or two, but I've been very busy."

He began to make tea, and it seemed to me that he avoided looking at me. I said, "I came as soon as I could, Dr. Langdon. Please . . . what happened? I mean, about Mr. Sabine?" I could feel my hands beginning to tremble as I spoke.

"I was able to do as you asked," Dr. Langdon said slowly, gazing at the kettle as it came to the boil, his face haggard. "I'll take you up to the cemetery later, Lucy."

It was difficult to speak, but I managed to say, "What happened? What did they do?"

He shook his head. "It's foolish of you to ask, Lucy. And it doesn't matter any more now. He told you not to think about it, not to think about him at all. Tell me your news of the Mission. How's Miss Prothero? Did you have to increase the medicine?"

It was a few moments before I could get control of my voice, but then I began to tell him of all that had happened, of Miss Prothero's death and the arrival of Mr. and Mrs. Fenshaw with their helpers. There was quite a lot to tell, and our tea was cool enough to drink by the time I had finished my story. Dr. Langdon showed no surprise when I spoke of Miss Prothero's death, but he listened to the rest very thoughtfully at first and then with growing pleasure.

"So you'll be going to live with a good family in England," he said, gazing down at his cup of tea as he sat holding it. "Well, that solves a lot of problems. But aren't you excited, Lucy? Good Lord, you tell it as if you were reciting a shopping list."

"I suppose that's because I don't really want to go. But I have to go because of the money this gentleman is paying the Mission. I can't refuse."

"It's best for you, Lucy." He nodded slowly, gazing absently into the distance. "There's going to be a lot of trouble here in China soon, a lot of danger. If I were a younger man I might clear out myself . . . if I had anywhere to go." He rose, unlocked a small cabinet, and took out a long brown envelope and a single sheet of paper folded in half. "If you're off in a few days I may not see you again, Lucy, so you'd better have this now." He handed me the envelope, and I saw on it a smudged thumb mark. "Those are all the papers concerning your marriage, and there's also the will."

I guessed that the thumb mark had been made by Nicholas Sabine's grimy hand. For a moment this brought him very close to me again in memory, and I shivered.

"There's something else," Dr. Langdon said slowly. "He gave me a message for you."

"A message?" I echoed, staring.

"Yes. I went to visit him again as soon as you'd left Chengfu that morning." Dr. Langdon fumbled with the paper in his hands. "I wanted to tell him you were safely on your way, and to ask if . . . well, if there was anything more I could do. He wrote this note and asked me to give it to you. I know what it says, because he showed me."

I took the paper and unfolded it. The message was quite short and written in a bold hand.

Dear Lucy,

I don't know when you will be going to England, but I would like you to delay approaching my solicitors and to say nothing of our marriage until six months have passed from the time Dr. Langdon gives you this. Also, would you leave some of your wedding-present money with him? I want to repay him for his help and kindness, and I have nothing left of my own.

> *Never change.*
> *With love from your devoted husband,*
> *Nick.*

There was a tightness across my chest and a pricking behind my eyes, and I wished that I could cry. I knew that the last line was a joke, but I did not think it was meant to mock me. More likely it was to mock himself, and I could almost see him grin as he wrote it.

"What does 'never change' mean?" I whispered.

"I guess it means just that, Lucy. He liked you the way you are. But what do you feel about the rest of what he says?"

I read the message again, then looked up. "I'll do as he asks, Dr. Langdon. I don't care about inheriting anything. I suppose I would have gone to see the solicitor if I could, because that's what Mr. Sabine wanted, but now I won't have to worry about it for a while."

Dr. Langdon looked very uneasy, and I realized that it was because of the money, so I went on quickly, "I'm glad for you to keep all the sovereigns. If I take any for myself I might have to explain where I got them, and it would be the same if I gave them to Mr. Fenshaw at the Mission, so please keep them, Doctor. I think you need the money for your work more than the Mission does now."

He hesitated, then nodded reluctantly. "Well . . . I'm deeply grateful to you, Lucy. Believe me, the money won't be wasted."

When we had finished our tea we walked through the town and out of the south gate, then up the hill to where the English cemetery lay. Dr. Langdon led the way to a new mound with a wooden cross on it. The name of Nicholas Sabine had been burned into the horizontal part of the cross with a hot iron, and that was all.

We did not speak. I stood there with my heart aching and felt almost glad to be leaving China, a place where such a cruel and terrible man as Huang Kung had the power to do these things. I spent ten minutes hunting for some of the small white flowers which were just beginning to show with winter's end, and which Miss Prothero had told me were like English snowdrops. When I had enough, I made a little posy and laid it on the grave. I knew that I ought to say a prayer, but no words would come into my mind. In the end I just said, "Sleep in peace, Mr. Sabine," and then we walked down the hill together, still in silence.

As we made our way through the town we passed a little group of muleteers squatting by a wall and watching two of their number playing *liu-po* with notched sticks and dice. One of the on-lookers picked up a clod of mud and threw it at Dr. Langdon, spattering the sleeve of his coat, and at this they all began to laugh, mocking him for a foreign devil. He took no notice, and we walked on. I was startled, but he said, "An omen of things to come. You'll be well out of it, Lucy."

When we said our goodbyes at the end of the street which led to his house he bent to kiss me on the cheek and said, "Take care of yourself, Lucy. And if you think of me sometimes, try to think of me as a friend." He had the same troubled and uncertain look I had noticed earlier, though I could not imagine why.

I said, "Of course I will, Dr. Langdon. How else would I think of you?"

He rubbed his brow, gave me a tired smile and said, "Well, you can never tell."

Later, as I stepped out along the road to Tsin Kai-feng, my thoughts kept returning to those last words Dr. Langdon had spoken and I tried to fathom what had been in his mind. I found no answer, but at least I was kept for a while from thinking about the future. Very soon now I would be starting on a long journey, and at the end of it I would have to live among strangers in a strange land. I had told myself that it was exciting and would be a wonderful new experience, but in my heart I was afraid, and now I tried not to think about it.

I had been walking for only an hour when I came to a part of the road which rose in a slight hill and then dipped down to wind between a straggle of trees. As I reached the point where the road sloped down ahead I saw a horseman some distance away and coming toward me. His horse was moving at a walk, and the rider sat with his head bowed forward on his chest, as if he were in deep thought or perhaps half asleep in the saddle.

I knew him at once, for I recognized the clothes he wore and the horse he rode, and above all the bright gold halo of his hair. It was Robert Falcon, the English foreign devil who had asked me that strange riddle and warned me to beware of a man I had never seen, a man I had since met and married, and who was now dead. I did not want to come face to face with Robert Falcon again, for I knew he would question me. With his head bowed, he had not seen me yet, and I was just about to move quickly into the trees beside the road when there was a sudden movement below, and I froze with alarm.

Three men had darted from the shelter of the trees as Robert Falcon passed. One threw a short wooden club, and I saw the horseman sway as it struck his head. Another man raced forward to seize the bridle, and the third jumped to catch Robert Falcon by the arm and drag him from the saddle. The club must have stunned him, for he simply fell to the ground. The attack by the robbers was all over in a few seconds, and I was still holding my breath from that first shock of alarm when I saw that one man was kneeling on the limp figure of the Englishman while the first robber moved to pick up his club.

Before I had time to think what I could do I found myself running down the road toward them and shouting at the top of my voice: *"Huang Kung's soldiers are coming! The soldiers of the mandarin are here! Run quickly! Run!"*

Three startled faces looked toward me. I knew they could not see along the road behind me because of the way the ground rose in a hillock, and I shouted again. Two of them ran, vanishing into the trees. The man holding the horse tried to mount it but was thrown off, and narrowly escaped a vicious kick. Next moment he too had vanished into the trees.

Robert Falcon lay still, but as I ran the last fifty paces I saw his leg move, then an arm, and as I reached him he lifted his head a little and stared dazedly. I said, "Wait, Mr. Falcon, I'll be back in a moment," and turned to make my way through the thin belt of trees. When I looked down the slope beyond them I saw the three robbers running hard, with the last man trying to catch up with his companions. I had been afraid that they might turn back, but evidently they were intent on getting as far away as possible. In great relief I went back to the road. The horse, Moonraker, had returned to his master and Robert Falcon was standing up now, holding the pommel to steady himself. Already there was a darkening lump on the side of his head. He stared at me blankly and said in a hoarse voice, "Lucy Waring . . . so it *was* your voice speaking to me just now. I thought I'd imagined it."

"Yes, it's me, Mr. Falcon. I was on my way home when I saw those robbers attack you. Are you all right?"

He looked up and down the road, then scanned the trees, and I saw that he held a pistol in his free hand now. "No, I'm not all right," he muttered, "but I'm a damn' sight better off than I might have been. What scared them off?"

"I shouted that the mandarin's soldiers were coming over the hill, and that made them run."

"Good God." He stared at me in astonishment. Slipping the pistol into an inside pocket of his coat, he led the horse to the roadside where a low outcrop of rock jutted from the ground, and sat down on it, putting a hand gingerly to his head and gazing at me curiously with his light blue eyes. "That was remarkably quick thinking, Lucy."

"I didn't think at all, sir."

He gave a short laugh. "Be that as it may, I rather fancy you saved my life. That fellow was about to use his club on me again. You're on your way home, you say? Well, the least I can do is to turn around and give you a lift to Tsin Kai-feng. I'm sure Moonraker won't object."

"No, it's quite all right, Mr. Falcon," I said hastily, for to ride home with him was the last thing I wanted. "It's very kind of you, but . . . but I'm not dressed warmly enough for riding. I mean, I have to walk to keep warm." This was an excuse, but it also happened to be true, and after looking at me steadily for a moment or two Robert Falcon nodded. Putting a hand in his pocket he said, "Well, I can scarcely repay you, but I'm sure you can make good use of a little money."

"No, it's quite all right, Mr. Falcon," I repeated, backing away. "I'm glad I was able to help, but please excuse me, I must go now."

He stood up with a look of surprise. The color had come back to his cheeks and he was quite steady on his feet once again. I went on hurriedly, "Some people have come to take over the Mission, so we have everything we need now, and I'll be going to England soon."

He shrugged, as if I baffled him. "Well . . . if I can't persuade you I suppose that's an end to it." He paused, then suddenly asked the question I had hoped to avoid. "By the way, you haven't seen that man I warned you about?"

I knew that if I told the truth he would at once ask more questions, and each would be harder to answer than the last, so I said, "There haven't been any strangers in the village apart from you, Mr. Falcon."

He nodded, his face grim. "Well, look out for him. It wouldn't surprise me to learn that he'd paid those robbers to attack me."

I was about to protest indignantly, but held my tongue just in time. It was strange that I should want to leap to Nicholas Sabine's defense, for I knew so little about him, yet the accusation had made me feel suddenly hot with anger. I watched Robert Falcon put a foot in the stirrup and swing up into the saddle. He slipped a hand under his coat where he had put the pistol and said, "I won't daydream on the road in future. I was puzzling over that riddle I asked you, Lucy. Have you thought any more about it?"

I shook my head. "No, I've been rather busy. Goodbye, Mr. Falcon."

"Goodbye, Lucy. And thank you again."

I turned and walked on my way. After a minute or two I reached the top of the slope at the far end of the ridge and looked back. He had not moved, but sat his horse with hands resting on the pommel, watching me. He lifted a hand, and I waved briefly in response before turning to continue on my way.

When I reached the Mission an hour later Mrs. Fenshaw came bustling into the hall, her skirts flying. "Lucy Waring!" she cried. "Where on earth have you been?"

"I just went into Chengfu," I said, startled. "I'm sorry, Mrs. Fenshaw, was there something you wanted me to do?"

"Do? Of course not, child! Everything's well in hand. You *just* went into Chengfu, you say? Heavens above, you've more energy than sense, wandering about China on your own."

"But I wanted to say goodbye to Dr. Langdon, and I've made the journey dozens of times, Mrs. Fenshaw. I've had to."

Her face softened. "Aye, so you have. Well, you're safe home again for the last time, lassie." She put an arm about me. "Come along now and have some dinner. You must be starved, and tomorrow will be a long day for you."

My heart turned over. I said, "Tomorrow?"

She looked down at me and smiled. "Aye. We've had a message from Mission headquarters at Tientsin. They're sending somebody to take you there tomorrow, Lucy. Your first step on the long road home. Aren't you a lucky girl, with a kind English gentleman like Mr. Gresham willing to have you?"

I swallowed, trying to ease the lump in my throat brought about by fear of the unknown. "Yes, Mrs. Fenshaw," I said. "I'm very lucky."

«FOUR»

NEXT MORNING when I said goodbye there were many tears from the children. I shed none myself, though I wanted to, for my heart was breaking and I felt that tears might ease the pain, but they would not come.

Mrs. Fenshaw had given me a large, well-worn suitcase, and in it I had packed my few treasures and my only set of spare underclothes, which left the case still three-quarters empty. The nearest railway station was at Yang-su, a four-hour drive in the mule cart. Mr. Fenshaw took me there, and we were met by a brisk English gentleman from Tientsin who had come to collect me. His name was Mr. Courtney.

I had never seen a train before, and was frightened when it came puffing and clanking into the station, but I set my teeth and just stared at it blankly, determined not to show my fear. I think Mr. Courtney was a very nice person, but I remember little about him for my mind seemed to have closed up, and I simply sat in the train as it roared along, staring out of the window without really seeing anything.

I spent ten days in Tientsin. It was much bigger than Chengfu, and I had my own little room at the Mission there, with a real bed. Here I was provided with English clothes which were no longer wanted by the ladies at the Mission and which they altered to fit me. The first time I put on a full set of clothes the lady in charge had to help me dress, and before she had finished I was scarlet with humiliation. I had never felt so uncomfortable or so stupid in all my life.

It was impossible to move easily with the long skirt flapping around my ankles, and I could not understand why I had to wear frilly cotton combinations underneath. As for the top part of the dress, which was called the bodice, this was much too tight and so were the long sleeves. Half a day's ditch-digging and the dress would have been in ribbons. When I told the lady so she looked rather shocked and said, "But you won't have to dig ditches, Lucy. You're a young English lady now, so you must dress and behave accordingly. No, don't stride about like that, dear. You're not a man. A young lady must never hurry. Just take small steps, and then the skirt won't get in your way."

The only thing that pleased me was the shoes, once I had got used to them. They made my feet look quite small compared with the feet of the other English ladies. I was something of a curiosity at the Mission, but everybody was very kind to me. I was told that the voyage home would take ten weeks, but that seemed a very short time in which to travel twelve thousand miles. I worked out a sum, and found that if I had to make such a journey on foot it would take more than a year, for I could scarcely have managed more than thirty miles in a day.

On the tenth day I boarded an English cargo ship which had cabins for thirty passengers. My companions on the voyage were Dr. and Mrs. Colby, an elderly couple who had served with the Mission for many years and were now retiring. He was not a real doctor, but a clergyman of some kind. The name of the ship was *Formosa,* and usually her northernmost port of call in China was Shanghai, but on this occasion she had cargo for Tientsin. I had never dreamed that any ship could be so splendid. The passenger saloon was like a hall in a great palace, with beautiful chairs and couches and rugs. The dining room was no less amazing, and when the long tables covered with fine white linen were laid with glistening cutlery and glassware it was a breath-taking sight.

There were two berths in my cabin, one above the other, but I had the cabin to myself because there was not a full complement of passengers and no other young woman was available to share with me. In the cabin was a large basin fixed to the wall, with a hole that allowed the water to run away when a plug was pulled out, and two taps protruding above it. I could scarcely believe my senses when I found that one of the taps gave hot water.

But that was not all. The lights on the ship worked by electricity. I had only to press a switch by the door of my cabin and a big glass bulb in the ceiling burned with a brilliant white light. Such lights were everywhere about the ship, and many of those in the passages were left burning all night. I had never imagined such a wonderful extravagance. In spite of all this, Dr. Colby told me that our ship was really rather small and simply equipped compared with some of the great passenger ships of today. It seemed impossible to me, but I had to believe him since he was a clergyman.

Among these many marvels there were two above all that delighted me. A little way along the passage from my cabin was a bathroom, with a huge bath and taps which gushed hot and cold water. There was one such bathroom for every ten passengers, and we could use them as much as we liked. The other special marvel was that adjoining our bathroom were three cubicles containing water closets. I had never seen one before, and I was entranced. When I remembered all the hours spent and trouble taken at the Mission, heating water on the range to bathe the children, digging cess pits, and carrying buckets, I decided in one of my rare daydreams that if ever I became rich I would buy a bathroom and some water closets and send them to the Mission at Tsin Kai-feng.

We sailed at noon, passing downriver to the Taku Forts at the mouth of the Pei Ho, and on into the open sea. This was a wonder of a different kind. For the first hour I stood at the rail and simply gazed at that immensity of water stretching to the horizon. Then my mouth grew suddenly dry, my stomach twisted and heaved, and I spent the rest of the day on my bunk in the cabin, unable to bear the thought of food, and convinced that I was going to die.

Gradually the seasickness passed. Within two days I was completely well and eating ravenously. There was so much food served that at each meal as much was left in scraps as would have fed the children at the Mission for two days. The other passengers were mainly merchants with business interests in China, but there were also two ladies from another Mission and two British Army officers. They all seemed to find me an object of some interest and tried to make me talk about my years of growing up in China, but although I was always polite I only answered their questions as briefly as possible, and said no more than I had to.

Our first stop was Hong Kong, and it was almost like visiting a human ant nest. So many people were crowded into the little island that thousands of them had to live on sampans and junks in the harbor and the sheltered bays. We were only there for twelve hours, but were able to make an excursion ashore. I enjoyed walking through the streets lined with shops and booths, and listening to the chatter of tongues. I could understand the Ning-po and the Wu dialects, but the very different Cantonese dialect of the south was beyond me. Dr. Colby bought me a beautiful green silk scarf as a present, and when we returned to the ship it was already growing dark. I left Dr. and Mrs. Colby and went to my cabin to enjoy a hot-water wash and to tidy my hair.

The key of my cabin had been taken from its place on the row of hooks in the passage and was in the door. I thought that perhaps the steward was inside, turning down the bed-clothes, a custom I still found strange and amusing, but when I opened the door I gasped with shock. The light was on, and the cabin was in turmoil. My clothes had been taken from the wardrobe and were scattered about the floor. All the drawers from the chest beside the bunks had been taken out and tipped upside down. The mattress and bed clothes from both bunks were lying heaped in a corner. My suitcase had been dragged from under the lower bunk, and my special souvenirs were strewn everywhere.

I took a step into the cabin, and even as I did so my nerves leapt with alarm, for I sensed a presence behind the half open door, but the warning came too late. A powerful hand clamped over my mouth from behind me, and in almost the same instant the door slammed shut and the light was switched off. The man held me with the back of my head clamped against his chest, and his other arm now whipped around my waist, imprisoning one of my arms. My heart was pounding with terror, and the noise of it seemed to fill my head.

As he lifted me, carrying me across the cabin, I tried to bite his hand, and failed, for he cupped it and pressed harder. I was kicking with my heels, but could not find his shins for he was carrying me half sideways now, with my legs clear of his body. I reached up and back behind my head with my one free hand to claw at his face, but he ducked his head and my nails slid across his hair. Next moment I was flung down against a wall and there came the slam of a door very close to my head. He had thrown me into the wardrobe.

I struggled to my knees in the cramped space, sobbing for breath, and pushed hard against the door, but it was locked.

With a great effort I crushed down the screams which were trying to burst from my chest, biting my lip until the blood came. At last the moment of near hysteria passed, and I was able to rest on my hands and knees, dragging in gulps of air to help me steady myself. When I pressed my ear to the door I could hear no sound. I turned so that my back was to the door, with my hands and knees pressed against the wall forming the back of the wardrobe. Summoning all my strength, I thrust backward. The flimsy lock snapped, and I tumbled out into the darkness. Getting to my feet, I blundered through the obstacles strewn about the floor and switched on the light. The cabin was empty. I tried to open the door, but it was locked from outside. He had turned the key as he left. I began to bang on the door and shout. In less than a minute I heard footsteps and the click of the lock. I wrenched open the door to find Mrs. Colby gazing at me with a startled expression.

"What on earth is happening, child?" she exclaimed. "Good heavens, your mouth is bleeding and your hair is—" She stopped short as she looked beyond me and saw the chaos in the cabin.

"There was a man here, Mrs. Colby," I said, trying to stop the breathless trembling of my voice. "He's turned all my things upside down, and he was waiting behind the door when I came in."

"A man! But *who?*" Her voice rose in a squeak of horror.

"I didn't see him. He put the light out and bundled me into the wardrobe. I—I think I surprised him while he was searching the cabin."

"Searching? For what?"

"I don't know, Mrs. Colby." I felt suddenly very tired. "I haven't got anything worth stealing, but perhaps he didn't know that."

The next hour was a nightmare. I had to tell my story to Dr. Colby, then to the Chief Officer and the ship's doctor, and finally to the Captain himself, a stout man with a beard who looked like pictures I had seen of the Prince of Wales. The doctor felt my pulse and my head, and wanted me to drink a draught he had made up to calm my nerves, but I refused stubbornly, which was very impolite and something I would never have done if I had felt myself. Mrs. Colby became angry with me for being stubborn, but I think this was mainly because she was so upset herself, and in the end the doctor gave her the draught to drink.

A score of questions I could not answer were asked me, and everybody was greatly distressed. The ship was searched for anybody aboard who should not have been there, but without result.

"A bad business," the Captain said at last, sitting behind the big desk in his cabin. "I'm very sorry, Miss Waring." He looked at Dr. Colby, who was there with me. "My apologies, Doctor. The prowler was some Chinaman who slipped aboard somehow, depend upon it. Every port has its complement of thieves. We keep close watch at the gangways and loading doors, but they've the devil's own cheek. I've even known them slip in through a porthole, and I'm afraid that's what happened here. He got in just after dusk, and this young lady surprised him." He turned to me. "Has anything been stolen, my dear?"

"I don't know yet, sir. I'll go and look now, if I may."

"Of course. And we shall certainly reimburse you for any loss." He frowned, looking very stern. "I see the brute has hurt your lip. Believe me, if we'd caught him I'd have raised some stripes on his hide before we kicked him ashore. And I'd like you to know that I think you're a very brave, steady girl."

I said, "He didn't hurt my lip, sir. I—I bit it to prevent myself screaming, because I was afraid that if I did I wouldn't be able to stop. I wasn't brave at all."

He looked at me curiously, then smiled. "Miss Waring, you've just defined bravery, whether you know it or not."

I could not work out what he meant, and was glad to

leave. Mrs. Colby wanted to help me tidy up my cabin, but I persuaded her to go and lie down, for she still looked white and shaken. When the steward had put the bedding in order I asked him to leave, closed the cabin door, and began to sort out the mess. Despite what the Captain had said, I did not believe it was a Chinaman who had attacked me. The man was too big for any average Chinese, and certainly too big to have wriggled through a porthole. In any event, he had gone out through the door and would surely have been seen before he managed to leave the ship, if he had been Chinese. I thought it more likely that he was one of the crew, a seaman perhaps, but I had not said so to the Captain, for it seemed wrong to make an accusation without proof.

When I had hung up my clothes and put everything back in place in the chest of drawers, I was left with the suitcase and the scattered souvenirs. One by one I found them and put them back in the case. Everything seemed to be there, the prayer book and the embroidery samplers, the framed photograph of my parents and the piece of blue ribbon, the sandals and some poor little gifts from the children on my leaving them—a pretty stone, a bright-colored feather, a piece of paper with a childish drawing on it. The piece of ancient canvas with the picture of the house, Moonrakers, was there and still rolled up, just as I had packed it.

I knelt gazing into the suitcase, trying to remember if anything was missing. Sudden shock made me catch my breath and press my hands to my cheeks. The envelope Dr. Langdon had given me was gone, the envelope which held my marriage papers and Nicholas Sabine's will.

I searched every inch of the cabin, but found nothing. Sitting on the lower bunk, looking down at my hands in my lap, I tried to think what I should do. Deep within me I had never been quite certain that I would go to Nicholas Sabine's lawyer and declare myself. It was something too far away both in time and distance for me to have any feeling of reality about it. Now I would be unable to go. I could tell nobody what had been stolen from me. For the next six months I was barred from doing so by Nicholas Sabine's wish. And after that, who would believe such a wild story when I had no proof?

A great sadness came upon me, for now that the thing was impossible I realized that when the time came I would surely have gone to the solicitor, regardless of my own feelings. Nicholas Sabine had been kind to me, saved me from mutilation, and I would have been bound to repay him by doing as he asked. But now I could never do so.

Something caught my eye. I was wearing a brown dress with long close-fitting sleeves which buttoned at the wrist, and something glinted on the cuff of my right sleeve. I lifted my hand, staring. A few bright golden hairs were caught between one of the buttons and the cuff. This was the hand with which I had tried to claw at the face of my assailant. He had ducked his head, and these few hairs had been trapped by the button. Bright gold hairs.

There were fair men aboard *Formosa,* both among the passengers and in the crew, but none so fair-haired as this. I knew only one man with hair of such a color, and that was Robert Falcon. I shivered as if someone had walked over my grave. Robert Falcon was not aboard the ship, and how could he be in Hong Kong?

I sat for a long time, my tired brain working slowly. There were many English people in Hong Kong, I thought, and among them must be some who had fallen on bad days, sailors who had stayed behind when their ships sailed, perhaps. Yes, and remittance men. I had heard Dr. Colby talking with another passenger about them, men who were black sheep and had been sent abroad by their families on a small remittance. Perhaps there were men as poor and desperate as I had been in Tsin Kai-feng when I went out to steal. Perhaps there was one with hair as bright as Robert Falcon's. I had surprised him just as he emptied the suitcase on to the floor, and he had snatched up the envelope because he thought it might contain money.

Yes . . . that was how it must have been. I told myself that there could be no other explanation.

The gong for dinner began to sound. I dreaded going to the dining hall, for I knew that everybody would be talking about what had happened to me. I would have given anything to go to bed and have a meal brought to my cabin, but that seemed cowardly. "Just do what comes next," I thought, and when I had plucked the strands of hair from my sleeve to put them out through the porthole, I bathed my lip, washed my face, tidied my hair, and practised a calm look in the mirror for a few moments before going to the dining hall.

*　*　*

The incident was less than a nine-day wonder, and for this I was grateful. When we stopped at Singapore and Penang great precautions were taken to make sure no prowler came aboard, and Dr. Colby would scarcely let me out of his sight, but apart from this, and perhaps because I would not talk about the matter myself, it was soon a thing of the past.

As the days went by, my mirror told me that my appearance was changing. I had been told that I must let my hair grow, since English young ladies did not wear their hair chopped off short all around the head like an inverted basin. My cheeks were filling out and there was more color in them. My nails, which had been chipped and broken, were becoming as smooth as a mandarin's nails—though I would never want to grow them so long.

We stopped at Colombo and again at Aden. I had never before lived so comfortably or eaten so well as I did on the ship, yet I was far less happy than I should have been. After the first wonder and novelty had passed I found that time hung heavily on my hands, for there was nothing for me to do—at least, nothing which had to be done. I spent hours walking around the deck, hours reading books from the little library the ship carried, and hours sitting with Dr. and Mrs. Colby while they made conversation with other passengers, but all this was just passing the time. It seems a foolish notion, but I think the truth was that I missed all the daily worries and difficulties I had known for so many years.

My happiest moments were when the sun had gone down and I could find a quiet corner of the deck to be by myself under the stars. Then I would think about the children at the Mission, each one of them in turn, and remember all the things we had done together; how we had struggled with our poor patch of land, the excitement when we gathered our first potatoes, the anxiety and the relief when Yu-lan and I sat up for three nights nursing baby Kimi through a fever we thought would kill her.

Sometimes I thought of Nicholas Sabine and that night in the prison. It seemed as remote as the stars in the sky above me, as if all that took place had happened to another Lucy Waring in another world. I remembered the last words he had said to me: "Try not to think about any of this . . . it's just a dream, really." That was how it seemed to me now, just a dream. But I never thought about him without an aching sadness in my heart. Perhaps he was a wicked man, as Robert Falcon had said, but he had the saving grace of laughter, could even laugh at his own fatal predicament, and he had been so full of life.

From Aden we sailed into the airless heat of the Red Sea and on through the Suez Canal, and as journey's end drew near my uneasiness grew greater. On the ship I was in a little world I had come to know, and I dreaded leaving it to be thrust into a huge new world that was alien to me. Although I now wore English clothes I knew that in many ways I did not think like an English girl, for my mind was still patterned by the Chinese way of life.

On a June evening, just before sunset, I saw my own

country for the first time as we sailed through the English Channel. All the passengers were at the rail, gazing at the distant coast, and those who had been away for a long time were full of emotion. My own feelings were mixed. I was curious and a little moved to be coming to the country of my own people, but this did not outweigh my nervousness.

Next day we sailed slowly up the River Thames, to tie up at the Royal Albert Dock early in the afternoon. There was a seemingly endless delay between the time we docked and the moment when we were at last told that we could disembark, and I grew more apprehensive with every passing minute. As we went down the gangway I was clutching Mrs. Colby's arm. All around us on the dockside excited greetings and reunions were taking place. I saw a man move away from a little group of ladies and walk toward us. He had a pale narrow face and thin dark hair. I judged him to be in his late fifties. His movements were quick and jerky, and he blinked his eyes rapidly as he approached, clutching his top-hat in one hand and waggling a slim walking stick in the other as if to attract our attention. As he reached us he smiled eagerly and said, "Good afternoon, sir. Your servant, ma'am. May I ask if you are Dr. and Mrs. Colby?"

"We are indeed," said Dr. Colby. "And you must be Gresham. Clever of you to spot us, my dear fellow."

"Oh no, no," Mr. Gresham protested with a modest laugh, tucking his cane under one arm to shake hands. "You were the only couple accompanied by a young lady." He turned his smile upon me, a rather toothy smile which seemed too big for him. "So I felt sure this was our little guest. Well, well, well, so this is Lucy Waring. How pretty you are, my dear. Welcome to England and to my family."

He put out his hand and I took it, dropping a curtsy as I did so, not realizing until it was too late that he had leant forward and drawn me toward him a little, to kiss me on the cheek. The result was that as I came up I butted him slightly in the face with my head.

"Oh, I'm sorry!" I cried, and went crimson with embarrassment as I straightened my hat.

He gave a quick, flustered laugh, said, "My own fault entirely," then turned to the Colbys. "Will you all come and meet my family?"

I was dimly aware of three female persons dressed in summer clothes, two of them girls and the other an older woman who was presumably Mr. Gresham's wife, but I was so upset by my clumsiness that everything seemed blurred and confused. I was afraid to put out my hand or to curtsy for fear of making another blunder. I forgot the girls' names as soon as Mr. Gresham had spoken them. And the only words of greeting which came into my head were Chinese.

Mrs. Gresham and her daughters found themselves being introduced to a flustered, red-faced creature who stared blankly at them and mumbled only a word or two of some strange language before lapsing into silence. My face felt stiff, and I knew that the expression I wore must be the one that Mrs. Fenshaw called sullen. Mr. Gresham kept laughing and talking in an attempt to make me feel at ease, but I was so numb with growing shame that even when somebody asked me a question I could not take it in, and only stared dumbly in reply. After what seemed an eternity, Dr. and Mrs. Colby said goodbye to us all, and ten minutes later we were in a motor tender and making our way up the Thames.

"The quickest way to Charing Cross," Mr. Gresham said, fidgeting with his cane and looking from side to side with quick movements of his head. "The traffic problem on the roads today is appalling."

Although it seemed unlikely, I wondered if Mr. Gresham was in any way nervous at meeting me, and it was not until later I came to learn that this was his usual manner. He was an impulsive and rather excitable gentleman, very different from the few other Englishmen I had now met. He had a strange, mechanical smile which came suddenly, accompanied by a glassy stare, and then was switched off again, almost in the way of an electric light.

The noise of the tender's engine made it difficult for us to talk, and for this I was grateful. I stared about me, pretending to be interested in the passing scene, but in fact I took in very little, and was simply aware of the hugeness of London because of the time it took us to reach Charing Cross. From the point where we disembarked we rode in a carriage for no more than two hundred yards to the forecourt of the station. The streets were busy with people going about their daily work, and I had never seen so many foreign devils all at once in my life. A porter took my case and we boarded a train that was waiting, while Mr. Gresham went to buy a newspaper. There was nobody else in our compartment, and as we sat down I thought how splendid this train was compared with the train in which I had traveled to Tientsin. This brought another thought to my mind. I was wearing the best of my three dresses, but now I realized how shabby I looked in comparison with Mr. Gresham's daughters in their beautiful dresses of heavy silk and their pretty hats decorated with big colored plumes. I had never thought much about clothes before, but suddenly I was very conscious of my drabness, and this made me shrivel up inside even more.

There was silence in the compartment, except for the two girls whispering together. I knew they must be whispering about me, and tried to think of something to say, anything to break the dreadful spell which had fallen upon me, but my mind remained empty. I sat with my head hanging, and glanced up furtively from the corners of my eyes. Mrs. Gresham sat waving a small fan in front of her face. She had lovely hair, the color of sandalwood, pinned up under a hat with ribbons which tied under her chin. She was small and plump, with blue eyes and a soft pink complexion. I saw her close her eyes for a moment and sigh, giving a little shake of her head as if faced with a problem she did not know how to solve, and I realized that I was the problem. When I thought

[99]

of the impression I must have given so far, I could scarcely blame her for showing signs of anxiety.

I was able to study the two girls by their reflection in the window. Now I saw that one was about eighteen and the other a few years younger. The elder girl was small and plump like her mother. The younger, almost as tall as her sister, was more like Mr. Gresham. They were whispering together, giggling, and darting little glances at me. At that moment I could almost have wished to be about to set out on a stealing expedition in Chengfu, rather than here.

Suddenly Mrs. Gresham seemed to come to herself, and said sharply, "Stop that whispering at once, you two! Emily, you ought to know better than to encourage Amanda, she's bad-mannered enough as it is. Sit up straight and chat with Lucy, there's good girls."

They looked at each other helplessly for a moment, then the elder girl, Emily, said to me, "Papa took us to see a comic opera all about China by Mr. Gilbert and Mr. Sullivan. It was called *The Mikado,* and he was the sort of king there. Have you ever seen him? I mean, the real Mikado?"

I shook my head. I had never even heard of him.

Amanda said to her sister, "It wasn't China, it was Japan, silly. The Mikado is king of Japan."

"Don't be rude to your sister, dear," Mrs. Gresham said, fluttering her fan. "After all, China and Japan are much of a muchness, I'm sure."

"I'm sorry, Mamma," Amanda said without sounding sorry. She turned to me. "Who *did* you see in China, Lucy?"

I managed to find my voice, and said in a whisper, "Just people. Chinese people. I saw Mandarin Huang Kung once. He's a very important person."

"There! You see?" Mrs. Gresham said hopefully. "Lucy's seen a mandarin, isn't that nice?"

"There was a Lord High Executioner in *The Mikado,*" said Emily. "Did you ever see an executioner?"

I nodded, and Mrs. Gresham looked pleased as she said, "You see, Amanda? I told you they were much the same."

"Did he have a big sword and cut people's heads off?" Amanda asked with a giggle.

"Not always," I answered, my voice emerging a little more strongly now. "If you were a thief, he was only supposed to brand you on the arm with a hot iron. But Huang Kung was very strict, so in Chengfu the executioner would cut your hand off."

Both girls stared at me round-eyed. Emily looked at her own soft white hand and made a mewing sound of horror. Mrs. Gresham made a strangled noise in her throat and I saw that she was leaning back with her eyes closed, fanning herself rapidly. "That's *quite* enough, Lucy!" she said in an agitated voice. "We don't want any silly tales of that kind, thank you!"

I shrank back into myself, wondering what I had said wrong. At that moment the door opened and Mr. Gresham climbed into the compartment. "We'll be off any second now," he said heartily, and threw his hat and cane on to the rack. Sitting down, he rubbed his hands briskly and looked around at us, blinking his eyes. "Well now, what shall we chat about?"'

"I think perhaps Lucy is very tired, Charles," said his wife in a meaningful voice. "We don't want to exhaust her with a lot of chatter the moment she's arrived, and I always feel it's difficult to maintain a pleasant conversation in these noisy trains. Why don't you read your newspaper, dear? We shall have lots of time to talk to Lucy later."

Mr. Gresham looked somewhat put out for a moment, but then leaned back in his seat and nodded several times. "Perhaps you're right, Becky. We must give her time to get her bearings." He gave me one of his sudden glassy smiles. "Besides, I expect you'll want to look out of the window as we go along. It's your first sight of England, and we don't want to spoil it for you."

I think I managed a small smile in response. Certainly I felt relieved, and I could tell that the others felt the same. I mumbled, "Thank you, Mr. Gresham," and turned my head to gaze with relief out of the window. It was several minutes before I really saw anything, because at first I just stared blankly into space, wondering how on earth I could ever recover from the dreadful start I had made with the Gresham family. Everything I had said and done had been wrong. And when I had said and done nothing, as we were being introduced, that was wrong too, for I had simply stood there dumbly, like a slow-witted ox.

Gradually I began to take in the surroundings through which we were passing. At first there were only long rows of huddled and smoke-grimed houses, and some buildings with tall chimneys which I knew must be factories, but after a time we came to big areas of countryside which lay between the towns and villages.

It was so beautiful I could scarcely believe my eyes. There were no flat plains of the kind I had always known. Here the ground rose and fell, always gently. There were no mountains. The fields made a huge patchwork carpet which seemed to ripple across the earth, so that it made me think of a wizard's flying carpet from a fairy tale. I saw giant horses with shaggy legs, working in the fields or drawing carts along the roads. Fine cows and sheep grazed on grassy slopes that were green as an emerald, and everywhere there were trees, clumps of them in fields, big patches of woodland, and even long avenues of trees lining the roads.

In China a road was simply a track between one place and another, and there were no boundaries to it. Here the roads were like a maze, and I wondered how people ever found their way about. In the towns the roads were bordered by rows of houses and shops. In the green spaces between they were bordered by hedges or common. There were wild flowers growing along the hedgerows, and roses on the walls of little cottages. Perhaps what surprised me most was seeing no walls built about the villages or even the towns. In China, the smallest village was protected by a mud-built wall. Each town was walled, often with stone, and within the town the rich people would build walls around their houses, and other walls within to make courtyards.

Here, all was open and unguarded, yet I sensed an atmosphere of peace and safety which seemed to lie like an invisible canopy over the land, from horizon to horizon. It may be that memory lingers like a ghost in the blood, for although I had never seen England before I suddenly knew myself to be a part of her, however strange she might appear to me until I knew her better.

Tears came unexpectedly to my eyes. I turned my head, and was stupidly surprised to find that I was not on my own; I had been so absorbed that I had completely forgotten my companions. Emily was staring at me. She wrinkled her nose and said to Amanda in a loud whisper, "Look, she's a cry baby."

Mr. Gresham raised his head with a jerk from the newspaper he was reading and glared in anger. "How dare you, Emily!" he snapped, blinking rapidly. "That remark was most unkind, and it won't do, it won't do at all, young lady. You will certainly not get the new hat you have been pestering your mother for."

Emily pouted as if about to cry herself. Amanda suppressed a giggle. Mrs. Gresham opened her eyes and said indignantly, "Really, Charles! How can you be so unkind to the poor pet? See how you've upset her now. Of course she must have the hat."

"There is no of course about it," Mr. Gresham broke in irritably, "and she is not a poor pet. She is a young lady who should know her manners. Unfortunately you spoil her, my dear, which is a great pity. I've no intention of withdrawing what I just said, and that's an end of the matter."

He shook his newspaper vigorously, frowned at his daughter, gave me what I think was meant to be a reassuring smile, and resumed reading. Mrs. Gresham bridled, and her elder daughter scowled sulkily. Amanda seemed to be rather pleased but was trying not to show it. A heavy silence fell, and the brief happiness I had known a moment ago dissolved. Without saying a word I had in some way caused at least three of the family to be angry with one another. I looked quickly out of the window again, feeling a great sense of guilt and scarcely daring to breathe.

I had no idea how long our journey would take, and could not bring myself to break the strained silence by asking, but after half an hour and several stops we came to a station called Chislehurst, and there we left the train. A porter took my case and Mr. Gresham led the way along the platform, talking with determined cheerfulness as if trying to dispel the uneasy atmosphere of the journey.

Waiting for us was a coachman with a big open carriage which I later learned was called a landau, and in this we set off along a country lane which wound up a hill and along a flat crest with woods on either side. Amanda was sitting beside me, and I could glimpse that her head was turned to stare at me as we rode along. Suddenly she tucked a hand under my arm and said, "It must be so difficult to come to a strange country. I was just wondering how I would feel if I was suddenly taken to China on my own, and I think I'd be quite frightened."

I could almost have wept with gratitude. I turned and smiled at her, and I know my whole heart was in that smile, then I looked at Mr. Gresham, who sat facing me with his wife beside him, and the words came tumbling out as I said, "I'm so sorry, Mr. Gresham, I know I've been stupid and impolite but I didn't mean to be, I was nervous, and—and everything seemed to go wrong."

"Not at all, not at all," he said quickly. "Quite understandable, my dear. You'll soon settle down and feel at home, I'm sure." He sat back with an air of relief and stopped fidgeting with his cane for a few moments. I noticed that

Emily still looked sulky and Mrs. Gresham somewhat doubtful, but Amanda bounced excitedly in her seat and said, "There, I knew she was just nervous. I'm exactly the same when we go calling on people I don't know. Oh, I'm glad you're coming to live with us, Lucy, we'll be able to talk and do things together. Emily's so stuck-up, now that she's eighteen."

"Amanda!" her mother exclaimed in horror. "Where *do* you learn such vulgar words? And don't dare to speak of your sister like that."

"Very well, Mamma," Amanda said meekly. "But I learned it from Emily. She said the Marchant-Yates boy was stuck-up."

"Ooh, I didn't!" Emily cried indignantly. "Mamma, I didn't!"

Mr. Gresham rapped sharply on the floor with his cane. "No quarreling, young ladies. Remember we have a guest." He gave me one of his mechanical smiles, but there seemed a little more warmth in it this time, and though Emily lapsed into pouting silence the atmosphere was suddenly far less strained and unhappy. I could have hugged Amanda.

The journey in the landau took less than fifteen minutes. As we rattled along I was able to look about me and take in the scenery now, and I marveled at the number and variety of the trees. In the only land I knew, the area where I lived had few trees to show. Here there was abundance, and the rich green countryside seemed to have a strangely healing effect on me. It was as if the heritage in my blood carried with it an indefinable need which had been sleeping all these years, so that I became aware of it only now, when the beauty of England filled my eyes. I wanted to drink it all in, and to learn the names of all the trees and flowers we passed along the way.

Mr. Gresham's house stood on the outskirts of the tiny village of Hawkfield and was called High Coppice. As we turned between the stout pillars of the gate and moved up the drive I saw that the house stood on a ridge and that beyond it the ground sloped down to a broad valley, then rose to another long ride on the far side, perhaps a mile away.

The house itself was huge, and at that time I thought it was ugly, for it was all straight lines. I had been used to the tall pagodas and upcurving roofs of Chengfu. High Coppice seemed too squat and without harmony. In China the rich people built their houses to harmonize with the spirits of earth and water and air, but the only harmony I saw in High Coppice was the natural beauty of the ivy which clung to the yellow brick walls, mellowing and softening them.

As the landau halted outside the big front porch the doors were thrown open and a very distinguished-looking servant, a butler, appeared to greet his master. A less important servant, a young man in shirt-sleeves and an apron, took my suitcase and carried it in.

As we stood in the big hall, with the stairs rising to a gallery above, I looked about me in astonishment. Some of the doors leading to other rooms were open, and I could glimpse what lay beyond. I had never in my life seen so much furniture, so many pictures, so many carpets, so many vases, mirrors, ornaments, statuettes. For a moment I thought of Miss Prothero's Mission. Apart from one picture in the chapel, the only ornament I could think of was the slim bronze shield which was fixed to the wall in my bed cubicle, and this had survived only because I could not bring myself to chip it out of the wall and sell it.

Mrs. Gresham said, "Ah, Edmund dear, you're here." I saw a man coming down the stairs. He wore a dark suit with a high stiff shirt collar, and there could be no doubting that he was Mr. Gresham's son. He was about twenty-six or twenty-seven, I thought, and he had the same pale narrow face, but his manner was very different. Where Mr. Gresham was quick and almost jumpy in his movements, the son was sober and precise in a way more suited to a much older man. His gaze was rather cold, but after a moment I realized that it was not meant only for me and was not hostile; I had the impression that he was a man who studied and appraised all that went on about him, and that this was his natural demeanor.

[106]

"Good evening, Mamma," he said politely. "Was it a good trip? I see you've brought home Papa's latest possession safely." He gave me what seemed a carefully measured smile, but his reference to me as his father's possession had made me feel ill-at-ease again as I remembered that Mr. Gresham had bought me from the Mission people.

Mrs. Gresham said, "Yes, this is Lucy Waring. Lucy, this is our son, Edmund."

"Welcome to High Coppice, Lucy," he said, and put out his hand. As I took it and said, "How do you do," I made a little curtsy, but remembering my earlier mistake I watched carefully to make sure I did not repeat the blunder.

"Edmund lives and works in London," said Mrs. Gresham, "but he has come down today especially to greet you."

"That's very kind of you, Mr. Gresham," I said.

"I think you would do better to call me Edmund." Another small smile. "Otherwise we shall be inviting a degree of confusion." He glanced away to where his father stood at the foot of the stairs, speaking with the butler and a female servant in a black dress and frilly white cap.

"Edmund's a lawyer, he's very clever," Amanda said, swinging her handbag. "Mamma, can I take Lucy upstairs and show her where her room is?"

"Not 'can I,' but 'may I,' " Mrs. Gresham said with a sigh. "Very well, dear."

I was glad to escape from the hall. I felt happier with Amanda than with anybody else. She led me up the stairs and along a broad passage to a room which looked out over beautiful gardens to a wooded valley below. It was a big room, twice as big as Miss Prothero's at the Mission, and the furniture was in proportion. I thought with some envy that the huge, solidly-built wardrobe would have provided enough wood to keep our kitchen range going for a week.

"Take your hat off, and you sit down while I unpack for you," Amanda said, busying herself with the clasps of my case. "Oh dear, wasn't that journey *awful?* I'm sorry Emily

[107]

was horrid to you, but she can't really help it. Partly she's silly, and partly she's just got a horrid nature. I take no notice." She began to lift the clothes from my case and lay them on the bed, chattering away busily. "I think I was a little bit horrid myself, and I *am* sorry, but I felt giggly because we'd never met a Chinese girl before, I mean a girl from China, like you. Did you really mean that, about the Lord High Executioner cutting people's hands off? No, that's silly, isn't it? I expect you read it in a story book. But did you see Mamma's face? And Emily's? I nearly died, trying not to laugh. Oh dear, you haven't got many clothes, have you? And those you have got aren't very nice."

I stood beside her and looked at the clothes on the bed. "They're what the Mission at Tientsin found for me," I said.

Amanda held a dress in front of her and looked in the wardrobe mirror. "I suppose they're missionary sort of clothes," she said. "I'll talk to Papa and persuade him to buy you some new and pretty ones."

"Yours are beautiful," I said. "I'm not used to wearing English clothes, or even seeing other girls in them, so I didn't know mine weren't very nice."

"What did you wear in China, then?" Amanda asked, staring.

"Just trousers and a tunic and a padded jacket, with sandals or boots. That's what everybody wears except rich people, and they wear silk robes."

"You wore *trousers?*"

"Yes. They're much more comfortable than a dress."

"Emily wore them once when we played Charades, and she says they're not comfortable, but I expect that's because she's too fat for them. Anyway, I've never heard of a girl wearing trousers all the time. What a funny place China must be." She looked at herself in the mirror again and fingered the pale blue silk of her skirt. "Yes, this is a nice dress. My best for traveling. But Emily has all the really nice things, because she's Mamma's favorite."

[108]

"You mean after the first-born son? After Mr. Edmund?"

"Goodness, no! I don't think Mamma really likes boys very much. I think she'd have been pleased if we'd *all* been girls."

I shook my head, bewildered. In China a girl baby was often considered a disaster. Evidently it was going to take me a long time to understand this strange new country, for though Miss Prothero had sometimes described the ways and customs of England to me, and though I had read about them in books, I had never been truly able to grasp that people could think so differently.

There came a tap on the door, and when Amanda called "Come in," a maid entered carrying a big copper jug of hot water with a woollen cover to keep it warm. "Pour some in the washstand basin, Beattie," Amanda said. "Have you put out soap and towel? Everything Miss Lucy needs? Very well, that will be all."

The maid went out after pouring water into the big china bowl on the washstand, and Amanda said, "Mamma and Papa have their own bathroom, but we're not allowed to use that. Look, there's a hip-bath in this cupboard. When you wake up in the morning, just pull the bell-ribbon here, and when the maid comes tell her to bring hot water for your bath. She'll see to everything. I expect there are lots of things I'll have to explain to you, but there's plenty of time. I'm going to change now, I won't be long."

When she had gone skipping from the room I sat down on the bed and stared about me in awe. Mr. Gresham was clearly an enormously rich man. That explained something I had puzzled over from time to time. From the beginning it had struck me as strange that anybody should go to the trouble and expense of fetching a young girl from China, but now I realized that he must be so rich that he could afford to indulge whatever whim might take his fancy.

I took off my dress, washed my hands and face, and combed my hair afresh. Now that it was long enough I had begun to wear it in a single thick plait which hung down level with my shoulders. I put on another dress, which had been patched at one elbow but was not so dull as the other two, and had just finished doing up the buttons when Amanda returned.

"Come along, I'll show you round the house," she said eagerly. "Papa says it's much too big and we can't possibly afford to keep it up because we're poor as church mice, but he's been saying that for as long as I can remember. Anyway, he'd never give up High Coppice as long as those dreadful creatures are there across the valley."

Mr. Gresham poor? After a moment of astonishment I realized that this must be some sort of English joke, and I said, "What dreadful creatures?"

"Come and look." She moved to the window, and as I joined her she pointed at an angle across the valley. "There. That's where they live."

I looked, and my mind whirled. The view shimmered and blurred. For long moments I wondered if I was asleep and dreaming. I had to let my breath out slowly and make an effort to focus my eyes again, but nothing had changed. On the far side of the valley stood a house I knew. The only English house I knew. There was a sketch of it, a perfect sketch, on the old piece of coarse canvas rolled up and put away in my chest of drawers now. The house was two stories high, with lofty chimney stacks and a long steep roof with hipped gables rising high above the parapet. The windows were rectangular, and there were ornamental stone balls set on squat pillars on each short section of parapet in front of the two end gables. When I had shown Miss Prothero my picture long ago, she had told me that the façade was Georgian but that the proportions of the house were not, and that it was probably an older house which had been rebuilt in the seventeenth century. I counted the windows. I studied the chimneys, noting the tall stack at each end and the other three just showing over the ridge of the roof from the far side. I saw the single semicircular window of what I had always thought must be an attic room, set in the central and shallower gable. Everything was the same as in my picture.

I became aware of Amanda holding my arm and saying, "Are you all right? Lucy, are you all right? You look so funny all of a sudden."

I shook my head, unable to take my eyes from the house across the valley. "I'm all right. I—I just felt dizzy for a moment."

"Perhaps your stays are too tight?"

"No . . . I don't wear them, they suffocate me. But please don't tell your mother. English ladies seem to think it's wrong not to wear stays. Mrs. Colby did."

"I won't tell. You *look* as if you're wearing them, so I don't think Mamma will guess."

Still looking out across the valley I said, "What do they call that house, Amanda?"

"Moonrakers." She giggled. "The Falcons live there, and Mamma says it's just the right name for them. Do you know what 'moonraker' means?"

"No." I had not been mistaken. This was the house which I had known for so long. "Does it have a special meaning?"

"Yes, Papa told me. It's a word they use in Wiltshire. A moonraker is someone not right in the head. He sees the moon reflected in a pond and thinks it's a big round cheese lying there, so he gets a rake and tries to rake it out, and they call him a moonraker."

"Oh!" I said blankly. "And you said it suited the Falcons?"

"Yes, they do all sorts of funny things. Edmund says they're very Bohemian, but I'm not sure what that means."

I said, "Is Mr. Falcon a young man?"

"Of course not, silly. How could he be? He's about the same age as Papa. His wife's younger than Mamma, though, and very beautiful. Then there's Robert, but he's gone abroad somewhere, and two daughters who are married and have moved away, and a younger son still at school."

I turned from the window. It was very hard to grasp that

only a mile away stood Moonrakers, the house an unknown hand had sketched an unknown number of years ago on a rag of canvas which had been left in the Mission at Tsin Kai-feng. Robert Falcon, the elder son of the family, had come to China from that house seeking something, with a useless map in his hands and a meaningless riddle on his lips. I wondered if I should tell Amanda now that I had met him in China, but felt I needed time to think about it first.

I said, "You called them dreadful creatures just now."

She giggled again. "Oh, that's how we always speak of them. We hate them, and they hate us, too. It's been going on for years and years. A feud, Papa calls it."

"It must have begun for a reason, I suppose."

"Yes, of course it did. It began when Mr. Falcon's father and Papa's father, that's my *grand*father, were young men in the Army together, ages ago, in a place called Ferozepur, in India. They were great friends, but then they quarreled over something and fought a duel with pistols, and they killed each other. Papa and Mr. Falcon were just babies at the time, but their mothers and the rest of both families started a feud, and it's gone on ever since."

"You mean the mothers handed it down to their sons?"

"Yes. I can just remember Grannie Gresham, and I was frightened of her. She had a terrible look, like a witch about to put a curse on somebody. She and Mr. Falcon's mother, that was the other wife, they hated each other as long as they lived. When old Mrs. Falcon died, my grannie was very frail and hadn't set a foot outside her room for months, but she insisted on being taken to the funeral, so she could watch it, and they say in the village that that's what killed her, because she took a chill and died herself only three weeks later."

Amanda paused for breath and shrugged. "I suppose the feud isn't quite as bad as that now, really, but it's become a sort of habit, and we just go on not liking each other and not speaking."

My head was beginning to ache with unanswered questions.

What had Robert Falcon been seeking in China? What had Nicholas Sabine been seeking there? It must be the same thing, for they had both asked me the same riddle. And it must surely be something valuable, for China could be a dangerous place for foreign devils who did not know her, as Nicholas Sabine had found. He had lost his life in the search, and Robert Falcon had come close to doing so. For a moment I wondered if they had been hunting for the sketch which now lay in my chest of drawers, but that was absurd; it was simply a sketch and could have no special value.

Amanda was at the door. "Come on," she said, "I'll show you over the house."

I nodded, trying to empty my mind of all questions and speculation. I was in England now. Mr. Gresham had paid a lot of money for me and I was living under his roof. There was enough for me to think about, without racking my brains for an answer to a mystery I could not solve. My new life was about to begin, and I hoped fervently that I would be able to meet whatever new demands were made upon me.

It was encouraging to know that the ordeal of first meeting my new family was now behind me, and I felt that with a little care and caution I would make no more blunders. I did not know that before the evening was ended I would make the most dreadful mistake of all.

«FIVE»

THERE WERE three floors to the house, and the servants' quarters were on the top floor. A back staircase led down to a big kitchen and the servants' dining hall in the basement. The servants outnumbered the people to be served, for Mr. Gresham employed two housemaids, a parlormaid and a lady's maid, and there were also the cook, the butler and a young footman.

"It's becoming terribly expensive to keep enough servants to run the house," Amanda said. "Papa says he has to pay over two hundred pounds in wages every year. That includes the coachman, but we're lucky that he does the gardening as well, with a boy from the village. Mamma says we couldn't possibly manage with a smaller staff."

I noticed that the maids wore shoes or boots with elastic sides, and Amanda told me that all servants had to use such footwear to avoid squeaking as they walked. After a tour of the gardens we returned to the house by way of the terrace and french windows leading from the dining room. The butler was there, supervising the footman and parlormaid as they laid the long table for dinner.

When I had first seen the butler on our arrival I had thought him to be quite old, but now I saw that I had been mistaken. His short thick hair was white, but the face beneath it was the face of a man much younger than I had imagined. He moved quietly but easily, not at all like an elderly person, and I realized now that he was probably younger than Mr. Gresham. He wore dark trousers and tailcoat, and his manner was one of polite authority. The footman was similarly dressed, though I was to learn later that in some houses the footmen wore livery.

Amanda said, "Has Mrs. Trowbridge made something special for dinner, Marsh?"

I was shocked to hear her address him so rudely by his surname, but he seemed to take this as quite normal and gave a grave smile as he replied, "I understand there will be some of her excellent haricot bean soup, followed by braised sweetbreads and roast saddle of mutton, Miss Amanda." He turned his head a little to look at me. "Has Miss Lucy found everything to her satisfaction?"

I scarcely knew how to answer an older male person of such great dignity, but Amanda simply said, "Yes, everything's quite all right. Come along, Lucy. We'll go to the drawing room, and I'll show you our photograph album. We went to Frinton for a holiday last year, and there are photographs of me in the sea, right up to my waist."

When we were in the drawing room I said, rather pink-faced, "Amanda, what are all those knives and forks on the dining table for?"

She stared at me. "For the different courses. Oh goodness, did you use chopsticks in China?"

"No, just spoons mostly."

"However did you eat meat with a spoon? I suppose you

must have minced it. Well, just start at the outside and work your way inwards with the cutlery, and if you're not sure, watch what I do."

We spent half an hour looking at an album of photographs, then Mr. Gresham and Edmund came in, followed shortly by Mrs. Gresham and Emily. They were all beautifully dressed. Edmund seated himself in an armchair, leaned back, placed the tips of his fingers together and said, "Well, you look very nice, Lucy. What a pretty dress."

Amanda sighed. "Men are so silly. Can't you see it doesn't fit her properly and it's not new? It was made for somebody else and it's been altered." She turned to her father. "She must have some proper clothes, Papa. Lucy hasn't anything that's suitable for paying calls."

"We shall have to see what can be done," Mr. Gresham said heartily. "Becky, my dear, I think that matter is to your address."

"Of course," his wife agreed with little enthusiasm. "We must do what we must do. But really, what Mrs. Collins charges for dressmaking nowadays is quite exorbitant." For the next few minutes there was a discussion between Emily and her mother about dressmakers and dressmaking, with Mr. Gresham and Edmund scarcely putting in a word. Even though I had to some extent become used to English ways during the voyage, I still found the behavior of the female persons quite astonishing. They spoke without being spoken to first, they showed displeasure if they felt it, and they would disagree and even argue with male persons.

In China the women did not eat with their menfolk, but served them at table. For a female person to dispute with a male was unheard of, and they were not allowed to chatter as English women did. Under Chinese law a husband was even permitted to divorce his wife for being too talkative.

Emily was sitting on a big couch, playing with a small white kitten she had brought in with her, and when there was a pause in the conversation Mrs. Gresham looked at me with a smile that seemed to be rather an effort for her and said, "Do they have cats in Japan, Lucy?"

I was taken by surprise by the unexpected question and replied in some confusion, "Yes, I think so, Mrs. Gresham. We certainly have them in China."

"That is what I meant, dear. I think you should not be *too* ready to correct your elders, but we'll say no more for the moment. So you have cats in China. Do you like cats?"

"Well, they're better than no meat at all, Mrs. Gresham, but rabbit is much nicer."

Her eyes went quite glassy. I looked round and saw that everybody was staring at me with a shocked expression. Emily was clutching the kitten to her breast protectively. I said hastily, "Oh, I beg your pardon, I didn't realize you were talking about cats as pets, Mrs. Gresham. Only the rich people have them as pets in China. But there are lots of strays, and when there's a famine—"

"Thank you!" Mrs. Gresham broke in, her voice icy. "That will do, Lucy."

I sat looking down at my hands in my lap, the blood rushing to my cheeks, wondering what I had said to shock everybody. Miss Prothero herself had shown me how to tell the difference between rabbit and cat when both were skinned, for they looked very much the same then, and sometimes the meat-vendors would try to sell cat as rabbit. I always looked at the kidneys, for in a rabbit these were low down and in line, whereas in a cat they were higher and off-set. If Miss Prothero knew this, surely it meant that people in England must sometimes eat cat when they were hungry? But perhaps not. It dawned on me now that after forty years in China even Miss Prothero had become accustomed to habits which would have shocked her in England.

I knew I had made another blunder. It was a relief when Mr. Gresham broke the chilly silence by starting a rather stilted conversation with his wife, and an even greater relief when Mr. Marsh entered to announce that dinner was served.

Although the sun had not yet set, the swan-necked incandescent gas lamps on the walls of the dining room had been lit, and as the six of us took our seats at the long oak table the silver cutlery sparkled against the white cloth. Mr. Gresham said grace, and a moment later the young footman and a maid began to serve dinner under the watchful eye of Mr. Marsh.

Once again it was Amanda who broke the strained atmosphere. "Mamma, *why* do we have to have dinner served like this?" she demanded. "It was much better when the dishes were put on the table and we served ourselves. Albert and Maggie takes *ages* fiddling with the servers."

"It is the fashionable thing, dear," her mother said firmly. "I've read about it in a ladies' magazine. It is called *service à la russe,* and is the proper thing with all the best people these days."

Even if I had not felt too nervous to be hungry, I could never have eaten all the food that was offered for each course, but it was wonderful food, even better than had been served on the ship, and as I gradually felt more calm I began to enjoy such a splendid dinner.

I was not drawn into the conversation, for which I was glad. Mr. Gresham talked very little. He had a faraway look in his eyes, as if reflecting on some weighty matter. When Albert and Maggie had withdrawn for the last time after serving a delicious dessert of peaches in syrup with cream, Mr. Gresham said that we would have coffee at table instead of in the drawing room. Mr. Marsh himself brought this on a silver tray with small cups and saucers, and busied himself at the sideboard where there was a little spirit stove to keep the coffee hot.

When we had all been served, Mr. Gresham seemed to emerge from his reverie. Leaning back in his chair, he dabbed his mouth with a table napkin and gave me one of his brief, glassy smiles. "Well, now . . . no doubt it was a considerable

surprise to you, Lucy, when you learned that you were to become part of an English family?"

"Yes, sir," I said meekly. I had been more distressed than
surprised, but did not want to offend him by saying so.

"You'll never guess why Papa brought you here," said
Amanda, and shot a mischievous glance at Edmund, who
shrugged with a rather bored air and murmured, "I imagine
not."

I could not understand why they should think I was mysti-
fied. So far I had closed my mind to this aspect of my future
because it made me nervous, but the situation was long
familiar to me as a bystander.

Amanda said, "Go on, guess."

I hesitated, for I knew that in a Chinese household the
purposes of the senior male person would never be discussed in
such a way. But this was England, where manners were different. Everybody was looking at me expectantly, so I bowed
my head politely to Mr. Gresham and said, "I know you paid
a lot of money to the Mission, sir . . ." I had to speak slowly,
for the phrases which came to my mind were the Chinese
phrases I would have used if this had been happening in that
country, and I had to translate them as I went along. "I am
greatly honored that you have chosen this insignificant person
to be your concubine now that your wife is becoming old."

There was the most terrible silence. It was as if everybody
had stopped breathing and every heart had stopped beating.
My face grew stiff and my blood seemed to turn to ice, for I
knew I had done something dreadfully wrong. I could not turn
my head, I could only move my eyes to look round at the
others. It was like a tableau, with everybody frozen in position.

Mrs. Gresham was white, her mouth open, her eyes bulging
with shock and indignation. Emily looked much the same as
her mother, except that there was a glint of horrified delight
in her startled gaze. Edmund's eyebrows had shot up so high
that they almost touched his hairline. Amanda was round-
eyed, but there was much puzzlement in her surprise; she was

not quite sure what had caused the shock, but in no doubt of its immensity.

His face dark red with rage, Mr. Gresham rose. *"How dare you?"* he said in a frightful whisper. "How *dare* you speak so, in front of my wife and family? Have you no shred of shame in you?" He pointed to the door with a shaking hand. "Go to your room, miss! *At once!"*

Understanding broke upon me like a thunderclap. I had been a fool a thousand times over. English gentlemen did *not* have concubines. I knew it well. If I had thought, if I had *allowed* myself to think, I would have remembered. But in my stupidity, when I learned that a rich man had bought me, I had at once assumed that it was for the same reason I would have been bought in China, and from that instant I had refused to think about my situation.

I was so dazed by Mr. Gresham's anger that I could not find the strength to get to my feet. I caught a glimpse of Amanda, and saw that even she was alarmed by her father's rage. Edmund dabbed his brow with a handkerchief and said, "Father, I think perhaps you should consider—"

"Be silent, Edmund!" Mr. Gresham snapped. "You will make no defense of evil talk at my table! Here, under my roof, in your mother's hearing, this . . . this child of corruption suggested that I had *bought* her for abominable purposes!"

My voice, when I could get it out, was not much more than a whisper. "I beg your pardon, Mr. Gresham. It's just that I'm used to Chinese ways, and—"

"That will do!" he cried. "I will have no pretense of innocence, miss! To your room *at once!"*

Behind me, Mr. Marsh's voice said, "If you please, Miss Lucy." He drew back my chair as I rose. When I turned, I saw that his face was as calm as ever. He moved beside me to the door, and opened it for me. Mr. Gresham called in a harsh voice, "Leave us, Marsh. I'll ring if I want you."

The butler said, "Very good, sir," and followed me out. In the moment before the door closed I heard Mrs. Gresham's voice as she said with a rising wail of anguish, "Dear Heaven, Charles, what *have* you done? I *begged* you not to be so impulsive! What kind of creature have you burdened us with?"

As I walked slowly across the hall to the big staircase I felt a crushing despair. Although I now realized my error, I was stunned by the extent of the shock it had caused. What was so abominable about concubines? The Chinese girls who left the Mission were always glad to become concubines rather than field laborers. I would have preferred it the other way for myself, but could have given no sensible reason for this, unless it came from some instinct born of the foreign blood in me.

I was at the foot of the stairs when a voice spoke behind me. "Miss Lucy."

I turned. Mr. Marsh had followed me across the hall and was looking down at me now with an odd expression on his face, an expression in which I saw, beyond the gravity, something of sympathy, wonderment, and even amusement. "Don't distress yourself too greatly, Miss Lucy," he said. "I fancy Mr. Edmund already understands that your offense was not intentional but due to your background, and he will certainly argue the matter with the master when Mr. Gresham's anger has cooled a little."

I felt an upsurge of gratitude so powerful that tears stung my eyes. "You're very kind, Mr. Marsh."

He smiled. "Only the other servants address me in that way. You must call me Marsh."

"Oh, I couldn't, sir. You're an older male person—"

"You are no longer in China, Miss Lucy. For your own sake you must behave according to your position here."

"Yes. I'm sorry. It's so difficult for me." I could hear my voice shaking, and I drew in a long breath to steady it. "I realize I've been very stupid, but I hardly know what to do. Whatever I say seems to make them angry, especially Mrs. Gresham. She thinks I tell lies all the time."

"What lies, Miss Lucy?"

"Well . . . Emily asked if I'd seen an executioner, and when I just told the truth Mrs. Gresham was cross. She called it a silly tale. And this evening they were all cross because I said rabbit was nicer to eat than cat."

"I'm not surprised that they think you're making up such things, Miss Lucy."

"But do *you* believe me, Mr. Marsh?" I said anxiously. "I'm sorry, I mean just . . . Marsh."

"That's better. Yes, certainly I believe you, Miss Lucy. But then, I know Hong Kong, Shanghai, Port Said, Bombay, and a score of places all round the world." He must have seen the surprise in my look for he went on, "I haven't always been a butler, Miss Lucy. I was for many years in the Army as an officer's servant, and I traveled overseas a great deal." He flicked a tiny piece of fluff from his sleeve. "May I offer you some advice?"

"Oh, please."

"You are with an English family of the upper class. They have their virtues and their faults. One of their faults is a kind of blindness to everything beyond the borders of their own little world. They believe in their hearts that God is an English gentleman, and it therefore follows that their customs and habits have in their eyes the stamp of divine approval."

I was astonished at the way Mr. Marsh spoke. He sounded more like a well-educated gentleman than a servant. Again he must have seen my surprise, for he paused and said, "Are you wondering at a servant who can express himself in this way, Miss Lucy? Well, I had the good fortune to serve an officer who was also a scholar—a rare combination, I may say. By modeling myself on him, I acquired the ability to converse with a modest degree of fluency. In time he honored me with a measure of friendship, and we spent many long hours talking together over the years."

I was reminded of Miss Prothero making me practise the

art of conversation, and said, "Yes, I understand, Mr. Marsh."

"Marsh," he said sharply.

"Oh, I'm sorry. Marsh."

He smiled his approval, then went on, "The word concubine would never be spoken in front of English ladies. You have lived all your life in China, and I have no doubt you wore trousers, as they all do. Here, the sight of a woman in trousers would shock most people. Even the legs of the grand piano are draped, as you may have noticed, because legs are deemed to be somewhat improper. If you have to refer to them, Miss Lucy, you must speak of 'lower limbs.'" He looked at me quizzically. "I hope this gives you some inkling of the shock which struck the family just now when you suggested that Mr. Gresham had bought you as a concubine?"

"Yes. Oh yes," I said feebly, and pressed both hands to my brow, staring at him. "But you . . . you *were* joking about piano legs, surely?"

"I fear not, Miss Lucy. No doubt you find it hard to believe, but perhaps it will help you understand why *you* were disbelieved when you spoke of the executioner, and of eating cat." He gave me a somber look. "I have seen the poor in India eat earth to ease their hunger. I have seen thieves punished by maiming in Jiddah, in Arabia. Like you, Miss Lucy, I have seen a hundred things that go beyond the imaginings of Mr. Gresham and his family. They will never understand the kind of life you have led. They barely understand how poor people here in England live. Try to remember that."

He glanced across the hall. "You must go to your room now, Miss Lucy. I'll see that some hot milk is sent to you. If I may advise you, try to carry on tomorrow as if nothing had happened. Ring for your bath at eight. Come down for breakfast at nine. I'm sure you will find matters have improved. Avoid speaking of your life in China, and devote

[123]

yourself to learning the ways of this country." He stepped back and gave me a little bow. "I'll wish you good night now, Miss Lucy."

I was so touched by his kindness that I could hardly speak, but I managed to say, "Thank you, Mr.—thank you, Marsh, with all my heart."

"It is my pleasure." He moved away with quiet dignity, and I went on up the stairs. The gas mantles in my room had been lit but were very dim, and it took me a little while to discover that I could make the light brighter by pulling one of the two little chains hanging from each bracket. Soon the maid called Beattie arrived with a glass of hot milk on a tray, and for an hour I sat in the bedside chair, thinking of all that had happened in the few hours since I had set foot in England. I had done very badly, but tomorrow I would make a new start, I decided, and I would keep my wits about me to avoid further catastrophes.

Sleep did not come easily, and I know my dreams were troubled, even though I could not recall them when I woke soon after dawn. By half-past seven I was becoming nervous and fretful at having nothing to do but wait for the time when I could ring for my bath, so I took out the Traveler's Friend Sewing Case which Mrs. Colby had bought for me and settled down to make sure that all buttons and seams of my clothes were in good repair.

There came a tap on the door, and before I could say a word it opened quickly and Amanda darted in, closing the door behind her. She was wearing a dressing gown, and full of excitement. "Oh, you're up!" she said breathlessly. "Lucy, how *awful* you were last night! Emily told me what a concubine is, it's like another wife. No wonder Papa was so furious!"

"I didn't mean to insult your parents," I said anxiously. "Truly, Amanda. I'm so used to the way people live in China, I didn't stop to think."

"That's what Edmund said. He's a lawyer you see, so he

has to think about things. Anyway, there was an awful commotion, but in the end Papa decided to do nothing more
about it." She giggled. "There's not much he *can* do, is there?
I mean, he can't send you back to China."

"I suppose not," I said slowly, trying to hide my regret. A
thought occurred to me, and I was surprised that it had not
come before. "Amanda, why *did* your father bring me to
England?"

"Oh, it's one of his schemes. He's always thinking of
schemes to make us rich, but they never work. Mamma said
this one was quite absurd, and Edmund thought the same,
but Papa gets furious if anyone criticizes his plans." She
turned to the door. "Don't say I've told you about it, Lucy."

"But you haven't," I said, bewildered. "Have you?"

"No, not exactly. He'll want to tell you himself. He's going
to talk to you after breakfast." She opened the door a little,
peeped through the crack, then darted out.

I might have enjoyed the luxury of my hot bath if my
mind had not been churning with questions. As the grandfather clock in the hall was striking nine I went down to the
dining room for breakfast. Edmund was already there and
had almost finished. I said a timid, "Good morning."

"Good morning, Lucy." He studied me in a manner that
was neither friendly nor unfriendly. "In England we serve
ourselves breakfast from the dishes on the sideboard." He
waved a hand in that direction. "You'll find kidneys, bacon,
kedgeree, eggs, etcetera. Take a plate and help yourself."

I thanked him, wondering what happened to all the food
that must be left over after every meal. By the time I had
taken some bacon and one or two kidneys, Edmund was folding his newspaper and rising from the table. "You will excuse
me," he said in his precise voice. "I must be at my office by
ten-fifteen, and I have a train to catch. I suggest you make
no reference to last night's—ah—misunderstanding, Lucy. It's
best left alone. No doubt I shall see you again when I come
down at the weekend. Good morning."

Again I thanked him and wished him good morning. Only a few minutes after he had gone, Mr. Gresham and Amanda arrived. The atmosphere during breakfast was uneasy, but still far better than I had dared to hope. It was a relief to learn that Mrs. Gresham and Emily would not be down for breakfast. They were in the habit of taking breakfast in their rooms, and rarely rose before eleven o'clock. I took little part in the rather stiff conversation, except to answer very politely and carefully whenever I was spoken to. When Amanda asked what we had for breakfast in China I simply said, "We had millet porridge mostly." I did not think there could be any danger in saying that, but even so I was anxious for a few moments.

After breakfast Mr. Gresham said, "Time for your piano practice, Amanda. Run along now. I have matters to discuss with Lucy in my study."

It was a large study, cluttered with a host of strange objects. I had expected to see quite a number of books, and indeed hoped to, but here they were everywhere, not only on shelves but in piles on the floor and on side tables. Yet even the books made only a small part of the great miscellany which filled the room.

There was a desk in one corner, piled with papers and bearing a large globe of the world. Beside the globe was a rectangular glass bowl of strange-looking fish, very tiny and of amazing colors. A human skeleton hung from a bracket on one wall. Along another wall were seed boxes covered with sheets of glass and containing what appeared to be sand with a few tiny green shoots sprouting from it. A dusty telescope was mounted on a tripod near the window. A magic lantern stood on a chair in one corner, and a model steam engine on a shelf, though it was only later that I learned what these were.

The more I stared the more I saw, large objects and small, familiar and unfamiliar, but with no kind of pattern. Mr. Gresham paced across the room with those quick, jerky movements which were characteristic of him. Pulling open a drawer of the desk, he took out a small box which was carved in oriental fashion.

"Well now," he said enthusiastically, waving an arm to encompass the room. "As you see, I am a keen student of the Orient, my dear."

I could not think of anything to say, and looked around the study again for help. Now one or two items particularly struck my eye. On the globe, a ring had been drawn with a red pencil around the Jehol province of China. On the wall beside the skeleton there were large-scale maps drawn by hand. I recognized a shape I had seen in Miss Prothero's atlas, the Gulf\of Liaotung, which was the nearest sea coast to our Mission.

"You see?" Mr. Gresham exclaimed, and pointed to a table near the fireplace. On it was a pile of books, and when I moved closer I could make out by the titles that they were books about traveling in China. Beside them was a large metal tray on which a landscape had been molded in some kind of clay. There were river valleys and plains, hills and ridges, with small wooden symbols for towns.

"Come now," Mr. Gresham said with a touch of impatience. "Surely you can see this represents the province of Shansi?"

"I'm afraid I've never been there," I said unhappily.

"Oh!" He gave me a blank look. "Well, never mind, I'm sure you are familiar with much else."

"I recognize that map on the wall," I said, anxious to please, "and I see you've marked Jehol province on the globe, but a lot of things aren't to do with China, Mr. Gresham. They would never display a skeleton, because it would be somebody's ancestor—"

"No, no, the skeleton has nothing to do with it," Mr. Gresham said testily. "That concerned an interest I have now discarded." He looked around the study and blinked as if vaguely surprised. "I seem to have one or two items here which hark back to former interests, but ignore them, Lucy, ignore them. We are concerned with *China,* eh?" He gave a chuckle. "And you are certainly an expert on that subject, I'm sure."

Lifting the small box he tapped it with one finger and looked at me significantly. "It's more difficult than seeking a needle in a haystack. We are hunting for *something* in a haystack, so to speak, but we are not at all sure what it is, or even where to find the right haystack. However, you were born in China, you know the language, the people and the customs, so you are the right person to assist me in my search. Oh, I expect no miracles, Lucy. Perhaps it will take months of patient deduction, but we shall persevere."

I found this all very bewildering, and said hesitantly, "Do you mean you will be going to China, Mr. Gresham, and you wish me to go with you to help find something?"

"Go there? Good heavens no, child!" He looked quite startled. "Somebody else will attend to the physical side of the matter, the traveling and so forth. My task is one of applying *intellect* to this affair." He gave a smug smile. "Like you, Edmund thinks that one should send a suitable man to carry out the search on the spot, but that would be seeking at random. Deduction must come first, and I have my methods, Lucy. Yes, I have my methods. You have read Mr. Conan Doyle's stories of Sherlock Holmes, of course? No? Well, never mind. He is a detective who solves mysteries by his powers of observation and deduction, and I have a similar cast of mind. That is how I shall solve this problem, Lucy. And you, with your knowledge of the Inscrutable East, will provide the framework in which the power of my intellect can operate. Do you understand?"

This was the moment when I told my first lie in England, by nodding my head. I was afraid that if he began to explain it all over again I would only be more confused than ever. Besides, he had paid the Mission a great sum of money for me, and he was entitled to have me understand him.

[128]

"I will give you a strange clue to think upon," he said, opening the box and taking out a slip of yellow paper. "Now listen."

Almost before he had begun to read from the paper I knew the words he would speak, but this sudden foreknowledge did not diminish the shock.

"Beyond the twisted giant's knife . . ."

I knew the riddle by heart. Mr. Gresham was the third Englishman who had recited it to me. Robert Falcon had done so by the Mission wall. And Nicholas Sabine in Chengfu . . .

Unwanted memories broke suddenly free in my mind, seeming to sweep me back into the past. I saw him now, in my mind's eye, as he crouched holding my hands through the bars of the prison cell . . . he had saved me from being maimed, and in gratitude I had become his wife for the few hours of life left to him, because he wished it so . . . and when that poor sad marriage ceremony in the dark prison was ended, I had gone away and seen him no more . . . I had laid a posy of wildflowers on his grave, and I still had the ring he had given me, but I did not want him to linger in my memory, for it brought me an aching sorrow.

". . . Rest the sightless tiger's eyes."

Mr. Gresham completed the rhyme. Then he must have looked up and seen my face, for his voice changed and he said sharply, "Lucy! What is it?"

I drew a deep breath and said, "I'm sorry. I was startled, Mr. Gresham. I know the riddle. I've heard it before."

"What? How's that, girl? When did you hear it?"

"In China. I met Mr. Robert Falcon there."

"What?"

"It's true, Mr. Gresham. Yesterday Amanda told me about

the family that lives across the valley, and she said the elder son, Robert Falcon, was abroad. Well, I met him in China, and I'm sure it must be the same person. He asked the same riddle."

"You *met* him? Good God, did you help him? Did you tell him the answer?" There was as much anger as alarm in Mr. Gresham's voice.

"No sir, no," I said quickly. "I couldn't help him. I don't know what the riddle means."

He exhaled a great sigh of relief, then began to pace the study, running a hand over his head. "Extraordinary! It's hard to believe such a thing—but no, perhaps it's not so strange. If the young whelp went out there to search the general area, it isn't altogether surprising that you met him." He swung round upon me. "What happened? Tell me about it."

As briefly as I could, I told of my meeting and what had passed, but I did not speak of Nicholas Sabine or of the sketch Robert Falcon had drawn when warning me against him. "I met Mr. Falcon a second time," I ended. "We passed on the road to Chengfu and he spoke of the riddle again, but I still couldn't help him."

Mr. Gresham rubbed his chin. "Well, in that case there's no harm done," he said grudgingly. "Did he show you a map?"

"Yes, but a lot of things were missing from it. He said they were on another map."

"I know, I know. His was the Falcon map. We have the Gresham map, which completes it. The two can only be read together." He jerked open a drawer and took out a rectangle of parchment. I had seen its twin in China.

"Here Lucy, look. Now, can you remember the map young Falcon showed you?"

I gazed at the features drawn in black ink on the parchment and shook my head. "I'm sorry, Mr. Gresham. I didn't memorize anything, and I don't think it would help very much even if you had both maps. There are so many places in China which look alike, just a village and a few groves and a river."

He frowned. "Oh, nonsense. A whole map must be better than half a map. Just give thought to it, and try to remember." He waved a hand to indicate the globe, the books, and the carefully made miniature landscape. "I am gradually assembling facts, Lucy, and I'm sure that if we persevere we shall be able to deduce the truth, able to narrow down the search to a small and definite area." He smiled one of his peculiar brief smiles. "My methods will prove superior to those of Robert Falcon, have no fear of that. Do you know the story *behind* this search, Lucy? Did he tell you?"

"No, Mr. Gresham. But Amanda said something about a feud long ago, when her grandfather and Robert Falcon's grandfather were in the Army together."

"Quite so. Sit down, Lucy. I think it best for you to know the whole story, so you will understand what I am trying to do. Have you heard of the Opium Wars in China?"

"Yes. Miss Prothero told me about them, though they were a little before her time."

"Well, my father, William Gresham, and John Falcon of Moonrakers were young officers serving with the British Army in China at that time. Both had been married the year before, in 1841. During the campaign they were sent as couriers on a special and secret mission which took them through territory where two war lords were fighting each other for control. Do you understand?"

I said that I did. There were still war lords in China, men who gathered an army and were able to impose their will on large areas, sometimes as big as a province, unless a more powerful war lord defeated them, or they offended against the Empress herself, who might send an army to punish them.

"These two young men skirted the battleground where the soldiers of the rival war lords were fighting," Mr. Gresham went on. "And then, at dusk, they came upon a dying man who had dragged himself from the battle. They could not understand a word he spoke, of course, but he was dressed in a fine uniform and they concluded that this was the defeated war lord himself. As they tried to tend his wounds, he died."

Mr. Gresham moved to his cluttered desk and sat down. "There are many details we can never know," he went on solemnly, "but on the dead man they found . . . something. A package, a bag, a case, we don't know what, but it contained something of great value—the dead war lord's personal treasure." He spread his hands. "Whatever it was, William Gresham and John Falcon decided to take it rather than leave it for whoever next found the body. They rode on, and later they rested for the night . . . somewhere."

He shrugged. "They spent a week on the whole journey, and we don't know their exact route, but I believe they stayed in an abandoned temple that night, because a temple is mentioned in the riddle. However, at some time during the night or in the morning they found that their presence had been discovered by enemy patrols of the Chinese Army, and they were in great danger of being caught. They therefore hid the treasure, so that if they were caught, but avoided death, they would be able to return in quieter times and recover what they had hidden."

He touched the old hand-drawn map on the desk. "They must have drawn the two maps later, perhaps from sketches made at the time. We only know that after hiding the treasure they continued on their mission, and had the good fortune to complete it safely. And then, two months later, their regiment was withdrawn from China and sent to India."

Mr. Gresham looked at me, blinking rapidly. "They had no chance to regain what they had hidden. No doubt they planned to take a long leave at the first opportunity and go back to China for that purpose. Meanwhile John Falcon amused himself by writing a cryptic piece of doggerel to indicate the whereabouts of this hidden fortune, and both men made wills, which they gave to their Commanding Officer for safe-keeping. Attached to each will was a brief account of their exploit, a copy of the riddle, and one of the two complementary maps." Mr. Gresham made a grimace. "All very romantic, no doubt. At that time they wanted to be sure that if anything happened to either of them, both families would share the fortune—if it could be recovered."

He shook his head dolefully. "And then they quarreled over some foolishness. An unmeant insult, perhaps. We shall never know, though I'm quite certain Falcon was the offender. The upshot was a duel, held in secret, of course, since dueling had long been made illegal. Both were mortally wounded. Both died in the same hour. Their wives were informed—my mother here in this house, Harry Falcon's mother in Moonrakers. He and I were babies only a few months old at the time."

Mr. Gresham was silent for a few moments, frowning, then he rose and began to pace the study again. "Now the two families are rivals for the treasure," he said. "There will be no sharing, for neither of us owns it as of right. It will go to whoever first lays hands on it. That hotheaded young fool Robert Falcon appears to be blundering about China in search of it. Well, let him waste his time! This battle will be won by *intellect,* Lucy." He tapped a finger to his temple.

Something was puzzling me, and I said, "Why has it been left so long, Mr. Gresham? I mean, why haven't you or Mr. Falcon searched for it before?"

"Because we first learned of it less than two years ago!" he exclaimed, interlinking his fingers and rubbing his hands together vigorously. "The story has only recently come to light."

"I'm sorry. I don't understand."

"It's quite simple. Soon after the duel there was a mutiny of the Indians in Ferozepur, where the regiment was stationed. It was rapidly put down, but the Commanding Officer was killed. His effects were packed up by his servant to be sent home to his widow, and the wills and attached documents entrusted to him by William Gresham and John Falcon were accidentally included with his own papers. His widow could never bring herself to go through his effects in detail. They were stored away in a trunk and put in the attic. Almost sixty years later, her grandson made a great clearance of accumulated rubbish in the house. He found the two sealed envelopes, marked with the names of the two men, and took them to the War Office, who forwarded them to Harry Falcon and to me respectively. Until that moment, nobody had ever known of our grandfathers' exploit in China—and both families have been careful to keep the secret since, you may be sure."

I thought to myself that he was mistaken in one respect. There had been somebody outside the two families who knew of the fortune, and that was Nicholas Sabine. He had been seeking it, too.

"If only we had some idea of what to look for," Mr. Gresham was saying, gazing dreamily at one of the maps on the wall. "Is it large or small? We can deduce an upper limit by the fact that one man was able to carry it—why do you look surprised, Lucy?"

"I was just thinking that it couldn't be very big, Mr. Gresham. I mean, emeralds don't take up much room, and even a small bag the size of a purse would hold a fortune."

For a moment I thought his eyes would start from his head. Twice he tried to speak before a word came out. *"Emeralds?"* he cried. "How do you know? Did you tell young Falcon? Were you lying to me just now? Answer me at once!"

I was hopelessly confused, and almost in despair at having angered him again. "But . . . but it *says* emeralds in the riddle," I stammered. "I thought you knew. I thought Mr. Falcon and *everybody* knew. That's why I didn't say anything."

"Knew *what?* There's nothing about emeralds in the riddle!"

"Tiger's eyes, sir. That's what they call them in China. At least, in Chengfu and all around that area. I can't speak for other parts." It dawned on me that I had been very stupid. "I—I'm sorry. It was obvious to me, and I thought it was obvious to everybody, but I can see now that I was wrong. I expect the young officer who wrote the verse must have picked up the local Chinese phrase for emeralds, and he used it for the riddle. Please forgive me for being so dense, Mr. Gresham."

He threw his arms up with a cry of delight, and his glassy smile remained fixed for several seconds as he gazed at me. "Thank heaven you were! It prevented you telling that fool Falcon! Oh, capital! I was right, you see, you don't realize how much you know, Lucy—but I shall draw it out of you. Your knowledge and my intellect will do the trick, my dear. I am delighted with you!"

At luncheon Mr. Gresham proudly announced that with my help he had already discovered exactly what the treasure was. Mrs. Gresham was not greatly impressed by the one small piece of information I had provided, and truth to tell neither was I, for it did nothing to tell us where the treasure had been hidden long ago. However, Mr. Gresham remained enthusiastically convinced that he was already well on the way to success and seemed to regard me more kindly now.

My greatest concern was to persuade Mrs. Gresham and Emily to like me a little better, but over the next two days I came to realize that my hopes of doing so were small. Edmund returned on the Friday evening, to spend the weekend at home, and I was quite pleased to see him because I felt that at least he did not positively dislike me. On the Sunday morning we attended Matins at the village church. I had been looking forward to this, for I felt that in church I would be able to stop worrying about making blunders and be at ease for a little while.

It was here that I first saw the Falcon family. It seemed that Mr. Falcon and Mr. Gresham were the most important gentlemen in the village, for their pews were placed between the main congregation and the pulpit, facing each other from opposite sides of the church. Mr. Falcon had the same bright hair as his son Robert, and wore a short beard. He looked like a picture I had once seen of an English king, Richard the Lionheart. His wife was also fair, with a beautiful oval face crowned by honey-colored hair. Slender and graceful, she looked a happy person.

There were three people with them, two men and a woman, all dressed more strikingly than most of the ladies and gentlemen I had seen so far. They seemed very full of self-confidence, and chattered in rather loud whispers while we were waiting for the service to begin. No nod or look of greeting was exchanged between the two families, but I heard Mrs. Gresham whisper to her husband, "They have some of their fast poet and painter friends staying the weekend with them, I see. How can they bring such scandalous people to church?"

The organ had been playing softly. Now it faded to silence. The vicar intoned a prayer and announced the first hymn. There was a rustle of hymn books, and I found to my delight that the hymn was *Onward, Christian Soldiers,* which was a great favorite at the Mission. Eagerly I drew a deep breath so that I would not be left behind. I was only just in front of the choir with the first word, but then I went steadily ahead, singing with all my heart.

I was surprised to find how slow the choir and congregation were, and thought that even the four-year-olds at the Mission could have beaten them, but evidently the organist did not want to lose the race, for he began to play faster, turning his head to glance in my direction with a startled look. Even so, at the end of the first verse I was almost a line ahead, and I glanced up happily at Mrs. Gresham beside me, hoping for a look of approval.

Her face was pink, her mouth tightly shut, and she was looking down sideways at me from the corners of her eyes. Beyond her, Mr. Gresham was leaning forward to glare at me, and on my other side Amanda kept urgently digging her elbow into my ribs.

"How *dare* you!" Mrs. Gresham muttered between stiff lips. "Follow the choir!"

I shrank inwardly, and felt sick. In all my years at the Mission, the morning hymn had been a race. But I remembered now that when I was still small, there had been a time when Miss Prothero tried to make the children sing slowly, as she and I sometimes sang together in the English way. She had soon given up the hopeless attempt. I wished desperately that I had remembered about it sooner.

The hymn continued, and I sang quietly, keeping strictly in time with the organist and choir. It occurred to me that this was really the way I liked to sing, the way I always sang on my own when working about the Mission. By the time we came to the last verse I was beginning to hope that Mrs. Gresham would overlook my foolish mistake, but I was careful to avoid letting myself be carried away again, and made sure that I sang no louder than Amanda beside me.

There was only one other anxious moment during the service. We were singing the *Te Deum,* and I was caught completely unprepared when all the Gresham family, together with quite a number of others in the congregation, stopped singing when we came to the line, *"Thou didst not abhor the Virgin's womb. . . ."* Because the volume of singing suddenly dwindled, my own voice seemed to ring out loudly, and again I was aware of Mrs. Gresham's darting look of displeasure.

When we left the church after the service, people stood chatting and greeting one another for a few minutes, and during this time I was introduced to the vicar. I was barely aware of what he said to me, or I to him, for I was conscious only of the black looks on the faces of the Gresham family. Even Amanda gave me a furious scowl, and Edmund's gaze was cold. Other people were looking at me, some with kindly amusement, others with disapproval. I saw the Falcons and their party briefly, and they seemed to be in great good humor as if they had relished the occasion.

Nothing was said until we were in the carriage and on our way home, then Mrs. Gresham let out a long hissing sound, as if she had been holding her breath all through the service. "Did you see them? Did you see the faces of those dreadful creatures, Charles?" she demanded in a shaking voice. "That child chose to disgrace us in front of *them*, of all people! I have never seen anything so deliberate in my life."

"She made fools of us in front of the whole village," Emily chimed in with a venomous look.

Edmund said, "You have no evidence that it was deliberate, Mamma. But it was certainly the most extraordinarily inept behavior."

My face had gone stiff, and I knew it wore the expression Mrs. Gresham would think sullen. I said, "I'm sorry. We used to sing fast at the Mission because of the children, and I—I didn't realize it would be different."

"Nonsense!" snapped Mrs. Gresham. "Oh, and another thing! You will *not* sing that particular line in the *Te Deum* in future. Such words are not for the lips of ladies."

Bewilderment was added to my misery. I could only imagine that wombs, like legs, must be considered improper. Mr. Gresham said nothing, but sat with his hands resting on his cane, glowering about him.

It was several days before the family unbent toward me. I doubt if Mrs. Gresham and Emily ever forgot or forgave me, but since I was living with the family they could not treat me as a leper indefinitely, and as time went by they began to speak to me again, though Emily rarely did so without some undercurrent of malice.

My first week at High Coppice set the pattern of my life there. An hour every morning was spent in the study with

Mr. Gresham, covering the same ground over and over again as I tried to help him make deductions from his clues. After this I was free until luncheon, and for at least an hour afterward but more often two hours. The rest of the afternoon was spent paying or receiving "morning calls"—a strange name for visits made in the afternoon, but that was what they were called. I hated them. We sat either in our own drawing room or in the house of one of Mrs. Gresham's friends, and made conversation while sipping tea and eating cucumber sandwiches.

At first I was an object of much curiosity, and many questions were asked me about my life in China, some of them silly. I had learned my lesson, and never said more than a word or two in reply, sometimes telling lies because I knew the truth would give offense. In a very short time I was considered a dull and timid little mouse, as I overheard one lady describe me. I was relieved, for it meant that they soon lost interest in me.

The evenings, before and after dinner, were spent in the drawing room, though often Mr. Gresham went to his study. This was a time for the ladies of the family to gossip while they did little pieces of embroidery or needlework of some kind. Amanda taught me to play draughts, and I learned quickly, but soon found that she did not like to be beaten, so I was careful to lose. Sometimes she played the piano for us, which I always enjoyed for she played very well. Occasionally, after dinner, we would play pencil and paper games for a little while before the ladies went to bed. The one I liked most was Anagrams. Each of us in turn would give the others two or three short words, from which they had to make a single long word using exactly the same letters.

But my moments of pleasure were few, for day after day went by and I could not find one single thing to do which was in any way useful. All my life I had risen each day with the knowledge that there were urgent problems to be met and work to be done if we were not to go hungry. Now there was nothing. Once I asked Mrs. Gresham if I could help in the kitchen or with the cleaning, but I received a very sharp refusal. "For better or worse, Mr. Gresham brought you here as a young lady of the family," she said sternly but with a note of regret. "And young ladies do *not* soil their hands with menial tasks, Lucy."

It had become quite proper over recent years for young ladies to play tennis, I found, and a net had been set up in the garden. There was no tennis court, but we were able to hit the ball back and forth across the net to one another. I enjoyed this, but again found myself in trouble. Emily's way of playing was to stand quite still and make no attempt to hit the ball unless it came easily within her reach, complaining loudly when it did not. Amanda would trot about daintily, squeaking with excitement whenever she hit the ball over the net. But Mrs. Gresham found me with my skirts and waist-petticoat gathered up in one hand, my legs exposed up to the knees, running about as I would have run when playing with the children at the Mission. For this I received another severe lecture on the way a young lady should conduct herself.

Bicycling was allowed. Amanda and Emily had a bicycle each which they sometimes rode in the country lanes and when going to the village. I learned to ride in the garden on Amanda's bicycle, which she very kindly lent me. This passed a few hours, and I would have loved to go out on my own and explore the countryside, but Mrs. Gresham would not allow it. I think she feared I would do something else to disgrace the family if I were not kept under her eye.

Each weekend Edmund came down from London. Although he had little to say to me, his manner was not unfriendly. To me he seemed a man without warmth or emotions, but he had a sense of what was fair, and I suppose this came of being a lawyer.

If I compared my life at High Coppice with the life I had known before, it seemed wicked that I did not feel happy. I was never hungry now, I had some pretty new clothes and every comfort, and there were no burdens of responsibility on my shoulders. Yet sometimes I lay in bed at night wondering how I could endure the months and years which lay ahead, for I lived with people who had no need of me and who did not like me much, except perhaps for Amanda. I had always been needed before, and the children had loved me. This was what I missed.

In the middle of July Mr. Gresham suddenly lost his enthusiasm for our daily task of trying to deduce the whereabouts of the Gresham fortune, as he called it. I was not surprised, for we had made no progress at all, and Amanda had warned me that her father was a man of sudden but short-lived enthusiasms. Over the years he had taken up many schemes for making a lot of money quickly, but had never followed them through. The seed boxes in his study were relics of his last scheme, which had been concerned with a system of mixing chemicals with sand so that crops could be grown in the desert.

I knew that both the Gresham and Falcon families needed to restore their fortunes, for this was often a subject of conversation. At first I could not believe it, but slowly I came to understand that Mr. Gresham lived on a private income, which meant that he did not work to earn money, and his capital was slowly dwindling because he had to use a little of it each year for living expenses. The same applied to Mr. Falcon, except that according to the Greshams he and his wife frittered their money away on their Bohemian friends in London, where they often spent several days at a time, mingling with painters and writers and theatrical people.

My failure to help solve the riddle of the war lord's treasure added to my uneasiness. I was another mouth to feed, and I gave nothing in return. When I thought how great a disappointment I must be, I felt that in all the circumstances the Greshams were more amiable toward me than I deserved. I only wished that Mr. Gresham had never sent for me in the first place.

One night toward the end of July, I found myself suddenly awake. I wondered what had disturbed me. The room was completely dark and I had no way of knowing the time, but I felt sure that it must be in the early hours. Something troubled me . . . yes, it was completely dark now, but in the moment of waking I felt there had been a pale light reflected on the ceiling, a light which had vanished abruptly as I stirred and lifted my head.

A faint smell touched my nostrils, and in a flash I was sitting upright, for I knew that somebody was in the room with me.

"Amanda!" I whispered. "Is that you?"

No reply came from the darkness, but I knew that distinctive smell. It was from an acetylene lamp. Amanda and Emily had them on their bicycles, though they never rode abroad after dark. Peering into the blackness I saw a tiny, curving thread of light hovering in the air. My skin crawled. This was no bicycle lamp, but a lamp with a shutter . . . a dark lantern. Who would be in my room with such a thing at this time of night?

A board creaked, and I bit my lip to hold back a gasp as the memory of that darkened cabin on the ship came back to me, when I had been seized and half suffocated. Strangely, I did not think to cry out for help, perhaps because during my last year at the Mission I had grown used to having nobody I could turn to, whatever trouble or danger might threaten.

The hairline of light escaping from the shutter seemed to move. I reached out and groped carefully for the candlestick on my bedside cabinet. My fingers touched . . . grasped it. Then I knelt up in bed with the heavy brass candlestick poised, and waited for that floating filament of light to come nearer.

« S I X »

I said sharply into the darkness, "Who's there?"

Silence answered me. The thin crack of light vanished, and I knew that the intruder must be shielding the dark lantern with his body. I sat straining my eyes and ears, the heavy candlestick raised.

There came the soft click of the door latch, followed by the faintest creak of a hinge. A pause . . . a sharper click from the latch, then complete silence. After a moment or two I knew I was alone. I could sense it. The intruder was on the hall landing now.

I fumbled for the box of matches, reversed the candlestick, found that the candle was still in its socket, and lit the wick with hands that shook. Jumping out of bed I went quickly to the door and opened it, lifting the candle so that the flame cast a wider ring of light. The landing was empty. I moved to the head of the stairs, then back and along the two passages which led to the other bedrooms. Nothing stirred but my own shadow, thrown on the walls by the light of the candle.

Slowly I made my way back to my own room, closed the door and sat on the bed. Should I tap on Mr. Gresham's door and tell him what had happened? It seemed the right thing to do, but I shrank from it, knowing that Mrs. Gresham would surely believe I was telling lies again, and her husband would be at least half inclined to agree with her.

I knew I had not been dreaming. Even now the smell of acetylene lingered. I looked about me, wondering why the intruder had come to my room rather than any other. When I looked in the wardrobe, in the drawers and in my suitcase, there was no sign that anything had been taken or disturbed.

At last I went back to bed and blew out the candle. The warmth of the bed did not dispel the coldness in me for a long time, for it was an inward chill. Perhaps I was in a more sensitive state of mind than usual, but I seemed to sense the first tendril of some nameless danger reaching out to touch me. For the rest of the night I slept poorly, and for the first time in many days I dreamed again of the prison at Chengfu, of Nicholas Sabine, and of Robert Falcon.

In the morning I realized that in only two months would come the time when I was supposed to go to Nicholas Sabine's solicitors and make myself known as his wife, but that was impossible now. I had no marriage papers, and did not even know the name of the solicitors, for I had never been able to bring myself to look closely at the will or the other papers. All I had read was his last letter to me. I told myself that I could not help what had happened, but I still felt guilty for having failed him.

At breakfast Mrs. Gresham and Emily joined us at table, which did not happen very often. Apart from this, everything was as usual. In the light of day, and after my nightmarish dreams, I began to doubt the reality of what had occurred during the night. Perhaps, after all, it had been part of a half-waking dream. Nobody in the house would creep stealthily into my room at such an hour, and any intruder from outside would have to break into the house first. If there had been any sign of this, Marsh would have informed us by now.

As I was thinking this, Marsh himself entered and made his way to the head of the table. Since he never attended during breakfast I knew that he must have a message. Mr. Gresham looked up. "Yes, Marsh. What is it?"

"Good morning, sir. I have just heard from Maggie that she saw Mr. Robert Falcon passing through the village in a carriage yesterday afternoon. I felt you would wish to be informed."

"Ah! So the young fool's back from China, eh?" Mr. Gresham pulled at his chin and looked at Marsh with a touch of anxiety. "Did Maggie say how he looked? Was he pleased with himself? Dammit, man, you know what he was after. The servants' hall always knows our affairs better than we do ourselves. Did he have a look of *success?*"

"I questioned Maggie closely, sir. In her own words, he was all sort of broody, and when another carriage got in his way he looked as black as Newgate's Knocker."

"Good! Good!" Mr. Gresham gave a satisfied chuckle. "I expected nothing else, of course. Nobody ever found a needle in a haystack by fumbling about blindfold. You and I must resume our labors, Lucy. We've been somewhat remiss of late. Very well, Marsh. That will be all."

When Marsh had gone Mrs. Gresham looked down the table and said to me, "It's much to be deplored, your meeting that dreadful creature in China, Lucy. I lay no blame upon you, I simply say it was a great pity. However, you realize that we do not acknowledge the Falcons, so if at any time you encounter Robert Falcon you must pass him by without recognition."

I hesitated, then said, "Couldn't I just say good day to him, Mrs. Gresham? I should feel very impolite if I ignored him completely."

She drew herself up in her chair. "Are you *defying* me now, Lucy? Are you presuming to instruct me in manners?"

"No," I said hastily, "of course not. I'm sorry, Mrs. Gresham. I'll do as you say." But inwardly I felt a dull anger. I had no part in the feud between the families, and whatever anybody might say, I thought it wrong and stupid to go on being enemies all these years. I felt sad, too, for I would have liked to talk with Robert Falcon. The knowledge of his return affected me quite deeply. He was a link with my past life. I bore no resentment for the time when he had struck me across the face, in fact I burned with shame whenever I recalled how I had tried to beg money from him that day, whining and cringing in the way of a beggar. I realized now how shocking it must have been for him to see an English girl in a foreign country behaving in such a manner.

I emerged from my thoughts to find that there was an air of excitement around the table. Mr. Gresham was holding a letter in his hand and wore a tantalizing smile, while Amanda and her mother were both speaking at once.

"What does it *say,* Papa? Don't tease!"

"Charles, has she been accepted?"

"All in good time," Mr. Gresham said smugly. "Lucy appears to be puzzled, so I had better explain." He looked at me. "In April last, Amanda became too old to continue at the private school in Chislehurst, and so we have sought a place for her at a splendid college for young ladies at Cheltenham." He waved the letter. "She has been accepted and will start there when the new term begins in September."

Amanda clapped her hands and exclaimed in delight, while Mrs. Gresham patted her hair and looked as smug as her husband.

"Heaven knows how we shall afford it," he went on genially, "but if only Lucy will make a real effort and help me to deduce the whereabouts of the Gresham fortune, then all problems will be solved."

With sinking heart I said, "Will you be staying at the college, Amanda?"

"Yes of course, silly. I can't travel to Cheltenham and back every day, can I? Oh, it's going to be so exciting. Lottie Fletcher was at the same college, and she told me all about it."

I was glad for Amanda, but not for myself. She was my only friend in the family, and I knew that without her I would be more lonely than ever. Almost feverishly I began to plan what I would do to help me through the endless days which seemed to stretch into infinity before me. Already I spent several hours each day in reading. There were few novels in Mr. Gresham's study, and most of them I had already read in Miss Prothero's small library, but there was a set of encyclopedias, and I was allowed to borrow a volume whenever I wished. At present I was simply browsing and picking out subjects which seemed interesting, but now I decided that I must try to select subjects to teach myself. I knew hardly anything of English history, and that would make a good start. Perhaps in time I would be allowed to ride Amanda's bicycle and go out into the countryside. If so, then I could begin to study the wild flowers and trees, learning about them from articles in the encyclopedia.

I quickly had a foretaste of what it would be like when Amanda had gone, for it appeared that the college had sent her special work to do in certain subjects, to bring her up to the standard of the girls she would be joining. This meant that she spent an hour each morning and afternoon studying in her room, and I was left to my own devices.

For a week Mr. Gresham had me come to his study each morning to resume the weary task of poring over maps, books, and that maddening riddle, seeking clues from which he could deduce the location of the war lord's treasure. I had now read a book of stories about Sherlock Holmes, so I realized what Mr. Gresham was trying to do, but I felt he had little hope of success. We were thousands of miles from China and had such scanty and uncertain information. Also, I had come to feel that his powers of intellect were not quite as great as he believed.

"This is the area," he said one day, spreading his hand on one of the wall maps. "Falcon was searching too far south. The boy's a fool, of course."

"I don't quite see why he was wrong," I said politely but perhaps incautiously. "He may have been, but there's no way to be sure, Mr. Gresham."

"No way? Heavens, child, don't you ever listen to a word I say?" He then proceeded to list a number of clues from the report of the expedition made by the two young officers, which he had secured from the War Office. I could not follow his reasoning, but at the end of it all he said, "There. It's quite conclusive, you see? The Chengfu area is out of the question."

I felt suddenly very obstinate, and for a moment I could not think why, but then it burst upon me as if a great light had been switched on in my mind. I had overlooked something so obvious that I could scarcely believe my own stupidity. I must have been gaping with shock, for Mr. Gresham said sharply, "What is it? Why do you look like that?"

"I've just thought of something!" I cried. "Excuse me just for a minute, Mr. Gresham."

I rushed from the study and ran up the stairs two at a time. It was as well Mrs. Gresham did not see me, or I would have been sternly admonished. Less than two minutes later I entered the study again.

"It's this," I panted eagerly, and began to spread the limp and ancient piece of canvas on the desk. "I've had it for years, Mr. Gresham. I found it in the Mission when I was quite small, and when I looked across the valley on my first day here I had such a shock. You see? It's a sketch of Moonrakers."

He touched the canvas gingerly. "Good heavens. This is a piece torn from an army kit-bag, I fancy. Why didn't you speak of it before?"

"I forgot." I put a hand to my head, trying to imagine how I could have forgotten such a thing. "I think I was too worried about making mistakes to remember anything else. But don't you see, Mr. Gresham? It means John Falcon was there, in our Mission, all those years ago. He sketched Moonrakers there. So surely our Mission must be the old temple where they hid the emeralds!"

He stood gazing down at the sketch for a long time, then pursed his lips and shook his head slowly. "Interesting, most interesting. That's John Falcon's work, no doubt. He was something of an artist, and it runs in the family. But you're making a false deduction, Lucy."

"Oh, surely not, Mr. Gresham! I mean, we know John Falcon was *there*."

"Don't argue, child," he said testily. "The soldiers were in China for several months and moved about a great deal. There must have been scores of more likely occasions for Falcon to make this sketch. Do you imagine he would do it in the middle of a dangerous venture, at a time when he and my father were surrounded by hostile forces? It's out of the question. Possibly he was quartered at your Mission for a time, or it may even be that he made the sketch elsewhere and it later found its way by chance to the Mission through other hands—wrapped round a loaf of bread or some such thing. Above all, one simple fact puts Tsin Kai-feng out of court, Lucy. The river there is not in accord with the map. You saw the river marked on young Falcon's map, and you have told me yourself that its course was different from that of the river at Tsin Kai-feng."

I felt almost sick with disappointment, but I could see that Mr. Gresham's reasoning was right. "I'm sorry," I muttered. "It came to me suddenly, and I was so excited I didn't think . . ."

"No harm done." Mr. Gresham shrugged. "And no good either, I fear. Never mind." He picked up the canvas between finger and thumb with a look of distaste, and handed it to me. "You'd better throw this object away, Lucy. It's not a relic I wish to have in the house. Run along now, and we'll try

[149]

again tomorrow. I think another word-by-word examination of the riddle might be of use. We'll see."

I left the study and went to my room, feeling guiltily determined that I would not throw the sketch away. It was mine, and a treasured souvenir. I rolled it carefully and drew out my suitcase from the bottom of the wardrobe to put it away. Just as I was about to close the lid again, something caught my eye. Along the back of the case a row of stitching which held the cloth lining to the leather had come undone, so that the lining hung slightly away from the stiff leather. I had not noticed this when last I used the case.

Wondering if I could restitch the cloth to the leather without an awl, by using the old needle holes, I reached down to find if the hem of the lining was sound. Something flat and rectangular lay between the cloth and the leather, something which rustled slightly as I touched it. Next moment I was holding the long envelope which contained my marriage papers.

I knew it by the smudged black thumb mark in one corner, which I thought Nicholas Sabine had made when he handled the envelope in Chengfu prison. My hands trembled as I drew out the papers. They were all there, together with the letter Dr. Langdon had given me after Nicholas Sabine's death. My eyes rested on the last words . . . *with love from your devoted husband. Nick.*

I held down the sadness that began to rise within me, and tried to focus my muddled thoughts. The envelope had been stolen from my cabin on the liner *Formosa* while we were anchored at Hong Kong. Now it had been returned. But how? I remembered the strands of bright gold hair caught in one of my sleeve buttons after the struggle in the cabin, and I remembered the intruder of a few nights before.

Robert Falcon? But he could not know of my marriage, could not know that the papers existed. Even if he had known, how could he have been waiting for me in Hong Kong when we docked? And if he had stolen the papers from me there, how had he contrived to enter High Coppice and restore them to my case?

And *why?* It all made no sense.

I looked at the open case again. Perhaps I had been careless when packing it in Tientsin, or when sorting out my things when I first settled in the cabin. I had certainly been very nervous and in something of a daze at that time. Perhaps the lining had been torn even then, and I had unwittingly pushed the envelope down behind it. If so, it had never been stolen at all, only mislaid.

I drew a deep breath and felt calmer. This was a much more likely explanation. Any other seemed beyond all reason. I looked at the papers I held, and felt glad for Nicholas Sabine's sake. Now I would be able to do what he had asked of me, though I dreaded the doing of it. I looked at the name and address of the solicitors, scribbled on the back of the will. *Messrs. Girling, Chinnery and Brand, 128a Grays Inn, London.* To visit them, when the time came, I would first have to explain to Mr. Gresham that I had married a man under sentence of death and had been widowed only a few hours later. I shrank from the ordeal. He would think that much of my story was a lie, but at least there could be no doubt of my marriage, for I had written proof of it.

One thing was quite certain. The Gresham family would be outraged that I had never told them my secret. I shrugged my shoulders in sudden anger. I did not care. It was not my secret, it was Nicholas Sabine's, and I would not break faith with him. He might have been a ruthless and dangerous man, as Robert Falcon had said, but I knew nothing of that. I only knew that he was brave, and had saved me from great pain and horror. I had married him and made promises. I would keep those promises.

After luncheon that day, when Amanda retired to her room to study, I went out on to the terrace and met Marsh as he returned from having a word with the gardener's boy about some matter. This was a quiet time of day. Mrs. Gresham and

Emily were resting in their rooms. Mr. Gresham spent most afternoons dozing in the armchair in his study, so I believed.

Marsh stopped and said, "Good afternoon, Miss Lucy. May I ask if you're feeling more at home now?"

"Well, yes, I suppose so, thank you. At least, I'm not quite so afraid of making blunders, but that's because I hardly say or do anything most of the time." A thought came to me. "Do you think Mr. Gresham would let me go into service if I begged him? I'd go to another house if he didn't want me to be in service here. I'd miss you, though, Marsh. I'd miss you very much."

"Why, thank you, Miss Lucy. I'm afraid the master would never allow you to go into service, though. You are his responsibility, and it would disgrace him."

I sighed. "Yes, I thought so. But having nothing to do makes me feel as if I were shut up in a cage."

He gave a sympathetic nod. "I know. It's very difficult for you, Miss Lucy. Idleness is not an art easily learned. One must be born to it."

His dry manner made me laugh. I looked out over the gardens. It was a beautiful day. Apart from trips in the carriage to church or to the village, and one journey into Bromley for my new clothes, I had never been more than a stone's throw from the house.

I heard a little note of defiance in my voice as I said, "I think I'll go for a walk."

Marsh raised an eyebrow. "A young lady does not go walking abroad on her own. And you have no hat on, Miss Lucy, no gloves."

"But it's hot. I only want to go for a walk, Marsh. Just to Bromley and back, or something like that."

"Bromley?" I saw amusement in his eyes. "Well now, that would take you two hours."

"Yes, I thought I'd better not go too far the first time."

I had never seen Marsh blink in surprise before, but he did

so now. Then he half smiled and gazed at me wonderingly. "You would think that a short walk?"

It was my turn to be surprised. "Yes. I often walked into Chengfu and back. That was twice as far."

"I see. Well . . . most young ladies in England might walk for half a mile, if they were feeling very energetic." He shook his head. "It won't do, Miss Lucy, it really won't do. But may I make a suggestion? If you take the path through the orchard you will find a footpath you can follow for half a mile or so down into the valley. It's all part of Mr. Gresham's land, so I think there can be no objection to your walking freely there."

I had not realized that the Gresham land extended beyond the gardens, and was delighted, but then a thought struck me and I said, "Will he be angry if I go without asking permission? I don't want to disturb him now."

"I shall be seeing the master shortly myself, and think it would be wise if you were to leave the matter in my hands, Miss Lucy. I shall say the suggestion was mine."

"Oh, but might he be angry with *you*?"

A smile flickered briefly in Marsh's eyes. "Be sure he will not dispute my opinion on a point of propriety."

I felt an impulse to run forward, throw my arms around Marsh and hug him. I had never forgotten how he helped me on that first terrible evening of my arrival, and he had shown me nothing but kindness and understanding ever since. I restrained myself, but words came tumbling out before I could stop them. "Oh Marsh, you're so good to me and I do love you for it. I never knew my father, but if I could choose one I'd want it to be you."

I stopped, and felt myself flushing. I was not ashamed of my impulsive words, for they were true, but I was afraid I had embarrassed him. His face lost its usual reserve and became more warmly human than I had ever thought possible. He took a step toward me, half lifting a hand as if to touch my shoulder, then checked himself. Lowering his hand he stepped back, but there was still a glow of pleasure in his eyes.

[153]

"That is the greatest compliment I have ever been paid, Miss Lucy," he said quietly. "I shall always treasure it. And if I may presume to say so, I return your feelings of affection. You also have my respect, and not only mine, but that of all of us below stairs." He paused, and gradually resumed his usual formal manner. "Now, when you reach the valley you will find that the path winds through tall bracken to a clump of trees with a wire fence and woods beyond. Don't go past the fence, Miss Lucy. That's Falcon land."

"I'll be careful. And thank you again."

"My pleasure, Miss Lucy." He smiled gravely, inclined his head, and moved on across the terrace and into the house. As I walked through the gardens I was happy to think that my impulsive outburst had pleased Marsh. Before coming to High Coppice I had never missed having a mother and father, perhaps because I had spent most of my life playing the part of a mother to the children at the Mission. Now I thought how wonderful it would be to have a father like Marsh, someone who liked me and really cared about me.

Beyond the orchard the path led down between pines and silver birch. The smell was beautiful, and the sunlight slanting down between the branches spread golden patterns on the grass. Below the trees the path followed a thick hedge for a while, then turned between two low shoulders of ground into a slope of high bracken.

I walked slowly, enjoying every moment, for my heart went out to this beautiful countryside. The smell of the greenery was fresh and good. Birds flashed between branches above me or rustled in the undergrowth skirting the path. When I reached the slope of bracken I saw three rabbits playing in a clearing, yet my mouth did not water and I had no thoughts of them as food. To me, this was like walking in fairyland.

Half-dreaming, I passed through a clump of chestnut trees. To my left, some way ahead, I saw a wire fence, and realized that I had almost reached the border of Mr. Gresham's land. As I turned reluctantly to go back, there came a scuffling from beyond a great bank of rhododendrons directly in front of me. The noise seemed too loud for a bird or fox to have made it. Puzzled, I walked on, moving around the mass of foliage which rose high above my head and stretched back quite some way to where the ground rose sharply.

Some of the rhododendron stems were as thick as my two arms together, and I saw now that there were several tall hollies and other evergreens mingled with them to make an almost solid wall. I crouched down low, peering through the twisting stems and thickly clustered leaves. In the dimness beyond I glimpsed something white . . . a face, a small face topped by fair hair.

I moved closer to the wall of foliage and said, "Hallo?"

From within a voice replied, "Wait a moment, please, I'm coming out." There was further rustling, then a big hanging branch was moved aside and a small boy of about nine or ten emerged from what appeared to be a tunnel running back through the bushes. He was dressed in knickerbockers and a jersey, and as he looked at me his fine-boned face held sorrowful resignation. I knew that this must be Robert Falcon's small brother, for his delicate features were so much like those of his mother.

"Are you going to tell them?" he said anxiously.

"Tell who? I mean, whom?"

He nodded in the direction I had come. "You know. Up there on the hill."

"You mean Mr. and Mrs. Gresham?"

"Yes. Are you going to tell them?"

"Tell them what?"

"Tell them I'm here."

"Oh, you mean this is their land? No, I won't tell them."

"Thank you very much. They'd write to my papa, and then I wouldn't be able to come here again. I know who you are. You're the Chinese girl who lives with the Greshams, the one my brother Robert met, but you don't look Chinese."

"No, I'm not. It's just that I lived in China all my life until now. I'm Lucy Waring. What's your name?"

"Matthew John Falcon." He put out his hand politely and made a little bow as I took it. "How do you do, Miss Waring?"

"How do you do, Matthew? Perhaps you'd better call me Lucy. It's more friendly."

"Yes, I'd like that. I haven't any friends here." He smiled at me, and it caught at my heart, for it seemed so long since I had known the simple warmth of a child's smile. "Would you like a cup of chocolate?" he asked.

I hesitated, and he went on, "Oh, I don't mean at home, I mean in my secret house." He turned and nodded to the towering mass of greenery behind him.

"Thank you, Matthew. I'd enjoy a cup of chocolate."

He pulled aside the leafy branch and said, "Excuse me for going first, but I'd better lead the way." We moved through a tunnel of branches and foliage which twisted and turned and dipped so that at times I had to duck low to pass through. Then we emerged into a small clearing hemmed by a semi-circle of thick shrubbery and backed by a miniature cliff about twenty feet high.

The clearing showed every sign of having been used for some time. There were half-coconut shells hanging from low branches for the birds to peck at, a roughly made pen in which a tortoise and a hedgehog were sleeping, and a small lean-to shelter made of branches and leafy twigs. On a piece of old blanket spread on the ground were some lengths of rope and string, a clasp-knife, two old tin bowls, and several oddments I did not recognize. There was a recess in the low cliff, not deep enough to be called a cave, but sufficient to give some measure of shelter if it rained. Set in the recess was a square biscuit tin with a saucepan resting on top.

Matthew Falcon gave a little sigh of relief. "It's all right for me to be *here,*" he said, "because the fence stops against the bluff on that side of the rhododendrons and starts again on the other side." He pointed as he spoke. "So I can pretend this is Papa's land, and you can pretend it's Mr. Gresham's."

"I think it's all your own," I said. "After all, you found it, and it's really an in-between piece."

"You're the only one who knows about it," he said, kneeling to lift the square tin from the spirit lamp it covered. "Not even Robert knows. He said you saved his life in China. That was ever so brave."

"It wasn't really. I only shouted to say some soldiers were coming, and the robbers ran away."

He pushed back a lock of hair from his brow, leaving a sooty mark, and said apologetically, "It won't really be a *cup* of chocolate. It's only a mug, and we have to share it."

"Then it's all the more kind of you to ask me."

He set a saucepan of water on the stove to heat. "I'd like to hear all about China. If I show you my zoo, will you tell me?"

"I'll tell you about China anyway, if you want me to, but I'd love to see your zoo."

"Come along then. I'm afraid it isn't very big." He took my hand, and I suddenly felt weak with joy, my eyes swimming. All my life children had been taking my hand, until a few months ago.

"This is my tortoise and my hedgehog," he said. "They're not always here, because I leave this part of the pen open so they can get out, but there's always food and water and straw to keep them warm here, at least while I'm at home during school holidays." He led me across the enclosed clearing and parted some foliage. On a bed of grass wedged in the crotch of a thick branch was a thrush with one wing held in a splint made of thin cardboard rolled into a fine tube.

"She's not really a part of my zoo," Matthew said, "because she'll fly away when her wing's better. I must find some worms for her this afternoon." Still holding my hand, he moved across the clearing to a point where the high mass of shrubbery met the miniature cliff. "Now I'll show you another secret," he said. "Listen."

We stood in silence for a few moments. "I can hear water, running water," I said in surprise.

Again he parted some bushes, then pointed down. At the foot of the little cliff a narrow trickle of water bubbled up among washed pebbles to make a clear pool only a few inches deep and no bigger than a tea tray. "It's an underground spring," he said, "and this is the only place where it comes to the surface." He crouched, pointing to a big damp stone. Beside it something green and black glistened in the shadows.

"That's one of my frogs, and there's another somewhere. Two squirrels live here too, but I haven't seen them today. They're rather silly. They gather nuts and hide them away, then forget where they've hidden them. Oh, the water's boiling." He ran to the recess and turned out the spirit stove. I was unused to boys, but felt completely at home with this little boy as I knelt on the blanket and watched him perform his duties as a host. He did not chatter, but gave his whole attention to what he was doing.

From a small tin he took a slab of chocolate, broke off a piece, put it in a chipped china mug and poured hot water into the mug. He had some lumps of sugar in a pocket, and after carefully blowing the fluff from them he put four lumps in the mug and stirred the liquid with a peeled stick. Standing the mug on a flat stone to cool, he trotted off to disappear into the wall of shrubbery for a few moments, and returned with an armful of dry hay from some secret store. He pushed this beneath the blanket to make a cushioned place for me to sit with my back against the wall, and said, "It's nicer with milk, but I haven't got any today."

Handing me the mug, he picked up the clasp-knife, sat down beside me, and began to strip the bark from a slender, newly cut branch. I took half a dozen sips, then said, "It's just right, Matthew. Here, your turn now. What are you making with that stick?"

"Well . . ." he eyed the stick thoughtfully as he drank a little chocolate. "There's a fox about, and I don't want it to get the thrush, so I thought I'd make little booby traps all around where the thrush is, using springy sticks tied back with thread. I think they'll frighten the fox away if he comes."

"Can I help?"

"I've only got one knife, but you can hold the sticks bent for me while I tie the threads." He returned the mug to me and resumed his work. We were silent for several minutes, but it was a comfortable silence. "I wish I could make a better splint for that thrush," he said at last. "The cardboard goes soft quickly, but wood's too heavy."

"What about whalebone?"

"What's that, Lucy?"

"A sort of thin bone, nice and light, but springy and easy to cut."

"Have you got any?"

There was plenty in my discarded stays. I said, "Yes, I'll bring a piece next time I come, if you like."

He looked up, a smile lighting his blue eyes. "I'm glad you're coming again. I'm here almost every day during the holidays, and I don't have to go back to school for nearly a month. Will you look after my zoo for me when I'm not here?"

"Yes, of course I will. But Matthew, if your parents don't know of this place, surely they must sometimes worry about where you've got to?"

"Oh, they know I like being in the woods and watching birds and insects and animals."

"They don't mind that you just disappear?"

He shaved a thin plume of wood from the stick. "As long as I'm home in time for lunch or tea, with my hands and face washed, they don't mind. Papa says a boy has enough discipline at school, and while he's on holiday he should do as he pleases as long as he doesn't cause any harm or trouble."

"Your father sounds a very nice man."

"Yes. He's not strict, and neither is Mamma. I just wish they'd talk to me more, sometimes, but they have a lot of

[159]

friends, you see, and they're always busy painting and things like that. Some of their friends are on the stage. A lot of people don't approve of actors and actresses, you know, but they've been quite nice to me whenever I've met them. They have rather loud voices, but they're quite nice. Robert gets cross with Papa and Mamma, though. He says they waste their time trying to paint, and mixing with artists and actors and people like that."

Matthew shook his head, puzzled. "It's funny, because Robert's a very good artist himself, at least *I* think so, but he's not very interested. He says we're living on capital, and the house will go to rack and ruin for lack of money if we're not careful. He loves Moonrakers. There's something else about Papa and Moonrakers that makes him very angry, but they don't speak of it in front of me, so I don't know what it is. I know that's why Robert went to China, though, to look for grandfather's fortune hidden there. That would make everything all right if he found it, but he didn't."

Matthew prattled on, and a picture of Moonrakers and the Falcon family began to form more clearly in my mind. I gathered that Mr. and Mrs. Falcon had little interest in the feud, but since they disliked the Greshams for themselves they made no attempt to heal the long breach. Robert had too much contempt for the Greshams to hate them, but since they were rivals for the fortune which he wanted for Moonrakers, he regarded them as enemies.

When he had drunk the last of the chocolate Matthew said, "I'm sorry to talk so much. I expect it's because there isn't usually anybody to listen. I talk to my animals quite a lot when I'm here, but it's much nicer with you. Will you tell me about China now?"

"Yes, but it's very different from England, so you won't think I'm telling fairy tales, will you? Some people think so."

"I won't. They must be silly."

"Well . . . let me see. Oh dear, I hardly know where to begin, Matthew."

"Why don't you tell me what one whole day was like, from when you woke up in the morning?"

"That's a good idea." I looked up at the sky as I tried to order my thoughts, and was startled to see how far the sun had moved. "Oh my goodness, Matthew, do you know the time?"

"Not exactly, but I heard the church clock strike the half-hour just now." He looked surprised. "It must be half-past three. Hasn't the time gone quickly?"

"Much too quickly." I knelt up and took his hand. "I'm sorry, dear, but I daren't stay longer. Mrs. Gresham will want me for morning calls, and I have to get ready. If I'm late she'll ask questions, and then I won't be able to come again. Can I tell you about China another day?"

"Yes, of course." He jumped to his feet and helped me to rise, looking anxious. "Hurry, Lucy. I don't want them to stop you coming again. When will it be?"

"I can't be sure. I'll just have to come when I'm free, and hope you're here. It might be tomorrow afternoon."

"I hope so. I'll wait for you here. Don't forget the whalebone, Lucy."

Little more than ten minutes later I was in my room and making a hasty toilet in readiness for our visit that afternoon.

When I went to bed that night I felt happier than at any time since my arrival in England. Two days passed before I was able to see Matthew again, and then we spent most of our time together talking about China. He was enthralled, asking a hundred questions, and as we talked we put a new whalebone splint on the thrush's wing. I was not greatly worried that anybody from High Coppice might come looking for me. For some time I had been reading about English flowers and trees in the encyclopedia, and I knew Mr. Gresham assumed I was pursuing my interest in nature study by walking in the wooded part of his land, looking for specimens. In fact I began to do so as I came and went from Matthew's secret house, and even spent some of my time there making little sketches of flowers on a pad I carried with me.

Mr. Gresham again lost his enthusiasm for our treasure hunt, and began to dabble with a scheme for making motor-car tires which could be blown up with air like balloons. I thought this a wild notion, but it meant that I was often free in the mornings as well. Within a few days everybody accepted the fact that I wandered away on my own for an hour or so at a time, but since I remained within the grounds nobody seemed to mind, in fact I think they were relieved to be without me.

Two weeks later we all attended the church Garden Party. This was on a Saturday, but Edmund did not come with us as he had brought home some urgent work to do. I had yet to see Robert Falcon since his return, for he had not been with his family at church the Sunday before. Matthew was with them then, and he had looked across at me just once, his little face very solemn, then sat gazing down at his hymn book for the rest of the service.

There were large grounds with fine lawns behind the Vicarage, and it was here that the Garden Party was held. The small parish had only a few families of gentlefolk, and these circulated to chat with one another, while the families of the shopkeepers and tradesmen mingled among themselves and the farm people formed yet another group. The Greshams and Falcons had long experience of avoiding each other on such occasions, but I wondered if Robert Falcon would be there, and if I might catch a glimpse of him across the lawns.

Mrs. Gresham had insisted on my carrying a parasol to keep the sun off my face, which seemed odd to me since I enjoyed the sun. I was having difficulty in manipulating the parasol gracefully as we moved about the Vicarage grounds, and was so preoccupied with this that I did not see Robert Falcon approaching until he suddenly appeared in front of me, raising his hat and smiling, his manner warm and friendly.

I saw that his hair was cut shorter than when we had last met, but his face was still deeply tanned. He looked very handsome in a light gray jacket and fine check trousers with sharp creases down the legs. I was too surprised, and even alarmed, to wonder at the fact that whereas I had once thought of him as the ugly stranger he now seemed handsome. It was only later I realized that living in England had changed my ideas.

A little way off I could see the rest of the Falcon family gazing in as much astonishment as I felt myself, and I knew that the faces of the Greshams on either side of me must be reflecting the same emotion.

"Lucy, how good to see you again," Robert Falcon said with pleasure and with no hint of embarrassment. "And what a remarkable coincidence." He made a little bow, first to Mrs. Gresham and then to the rest of the family. "Your servant, ma'am. Young ladies. Good afternoon, sir."

I shot an urgent glance at Mrs. Gresham for help and guidance, but her face was blank with confusion, and Mr. Gresham was in no better case. The only sound was a smothered titter from Amanda.

I said feebly, "Good afternoon, Mr. Falcon."

Still smiling, he addressed Mr. Gresham in the same friendly manner. "No doubt Lucy has told you that we met briefly on two occasions in China, and the second time she saved my life when I was attacked by robbers. I'm greatly in her debt, sir, and so are my parents. I'm sure you'll be so kind as to permit me to steal her from you so that I may introduce her to them."

Mr. Gresham made a bewildered sound. "Eh? Uh?"

Without waiting for more, Robert Falcon turned his smile upon me and offered his arm. "Most kind of you, sir. Will you take my arm, Lucy?"

I flashed a last look of appeal at Mr. Gresham, but he

simply stood as if transfixed, blinking rapidly. Without help from him I found it impossible to refuse, and I put my hand in the crook of Robert Falcon's arm. Next moment we were strolling across the lawn toward his parents and Matthew.

"Mamma, Papa, this is Lucy Waring. Lucy, I present my mother and father. And this is my young brother, Matthew."

I shook hands and curtsied twice, then shook hands with Matthew, glimpsing a momentary twinkle in his eyes as he politely wished me good day.

"My dear, we can never thank you enough," Mrs. Falcon said, and I saw that her beautiful eyes were moist. "I've wanted so much to try, ever since Robert told us what you did, but I simply didn't know how to arrive at speaking with you. Now Robert has taken the bull by the horns, and I'm very glad."

"More than one can say for old Gresham," Mr. Falcon said with some amusement. "Robert, my boy, I think you may be the cause of him having a fit, by the look of him."

"Now Harry, behave yourself," his wife said gently. "Lucy lives with the Greshams, and you mustn't embarrass her."

"Sorry," Mr. Falcon said cheerfully. Then, to me, "I left my wife to thank you because she does such things far better than I could. But never doubt how grateful I am to you for saving this young idiot, Lucy. It's a pity you couldn't help him find that confounded treasure, whatever it is. Might have stopped him fretting and worrying all the time, like a tailor waiting for his bills to be paid."

"Somebody has to worry, Father," Robert said rather grimly. Then his face cleared and he smiled again. "But let's not talk of that now."

"Let's not talk of it at all," Mr. Falcon replied, and chuckled. "Well, Lucy, have you been able to help Mr. Gresham find a solution to the mystery?"

"No, sir. I'm afraid I've been of little use."

"Oh, never say that. He should be content just to have

you in the house. You're a pleasure to the eye, my dear."
He turned to his wife. "My word, isn't she a lovely girl,
Tina? I'd like to paint her, wouldn't you?" He suddenly put
his hand to my chin and tilted my head. "Look at those
bones. Nothing wishy-washy there. And the eyes. Beautiful.
Older than eyes should be in a girl this age, but even that's
an enchantment." He took his hand away. "You can see
character wherever you look." He chuckled again. "There's
a girl to send robbers packing."

Robert said, "If you've done with embarrassing her,
Father, I suggest we stroll together for a while. I'm sure
we'd all like to hear how Lucy is settling down in England."

For the next half hour we strolled and chatted, though I
said very little myself. Every now and again I caught a
glimpse of the Gresham family. Mrs. Gresham would roll
her eyes at me and pretend to fiddle with her blouse while
she crooked a finger in an urgent beckoning motion. Twice
I tried to excuse myself, but each time Robert forestalled me
by asking another question, and it seemed an eternity before
he conducted me to where the Greshams now sat at one of
the tables, taking tea.

"I really can't thank you enough for allowing me to renew
old acquaintance with Lucy, sir," he said. "And be sure I
speak for my parents also when I say it has been a great
pleasure." He bowed to us all. "Your grateful servant."

As he moved away, Mrs. Gresham let out a sound like an
enraged goose. Within five minutes we had left the Garden
Party and were on our way home. Once we were in the
carriage, the explosion came. Mr. and Mrs. Gresham both
talked at the same time. He was frantic to know if I had
been questioned about the Gresham fortune, and whether
I had revealed that it consisted of emeralds. Mrs. Gresham
was concerned only with my disloyal and disgraceful behavior
in having consorted with the Falcon family before the eyes of
the whole village, and in having refused to leave them when
she kept beckoning me.

Amanda made one attempt to defend me, but was quickly silenced. Emily entirely supported her mother, whose words she kept echoing. I apologized, tried to explain that I had been unable to help myself, and even dared to say that I wished Mr. Gresham had not allowed Robert to lead me away, but my protests were brushed aside almost before they were spoken, and the last provoked a fine outburst of indignation.

For the next few days the atmosphere at High Coppice was icy. I felt very unhappy, but on this occasion I also felt resentful. I was sure that for once the fault for what had happened did not lie with me. However, I tried hard to conceal my feelings, answered with a bright smile when I was spoken to, and tried to behave as if nothing had happened. I reasoned that Mr. and Mrs. Gresham were people who had to vent their anger on somebody, and I was the most convenient person for it.

On the day after the Garden Party, Mrs. Gresham said I was not to accompany the family to church that morning, and she would explain to the vicar and to her friends that I had a slight fever. Apparently everybody would understand that this was not true, but meant that Robert Falcon was not to attempt to breach the barrier between the two families again.

While they were at church, I was able to talk with Marsh. He already knew what had happened, as it was the talk of the servants' hall. "Most unfortunate, Miss Lucy," he said regretfully. "I fear you will be out of favor for a while. However, I see you have made up your mind to grin and bear it, which is by far the best thing you can do. Would you like to come down to the kitchen and have a cup of tea with us? The servants won't tell, and I'm sure it will cheer you up."

When I went walking and met Matthew in his secret house next day, he was very troubled. It seemed Mr. Falcon had predicted that I would be in hot water following Robert's behavior at the Garden Party.

"I was cross with Robert when Papa said that," Matthew told me as we made a repair to the little pen. "It was unkind of him to get you into trouble. Have they been horrid to you?"

"Not really. Just a little unfriendly, but they'll soon get over it. They always do."

"I hope so." He looked relieved. "Tell me some more about China. Why do they have such funny names, Lucy?"

"They're not really funny, just different."

"Say some names now."

"Oh, let's see. Chang, Wang, Li, Chen. They're the most common family names, like Smith, Jones and Brown in England. But in China the surname always comes first, and all names have a meaning."

"What sort of meaning?"

"Well, it might be a bird, a color, a fish, a tree. All sorts of things."

"What do those ones you said mean?"

"Chang, Wang, Li, Chen? They mean Draw-bow, Prince, Plum, and Spread."

He gave a snuffle of laughter. "There! They *are* funny, Lucy."

"Yes, I suppose they are. You know how in England people might say Mr. So-and-so? Well, in China they say Chang-three-Li-four to mean that."

He laughed again, then gradually his face grew thoughtful. "I suppose English people would seem funny to them, Lucy, so we must have seemed funny to *you*, at first."

"Well, everything seemed very strange here. I'm getting used to it now, though."

"It must be awfully difficult."

We talked easily as we worked, and as usual I was sorry when the time came to leave, for I had a growing affection for this rather solemn little boy who in many ways seemed older than his years.

At five o'clock the following afternoon I was sitting in the drawing room with all the family, taking tea. Two ladies and a young man who showed signs of becoming interested in Emily had called earlier, and Mrs. Gresham was speculating upon the size of the private income the young man was known to have, when Marsh entered carrying a small silver tray with a card on it.

I knew at once that something unusual had happened. It was not obvious from his expression, which was as calm as usual, and nobody else seemed to sense anything, but perhaps I knew him better than the others because he was a real person to me and not just a butler. Mrs. Gresham took the card, and as she looked at it her eyes widened with shock. "Robert Falcon?" she said angrily. "Good heavens, Marsh, you know very well that we are *never* at home to a Falcon!"

"Quite so, madam. However, the young gentleman brought what I understand is a very special gift for the master." He placed a long envelope on the tray and moved toward Mr. Gresham. "Under the circumstances I thought it my duty to ask the young gentleman to wait in the hall while I ascertained your wishes."

"Confound his impudence!" Mr. Gresham stood up and snatched the envelope from the tray. "What the devil makes him imagine I would accept any gift from *him?*" The envelope was unsealed, and as Mr. Gresham spoke he flicked open the flap. "Here, you can take it back to him, whatever it is. What the deuce is it, anyway? Good heavens!"

He stared at the folded parchment which had slid partly from the envelope, his eyes wide with astonishment. Mrs. Gresham, Emily, and Amanda clustered about him, all speaking at once in urgent whispers.

"What is it, Papa?"

"Why do you think he brought it?"

"Charles, you simply cannot accept anything from a Falcon!"

"Be quiet! All of you, be quiet!" He had unfolded the parchment and was gazing at it, his eyes alight with excitement. Lifting his head, he looked across at me. "Lucy! Do you know what this is?"

"I think so, Mr. Gresham. Is it the other map? The one Robert Falcon had in China?"

"Charles! You are surely not going to take up that wild-goose chase again? Really! Have you not brought us enough problems with it already?"

"Be quiet, Becky. You don't understand these things." His hands were unsteady as he folded the map. "This could answer *all* our problems, my dear. At least there can be no harm in seeing young Falcon for a moment, to hear what he has to say." He turned to Marsh. "Very well, show him in. And you ladies, kindly be seated and compose yourselves."

Marsh went out. Emily and Amanda and their mother sat down again, attempting to look cool and unruffled, though Mrs. Gresham remained tight-lipped with disapproval. Blinking rapidly, Mr. Gresham stood with his back to the fireplace, holding the lapel of his coat with one hand and striking a dignified position.

The door opened again. Marsh entered and stood to one side. "Mr. Robert Falcon," he announced.

« SEVEN »

HE WAS beautifully dressed, with a carnation of the correct size in his buttonhole, carrying hat and cane in one hand. His manner was warm but respectful.

"How very kind of you to receive me, ma'am." He greeted Mrs. Gresham first, bending over her hand, then made a little bow to Mr. Gresham. "I hope I find you well, sir." Another bow. "Your servant, young ladies."

After a moment of silence I said, "How do you do, Mr. Falcon?" and received a glare from Mrs. Gresham. Her husband cleared his throat and blinked half a dozen times. "I should be obliged if you would tell me the reason for your visit, Falcon, and for this—ah—unexpected gift." He lifted the hand holding the map.

Robert Falcon smiled engagingly. "Very simple, sir. During my journey abroad, I had much time to reflect, and I concluded it was a great pity that our two families should be bad friends as a result of events which occurred long ago. I come for a double reason. First, to extend the olive branch of peace, and in token of my sincerity I have brought you the gift I thought you would be most pleased to receive."

Mr. Gresham weighed the map in his hand solemnly. "Does your father know of this?"

"Naturally, sir. I have his approval. As you may know, he is a man who concerns himself only too little with material fortune. I myself have tried to find the war lord's treasure, and failed. I hope that you may have greater success."

Mr. Gresham looked baffled. "Extraordinary," he muttered. "Most—um—unexpected. You mentioned a double reason, I believe?"

"I did, sir. I confess I have a somewhat selfish reason for wishing to dispel the regrettable ill-feeling which has existed between our families." He turned to smile at me, then faced Mr. Gresham again. "I would like to be allowed to call upon Miss Lucy, and hope you will give your permission for me to do so."

I heard Emily squeak with surprise. Mrs. Gresham put a hand to her breast and stared as if thunderstruck. Amanda gasped and wriggled. Mr. Gresham began to blink again. There was a long silence, during which Robert Falcon stood quite at his ease, a polite smile on his lips, waiting. I saw Mr. Gresham glance frantically at his wife for guidance, and expected to see angry indignation on her face, but to my surprise she looked suddenly thoughtful, as if weighing up some unexpected consideration which had struck her.

"Ah . . . hum," Mr. Gresham said uncertainly. "Would you care to sit down, Falcon? Have some tea?"

"Thank you, sir, but I feel I've intruded long enough for this occasion. No doubt you will wish to give thought to my request and discuss the matter with Mrs. Gresham." He smiled warmly again, his teeth very white against the tan. "I shall await your decision with some anxiety, but rest assured that my small gift is yours no matter what your answer may be."

He turned to Mrs. Gresham. "With your permission, ma'am, I will take my leave."

Mr. Gresham, looking dazed, tugged at the bell-pull, and by the time Robert Falcon had made the correct goodbyes to us all, Marsh was there to show him out. No sooner did we hear the sound of the carriage driving away than there came an outburst of excited chatter, with everybody talking at the same time, except for me.

Emily was shrill with annoyance. "It's absurd! Why ever would he want to court Lucy? Mamma, you'll never allow it, surely!"

Mrs. Gresham was saying: "We must discuss this alone, Charles. I certainly don't wish to be *friends* with the Falcons, but one must consider that Lucy's chances of marriage are not particularly glowing, and our responsibility for her may continue indefinitely."

Mr. Gresham was exulting over the map. "Yes, Becky, yes. We'll talk about it. But not now, my dear, not now. Look! We have the Falcon map! With this, Lucy and I can surely make a huge stride forward in our quest."

"Charles, do try to put first things first! I'm sure the wretched map will be quite useless, otherwise that young man would never have given it to you."

"Nonsense, Becky. The point is that he knows nothing about the deductive process, and neither do you."

"Emily's cross, Mamma! Look, I think she's jealous!"

"I am *not!* Mamma, tell Amanda not to say such things!"

"Will you both be *quiet?*"

I was busy trying to untangle my own confused thoughts. Did I want Robert Falcon to call upon me? This, I knew, was the first stage of courtship. Did I want to be courted? I became suddenly aware of a tingling in my legs and arms, and a strange warm feeling in my stomach, as if a small fire had begun to burn there, and with it came an obscure yearning.

Yes . . . I would like to be held in the arms of somebody who loved me. In China the females were grown-up while still young in years, and I had sometimes heard girls of four-teen at the Mission speak longingly of handsome young men in the village. In those days I had been amused. Now I knew something of what they had felt. Perhaps if I had been brought up in England, perhaps if I had not been delivering babies since I was fourteen, I would have thought my feelings immodest, and been ashamed. As it was, I felt only intrigued and curiously excited.

But did I want to be courted by Robert Falcon? Panic touched me, startling me because I did not know its source. Then Nicholas Sabine's face was suddenly in my mind's eye, clear in every detail, and with it came an aching sense of loss, stronger than I had known before.

With an effort I roused myself from the turmoil of my thoughts, just as an argument between Emily and her mother abated for a moment or two while they caught their breath. Mr. Gresham had taken a folding magnifying glass from his pocket and was absorbed in a study of the map.

I said, "Excuse me, but I really would rather not have Robert Falcon call upon me, Mrs. Gresham."

Emily looked astonished but cried in triumph, "There, Mamma! Even she can see it would be ridiculous for her to have a beau before I do!"

Mrs. Gresham ignored her and looked at me coldly, with an air of one suffering a bitter injustice. "It would make a pleasant change, Lucy, if we were to see an occasional sign of gratitude in you for all we have done."

"Oh, but I *am* grateful, Mrs. Gresham," I said hastily. "I never forget that you've taken me into your family and given me everything anybody could want for."

"In that case I'm sure you will be content to let your elders decide whether or not Robert Falcon shall call upon you. That is our duty, and not a matter for a young girl to make up her own mind about."

Mr. Gresham looked up from the map and said, "Exactly. But we'll discuss it later, Becky. I want Lucy to come to the study with me now, so that we can compare the two maps. By George, if we're lucky we may be able to narrow the search to a very small area!"

That evening, before and after dinner, was spent in tracing out a new map with all the features from the two old maps marked on it. When this was done I sat and gazed at it while Mr. Gresham rustled through books and papers, reading out names of towns and villages in such a strange accent that I would scarcely have known they were Chinese names. I had seen few villages apart from Tsin Kai-feng. As for the area we were now dealing with, I had never seen it at all, and could not possibly identify anything on the map. Even now that the map was complete, it could have represented any one of a dozen different places similar to the surroundings of Tsin Kai-feng, for so much of China was the same.

After the new hope and excitement brought about by Robert Falcon's gift, Mr. Gresham's enthusiasm lasted for almost a week before beginning to dwindle once again, though he was reluctant to admit his waning interest. "It's a matter of patience," he said, slowly filling a pipe with a curving stem which he had recently adopted. "We need one or two more pieces of the jigsaw, Lucy, and no doubt they will come our way. Perhaps just one more fact will give us the pattern, and then everything will fall into place." He set a match to the pipe. "Just one more clue."

I thought wearily that one more clue would be of as little use as all the rest. I did not know how wrong I was.

A brief note had been sent to Robert Falcon to say rather coolly that he might call upon me for the time being. Mrs. Gresham did not want to commit herself too far. I realized now that even in England daughters were something of a problem. Few young women of good family worked, so if they failed to find a husband their parents had to keep them indefinitely. The great matter which concerned all parents was to make a suitable match for their daughters. I knew very well that Mrs. Gresham would never have allowed a Falcon to call upon her daughter Emily, but I was not a daughter, I was an extra young female who should be married off as quickly as possible to any young man of reasonable position who would have me. Even a Falcon might be considered.

Twice a week Robert called to see me, and we sat in the drawing room with Mrs. Gresham, making conversation. For me this was an ordeal. It was impossible to be natural, and I found that everything I said sounded stilted. Robert was very good, talking freely and amiably as if quite unaware of my awkwardness. Later, if Mrs. Gresham decided to let the courtship continue, I knew we should be left alone together for a little while during each visit. I hardly knew whether this would make things easier or more difficult for me. I could have talked with Robert more readily in Mrs. Gresham's absence if only he had not been courting me.

Because of these visits, my meetings with Matthew were less frequent. "Do you think you'll marry Robert?" he said one day as we watched the hedgehog suckle some babies she had unexpectedly produced. "I'd like you to be my sister."

"Well, he's very handsome and very friendly, but I never feel that I really know him, Matthew."

"Yes." Matthew nodded agreement. "It's funny, he's my brother but I know you much better. I'd like to marry you myself, Lucy, but I'm too young."

"It's a lovely compliment just the same, Matthew dear, and thank you. I'm sure there's a very small girl growing up somewhere who'll be just right for you."

"She'll have to be like you, Lucy. I mean, not frightened of spiders like most girls are."

"Yes, that's very important."

A week later Matthew went back to his preparatory school, and amid great excitement Amanda was taken by her parents to the school for young ladies at Cheltenham. Then my life seemed more useless and empty than ever. Mealtimes and morning calls were more of an ordeal without Amanda to brighten them, and I so much missed arriving at Matthew's secret house, to have him take my hand and show me some new feature of his zoo.

I read more than ever, and began to make a small garden near the spring in the hidden clearing, transplanting wild flowers from the woods, but sometimes I was so lonely as I worked that I talked aloud to Matthew just as if he had been there with me. I even found myself looking forward to Robert's visits because they broke the gray monotony of the days. He was always kind and friendly, trying to put me at my ease, but in spite of this I still felt that I did not know him. This smiling, attentive man was very different from the brusque and quick-tempered stranger I had met in China. I wondered which was the real Robert Falcon.

The weekends brought Edmund to High Coppice. I looked forward to this because his was another voice to hear, another face to see. He was always pleasant to me in his formal way, and would sometimes play a game of draughts with me or give me a lesson in chess.

The best times were when I was able to talk with Marsh for a little while, but this did not happen often. On one occasion I said, "There's something I thought of asking Mr. Gresham, but I'd like to know what you think about it first. Do you mind if I ask your advice? I'd be so grateful."

"Not at all, Miss Lucy. What is it?"

"Well, I've met Dr. Cheyne once or twice when we've paid morning calls on his wife, and he seems a nice man. I wondered if I could help in his surgery and go on his rounds with him as a sort of nurse. He's always busy, and I could help with delivering babies."

For the first time I heard Marsh catch his breath in a gasp. "Delivering *babies?* But good heavens, my dear—I beg your pardon, Miss Lucy—do you know what you are saying?"

"Yes. I helped Miss Prothero deliver babies from when I was fourteen, and after she was taken ill I had to do it on my own, so I'm quite good at it, truly. I've done simple nursing, too, like cleaning and stitching gashes, or splinting broken fingers. Perhaps I could help in that way as well."

He almost laughed in wonder. "You continue to surprise me, Miss Lucy. But I beg you never to mention your midwifery as a topic of conversation. It wouldn't do at all."

"Oh, I won't. I've been careful not to talk about having babies ever since that first Sunday, when Mrs. Gresham said I mustn't sing the line in the *Te Deum* about the Virgin's womb. That was after you told me about piano legs. But I thought helping Dr. Cheyne would be all right. After all, ladies do *have* babies."

"Indeed. But the having of them is not discussed or acknowledged, Miss Lucy." Though his face remained straight, his eyes twinkled. "Many ladies feel that the Good Lord might well have devised a less vulgar procedure. I'm afraid I must advise you against asking Mr. and Mrs. Gresham if you may help Dr. Cheyne. You will certainly be refused, and probably scolded for making such a suggestion."

This was a great disappointment to me. My spirits had risen when I first thought of the idea, but now they fell even lower than before. It was Marsh who came to my rescue, and in a very diplomatic way. Unknown to me, he approached Mr. Gresham and suggested that my ways and behavior were much less polished than a young English lady's should be, owing no doubt to my Mission background in the Far East. He therefore offered, for the general good of the family reputation, to devote an hour each day to coaching me in the many fine points of custom and etiquette which society required its members to know.

The first I heard of this was as we were taking coffee in the drawing room after dinner one evening. Marsh had just served us when Mrs. Gresham said, "Now, Marsh, what is this idea you've mentioned to the master about teaching Miss Lucy her manners?"

"No more than a suggestion I hoped might please you,

[177]

madam. I can find an hour each day without detriment to my other duties, and if you so wish I shall be happy to instruct Miss Lucy."

"It's most unusual," Mrs. Gresham said slowly. "But then, Lucy is an unusual problem, and we want to do the best we can for her, particularly now that Robert Falcon is calling. How exactly would you go about it?"

"I had in mind to use the sewing room immediately after luncheon, madam. Of course, in instructing Miss Lucy I shall have to make so bold as to act the part of a gentleman at times, and even the part of a lady." Marsh's face was as grave as ever, but I knew him far better than the Greshams did, and I could tell that his considerable sense of humor was alive now behind his butler's mask of dignity.

Mr. Gresham said, "Seems a very good idea to me, Becky."

His wife looked across to where I sat. "What do you think, Lucy?"

I was watching Marsh, and saw the faintest movement of his head, a tiny shake from side to side. Looking down into my lap to hide my hope, I said reluctantly, "Well . . . I thought my behavior was very good now, Mrs. Gresham. I don't feel I need extra instruction."

Emily said, "Pooh! She still can't climb into a carriage without showing her limbs, Mamma, and when we go visiting she smiles at the servants and thanks them. Have you heard her?"

"We must be charitable toward ignorance, Emily dear," her mother said fondly. "I suppose Lucy is doing her best, but there's no doubt she has much to learn, and Marsh will make an excellent teacher. I'm sure I'm much too busy myself. Very well, Marsh, that is settled and your suggestion is approved. You may go now."

"Very good, madam."

When Marsh came to the sewing room after lunch the next day I went straight to him and hugged him, much to his alarm.

"Miss Lucy, behave yourself!"

"Yes, I will, I promise. But thank you with all my heart, Marsh. You're such a dear."

From then on, my hour with Marsh was the best time of the day. I listened carefully as he explained bewildering points of etiquette to me, and practised such things as the correct way to stir my tea, and how I should extend my hand to be shaken so that only the fingers were grasped. When he pretended to be a lady or gentleman so that I could practise various formalities, we often had to pause and stifle our laughter, but I took care to learn quickly, for I knew that the better pupil I was the more time we would have for practising the art of conversation, which really meant chatting happily with Marsh about all kinds of things. He told me of his years in the British Army, and listened with interest when I talked of my life in China.

I told him of Miss Prothero and of Dr. Langdon, and sometimes felt I would like to tell him about Nicholas Sabine, but though I trusted Marsh completely I knew that this was not my secret to tell. If I was to carry out the wishes of the man I had married under such strange circumstances I should speak to nobody of it until I had seen the solicitor.

And there lay a huge problem. The six months Nicholas Sabine had asked me to wait had almost passed, and I was beginning to have sleepless nights wondering how I could ever go to London and see the solicitor without first explaining to Mr. Gresham. That, I knew, would be a very unpleasant occasion, and I wanted it to come only after I had done what Nicholas Sabine wanted of me, for otherwise Mr. Gresham might even refuse to let me go to the solicitor.

I had no money of my own for the train fare, and had thought of walking. If I started early in the morning, at about seven, and wore my old felt boots which I had brought with me from China and never thrown away, then I could cover the sixteen miles to London before midday. Allowing two hours to see the solicitor, I would be home again by six or seven. But this was far too long for me to be absent from High Coppice without explanation. In fact, when I worked it out carefully, I found that even if I borrowed money from Marsh for the train fare, I would still be away too long.

In the middle of October I decided that if the worst came to the worst I would go to London next week, leaving a note for Mr. Gresham to say that I would return later in the day and explain. But once again Marsh came to my rescue, this time by chance. He was allowed one day off each month, and when the day came in October he suggested to Mr. Gresham that it would improve my education if I were taken to London to see the sights, for this would provide me with topics of conversation.

As usual, the idea was referred to Mrs. Gresham. She was somewhat dubious about allowing me to be escorted by a butler, but since she was pleased with the results of Marsh's tuition over the past week or so, she finally concluded that a visit to London would be a good thing for me, and said that Mr. Gresham would give Marsh money for the train and the carriages we would have to take, as well as for a meal in a modest restaurant at lunchtime.

The day was a Wednesday, and I was careful to pack in my handbag the envelope containing my papers before leaving with Marsh to catch the ten o'clock train. We had a compartment to ourselves, and I waited until the train had pulled out of Chislehurst Station before saying, "Marsh, will you do something very special for me?"

"Why yes, if I can, Miss Lucy. Is there somewhere in particular you wanted to visit? I had in mind to show you the Tower of London first—"

"No, it's something I have to do," I broke in anxiously. "It's awfully hard to explain, because it's a secret I can't tell you about until afterward. But I want to go to an address in Grays Inn, a solicitors' office."

"A solicitors' office?" He looked at me very hard, his eyes

puzzled. "I've no wish to pry into your business, Miss Lucy, but surely you should have spoken of this to the master?"

"I will this evening, I'll have to. But I *couldn't* speak before. You see, something happened in China, and I promised faithfully that six months after leaving there I would . . . deliver some papers to a firm of solicitors, and that I wouldn't breathe a word to anybody until I'd done so."

Marsh shook his head, frowning. "A promise should always be kept. But wasn't this a rash one to make? Are you sure it isn't some underhand matter?"

"I know it isn't. Oh, please believe me. I made the promise to a man who saved me from something horrible. I—I didn't want to tell you this part, but I must. We had no food at the Mission, and I tried to steal in Chengfu. I'd done it before . . . but this time I was caught, and they would have cut off one of my hands if this man hadn't given Dr. Langdon money to bribe the officials."

"Oh my God, child," Marsh said in a low voice. He rubbed his eyes with finger and thumb, then took my hand and held it gently. "So you made a promise. I imagine the man was English, since he wanted you to go to an English solicitor. Is he still in China?"

"No . . . well, yes, in a way." My throat ached and I swallowed hard. "He'd desecrated a tomb, and the mandarin had him killed next day. I saw his grave later, when I went to say goodbye to Dr. Langdon."

"So this was the request of a dying man," Marsh said slowly. He lifted his chin. "Certainly you must not fail him, Miss Lucy. We shall go to Grays Inn, and if Mr. Gresham is displeased, as I don't doubt he will be, then we shall meet his displeasure together."

I was startled. "Oh, Marsh! You'll get into trouble too. I'm so sorry, I didn't think."

"Don't concern yourself on my account, Miss Lucy." He held my hand tightly for a moment, then released it. "Believe me, if Mr. Gresham chose to dismiss me for helping you fulfill a promise to a man about to die, then I would much prefer to serve another master."

There was silence for a while, except for the rhythmic rattle of the wheels on the rails. I was relieved, but at the same time I was deeply ashamed, for now Marsh knew I was a thief. At last I said miserably, "I know it was wrong to steal, but I was so worried about the children. Please don't think too badly of me."

He roused from his thoughts and turned his head to stare down at me as if I had shocked him. "Think badly of *you*, Miss Lucy? Never fear I'll do that. I've seen starvation, and it's not hard for me to imagine your situation. You risked mutilation for the sake of those children who were in your care." I saw the muscles of his jaw tighten for a moment. "And here they find fault with you for not stirring your tea correctly."

That was when I began to cry, slipping my arm through his and pressing my cheek against his shoulder because I was so happy to know that he was still my friend.

From Charing Cross we walked to Grays Inn. I asked if we might do so, partly because I could take in the London streets, the buildings, the traffic and the passers-by much better than if we had been in a carriage, but also because I was nervous and wanted to delay the moment when I would have to see the solicitor. Nobody would have known that Marsh was a butler. He wore a dark suit, rather old-fashioned in style but beautifully kept, and a gray tie with a small pearl tie-pin. His hat was a black bowler, and he carried a rolled umbrella. As we walked, I noticed how erect he was and how lightly he carried himself. It was hard to believe now that on my first sight of him I had been deceived by his prematurely white hair.

The walk took us less than half an hour. We went by way of Covent Garden, the great fruit and vegetable market where scores of laden carts jostled each other in seeming chaos. Yet this was a slack time, Marsh told me. The market was busiest at dawn.

In Holborn I saw a Steam Omnibus. It was full of passengers inside, with five more in a long seat above the driver's cab, and another one on either side of him as he sat at the steering wheel. At any other time I would have been full of excitement at all the new sights in this great city, but the coming ordeal lay heavily upon me. Grays Inn was a big square with tall houses around three sides of it and heavy iron railings on the fourth side. In the middle were some trees set in a large rectangle of grass.

"Do you wish me to go in with you, Miss Lucy?" Marsh said as we halted on the corner of the square. "No doubt I can sit in a waiting room while you see the solicitor."

I hesitated, for I would very much have welcomed his company and support, but then I screwed up my courage and said, "I think I ought to do it alone."

"Very well." He nodded approvingly. "I shall wait on that bench under the tree." He pointed with his umbrella. "Please understand that there is no need for you to tell me anything more of this matter, Miss Lucy. I am not inquisitive, and I shall ask no questions when you rejoin me. I recommend that you act according to whatever advice the solicitor may give. That is the best way."

Two minutes later I stood outside a house which bore the brass plate of *Girling, Chinnery and Brand, Solicitors and Commissioners for Oaths.* On the far side of the green, under a plane tree, I could see Marsh settling himself on a bench. When I rang the bell, the door was opened by a thin, elderly man in a black suit and white shirt with a very high stiff collar. He invited me to enter, led the way along a hall to a musty room where some copies of *Punch* lay scattered on a table, asked me to be seated, and inquired my business.

I drew a deep breath and recited the words I had prepared for this moment. "I am Mrs. Nicholas Sabine. My husband died abroad six months ago. He asked me to come here at this time, and to see his solicitor. I have a number of papers with me, including my husband's will, which he made shortly before he died."

The little gray man nodded solemnly, but showed no surprise. "Quite so, Mrs. Sabine. Pray accept my sympathy. I am the firm's chief clerk, but your husband rarely called here, and I must confess I do not recollect him. May I ask which of the partners deals with his affairs?"

"Oh! You mean, Mr. Girling or one of the others?"

He smiled sadly. "There is no longer a Mr. Girling or a Mr. Brand with us. Several new partners have entered the firm since their day, Mrs. Sabine."

"I don't know which one Mr. Sabine dealt with. I'm sorry."

"Never mind, Mrs. Sabine. If you will be so good as to wait a few moments, I will inquire. There are some magazines to glance at if you wish. I fear *Punch* is not what it was. Far too radical. However . . ."

His voice trailed away as he moved slowly out of the room. I stared at a magazine, but saw nothing. Five minutes later he returned, and conducted me along a wide passage to the last of several doors. He tapped, opened the door, and held it wide for me to enter. "Mrs. Nicholas Sabine," he announced. I thanked him with a smile, and went in.

Edmund Gresham rose from behind the big desk at which he sat, and said, "Good morning Mrs. Sab—" He stopped short, staring. I heard the door close quietly behind me.

Edmund? I had begun to feel more calm once I was launched on the ordeal, but now I froze with shock. Edmund was no less astonished. We stared at each other blankly for long seconds, and I could see that he was struggling to believe his own eyes. Even so, he was the first to recover.

"*You,* Lucy? What on earth does this mean?"

"I'm sorry, I had no idea . . . Mr. Sabine didn't say it was you. I mean, he just wrote the name down. The name of the firm. I didn't know it was yours. I mean I didn't know it was the same firm. I mean the same firm you work for . . ."

I stopped in confusion. Edmund was looking at me sharply.

He moved around the desk and brought a chair forward. "Come and sit down, Lucy, then wait till you've got your breath back. We must take this calmly." He returned to his chair and sat with his hands linked on the desk, his face very thoughtful, watching me.

Slowly the worst of the shock faded and I was able to collect my wits a little. I had always known that Edmund was a partner in a firm of solicitors, but he rarely spoke of his work when he was at High Coppice, and I had never heard the name of the firm mentioned. It was an astonishing coincidence that he should be Nicholas Sabine's solicitor . . . or was it? I had thought that to find myself a neighbor of Robert Falcon's was a coincidence at first, but the two families were linked by the war lord's treasure. Nicholas Sabine had been seeking an answer to the same riddle, so perhaps it was not so strange that he should have some connection with Edmund Gresham.

I was still trying to decide where I should begin to tell my story when Edmund said, "I think it will be best if I ask a few initial questions, Lucy, then we can proceed in an orderly manner. Now first, did you come here on your own?"

I shook my head. "No. It's Marsh's day off, and he had permission to show me some of the sights of London. While we were on the train I asked him to bring me here. He's waiting on a bench outside."

"My parents know nothing of this?"

"No. I'll tell them when I go home. I couldn't tell them before, because I'd made a promise. You see—"

"Just a moment, Lucy. We'll come to the whys and wherefores later. First I want to establish the essential facts." He looked at me curiously. "You say you are Mrs. Nicholas Sabine?"

"Yes."

"And that your husband is dead?"

"Yes."

[185]

"Can you prove what you say?"

"Yes, Edmund." I took the envelope from my handbag and passed it across the desk. He drew out the papers, and there was silence for five or six minutes as he read through each one of them carefully.

"H'mm!" he muttered at last. "These will certainly stand up in court if need be. Trust Nick to make a job of it." He held up the letter Nicholas Sabine had written to me shortly before he died. "Do you know why he wanted you to delay for six months before coming to me?"

"No."

"I see. Now, have you ever spoken of this to anybody? To Robert Falcon in particular?"

"No. I told Marsh I wanted to come here because of a promise I'd made in China to a man who was about to be executed, but I didn't say Mr. Sabine's name."

"Executed?" Edmund's eyebrows rose, and for the first time I heard a note of genuine feeling in his usually cool voice. "Was that how he died? My God . . . poor Nick. So he took one gamble too many at last. I think you'd better start telling me the story from the beginning now, Lucy."

My nerves had steadied again. I was not in any awe of Edmund, and I felt that it was my turn to ask a question. I said, "From the way you speak of him, you seem to have known Mr. Sabine quite well. Did you know about him going to China?"

"Know about it?" Edmund arranged the papers neatly in front of him and gave a small, unhappy smile. "It was I who engaged him to go there, Lucy. That was *my* way of trying to find the Gresham fortune. I was sure Nick Sabine would succeed if any man could, and I offered him one fifth of whatever he brought back." He looked down at the papers. "But it seems I was wrong. He won't be coming back."

I stilled the familiar ache that came with remembering the humble grave with my little posy of flowers on it. "Did you know him well, Edmund?"

He pursed his lips. "I doubt if any man could claim to have known Nick well. A few women, perhaps, but no man. We were at the same school together—Nick and I, and Robert Falcon."

"*Robert Falcon?*"

"Yes, to my regret. I was never a very active person, and as you can imagine, Falcon hated me as a Gresham. He certainly did his best to make my life unpleasant, and it amused Nick to protect me from him to a great extent." He shrugged. "But that's long ago now. I went on to study law. Nick preferred to enjoy himself at whatever might take his fancy for the time being. He was an adventurer, Lucy. He's been a gun-runner in South America, an ivory poacher in Africa, a river-boat gambler on the Mississippi, and Heaven knows what else."

"Robert Falcon said he was a bad man, very ruthless and dangerous."

Edmund frowned. "You told me you had never spoken of him to Robert Falcon."

"I haven't." I explained how Robert Falcon had warned me against Nicholas Sabine before I had ever seen him.

Edmund nodded thoughtfully. "Well, what Falcon told you was probably right. Ruthless and dangerous, certainly, I would say. A bad man? I'm not at all sure. But he was definitely the kind of man for the job I invited him to do. I'm sorry he failed, and sorry he's dead. Bad or not, Nick was one of the few people I've ever liked." He tapped the papers in front of him. "And now I shall be obliged if you'll tell me how all this came about, Lucy."

It must have taken me almost a quarter of an hour to tell my story, even though I left out all unimportant details. For the second time that day I had to confess my attempts to steal, but Edmund's expression did not change in the smallest degree when I came to that point. He listened carefully, making an occasional note on a pad of paper, and did not once interrupt with a question. This was Edmund the lawyer, and it was not until my tale was told that he gave any sign of his personal feelings. Then he capped his pen slowly, shook his head and exhaled a long breath.

"I might have guessed Nick would go down with his colors flying," he said dryly. "Dead or alive, he'd never let Falcon come out on top."

"Mr. Sabine said he wanted a wife to inherit something which an enemy of his might get otherwise. I thought he meant some sort of right to whatever he was looking for. Oh, but that was the war lord's treasure, so I suppose it must have been something else."

"Indeed it was. What Nick told you was a simplification of a rather complex affair."

"But the enemy he spoke of was Robert Falcon?"

"Yes." Edmund stood up and paced slowly to the window. "They were always rivals, Nick and Falcon. It began at school. Nick was a scholarship boy, and very poor. I think his father must have died when he was young, for Nick never spoke of him. His mother worked as a nannie, and I saw her only once. She died just before I went up to Cambridge. The life of a scholarship boy isn't an easy one, you know. He's looked down upon, often by thickheaded oafs with no brains but rich parents. Nick didn't give a damn . . . except with Robert Falcon."

Edmund turned back to his desk. "Something about Falcon got under Nick's skin, and vice versa. I'm not sure why. In any event, they were always at each other's throat, on the playing fields or in class. Nick had the best of it though, mainly because he didn't care as much as Falcon did. Everything was a game to him, just as this treasure hunt in China was a game, even though it cost him his life. There was a devil in Nick, you could see it in his eyes."

Edmund looked down at the papers on his desk. "I take it you've studied the will carefully?"

"No. I've just looked at it once, without really reading it."

He stared. "Why ever not?"

[188]

"I don't know, Edmund. I suppose because it made me sad to be reminded of what happened."

"Well, you'd better look more closely at it now." He passed the will to me. "As you see, Nick appointed the junior partner of this firm to execute the will, in other words myself. By nominating the junior partner he provided for continuity in the event of my unexpected death or disability. Our Nick had a few streaks of caution in him, it seems. If you read on, you'll see that he leaves his whole estate to you." Edmund gave a brief smile, and looked at me with the air of one who is about to spring a surprise. "In simple terms this means, among other things, that you will inherit Moonrakers in approximately one year's time."

My head reeled. "Moonrakers? But . . . I can't see it mentioned here, Edmund."

"No. It is included among his instructions to the executor regarding mortgages held on property."

"But I still don't understand! Moonrakers belongs to the Falcons, surely?"

"At present, yes. But Harry Falcon is not a prudent fellow. A rather gay and reckless fellow in fact, one of those who think, like Mr. Micawber, that something will turn up. That is why he borrowed a substantial sum of money from one of the wealthier of his Bohemian circle of friends, against a short-term mortgage of five years on Moonrakers."

"Does that mean he has to pay back the money in five years?"

"Yes. And if he should fail, Moonrakers would be taken over by the lender of the money."

"But how does Mr. Sabine come into it?"

"Your husband . . ." Edmund smiled slightly and repeated the words. "Your husband, Lucy, belonged to the same club in Whitehall as the wealthy friend, Ramsey by name, who fancied himself a dab hand at the card table. Nick engineered a game which ran to high stakes, and proved Mr. Ramsey to be less of a dab hand than he imagined. It's quite a dramatic tale, still recounted with awe at the club, but the simple upshot was that Nick won the mortgage deed on Moonrakers. So when repayment falls due in a year's time, and if Harry Falcon fails to meet it, Moonrakers will belong to Nick—or rather to his widow now, which is you, Lucy."

Edmund shook his head with admiration. "Oh, Nick made no mistake about it. He could simply have made a will leaving his rights in the debt to you, but that might have been challenged, and it would certainly take a long time to prove such a will, especially with the witnesses in China. And for all we know, he may have had some distant relatives to complicate matters. So he made you his wife." Edmund tapped the desk with his finger. "But please note, Lucy, that as executor I am instructed to sell the property deriving from the Ramsey mortgage, if and when the debtor fails in his repayment. The proceeds from the sale of Moonrakers will come to you, of course. A very substantial sum, no doubt."

If I felt anything at all it was a sense of emptiness. To find myself about to be rich was too unreal for me to comprehend just yet. For the moment I felt only a small quiet sadness that Nicholas Sabine had made me his wife only to strike at his enemy. With an effort I tried to concentrate on what Edmund was saying.

"There is the rest of Nick's estate, of course. He tended to spend money as fast as he made it, so I doubt that he'll have more than a thousand or two tucked away. But he'll not have less, he always kept a reserve of stake money for his ventures. I'll consult his bank, and let you know what to expect. However, the first necessity is to take out probate in common form at Somerset House, and I'll put that in hand at once. Are you listening, Lucy?"

"I'm trying to, Edmund, but it's all rather a lot to take in at once."

"Quite so. Never mind, I can go over it again with you at leisure. Since you're in the care of my parents I think you are bound to tell them all about this. Do you agree?"

"Yes, I must. Do you think they'll be angry?"

"On the contrary. They will be amazed, of course, but when they know the full story they will be well satisfied, for it means their responsibility for you will end as soon as you have substantial funds of your own, and that relieves them of a financial burden. I advise that you continue your day's sightseeing with Marsh, and return here at four o'clock, so that we can all go home together. Then I shall explain everything myself."

"Oh, I'd be so grateful, Edmund. I've dreaded that part."

"Then you need worry no more. I urge you not to speak of this to Marsh or to anyone at all. For the time being we should also keep it from Emily, who will *not* be pleased, and from Amanda when she returns for her half-term holiday. The more closely the secret is kept, the better. If Robert Falcon came to know of it, he might attempt some sort of delaying action to gain time. With Nick absent for so long, Falcon no doubt hopes that he has met with some accident in China, as indeed he did, and that in consequence there will be a long delay before the slow process of the law requires Moonrakers to be yielded to Nick's estate. So not a word, Lucy." He gave me a small conspiratorial smile. "Let us take the Falcons by surprise when the time comes."

I could not share his pleasure, and felt again that sense of emptiness as I said, "Very well, Edmund, if that's what you advise."

Five minutes later I was with Marsh again. I told him that the solicitor had proved to be Mr. Edmund, and that we would all three travel home together that afternoon, but explained unhappily that I was not allowed to say more.

"Then try to put the matter out of your mind, Miss Lucy," he said gently. "I'm sure Mr. Edmund is a very good lawyer and can be relied upon to do whatever is best for you."

For Marsh's sake I made a great pretense to be enjoying myself during the next few hours, but inwardly I felt a weariness of spirit. I did not want to take Moonrakers from the Falcons,

I did not want to cause unhappiness to anybody, but I could see no way of avoiding what Nicholas Sabine had set in motion. I could not reject the inheritance he wanted me to have, even though his reasons saddened me.

That evening, when Emily and I had gone to bed, Edmund told his parents the strange story. At breakfast next morning I could see that Mr. Gresham was full of suppressed excitement, but he said nothing until breakfast was over, then summoned me to his study.

"You said nothing to Marsh?" he asked in a tense whisper as soon as the door was closed.

"No, Mr. Gresham. I'm sorry I couldn't speak to you about this before. Did Edmund explain?"

"Yes, yes, we'll make no fuss about that," he said, blinking, rubbing his hands together and flashing his strange smile on and off rapidly. "Leave everything to Edmund, and next year you'll be able to send the Falcons packing. Naturally I've discussed with my wife the matter of Robert Falcon. Under the changed circumstances we'll not have him paying any further calls on you. No need for that now, and it would be quite improper in any event, for you are technically a widow of only six months, so to encourage a suitor is out of the question. I shall write and tell him not to call again."

I felt an unexpected pang of disappointment. Robert Falcon's visits had been something of an ordeal, but he had been more friendly toward me than anyone except Marsh and little Matthew.

"When the will is proved," Mr. Gresham was saying, "you will inherit some money as well as the Moonrakers mortgage, so Edmund tells me. Sabine should have left it in trust for you, but since he didn't I shall be happy to advise you on the handling of the money when the time comes."

I made no answer to this, at which he frowned almost sulkily, but I was not greatly troubled by his displeasure on this point, and excused myself as soon as I could reasonably do so. During the next week or two I came to hate the occasional gloating look that I sometimes detected on the faces of Mr. and Mrs. Gresham. They were reveling in the coming downfall of their enemies, and this was something which left me with a bad taste in my mouth, for I knew I was to be the instrument of that downfall.

In the first week of November, Amanda came home for her half-term holiday. My first pleasure at her return soon vanished, for she had changed greatly and become very condescending. I knew this was something which would pass when she had grown out of the novelty of becoming a young lady, for at heart she was a good-natured girl, but for the present it made us strangers.

Through the servants, I heard to my dismay that Matthew Falcon had chicken pox and was being kept at school in the sick bay over the holiday, so I missed the longed-for few days of his company in the secret house, and my visits there to care for his little zoo were lonely.

On November the Fifth came the day when the English people remembered the Gunpowder Plot. In China, many important days and festivals were celebrated by setting off fireworks, though I had seen this only once myself, when the people of Tsin Kai-feng had an especially good year for crops and there was a little money to spare. This happened when I was thirteen, and Miss Prothero and I took all the children down to the village to watch.

Here in England people made an effigy of Guy Fawkes and burned it on a bonfire. Amanda pretended she thought Guy Fawkes Day a childish occasion, but when Mr. Gresham suggested that we should not trouble to celebrate it at High Coppice this year, she became angry and said that of course we must, because the servants enjoyed it so.

The bonfire was built the day before, on a piece of open ground halfway down the valley, where the slope flattened out for some distance to form a wide platform. Most of the servants were allowed to attend, and Marsh was in charge with Albert the footman as his helper. Mrs. Trowbridge had prepared small packets of bread-and-butter for each of us, and some sausages were to be cooked later on a coke brazier near the bonfire.

By six o'clock, when the bonfire was lit, it was quite dark. All the family was there, for Edmund had come down from London that afternoon. Well-wrapped against the cold, we stood scattered about at some distance from the fire as the wood crackled and flames leaped up to engulf the effigy with its ugly mask. Marsh brought us some fireworks which could be held safely in the hand, and Amanda was soon squealing with excitement, all her grown-up scorn of the occasion forgotten.

Soon there were rockets soaring into the sky, leaving trails of golden fire. Other fireworks threw glowing spheres of green and red and blue high in the air, and once there was a great commotion and shrieks of laughter from where the servants stood watching, when the gardener's boy dropped a jumping cracker among the maids, for which he received a sharp reprimand from Marsh and a cuff on the head from Albert.

Along the valley and on the far side I could see other fires, and from all around came the distant sound of cracking and banging as the people of the village set off their fireworks, while every few moments a rocket curved across the dark sky.

The smoke thickened, so that soon the valley was filled with a foggy haze. When Albert threw fresh wood on our fire it produced such heavy coils of smoke at first that I found my eyes were smarting, and moved back some little way. As I stood alone, watching, a strangely dreamlike sensation came upon me. I saw dark figures flitting here and there through the smoky gloom, or silhouetted against the glow of the fire, but they were like shadows without substance; I heard voices and laughter, but they seemed disembodied sounds. It was as if time had stopped for me, while the rest of the world went on its way. I do not know how long I stood lost in this half-sleeping state, but suddenly I was no longer alone, for a man was walking toward me through the tendrils of smoke, and it was Robert Falcon.

He wore no topcoat and was hatless. On his face was a hard, intent look, and the blue eyes seemed almost to shine in the darkness. I did not move. I think I could not have moved even if I had wanted to, for I seemed to be suspended in a void. He stood in front of me, staring from those fierce blue eyes with an expression I could not fathom. Slowly he lifted his hands, reached out toward me, hesitated, then gripped my shoulders. I felt myself drawn toward him, and did not resist.

His arms went about me and held me close to him. Moments later he lifted a hand, put it under my chin, and tilted up my face. Then his head came down and he kissed my lips. There was a stirring, an awakening within me. I found that my arms were about him, and knew that I was answering his kiss. He broke from me almost roughly, holding me at arm's length and staring at me with a baffled gaze, as if wondering what he had done. His grip on my shoulders was almost painful. I wanted to speak, but did not know what I wanted to say, and long before I could find words he let his hands fall, turned on his heel and walked quickly away.

In seconds he was lost to my sight in the smoke and darkness. I shook myself, trying to throw off the numbness that held me, then started after him, blundering over tussocks of grass which seemed to snatch at my feet. He could not go like this. Something must be said. I had no clear idea of what I felt for Robert Falcon, but he had come to me out of the darkness, held me in his arms and kissed me. Surely he could not go without a word?

The sound of voices around the bonfire became still more distant, for the thickening haze of smoke seemed to blanket all noise. I blundered upon a bush, turned to move around it, then glimpsed his figure to one side, where I had least expected to see him, for now he was moving past me as if going up the valley side away from Moonrakers. I began to hurry after him, and he must have heard me, for he stopped and turned his head, peering through the shifting wreaths of smoke. A feather of wind blew the gray coils aside, and in that moment my dreamlike sensation was shattered as if by a hammer blow, and my legs almost gave way beneath me, for this was not the face of Robert Falcon. This was the face of a man who lay buried on the other side of the world, the face of Nicholas Sabine.

I found myself half crouching, hunched over, covering my eyes with my hands, and wondering if I had gone mad. The image of his face still burned in my mind. I saw the thick black hair curling over the brow, the lean jaw and wide mouth. One thing only was different. The wicked laughter, the devils that lived in his eyes, were no longer there. Instead there was emptiness.

Slowly I lifted my head, drew my hands down over my face, and looked again.

Nothing. Darkness and curling smoke. Nothing more.

My teeth were clenched so tightly that my jaws ached. I did something I had never done before but only read of in books. I pinched the flesh of my cheek hard, and twisted, feeling the sharpness of pain and knowing that I was awake. I had seen Nicholas Sabine, or a man who was the image of him. Or I had seen his ghost. Or I had suddenly lost my mind.

I felt like a ghost myself as I turned and began to move slowly toward the glow of the bonfire, a hundred paces away now. I could not bear to meet anybody, could not dare to, for I knew that if anyone so much as spoke to me I would give way to the shock that tore at my nerves. I moved to my right, acting by instinct, to make a wide circle around the fire and then go back to High Coppice, to be alone in my room until I could get a grip on myself again.

My legs felt like lead, yet I broke into a stumbling run, for the need to be away from this haunted place and safe in High Coppice flared urgently within me. My foot came down on air, and I plunged forward helplessly. Next moment I was rolling down a steep slope, gasping as I bumped bruisingly over thick clumps of grass, and clawing for a hand-hold. I had forgotten that I was on a flat promontory set in the valley side, and I had run over the edge at a point where the slope was steep.

As I tumbled on, I spread my arms and legs so that I could stay face-up and prevent my face being scraped. The slithering fall lasted only for a few seconds, and I was slowing down as the slope flattened, when my foot caught in some obstruction and I swung around.

Next instant a great light seemed to explode in my head, and the world ceased to exist.

«EIGHT»

I WAS COLD to the bone. There was a dull, pounding pain in my head and a sharper pain an inch or two above my ear. I was lying on my side, on cold damp stone. With a great effort I pushed myself into a sitting position and gently felt the lump on the side of my head where I had banged it against rock. I had the strange sensation of rousing not from complete unconsciousness but from a dream. There was the lingering impression that I had been carried in strong arms, and that a voice had spoken whisperingly to me, but the impression was fading with every passing moment.

Nausea swept me, and my face broke out in an icy sweat as I struggled against the onset of sickness. Slowly I got to my knees and looked about me, then fear tore the breath from my lungs in a great gasp, for I was totally blind. I could see no glimmer of light, whether from a star, from the fires along the valley, or from the rocket trails in the sky. There was only complete blackness.

In panic I began to crawl, feeling for the grassy tussocks which dotted the slope I had tumbled down, but there was no grass, only stone. And there was no slope. I was on flat, rocky ground. This was not the place where I had fallen. Could I have stumbled some distance in a semiconscious state before collapsing again?

The air about me was strange, and suddenly I realized that I could feel no breath of wind, hear no whisper of sound. I drew my coat more tightly about me, and as I did so there came a faint rattling sound from it. Matches . . . a box of matches, less than half full. I remembered putting it in my pocket before leaving the house, in case I had the chance to light some of the fireworks. With my cold and trembling hands it was difficult to take out a match and strike it, but the sight of the flaring match head brought me relief so great that I almost wept.

I was not blind.

I lifted the match. Beside me a slightly curving stone wall stretched away for as far as the light of the match revealed. Opposite the wall, perhaps twenty feet away, was another rough-hewn wall; and above me, a roof of curving stone that dripped with damp. The match burned my fingers and went out as I dropped it, bringing the weight of darkness upon me once again. Now I knew where I was, and with the knowledge came fresh terror.

I was in the Chislehurst Caves, a great maze of tunnels which spread far underground. Some said they were the work of men in a time before history began, others that they were chalk diggings only a few centuries old. Nobody knew for certain their origin or purpose, but this vast labyrinth had been explored for twenty miles without its limits being reached.

I had been scrabbling frantically to strike another match, but now I stopped myself, though with an effort that left me shaking. Those matches were my most precious possession. I dared not waste them. Very carefully I put the matchbox back in my pocket, then crouched down with my back to the wall and put my head in my hands to help me think.

Whether I had walked here unwittingly, or been carried as in my half-remembered dream, I could not conceive how I came to be in the caves. The only entrance I knew of was close to Chislehurst Station, a mile or more away even in a direct line, and much farther by road. There, the caves were open to the public at certain times. Guides would take small parties on conducted tours of a limited section, a few hundred yards or so, but no more than that, for wooden barriers were set across the maze of tunnels at different points, to prevent foolhardy people going too deeply in and losing themselves.

I had heard that there were other ways into the caves. According to a small book in Mr. Gresham's library, secret tunnels had been dug from one or two of the great houses at the time of Cromwell, tunnels which led into the caves and provided a way of escape for hunted Royalists. But even people whose families had lived in the area for generations seemed to have lost those secrets.

The cold was biting more deeply, and I knew that if I did not find my way out within a few hours I would die here from exposure. Yet my hope of escaping from the labyrinth was so small that I hardly dared to think about it. All I could do was to beat down the panic within me and try as doggedly as possible to make the best use of my one advantage—the matches.

I tried to think what else I might make use of. My handbag was gone, I had no idea where, and I had nothing in my pockets except a handkerchief and the small packet containing two bread-and-butter sandwiches which Mrs. Trowbridge had made for us to eat with the hot sausages Marsh intended to serve during the firework celebration. I still wore my hat, a felt hat with a long pin which had kept it on my head during my fall and whatever had happened to me since. I wished it had been my summer straw hat, for the straw would have made a good torch.

Lifting my skirt I began to tear strips from my petticoat,

fumbling in the darkness. When I had several strips I plaited them together in short lengths, then put all but one length in my pocket with the matches. My teeth were chattering as I opened the packet of sandwiches and began to smear some of the butter on the plait, finding a moment to bless Mrs. Trowbridge for using a liberal hand with the butter.

I drew out my long hatpin and pierced the ungreased end of the plait, so that when it was lit I could hold it without burning myself. Only then did I stand up and strike one of the matches. I moved to the center of the tunnel and stood quite still, facing one wall. I could feel no breath of air, and the flame burned steadily, but as I watched closely I felt that it was drawn a little toward my right. I put the match to the dangling, greasy plait of my primitive torch, and felt almost dizzy with relief as the material took the flame and began to burn slowly.

Without wasting a second I set off along the tunnel, taking the direction in which the match flame had leaned. I knew well enough that I might be quite wrong in thinking that whatever faint current of air might be in the tunnel would tend toward an aperture. I could well be going deeper into the maze. But I had to make a decision one way or the other, and it was better to follow some pattern than to wander at random.

After only thirty paces I found myself passing the end of another tunnel which ran at right-angles to the first. Quickly I crushed out the end of the rag torch under my foot, to avoid wasting it, then struck another match. I did so with agonizing reluctance, for every match used was a tiny hope destroyed, but having decided to follow the flame I was not going to start guessing, and the flame from the torch which hung from my hatpin was too big and uneven to give any guidance.

It was hard to detect which way the flame leaned, but I fancied that it was in the direction I had been going, so I ignored the side-tunnel and walked on, relighting my torch just before the match burned out. I was counting my paces, and after another forty-seven I came to a point where the tunnel forked. The flame of my third match leaned very positively toward the left fork, and I followed that direction. Now I moved quickly for a hundred and twenty-three paces, for though the tunnel curved and recurved there were no branches leading off. My torch died out, and I squatted down to rub melted butter into another rag plait.

In the next few minutes I walked only four hundred paces but used up three torches and eight matches, for now I was in a section of the caves where many tunnels linked and crossed. My eyes were becoming blurred with the strain of trying to detect the direction in which the match flame was drawn when I paused at each intersection, and it was sometimes hard to see any movement at all. Despair began to ferment within me, and I bit my lip hard to prevent panic overwhelming me.

There was little butter for the last torch. At first it refused to light, and then, when I teased open the plait to make it burn more easily, the material flared up and was quickly consumed. I stood in the darkness, knowing that I had only eight matches left, wondering if I should tear long strips from my petticoat and keep lighting one from the other while they lasted.

The tiny spark which was dying on the charred torch I held grew suddenly brighter for a few seconds before vanishing completely. My heart jumped. Surely that meant there must be a definite current of air? I struck a match and watched the flame carefully. It flickered distinctly toward me, and that was absurd, for I was standing with my back to one wall. I turned, and there was nothing to be seen but a long, dark shadow on the wall.

Shadow? What could throw a shadow except my own body? And I was behind the flame now. As I moved forward the match went out. I did not strike another, but groped my way onward.

My hands found it—a long, irregular aperture stretching

from the ground to as high as I could reach, and no more than a yard wide. As I moved through the gap I felt the touch of warmer air on my face, and hope leaped so violently within me that for a few moments I was again swept by nausea and had to lean against the wall until my stomach grew steady once more.

I rubbed greasy bread into the remains of my torch, twisted the fabric a little tighter, then struck another match. The flame flickered so much that it almost went out, but I turned to shield it with my body and relit the charred stub of torch. Ahead of me the gap widened, then grew narrow again. The ground sloped steeply up. I moved forward, and heard myself give a quivering sob as I exhaled the breath I had held. The sound shocked me, and again I took my lower lip between my teeth. The passage wound through rock, rising at each step. I was in dread that the walls would narrow to a crack, but suddenly there were no walls hemming me in, and I felt the crunch of dead leaves underfoot.

I was in a thicket, a mass of bush and bramble with a narrow path running through it. I turned to look behind me, lifting the torch. The opening I had emerged from could be seen clearly enough, but only from just where I stood, for it lay in a deep cranny which seemed no more than a recess in the bluff that rose steeply from the ground, and one side overlapped the other to hide the passage beyond.

The torch died out, but I could still see the shape of the bushes and foliage about me, and when I looked up there were stars in the sky beyond the evergreen pine branches which spread above me. I sank to my knees and let the tears come. I had never in my life been so glad to see the stars. After a little while I dried my tears on my petticoat and began to move through the thicket. In less than a minute I found myself in the open. Behind me lay the thicket and the stand of trees which mingled with it. I knew where I was now, for I had often noticed these trees from a distance when making my way down into the valley to visit Matthew's secret house. They stood against the valley side only a stone's throw from the public footpath which ran between them and Mr. Gresham's land.

As I looked along the valley I could see the glow of the Gresham family's bonfire, high up and to my left. On the far side other bonfires gleamed red and yellow in the darkness. I crossed the footpath and climbed the slope, bypassing the Gresham fire by a good distance. I did not want to meet anybody, for I was weary to my soul. When I entered the house by the kitchen door there was nobody about. I guessed that Mrs. Trowbridge and the maid left on duty were at one of the upper windows watching the fireworks. The hands of the kitchen clock stood at twenty-five minutes past seven, and I thought it must have stopped. But no, it was still ticking. I could not believe my tired and smarting eyes.

I had fallen and hit my head at about half-past six, and woken perhaps ten minutes later. It seemed to me that I had been in that dreadful labyrinth of the Chislehurst Caves for hours, but in fact I had been there no longer than thirty minutes. I went to my bedroom, washed my face, brushed and combed my hair, then changed my dress and lay down on the bed. My head throbbed, and there was a lump on the side of it just above my ear, but the skin was not broken and my hair, which had saved me from the full force of the blow, hid the swelling.

As I lay with a cold flannel covering my brow and eyes, thoughts churned chaotically in my head. So much had happened. There had been Robert Falcon, coming to me out of the darkness, taking me in his arms and kissing me, going away without a word spoken. Then . . . then there had been Nicholas Sabine. But that was impossible, a trick of the imagination. Nicholas Sabine had died more than six months ago. Dr. Langdon himself had shown me the grave.

Who had carried me into the caves and left me there? Fear began to creep over me again as I sought an answer to that question. Whoever had done so was a dreadful enemy, for it was only by good fortune that I had not wandered in utter darkness until I died. Was my enemy an unknown? Or a Falcon? Or a Gresham?

All answers seemed to make as little sense. Could Edmund, that precise man of the law, be working against me for some unfathomable reason? Or his father? What of Robert's father, or Robert himself?

Not Robert. If he had wished to harm me he could have done so easily enough when he held me in his arms. Would he kiss me, and go away only to come back, find me unconscious at the foot of the slope, and carry me to my death? Edmund surely was no man of violence, neither was Mr. Gresham. As for Robert's father, I had met him only once, but I could not imagine him as a coldly ruthless man, and only such a man could have attempted such a fearful act.

Nicholas . . . ? But I had not seen Nicholas Sabine, only imagined him.

There was one other answer—that I had wandered without memory after my fall, and by sheer chance stumbled upon the hidden entrance to the caves.

I heard sounds from below me as the family returned to the house, and a few minutes later Amanda rapped on my door and entered. I took the damp flannel from my brow.

"So there you are!" she said, staring. "What a thing to do, going off home without a word. Really, Lucy!"

"I'm sorry. I didn't feel well."

"You don't look it, either. You're as white as a sheet."

"It's just a headache, I'll be all right in the morning." Without making any conscious decision I knew that I was going to tell nobody of what had happened. The Greshams would never believe me, and even Marsh would find such a story hard to accept. I said, "Will you apologize to your parents for me? I don't think I'll come down to dinner."

"All right. My goodness, you do look pasty. Well, I'm going to change. Why don't you ring for Maggie and have her bring you a hot drink and something on a plate?"

"Perhaps I will."

When Amanda had gone I lay with eyes closed, trying not to relive the terror I had known in the caves, and at last I fell into an uneasy doze. An hour later Maggie brought me some hot milk and a chicken sandwich. Marsh had heard Amanda explaining my absence at dinner, and had sent Maggie up with a light snack and his good wishes that I should feel better soon.

I was afraid my sleep would be filled with nightmares. If it was, I remembered nothing of them when I woke in the morning except a fragment of dream in which I was back in China again, walking through the dark and deserted Mission with a spluttering torch held on a hatpin, and hearing a voice that whispered in the darkness, Nicholas Sabine's voice, saying: *"Beyond the twisted giant's knife . . ."*

Throughout the next day I had a dull headache, but after another night's sleep I felt myself again. I closed my mind against thinking about my experience on that night of the firework celebration, partly because it seemed more and more unreal as time went by, but mainly from cowardice. I did not want to think about it.

At the end of the week Amanda went back to Cheltenham. Christmas was little more than six weeks away, but to me that seemed a long and barren period stretching out before me. At the Mission I would have been so busy, planning and maneuvering to save food and money so that the children would be able to have something special for Christmas dinner, making decorations, stitching and sewing to make a present for every child.

Here, in High Coppice, preparations had not even begun yet, and when they did the servants would see to everything. Mr. Gresham made me a generous allowance of pocket money, one shilling each week, and with this I had bought some fine linen from a shop in the village, to make an embroidered handkerchief for each of the family as my Christmas presents to them. But this took very little of my time, and the days seemed long. My hands twitched for something useful to do, my legs for the need to walk, and even my back for the yearning to dig in the good earth and plant for growing.

The atmosphere at High Coppice did not improve. Mrs. Gresham and I seemed forever doomed to misunderstand one another. She could not even begin to believe that idleness could make a young lady unhappy, and became increasingly bitter at what she considered my ingratitude in failing to enjoy my wonderful life with the Gresham family after the hardships of Mission life in China. On the other hand, I found myself feeling that no matter what she said to me was said in a spirit of criticism, and I have no doubt that in this I sometimes did her an injustice.

In the middle of November, Edmund told me that he had received some information from Nicholas Sabine's bankers, and it appeared that when probate of the will had been obtained, as Edmund put it, there would be rather more than sixteen hundred pounds to come to me. My only response to this news was that I sometimes thought about running away from High Coppice. With so much money I could easily find somewhere to live and some work to do. The thought of continuing to live with the Greshams in such an unhappy atmosphere was unbearable to me.

Such thoughts made me feel guilty. Although Mr. Gresham had brought me to England for his own purposes, he had still housed and fed me and been not unkind to me for all this time, and I was in his debt. I consoled myself with the thought that if I did leave the family I could at least pay back my debt in money before I went, and I knew that my going would be a relief to them.

Meantime, my happiest moments were those I spent in the sewing room each day after luncheon, for Marsh's lessons in behavior and etiquette still continued. One day in the second week of December, Marsh was several minutes late in coming to the sewing room, and I busied myself finishing the last of the handkerchiefs I was embroidering. When I heard the door open I said, "Hallo, Marsh. Look, I'm not sitting cross-legged on the floor, I'm sitting gracefully with my knees together, just as a young lady should. Are you pleased with me?"

I heard the door close, but he did not answer, and when I looked up from my embroidery I saw that he was unsmiling and his face was pale. He moved to one of the chairs, looked at me strangely, and said, "May I sit down, Miss Lucy?"

"Oh Marsh, don't ever behave like a servant when we're alone together," I said quickly, and jumped to my feet. "Yes, please do sit down. Aren't you feeling well?"

He lowered himself into an easy chair, leaning forward, his elbows resting on his knees, hands clasped, gazing through me rather than at me. "I'm . . . not quite myself at this moment, Miss Lucy. An incident occurred only a few minutes ago . . ." He fumbled in one of his pockets. "Beattie found this on the landing outside your room, and brought it to me. Is it yours, Miss Lucy?"

He held out his hand. On it lay the signet ring Nicholas Sabine had given me when we were married. I had always worn it since, on a piece of thin ribbon, hung round my neck under my dress. Stupidly I clapped my hand to my chest, as if to make sure that the ring was no longer there. "Yes, it's mine," I said. "Oh, thank goodness Beattie found it." I felt round my neck with one finger, and drew out the piece of ribbon. "Look, the ribbon's broken and the ring must have slipped down under my clothes, but I didn't feel it."

I put out my hand, but Marsh made no move to give me the ring. He held it between finger and thumb, gazing at it with a look in which pain and unbelief were mingled. "May I . . . may I make so bold as to ask how you came by this ring, Miss Lucy?"

I hesitated. "I can't tell you exactly. Mr. Edmund said I wasn't to tell anybody. But it was given me by the man I told you about, the one I met in China, who asked me to bring the papers to England for him."

"The man who . . . died?"

"Yes. But Marsh, what's wrong? You look so shaken."

"I know this ring, Miss Lucy." His voice was very low. "It has an unusual design. I bought it in Hong Kong when I was a young soldier, and later gave it to my wife."

"Your *wife?* I didn't know you were married. But how—? I mean, if you gave it to your wife, how could . . . ?" I left the question unfinished.

Marsh turned over the ring. He did not seem to have heard me. "I gave it to her as a keepsake," he said, his voice quiet and heavy. "That was long ago, and my own initials were on it then. Now I see they have been replaced by the initials N.S." He blinked, then seemed to drag his eyes from the ring to look up at me. "Would these initials stand for Nicholas Sabine?"

I stared at him, dumbfounded. "Yes," I said at last, wonderingly. "But—but how did you know?"

"Because I know the ring, Miss Lucy. And because Nicholas Sabine, the man who made that request of you just before he died . . . was my son."

I could not believe it. Yet I could not disbelieve it, for Marsh would not lie to me, of that I was sure. A dozen questions were in my mind, but none would come to my tongue. My heart went out to him in sorrow as I saw the grief in his eyes. I sank down on to my knees in front of him and took the hand that held the ring in both my own. He drew in a long breath and braced his shoulders a little more.

"Was it Nick?" he said steadily. "You're quite sure? Not a different man who'd come by the ring in some way? Black, curly hair. Strong. A long jaw, like his mother. And eyes always laughing at some strange joke only he could see."

I held his hand tightly, feeling the ring between our palms. "It was Nick," I said. "I'm so very sorry, Mr. Marsh."

The "Mr." came naturally to my lips. This kindly man had become more than a household servant in the last few moments. Much more. And I could no longer keep secret from him what had happened in Chengfu. I said, "I have a story to tell you, about Nick and what happened to us in Chengfu prison. But will you tell me first how it is that his name was different from yours? And why you've never spoken of him in all the times we've talked together?"

He nodded, then seemed to become aware that I was kneeling. "Please, sit down, Miss Lucy."

"No. I'm comfortable like this. And you mustn't call me Miss Lucy any more. I'll explain why later, but you speak first."

"Well . . ." There was grief in his eyes, but his face had regained its usual calm now. "It's a sad and simple story. I married above me, you see, and my poor wife paid the price. I was a young soldier, signed on for twenty-one years. Most of that time I was abroad, and my wife was alone, for when we married against her parents' will they rejected her. We had one child, Nicholas, and in the first ten years of his life I saw him only three times." He made a little grimace. "After that, he did not wish to see me even on the few occasions when I came home on leave, and neither did his mother."

Mr. Marsh's eyes became distant, remembering. "It was understandable that my wife should be embittered. She lived in poor lodgings in London, the best I could afford on a soldier's pay, and even then she had to take work as a seamstress to make ends meet. But she brought the boy up well, educated him herself in the early years, and taught him the ways of a gentleman. It was a great credit to her. He won a scholarship to a fine school."

I said, "He was there with Robert Falcon and Edmund, wasn't he?"

Mr. Marsh stared, his eyes tired and perplexed. "How did you know about that, Miss Lucy?"

"Lucy. Please, just Lucy. Edmund told me. Nick was his friend at school. Does Edmund know about you? I mean, that you're Nick's father?"

"No, no!" He shook his head quickly. "Nobody knows. When I had served my time in the Army, ten years ago, and took this position with Mr. Gresham, it was a shock to discover that young Master Edmund was at Bellwood, where I knew Nick was also a pupil." He gave a humorless smile. "My wife, Clara, wanted no more to do with me, but I used to send every penny I could spare to her, to help pay for Nick's clothes and books. Poor soul, she worked herself to an early grave for the boy. I have always blamed myself . . . it is foolish to marry outside one's station in life."

"But did Nick never tell Edmund that you were in service here?"

"Nick didn't know."

"Didn't *know* where his own father was?"

"No. You see, he grew up with a great contempt for me. Even when he was ten years old it was there. He hated his father being a servant. I suppose that feeling came from his mother, though I'm sure she never spoke badly of me to him. When I saw him for the last time, at fourteen, he spoke bitterly, saying that he would never be a servant to any man, soldier or civilian. I tried to explain that this was the station I had been born to, and that I was very proud to be an excellent servant. Capable, reliable, and trustworthy. But Nick saw no virtue in that. When he went to Bellwood, he took his mother's maiden name, Sabine, and he has kept it ever since. He wanted nothing to do with a father who was not his own master."

"That was very cruel," I said sadly.

"Perhaps. But the young are inclined to measure yesterday's ways by tomorrow's standards, and now I begin to understand the boy a little better. Not so many take pride in service nowadays, and who can say they are wrong? But I think it was something else that lay behind Nick's contempt. He saw his mother neglected, as it seemed to him, left uncared for by her soldier husband who spent his life in foreign parts. He was right, of course. For the soldier's wife or the sailor's wife, marriage is a lonely business."

"So . . . you haven't seen him since he was a boy?"

"I saw him by chance, three years ago. But I'd heard about him from time to time. Occasionally, when serving at table, I've heard Mr. Edmund recount the latest of Nick's exploits to his parents, so I know something of his adventures."

"Did you speak together when you saw him?"

"Yes. It was my day off, and we came face to face in Piccadilly. I knew him at once, but I was astonished that he recognized me."

"How was he? I mean, was he pleasant to you—or not?"

"I've never been quite sure." Mr. Marsh gave a little shrug. " 'Hallo, Father,' he said, 'I see your back's as straight as ever.' It was a strange thing to say, and I scarcely knew how to answer him, Miss Lucy. Truth to tell, I was close to tears. We talked for a few minutes, and I told him I was butler to the Greshams. 'Well I'll be damned,' he said. 'I hope they treat you well, for I've saved that dry little stick Edmund from a few bloody noses.' "

Mr. Marsh shook his head. "I'd almost have said Nick felt awkward with me, except that I doubt if he ever felt awkward in all his life. So perhaps he was mocking me in some way of his own. I've never been able to make up my mind. He was off to South America next day, but in any event it's hardly likely that we'd have arranged to meet again."

There was a long silence. At last Mr. Marsh roused himself from his memories and looked at me. I was still holding his hand in my own. "Won't you be seated now, Miss Lucy?" he said, troubled. "It's not my place to sit here like this with you at my knee."

I did not move, but said, "Yes, it is your place, Mr. Marsh. It's strange to feel sad and happy at the same time, but I do. I'm truly sad for you about Nick, and I'm sad for myself, but I'm more used to it now. In another way I'm happy. I once said I wished you were my father. And Mr. Marsh, in law you *are* my father. I was married to Nick in Chengfu prison that night. The ring was all we had for a wedding ring."

Mr. Marsh sat without moving for several seconds, then he rubbed his eyes with finger and thumb, shook his head slowly, and stared at me as if still trying to take in my words. "You . . . married Nick?" he said at last.

"Yes. That's when he gave me his signet ring, and I've worn it ever since." I told my own story now, even the parts I had already told on the train to London, beginning with the moment when Robert Falcon first warned me against Nicholas Sabine. By the time I ended my strange tale, with the moment when I had stood with Dr. Langdon beside the mound of earth that was Nick's grave, Mr. Marsh had recovered from the first shock of surprise and was watching me with wondering eyes in which a trace of happiness was beginning to show through the sorrow.

"Why, Lucy child," he breathed after a little silence, "I am . . . a greatly honored man." He leaned forward to kiss my cheek. I knelt up, put my arms round his neck and hugged him.

"Come now," he said in a husky voice, and stood up, helping me to my feet, then moved away and turned to stand looking at me with his head a little on one side, a shadow of anxiety in his eyes. "We must keep this as our secret, Lucy. It would never, never do for the family to know that you are married to their butler's son."

I was startled. "Oh, but why not? I'm not ashamed of it!" I said hotly.

"It simply won't do." His voice was very firm. "It is socially impossible, Lucy. You have been accepted as one of the family, and as such you are a young lady. I am a servant. It would cause even greater difficulties than you face already. I beg you to be guided by me in this."

"Well . . . of course I'll do what you want, Mr. Marsh," I said reluctantly. "But couldn't we go away together? Couldn't I go into service with you somewhere? I don't think I'm really cut out to be a young lady. And in a few months everything will be different, because I'll have some money, a lot of money that Nick left me. Later I inherit Moonrakers, too, though I don't really want that."

"Moonrakers? What do you mean, Lucy?"

I told him of Nicholas's will, and how I would inherit the mortgage on Moonrakers. He rubbed his brow and gave a perplexed sigh. It was small wonder he was confused after all he had learned in this past hour.

"We'll talk of this again, Lucy, but for the moment my head is in a whirl." He took out his watch and looked at it. "I must be about my duties. Here, child." He put the ring in my hand. "I have a silver chain that belonged to Nick's mother. I'll bring it to you later, and you can wear the ring on it." He put a hand on my shoulder. "We neither of us knew the boy well, but he was my son and he was your husband. It gives me pleasure to know that you wear the ring he gave you in his memory."

He drew himself up, and his face became calm and formal again. Only the pallor of his cheeks bore witness to the shock and stress he had passed through. He was Marsh the butler again as he said, "With your permission I will take my leave of you now, Miss Lucy." He inclined his head in a little bow, moved with his usual unhurried pace to the door, and closed it quietly behind him.

I sat pretending to be busy with my embroidery in case anybody came in, and tried to collect my thoughts. I wanted to have no secrets from Mr. Marsh now, and decided to tell him of my meetings with little Matthew Falcon. As for what had happened to me on the night of November the Fifth, that was another matter. I still did not really know what had occurred, but I could tell none of it without saying that I had seen, or imagined seeing, Nicholas Sabine. The mental picture of him standing there in the smoke was as clear now as it had been during those frightening moments on the valley side, yet I knew my mind must have played me false. Nick

Sabine was dead. It would be cruel to speak of what I had imagined to his father.

It hurt me to keep secret from the family that Mr. Marsh was my father-in-law, but I realized he would probably be dismissed at once if Mr. Gresham learned the truth, and I could not let that happen while I had no money to help him until he found a new position. I would have to be patient, I decided, but as soon as I had some money I would beg Mr. Marsh to take me away.

I expected the days that followed to be happier for me, knowing that Mr. Marsh was something much more than a friend now, but I was wrong, for I found the situation deeply distressing. I hated to have him wait on me at table or in the drawing room, and it was even worse when he was serving Emily in any way. She was always disagreeable with the servants, puffing and sighing as if their stupidity made her life a burden. I had seen Albert flush dark red at some of her cutting remarks, and seen Maggie reduced to tears. Mr. Marsh always remained quite unruffled; but now, when she made some scathing remark as he served her, I felt my fingers twitch with a longing to pull her hair until she squealed.

I spoke of my feelings to him in the sewing room one afternoon, and he looked surprised. "Good heavens, child, you don't imagine that Miss Emily's little tantrums trouble me, do you? Part of a good servant's duty is to be an outlet for the occasional bad temper of members of the family he serves."

I did not argue, but the idea was hateful to me, and I knew now how Nick Sabine must have felt.

Amanda came home a week before Christmas, and Matthew the next day. I had not been able to discover exactly when he was coming home, so I had taken to waiting in his secret house for an hour each afternoon, even though it was cold. On this day he was already there when I arrived. It was a joy to see him. We made hot chocolate together, and with great pride Matthew introduced me to a tame rabbit he had brought from school with him. The Falcons' gardener had made a hutch from an old crate and some wire netting, and this Matthew had brought down the path which wound through the wooded slope below Moonrakers, dragging it over the carpet of wet leaves without too much difficulty.

I held the rabbit while he spread straw in the hutch and set out two small bowls of food and water. "There," he said at last, "we can put him inside now. Do you think he'll be all right, Lucy?"

"It's a lady rabbit," I said. "I'm sure she'll be all right, but we mustn't leave her for more than two days without bringing fresh food and water. And we ought to make a long leash of string, so we can let her have a little run whenever we come."

"I shall come every day."

"Won't that be difficult over Christmas?"

"Oh, no. Mamma and Papa will have some of their friends staying, and they won't mind if I'm away for a little while, even on Christmas Day. They like me to do what I want to do. I say, could you come too, Lucy? I'll bring two Christmas crackers, and we could have our own special party, just for a little while."

"I'd love to, Matthew, and I'll try, but I don't think it's likely I'll be able to get away, so you mustn't get cold waiting for me."

As I walked home I wondered what Matthew would feel when the Falcon family lost Moonrakers—to me, his friend. It would seem the most terrible betrayal to the little boy, and even to think about it made me feel a sick despair. But there was nothing I could do, for Edmund was bound to carry out the terms of the will.

That evening I suffered again the regular ordeal of watching Mr. Marsh serve the family at dinner, and of hearing Emily make a sarcastic remark when he asked if she would like another slice of roast beef. I went to bed feeling that more than anything in the world I wanted to go away from High Coppice and never come back.

[216]

On the evening before Christmas Eve we sat in the drawing room after dinner, playing Anagrams. Edmund had arrived later than expected from London, because of the snow. Until midday the skies had been clear, but then, within an hour, they grew leaden. Snow began to fall in enormous white flakes, and so heavily that by teatime the countryside lay under a great blanket of it. The trains were held up, no carriage could climb the hill from Chislehurst Station, and Edmund told us the snow had gathered in such drifts down there that the porters had to dig a pathway for passengers leaving the station. It had taken him twenty minutes to climb the blizzard-swept hill, almost knee-deep in snow. At the top he had found a carriage at the inn, and this had brought him to within a hundred yards of High Coppice before the driver decided that he would turn back while he was still able to do so.

The snow was still falling. In the drawing room a huge log fire roared in the grate. We were cosy and well-fed, and to-night we would sleep in warm beds. I thought about the children at the Mission, and wondered how they were faring at this moment.

On my knee was a little pad, and there I had written down the anagram Edmund had just given us to solve, for it was his turn to provide the puzzle. The words he had given were *string manor,* and we had to make a single word from those letters. Amanda had forgotten how grown-up she was now, and kept shouting a word before realizing that it contained some wrong letters. Emily sat gazing at her pad and eating chocolates. Mrs. Gresham toyed with her pencil rather sleepily, and Mr. Gresham sat with an expression of profound concentration, lips pursed.

I could not solve the anagram, and began idly to reflect that the game would be impossible to play in Chinese, because the language had no alphabet. Each word was a character or collection of characters in itself. That much I knew, although I had never learned to write Chinese. For no particular reason

I wrote down *Chengfu* on my pad, setting the letters in a circle. This was the way I had written down the letters of *string manor,* because I had found it the best way to solve anagrams. Still hardly thinking about what I was doing, I wrote down *Tsin Kai-feng* in another circle, then *Tientsin* and *Shanghai,* wondering if it might be possible to make an English word from the name of a Chinese town.

"Oh, I give up," said Amanda. "Tell us, Edmund."

"You have another fifteen seconds before the three minutes is up," Edmund said reprovingly, looking at his watch. "Father, are you having any success?"

"I believe I'm on the verge of it," Mr. Gresham said slowly, frowning at his pad. "Now, let me see . . ."

"Time's up!" cried Amanda. "Oh, it must be. Go on, Edmund, what's your silly old word?"

"The word is '*morningstar.*'" Edmund smiled a little smugly.

"But that's two words! Papa, he cheated. It *is* two words, isn't it?"

Edmund spoke before his father could reply. "Not at all, Amanda. I am not referring to the morning star which shines in the sky, but to the ancient weapon, like a mace or club with spikes on it, called a morningstar."

"Oh, that's still cheating! How do you expect us to know words like that? Papa, tell him not to be so mean!"

I did not hear Mr. Gresham's reply, for I was staring at the jumble of letters on my pad, and the rest of the world seemed to have dwindled away. Something had leaped out at me, so clearly that I could not understand why I had never seen it before. I was holding my breath, and my body was taut with excitement. A fragment of the riddle John Falcon had written sixty years ago was suddenly plain to me. And then, in the long strange moments of clarity that followed, another and another fragment fell into place, like the last few pieces of a jigsaw puzzle.

I drew in a shaky breath and was about to cry out with

excitement, when the drawing-room door opened and Mr Marsh entered. There was a hint of urgency lurking under his usual unruffled manner, and without waiting to be spoken to he broke into the conversation. "Excuse me, sir. A matter of some importance. Mr. Harry Falcon begs a moment of your time."

For several seconds there was complete silence, then Mr. Gresham got slowly to his feet. "Harry Falcon? Here?"

"Yes, sir. He is waiting in the porch, in view of the snow upon his boots and his person."

"Really!" Mrs. Gresham exclaimed. "Tell him we are not at home, Marsh."

"If you will forgive me, madam, this is not a social call but an emergency of some nature, so he informs me. Certainly he is greatly disturbed."

"Well . . . I'd better go and see what it's about," Mr. Gresham said reluctantly. As he went out with Mr. Marsh, and the door closed behind them, there was a burst of chatter in the drawing room. For myself, I found it hard to turn my mind to the puzzle of Mr. Falcon's visit, or to wonder what the urgency might be, for I was still befuddled by the staggering discovery I had made only a few moments ago.

Edmund was saying: "All this eager speculation among you ladies is really quite pointless. We shall learn the facts of the matter in due time. I suggest we contain our curiosity till then, and continue with the game. Come along, Amanda, it's your turn to provide an anagram for us to solve. Do you have one ready?"

Nobody much wanted to continue, but at Edmund's insistence the game went on in a half-hearted fashion. I had managed to collect my wits now, but gave only a small part of my attention to what we were doing. I was suddenly glad that the interruption had prevented me blurting out my discovery, for now I was by no means sure that I wanted the Gresham family alone to know it. If the war lord's emeralds existed, if they lay hidden where I now believed, and could be found and brought home, then I wanted the fortune to be shared by the two families, as their forebears had originally intended. To bring such a thing to pass seemed hopeless, but I decided to wait a while and think hard about what I had discovered.

A full ten minutes passed before Mr. Gresham re-entered the drawing room. During that time we once heard his voice in the hall, calling to one of the servants, but though we strained our ears we heard no more. He looked flustered as he came in, and was blinking rapidly. Questions burst from his wife and daughters, and he gestured impatiently for silence.

"It appears the Falcon boy is missing," he said. "They're searching, but this blizzard makes all movement difficult."

"Robert?" Emily said, gaping.

"No, no. The little boy, Matthew. He was in the house an hour ago, or a little more, but now he's missing. Falcon says he wanders off on his own a great deal, but they didn't dream he'd go out in this weather." Mr. Gresham shrugged. "The child must be touched, like his parents. Robert Falcon and the male servants are out searching now."

"Why did Falcon Senior come here?" Edmund asked.

"First to ask if the boy had taken shelter here, since we're the nearest neighbors, and then to ask for help in the search. I told Marsh and Albert to put coats and rubber boots on, and I've sent them off with Falcon." He looked almost guiltily at his wife. "I felt bound to—um—co-operate under the circumstances."

"No question of that," Edmund said firmly, and stood up. "It's a bad business. If the child is in a drift, there's little hope of finding him, and he'll not survive long in such cold." He moved to the door. "I'll wrap up and search the lane from the end of the drive to the main road."

"For Heaven's sake be careful, dear!" Mrs. Gresham called anxiously as he closed the door.

All this I heard as if from a great distance, for I was

stupefied by fear. My face felt pinched and drained, my hands were like cold damp clay. Once, at the Mission, a weeping young woman had come to tell me that her husband had taken their girl baby to leave out in the snow. I had run with her to a grove by the river, and found the baby within ten minutes, for the snow was only two inches deep. Even so, I was too late.

Something was stirring slowly in my benumbed mind, but I could not grasp what it was. I only knew that it was important, and pressed my hands to my eyes in an effort to capture and recognize it. Time stood still. Then abruptly I cried out, jumped to my feet and ran to the door. Wrenching it open I shouted, "Edmund! Edmund!" Maggie was passing across the hall, and she jumped with alarm, then said, "He's gone, Miss Lucy. Went out a minute or two ago."

Mr. Gresham was beside me. "What on earth is the matter with you, Lucy?" he said angrily. "You startled us out of our skins, shrieking like that!"

"I know where he is!" I said frantically. "I know where Matthew is! He's down in the secret house—*he went there because of his rabbit!* He was afraid it would die in the snow!"

Mr. Gresham gazed at me as if I had gone mad. Then with a tight, angry set to his mouth he gripped me firmly by the arm, closed the door, and marched me back across the room to stand facing him in front of the fire. Lifting a finger, he wagged it to emphasize his words. "How dare you? I hoped you had outgrown this habit of making up fantasies! At a time like this it is nothing short of *wicked* to do so!"

My voice was a croak. "It's not a fantasy, Mr. Gresham. Please come with me. I *know* where Matthew is."

He puffed out his breath with an explosive sound of anger. "Nonsense! Secret house? Rabbit? Do you think I'm a fool, girl?"

"But it's true! There's a place in the valley, hidden by lots of bushes. He has a zoo there, and I often go to meet him when he's home from school. He makes chocolate on a stove—"

"Rubbish!" Mr. Gresham almost shouted the word, and his

face was mottled with fury. "You would never *dare* to consort with the Falcon child!"

Emily said, "Perhaps he makes *chocolate* rabbits on a stove, Papa." She giggled, and the sound of it brought anger surging up within me.

"I—I don't *care* whether you believe me," I stammered, "I'll go on my own if you won't help!"

"You will go nowhere except to your room," Mr. Gresham said, speaking between his teeth. "You are a wicked, lying young woman, and I regret the day I brought you to this house. Now go to your room *at once!* Not another word!"

There was an awful silence. With an enormous effort I took hold of myself and said in a low voice, "Very well, Mr. Gresham. I apologize for making you angry." I turned, made my way across the room, and went out. The instant I had closed the door behind me, I gathered up my skirts and raced up the stairs two at a time. Maggie was busy turning down the beds, and she emerged from Edmund's room as I hurried across the landing.

"Maggie! Come here!" I whispered urgently, and ran on into my room. She followed, her eyes round with surprise. I was already struggling out of my dress. "I need some trousers, Maggie. Yes, *trousers.* Go and get me a pair from Mr. Edmund's room, the oldest pair you can find."

"Ooh, miss, I daresn't!"

"I'll say I took them myself. I promise. *Please,* Maggie. It will save me a minute or two. The little Falcon boy is dying in the snow, and I know where, but they won't believe me."

She blinked, then her thin peaky face grew stern. "Right, miss. I'll be back in a jiffy."

Three minutes later she was in the hall below, keeping watch on the drawing-room door for me as I ran stealthily down the stairs and darted across the hall to go on down to the servants' hall. I had taken off my dress and waist-petticoat, and put on three blouses and a woolen jacket under my topcoat. A pair of Edmund's trousers were tightly belted about my waist with the strap from my suitcase, the bottoms tucked into the high felt boots I had brought with me from China. My hands were gloved, and a long woolen scarf was wrapped round my head and neck. Under one arm I carried a folded blanket.

There was a side door which allowed me to leave the house without going through the kitchen itself, and for this I was thankful since I did not have to delay for explanations to Mrs. Trowbridge and Beattie, who were in the kitchen together.

Before I had gone fifty yards across the garden I began to wonder if I would ever reach the secret house in the valley bottom. The snow was more than twelve inches deep, and though I could plod through it here without too much difficulty I knew that on the path running down into the valley there would be treacherous drifts. The snow still fell heavily, slanting against me in the bitter wind that whined across the valley. The moon and stars were blotted out, but there was some reflected light from the great white blanket hiding the earth, and I was able to see a dozen or fifteen paces ahead of me. Once through the orchard I altered my direction a little to avoid the path. This meant I had to clamber over rocks and between snow-crushed bushes which lay on the higher ground bordering the path, but it was better than fighting through drifts several feet deep.

I slithered, I fell, I bruised my legs painfully on hidden rocks, but at least I made steady progress, for I was moving downhill. I did not dare to think what the return journey would be like. When I reached the stand of trees, their boughs were groaning under the weight of snow, but there were no drifts or obstructions here, and I was able to move a little more quickly, though even then it was like wading rather than walking.

I came at last to the great mass of shrubbery and undergrowth which hid Matthew's secret house, and found that the snow had made the foliage sag so low that it was impossible to walk through the tunnel. I could only crawl. Here the ground was sodden and muddy, but no snow had penetrated. As I crawled I began to shout against the noise of the blizzard.

"Matthew! Matthew!"

There was no answer. I felt sick as I realized that Matthew might have started back home before exhaustion overtook him; or he might never even have reached the secret house. He might be anywhere, lying under the snow. In the clearing beyond the ring of bushes the snow lay as deep as ever, but I could see faint indentations under the most recent layer, as if someone had trodden there. I blundered forward to the low cliff wall, looking frantically about me, but there was no sign of him. I rubbed the snow from my face and eyes, and peered again through the darkness. Then I saw him, huddled on all fours in the recess, with his arms curled about his head. A thin layer of snow, which grew thicker every moment, spread like a sheet over his hunched form.

"Matthew!" I knelt beside him, taking him by an arm and trying to lift him, but he only rolled on his side. In the dim, eerie snowlight I saw that his eyes were closed and his face was like marble. I took him under the arms and dragged him to his knees, shouting at him, holding him pressed close to me, blowing hot breath on his face and eyes. For a moment the lids flickered and half opened, but then they closed again and he sagged in my arms.

I ached with cold and fatigue, but now I felt an even deeper cold, for I knew that Matthew would never wake again unless I could bring him to warmth and safety very soon. And I knew, too, that I could never carry him back up the hill to High Coppice. Burdened with his weight, I could not climb the rough and rocky slope beside the path, and on the path itself the drifts would engulf us.

There was no time to go for help, even if I had known where to find any of the searchers. I knew with bleak certainty that whatever was to be done I would have to do it alone. And I did not know what to do.

With a great effort I stilled the terror that rose within me, and spoke to myself through sore and frozen lips as I began to unfold the blanket. "Do what comes next, Lucy. First, do whatever comes next, then think about it again."

« N I N E »

I SPREAD the blanket on the snow, and dragged Matthew's limp form to the middle of it so that he lay diagonally on the rectangle. Two corners I brought across his middle and knotted there. I took the other two corners, at his head and feet, brought them together and tied the ends in a big double-knot. My fingers were numb and the blanket seemed to have a perverse will of its own, but at last it was done.

Turning my back on Matthew, I went down on my hands and knees in the snow, then reached back, grasped the knot and struggled to bring the loop of the blanket forward over my head. I felt Matthew's curled body against the small of my back, and with a final heave managed to bring the knot over my head so that it rested hard against my brow. This was the way I had carried heavy burdens in China, the way the peasants used. Matthew was huddled in the blanket and resting against my back, with the loop acting as a sling around my forehead. I did not stand up yet, because that would be the most difficult part and I still had to crawl through the tunnel. On hands and knees I moved forward across the clearing, sometimes sinking almost to my shoulders in the snow.

I reached the tunnel and crawled on through the creaking foliage with its great weight of snow above. It was not until I came into the open again, and into the deep-piled snow, that I hunched my shoulders, tensed my neck, and used all the strength of my legs to stand up with my burden. Once I was on my feet, and leaning well forward against the pull of the blanket across my forehead, Matthew's weight seemed less formidable. But I knew that I dared not fall too often, for the struggle to rise would sap my strength.

Well . . . I had done what came next. But what came next now? The answer slipped into my mind as I watched the snowflakes hurtling away from me, vanishing into the darkness. The wind was blowing across the valley from Moonrakers to High Coppice, so the drifts would be on the southern slope, the slope I had descended. I had never crossed the fence and traveled up the path which led to Moonrakers, but I knew it was a gentler slope, and that for much of the way the path ran through the woods. I also knew that with the wind southerly there would be no drifts.

Two minutes later I had trudged fifty yards to the fence, and there I had good fortune, for a short section of it had been brought down by the weight of snow driven against a rotted post, and I did not have to find a way over or through it. But then the struggle began, a struggle so unending that at times, in my fatigue and mental confusion, I felt I must be a lost soul wandering for ever in some dreadful and eternal limbo.

Three times I strayed from the path that wound through the woods, for it lay hidden under the snow. Twice I had to retrace my steps for a little way, and the third time I blundered desperately on through a tangle of snow-laden bushes to reach the path again by lucky chance. I was bent double now under Matthew's weight. The muscles of my shoulders and neck burned like fire, and the breath rasped in my throat.

After what seemed an age, my wits became so dull that I had to tell myself to lift up a foot and put it down again with each pace I took. I began counting my steps. The snow whistled down the valley side, swirling through the trees and driving into my face. My eyes felt raw, and it became steadily more difficult to make out what little of the path lay within my range of vision, for here under the trees it was very dark.

All the time I was desperately aware that Matthew, lying still and unmoving across my back, would be sinking deeper into that soft, murderous coma by which cold claims its victims. Half a dozen times I knew that I could not take another step, then roused from a period of unawareness to find that I was still plodding on, still counting. My mind fluttered and reeled. It would never end. I would take a million steps, and still it would be only the beginning.

A dull despair grew within me as I found that the snow underfoot was becoming deeper. Slowly I reasoned that this must be because the trees were left behind and I was nearing the top of the ridge—

The top? I lifted my head and stared. Through the swirling flakes I could see lights, rectangles of light, the windows of a great house with every light burning and every curtain drawn back. Moonrakers. Two hundred paces away.

I stumbled forward. Several minutes and a hundred paces later, I fell. Somehow I came to my feet, and went on. Twice more I fell, but struggled up again. The third time my muscles refused to obey me, despite all the fierce insistence of my mind. I moved slowly forward, crawling on hands and knees, plowing a channel through the snow, my face sometimes buried. The weight on my back was no longer that of a little boy. It was a boulder, a house, a mountain.

There was gravel beneath the snow. I could feel it through my gloves and against my knees. I looked up. The great warm house was so near now, looming only thirty paces away. I could see two figures moving, each with a lantern. They stood close together as if speaking, then moved in different directions. I crawled on, but my arms gave way. I lifted my head, drew in a shuddering breath, and shouted. Not a sound came from my throat.

One of the figures was striding past, a man, head bent against the snow, no more than ten paces away. I shouted again, almost beyond hope now, for I knew I could neither walk, nor crawl, nor drag myself another inch. My shout was a thin shrill noise.

The man stopped, turned, moved slowly toward me, lifting the lantern, then suddenly lunged forward with great strides and dropped to his knees beside me. I was lying face-down, with the blanket-wrapped form of Matthew across my back. My head was lifted, but only because the blanket sling dragged it back, otherwise it would have fallen forward, for my strength was gone. I found myself looking up into the haggard face of Matthew's father.

"I've got him," I whispered, fighting to lift my voice above the wind. "I found Matthew. He's in the blanket. Please, get him warm . . . quickly."

Then there was a great roaring in my ears, and my mind slid down a long dark slope into nothingness.

* * *

The aching of my neck and back woke me. I was propped on pillows in a big fourposter bed which stood facing a curtained window. The large and rather shabby room held far less furniture and fewer knickknacks than the bedrooms at High Coppice.

A log fire crackled in the grate, and I was almost too warm with the featherbed below me and the blankets and eiderdown upon me. I put my arms outside the covers, and saw that I was wearing a pretty pink nightdress with lacy cuffs. Mrs.

Falcon sat in a chair beside the bed, her beautiful face tired but calm.

As memory returned I started up on one elbow. "Matthew? Is he all right? You have to rub him hard all over with rough towels, Mrs. Falcon—"

"Hush, dear. Don't worry about Matthew, he's safe." She stood up and took my hand. "It's more than three hours since Harry found you crawling through the snow with Matthew on your back. Dr. Cheyne has been, and he's seen you both. We sent word to the Greshams at once, so they know you're safe."

I lay back thankfully. Mrs. Falcon had told me everything that mattered in those few words. It would have taken Mrs. Greshan ten minutes to say as much.

"Matthew woke a little while ago," she went on. "Only for a few minutes, and he's asleep again now. But he told us where you found him, and how you've been meeting there, down in the valley. What a silly boy. We wouldn't have minded." She shook her head wonderingly. "Harry and Robert still can't understand how you carried him up out of the valley in that dreadful blizzard."

Despite the warmth of the bed, I shivered as I remembered. "I'm quite strong for my size, Mrs. Falcon . . . but I was so frightened I wouldn't be strong enough."

"My dear, you're strong in your heart, where it counts most." Tears suddenly filled her eyes. She bent to put her head close to mine, and kissed my cheek. "God bless you, Lucy. Once you saved Robert's life, and now my little boy's. I've no words to thank you."

I was close to tears myself, with relief. "It just happened in that way, Mrs. Falcon. I'm glad I could help. Please, need I go back tonight? I'm so tired, and . . . and I'm afraid Mr. Gresham is going to be terribly cross with me."

"Go back tonight? It's out of the question, Lucy. In any case, Dr. Cheyne said you must stay in bed until he's seen you again. But why will Mr. Gresham be angry?"

"I—I shouted at him because he wouldn't believe I knew where Matthew was. He thinks I make up fantasies. He said he wished he'd never brought me to his home, and sent me to my room, but I disobeyed him."

"Thank Heaven you did, or Matthew would have been lost to us by now." Her voice shook and her hand tightened on mine. "But you proved Mr. Gresham wrong in thinking you were making up a fantasy, so surely he can't be angry?"

"Well . . . he doesn't like to be wrong, Mrs. Falcon."

"I see." She sighed. "Could you take a bowl of hot soup if I brought you some? And may Harry and Robert come to see you for just a moment? I know Harry won't sleep until he's thanked you."

"I'd like the soup, Mrs. Falcon. Thank you very much." I hesitated. "I must look horrid. My face feels all swollen and my hair must be like a bird's nest, but if they really want to see me will you explain that I'm not always like this?"

She smiled, and there was warm understanding in her eyes. "We've all seen you looking your own beautiful self, dear, and they do realize what you've been through tonight. They were out in the blizzard themselves for hours."

It was not until she had brought me a bowl of soup herself, and watched me swallow it, that she allowed her husband and Robert to enter. I felt very foolish and awkward. Mr. Falcon still looked haggard from the hours of anxiety, but he smiled and kissed me on the forehead, and thanked me with such warm simplicity that I was quickly at ease with him. Robert seemed quite at a loss. He stood grim-faced and troubled, muttering a few stilted words. His manner was so different from the confident air habitual to him that I would scarcely have known him for the man I had spoken with in Tsin Kai-feng, the man who had walked boldly into High Coppice to ask if he might call on me, the man who had appeared out of the darkness on the valley side only a few weeks ago, and kissed me.

My sleep was deep and dreamless that night. When I woke

next morning the curtains had been drawn back and I saw that the snow had stopped falling. My shoulders still ached, but apart from that I felt well and even hungry. A maidservant was sitting beside me, and as soon as I opened my eyes she hurried away to tell her mistress. Ten minutes later she returned with a breakfast tray, followed by Mrs. Falcon.

"Hallo, Lucy dear. I hope you slept well. Matthew keeps asking for you, but I've said he must wait until the doctor has been to see you."

As I ate my breakfast, she stood by the window, looking out over the snow-covered valley and talking easily about the beauty and cruelty of nature. I found myself responding readily, and thought how different this household seemed. Mrs. Gresham had never talked of anything but domestic matters and general gossip.

Later that morning Dr. Cheyne came, a cheerful red-faced man who took my pulse and temperature, and said, "Well, young lady, how d'ye do it? That little jaunt of yours would put most people in bed for a week. What the dickens d'ye mean by being back to normal this morning, hey? You're out to ruin my business, is that it?"

He turned to Mrs. Falcon. "You'll keep young Matthew in bed another day if you please, ma'am. But if this one wants to get up, better let her have her head. She's a freak, ma'am, that's what she is." He winked at me, gathered up his bag, and departed.

I said to Mrs. Falcon, "Must I go back this morning?"

"Of course not, dear. I'm sure the Greshams won't expect you to be recovered so soon. Now, would you rather stay in bed or get dressed? I've had your blouses and underwear washed and ironed, and the little maid, Peggy, says you can borrow her best skirt. I'm afraid one of mine would be too big for you."

"I'd like to get up, please."

"Good. Sit up and let me do your hair for you, then I'll have hot water brought up for your bath."

An hour later, wearing my own blouse but in a borrowed skirt and shoes, I was in Matthew's bedroom. He did not have much recollection of his ordeal the night before, in fact his main concern was for his rabbit, and I found it hard not to look taken aback when he asked me reproachfully why I had left it behind. His mother rolled her eyes up at me in comic despair, and gave an apologetic shrug. I promised to tell Robert exactly how to find the secret house so that he could go and look for the rabbit, and this satisfied the little boy for the time being. We left him to sleep, and Mrs. Falcon took me along to the studio, which was a great light room at the top of the house.

There, Mr. Falcon laid down his paint brush and palette to greet me warmly. The haggard look had gone now, and he was as smiling and easy as I remembered from our meeting at the garden party. The studio was gloriously untidy, with half finished paintings stacked at random, and on the walls some colorful theatre bills, unframed, and even theatre programs.

"I'm trying a winter scene," Mr. Falcon said, nodding toward the big window and putting an arm around his wife's waist. "Going badly, isn't it? Ah well, we're both of us mere daubers, aren't we, Tina? But the flesh is willing, even if the talent is weak." He took off his paint-smeared smock. "Who's for coffee? Mrs. Cox, our cook, doesn't hold with it, of course. She firmly believes God gave us tea for hot drinks and gin for cold, but she produces quite a respectable brew these days, now she's got the hang of it. Let's go down and have her show her skill, shall we?"

In many ways Moonrakers was a shabby home, but it had an atmosphere I loved. Though the furniture was old and worn, and the carpets a little threadbare here and there, the style of decoration was full of casual artistry. Instead of rooms crammed with furniture there was spaciousness; instead of fussy knickknacks there were fascinating objects set sparingly on shelves and mantelpieces and small tables—carvings in wood and stone; a slender vase holding some stalks of strange

[233]

dry grass, delicately arranged; a stone as big as a coconut, broken to show amethyst within it and set on a base of beautifully grained wood. There were pictures everywhere, some painted by Mr. or Mrs. Falcon, I was told, but many by their various friends.

"Nothing of any value," Mr. Falcon said cheerfully as we settled down in the drawing room with cups of coffee. "The amethyst is worthless for cutting, but it's pretty. As for the paintings, well, perhaps one of our friends will turn out to be an unsung genius in a hundred years. Who knows?" He turned in his chair as the door opened. "Ah, Robert. Come and pour yourself some coffee. Any luck with the rabbit?"

"I found it alive. Isn't that extraordinary? The hutch was almost buried, but I suppose the snow kept it warm, like an Eskimo in an igloo." He shook his head. "You'd never believe the journey Lucy made with Matthew last night. It's bad enough now."

Robert Falcon had recovered his old manner. Quite at ease, he crossed the room, took my hand and bent to kiss my cheek. "Already out of bed, Lucy? What an astonishing girl you are. And how nice it is to see you here."

"Hallo, Robert. I'm very happy to be here." I had expected to feel embarrassed meeting him this morning, for we had seen nothing of each other since Mr. Gresham had brusquely forbidden him to call on me any more, except for that moment in the darkness on the valley side. But Mr. and Mrs. Falcon seemed to create such a warm atmosphere that it was impossible to feel ill at ease. Before I could think what I was saying I added, "It's so different here, I don't like to think about going back."

At the coffee table, Robert shot a glance at his father.

"Can Gresham make her?"

Mr. Falcon scratched his beard. "Damned if I know, boy. If he's legally her guardian, I suppose he can."

I said, "He isn't my guardian," then added hastily, "but

please don't think I was suggesting I could stay. I shouldn't have said what I did."

"Why not? You'll always be welcome here, Lucy." He looked at his wife, and grinned. "We could manage somehow, couldn't we, sweetheart?"

"We always have, Harry." She turned her clear, candid gaze on me. "I'd be very happy to have you, dear."

I said reluctantly, "You're very kind. But Mr. Gresham brought me from China and has looked after me all this time. It wouldn't be right for me to come to you if he wants me to stay."

"Well, we won't try to persuade you, Lucy," Mrs. Falcon said quietly. "This isn't a family where the master lays down the law and decides what's best for each of us. Harry won't have it so. We believe everyone should follow his own way of thinking and acting." Her glance touched Robert. "As long as no hurt is caused to others."

Mr. Falcon chuckled. "I'll wager old Gresham considers us a feckless crew, with a lot of wild and loose-living London folk for our friends. Well, perhaps Tina and I don't worry about material things as much as we should." He glanced at Robert with a half-apologetic grimace. "Robert there certainly thinks so, and that's his privilege. But we don't tell him how to live his life, and he's learning not to tell us how we should live ours now. We like our friends, for better or worse, and most of them are decent folk, just a little unorthodox. We live the way we want to, cause no harm and don't complain when life gives us a few buffets." He stood up, moved to where his wife sat, and bent to kiss her without any hint of embarrassment. "And we're happy, aren't we, sweetheart?"

I felt so glad for them that my eyes stung. I had never seen Mr. and Mrs. Gresham display such affection. Later, when we ate a simple but good lunch in the dining room together, I was constantly aware of this great bond between Mr. Falcon and his wife. Robert was not a part of it, though. Unlike his parents, he gave thought to the future, and it was clear that concern for Moonrakers ran strongly within him. As they talked at table, I realized that this was an issue between them.

"Your happy-go-lucky philosophy is all very well in theory, Father," Robert said amiably enough, refilling his glass from a decanter of white wine, "but one day you'll come to the crunch." His face grew somber. "It could well be next year."

"Oh, don't be a pessimist, boy," Mr. Falcon said heartily. "George Benton was saying the other day that if I put my mind to it I could make a pretty penny doing portraits for rich, vain women."

"But you won't, will you? Because you don't like that sort of painting."

His father grinned. "True. Oh, well. Something else will turn up."

"If it doesn't, we'll lose Moonrakers."

Mrs. Falcon said, "Even that doesn't mean the end of the world, Robbie. Your father and I might take a little cottage in Cornwall, if we have to go. I love Moonrakers, but a house isn't the most important thing."

"Moonrakers is important to me, Mother."

"I know. It's an obsession with you, Robbie, and I wish it weren't. But perhaps Mr. Sabine will extend the mortgage when the time comes."

"Nick Sabine? You're dreaming, Mother. The only chance we have of the mortgage being extended is if he never comes back from China. What happens then I don't know. His heirs and assigns would have to be found, if he has any, and then it would be up to them, I suppose. In any event we'd have more time. I've heard no word of his return, so perhaps we'll be lucky."

"Never wish him dead, Robbie," his mother said quickly. "That's an awful thing to hope for."

Robert shrugged. I felt guilty to be sitting at their table in silence when I could have told them so much, but I needed time to think before I could decide whether it was right for me to speak. A little later Robert excused himself to arrange for Matthew's rabbit to be properly rehoused. When the door closed after him, Mr. Falcon looked at his wife and lifted an eyebrow. "Our Robert seems to be mellowing somewhat," he said with pleased surprise. "It must be Lucy's influence." He smiled at me. "Robert doesn't usually reproach us so gently for our follies. It seems you have an excellent effect on him."

An hour later I was sitting in Matthew's room, playing Snakes and Ladders with him, when the front doorbell sounded. Three minutes passed, then Mrs. Falcon came into the room. "I'm sorry, Lucy," she said sympathetically, "but it's Edmund Gresham."

"Oh!" My heart sank. "Has he come to take me back?"

"I don't quite know, dear. He inquired after you, then asked if he could speak to you. He's waiting in the drawing room now. I must say his manner was very courteous."

"Yes. He's not quite like the others." I got to my feet reluctantly. "I'd better go down, then."

Edmund rose as I entered the drawing room. We greeted one another a little awkwardly, and when he asked how I was I replied that I felt almost myself again now. Then we fell silent. I had never seen Edmund embarrassed before, but he seemed very much at a loss. To fill the silence I said, "I'm sorry I took your trousers, Edmund, but I had to. I could never have got down into the valley wearing skirts."

"Oh, quite so, quite so," he said hastily, flushing a little. "I —um—what I have to tell you, Lucy, is that . . . well, as perhaps you realize, my father is not always a logical man. The fact that you were entirely right last night, and that the boy would have died but for your disobedience, has not in any way lessened my father's ill-temper with you." He shrugged apologetically. "Perhaps without realizing it he is ashamed, and in the way of impulsive people he tends to convert this into anger toward you."

"I'm sorry I disobeyed him, but I had to, Edmund."

"I know that. But there is something else I must say. Marsh returned some time after we found that you were not in your room and had left the house. He learned what had happened from Maggie, and as a consequence forgot his position as a servant, and—ah—criticized my father in terms more suited to a sergeant major than a butler."

I put my hands to my mouth in dismay. "Oh! What happened, Edmund?"

"In the course of his—um—surprisingly articulate expression of opinion, Marsh revealed the astonishing fact that he is Nick Sabine's father, and therefore your father-in-law. No doubt this was the cause of his extreme alarm for your safety, and his anger toward my father."

"Yes, it's true, Edmund. I have Nick's signet ring, and Mr. Marsh recognized it. That's how he found out. I didn't tell anybody, because I was afraid Mr. Marsh would have to leave High Coppice if I did."

Edmund tapped his fingertips together. "Quite so. In the event, and after his unfortunate behavior last night, he was dismissed on the spot. He left the house this morning." Edmund drew an envelope from his pocket. "This is a note he asked me to bring you."

My hand shook as I took it. "May I read it now, please?"

"Of course."

I was all thumbs, trying to open the envelope. "It was . . . very kind of you to bring this, Edmund."

He looked slightly surprised. "I have no animosity toward Marsh. In my view his offense was justified by the fact that he is your father-in-law."

I took out the note and unfolded it.

My dear Lucy,

Thank God you are safe, and the little boy, too. Mr. Edmund has kindly promised to deliver this for me. I shall be lodging with an old army friend of mine in Greenwich while I seek a new position. Please do not worry about me. I have my army pension, and am sure that my old master, who is now an important person in the War Office, will

help with a good recommendation. It would be a great joy
to hear from you, and perhaps to meet occasionally if this
can be arranged. My address will be, 14 Ludford Road,
Greenwich.

>*With love from your affectionate father,*
>*Thomas Marsh.*

I folded the note and looked up. "It's just to give me his address and tell me not to worry about him. Thank you again, Edmund."

"Not at all. Have the Falcons taken good care of you?"

"Oh yes, they've been wonderfully kind."

"You—um—quite like it here?"

"Yes. Very much."

"I suppose it would hardly be possible for you to—er—stay? I mean . . . well, to be frank, I know it would be a relief to my parents if you did not return to us, Lucy. I'm sorry to say this, and I bear you no ill-will myself, you understand." He stood up and began to pace slowly across the room. "The fact is, however, that your presence creates an atmosphere of strain. My father is to blame for bringing you to High Coppice in the first place, and I have said so to him, plainly. My mother has never approved, of course. You have been unable to help my father in the way that he hoped, though this is not your fault, but it has had the effect of severely abating his enthusiasm for having an extra member of the family."

I could hardly speak for delight, but struggled to hide the fullness of it, for this would have been too unkind, so I simply tried to look thoughtful and said, "If he doesn't want me back, Edmund, I'm sure I could stay on here. Mr. and Mrs. Falcon have said so."

"Really?" It was hard to tell whether Edmund was more relieved or surprised. "Well, that's really most convenient, Lucy. My parents would never neglect their duty to you, of course, but this offers an excellent solution. My father felt the Falcons might be willing to take you, in the hope that you

[239]

might help them discover the secret of the war lord's treasure. I thought otherwise, but evidently I was wrong."

"That isn't the reason, Edmund. They're just grateful to me. I'll write to your parents, I want to thank them for all they've done for me. Do you think I could have some of my clothes?"

"Eh? Yes, yes, of course. I'll have all your clothes and belongings packed up and sent across." He lowered his voice. "Will you tell the Falcons about Nick? I mean, that you were married to him, and will inherit Moonrakers?"

"I don't know yet. It's awfully difficult, and I haven't had time to think about it. Oh Edmund, *must* you do what Nick said in the will? Couldn't the mortgage be extended?"

"Certainly not, Lucy." He looked shocked. "I am bound by law to follow Nick's instructions and take possession of his whole estate for your benefit. I realize it will make an awkward situation for you, but that can't be helped."

"It all seems such a pity. Edmund, don't you think it would be good for both families to agree that if the war lord's fortune is ever found it should be shared equally, the way your grandfather and Robert's grandfather intended? Then the feud would end and the families could work together in trying to find the treasure."

Edmund nodded. "I think it would be excellent, Lucy. But my parents would never agree, and neither would Robert Falcon, even if his parents were willing." He shrugged. "Frankly, I don't think the emeralds will ever be found. Nick Sabine failed, Robert Falcon failed, and my father's plan failed. That's enough for me. I see no virtue in wasting further time and money."

My feelings were divided. I was sure I knew where the fortune lay, unless it had been removed since it was first hidden. If I told the Falcons, it would be a betrayal of the Greshams. I had not been happy at High Coppice, but I had lived under Mr. Gresham's roof and eaten his bread for the past seven months, and I could not give the secret he sought to his enemies, even though they were my friends. Neither could I give my solution of the riddle to the Greshams, for it seemed to be the one way which offered hope of saving Moonrakers for the Falcons, and this I wanted desperately.

Edmund stood up. "I'll leave you now, Lucy. Perhaps I should speak with Harry Falcon before I go, to make sure he is willing to have you."

"Yes, I'll go and call him. Edmund, please know how grateful I am for all your kindness."

"Kindness?"

"Yes. You've always been very nice to me."

"Really?" He gazed out of the window. "I've done my duty, I hope, but I hardly think I can take credit for kindness. It's strange, but I don't seem to feel things the way most people do. My family hates the Falcons, but I've never been able to do that, even though I was so afraid of Robert at school. I don't bear them any particular goodwill, either." He looked at me. "You know, the law doesn't have any feelings, it simply tries to be just and fair. That's all I've ever been to you, Lucy. Perhaps I'm rather like the law."

I thought those words were among the saddest I had ever heard, and a wave of pity for him touched me, but I could find nothing to say. After a moment I gave him my hand and wished him goodbye, then went to fetch Mr. Falcon.

* * *

Living at Moonrakers was like living in another world, though I did not fully realize this until after Christmas. It appeared that the Falcons usually had several guests for Christmas, but after the shock of Matthew's narrow escape from death they sent telegrams to their friends the next morning, canceling these arrangements.

On Boxing Day, Matthew was allowed out of bed, and within another three days he was quite better. I was glad to spend Christmas quietly, just with the Falcons, for I felt that I wanted time to settle down and learn to fit in with my new family. I need not have worried, for as Mrs. Falcon had said, Moonrakers was a house in which each member of the family was free to do as he pleased, as long as it caused no trouble to others.

Apart from Mrs. Cox, there were only two maids, a young footman and a gardener-handyman who lived in a small lodge with his wife. She was sometimes called in to help when Mr. and Mrs. Falcon entertained friends. The butler had retired a year ago, and had not been replaced for reasons of economy.

I was allowed to help the servants in any way I wished, with cooking, cleaning, or in the garden once the big thaw came in early January. They were all friendly people, and although their wages were a little lower than other servants in similar houses received, they seemed to count themselves fortunate to be in service with the Falcons. My time was much more happily occupied now. Some of it I spent with Matthew until he returned to school during the second week in January, though his mother gently made him understand that he must not monopolize my time. In the kitchen, Mrs. Cox welcomed my help and began to teach me how to cook some English dishes. I no longer had to lie awake from dawn until it was time to get up, but could rise and help the maids with the fires and dusting. It was good to feel useful again.

Mr. Falcon encouraged me to try my hand at painting, and I spent an occasional hour or two in his studio, working on a small canvas he provided for me, but I had no talent for this, and did not continue long. I showed the Falcons the sketch of Moonrakers I had found in the Mission, drawn by Mr. Falcon's father. To me it was fascinating because it proved that one of the places where those two young officers had been quartered sixty years ago and on the far side of the world was the very place where I had lived most of my life. But Mr. and Mrs. Falcon were more interested in the quality of the sketch itself.

[242]

"Sheer natural brilliance," Mr. Falcon said, and smiled. "Doesn't it make you feel green with envy, Tina?"

His wife nodded, her eyes on the canvas. "I wonder if he cared? I mean, about his ability. Or whether he was like Robbie?"

"Like Robbie, I imagine. Why else would he become a soldier when he had this talent?" Mr. Falcon looked at me ruefully. "Robert simply doesn't care to paint or draw, yet he has twice the ability Tina and I share between us."

I knew that. I had seen him bring Nick Sabine to life with a few bold strokes of charcoal on a rough wall.

Soon after Christmas I wrote to Mr. Marsh and received an affectionate letter in return. At present he was working as a valet at the small London house of his old master, who was now a Lieutenant General at the War Office. He seemed well content, was delighted to learn that I was happily settled with the Falcons, and hoped that he might be allowed to visit me soon, when he had a day off.

The first time I saw the Greshams again was when we went to church. It was strange to sit in the pew facing them, and naturally all the village was agog with the news that "the Chinese girl" had moved from High Coppice to Moonrakers. After the service, as the two families passed, I dropped a little curtsy and said, "Good morning." Edmund raised his hat and responded. Amanda, looking embarrassed, said, "Hallo, Lucy." Emily ignored me. Mrs. Gresham inclined her head haughtily, and Mr. Gresham half lifted his cane in a vague acknowledgment. I was very glad to have this first meeting over and done with, as it set the pattern for future encounters at church or in the village during the following weeks.

I had not been able to bring myself to tell the Falcons my secrets—about my marriage to Nicholas Sabine, and the reason for it. I simply could not find the courage to tell them that before the year's end I would inherit Moonrakers and they would have to go. One day the truth would have to be told, but I kept hoping that before the day came something wonderful would happen to prevent what Nicholas Sabine had planned.

One evening in February, as we sat at dinner, Robert said with a frown, "You've polished this silver beautifully, Lucy, but it annoys me to see you doing work about the house and in the kitchen. You've had enough of it in your young life."

"That's for Lucy to decide," his father said cheerfully. "The trouble with you, boy, is that you imagine how *you* would feel if you were someone else, and then you can't understand why they feel differently. But Lucy's not you. She's herself, and unique, like each one of us. So just let her do what she wants."

I did not say anything myself just then, for I knew why Robert had spoken in this way. In the last month, since Matthew had gone back to school, Robert had begun to court me again. At least, I was almost sure of it. He sought my company, especially when we could be alone together. He was attentive, kind, and affectionate. But he was not in any way pressing, and this puzzled me a little, for I could never think of him as a diffident man. He had never mentioned the strange occasion when he had kissed me in the darkness on the valley side, and I had the feeling that something held him back from saying what he really wished to say to me.

If I was right in my belief that he was courting me, I did not know whether I felt glad or sorry. I had never been in love, or had much time to think about it, and I found it hard to know what my feelings for Robert were. In China I had seen him away from the safe and easy life of Hawkfield, and I knew that he was a strong, capable and determined man. For this I admired him. Certainly I thought him handsome and exciting, as I think any English girl would have done. It was hard to understand why I had once thought of him as "the ugly stranger." Living in England had changed my ideas of good looks in a man and beauty in a woman.

I knew that I was attractive to him, for he had made that plain long ago, during his visits to High Coppice, and I had overcome the shyness which this at first made me feel. I believed that sooner or later he might tell me that he loved me, and I wondered what I would do then. Whenever I saw Mr. and Mrs. Falcon together, I felt that I knew what love should be. There was a golden current flowing between them, as warm and natural as the sun's rays flowing to earth. No, I did not feel that for Robert or any man, but perhaps it only came with time, with being together and merging with one another. And then, perhaps, it came only seldom and to the very fortunate.

Later that day I was in the studio with Mrs. Falcon, who had begun to paint a portrait of me. We had been silent for some time because she was concentrating, but when she paused to mix some fresh paint on her palette she said quietly, "I think Robert wants to marry you, Lucy."

"Oh!" I felt myself color a little. "Has he said so?"

"No. Robert tells us very little of what he thinks and feels, but we've learned to guess over the years." She looked at her paint brush, but as if scarcely seeing it. "He's a strange boy, to be born of such parents. So much unlike us both. But there, we're all ourselves, each one of us, and we can't change it." Now she looked at me, her eyes troubled. "If he asks you to marry him, I . . . I hope you won't accept."

For a moment I was startled, and even hurt, but then I realized how stupid I had been. The Falcons might not be wealthy, but they were of the gentry, and I knew very well that a young Englishman of good family had to choose his wife carefully, and make a good match. I was an orphan from a Mission in China, and penniless as far as they knew. Mr. and Mrs. Falcon had been wonderfully kind to me and given me their friendship, but in their eyes I was quite unsuitable as a wife for their son. They would not forbid him, and Robert was not a man to be forbidden, but Mrs. Falcon was trying gently to make me realize how she and her husband felt.

I said, "I hadn't thought about it before, Mrs. Falcon, but I can understand your feeling that I wouldn't be a suitable person for Robert to marry."

She looked at me quickly, and for a moment I thought she was about to protest, but she hesitated, seemed to change her mind, and said, "It's something like that, Lucy, but I won't speak of it again." She laid down her brush, and the smile she gave me was a little tired. "I think I'll stop painting for today, it's not going very well."

A week later Robert asked me to marry him. I was not unprepared, but even so I felt very strange and muddled. In a stumbling fashion I thanked him for the great compliment he had paid me, and said I did not think I was the right person to be his wife.

He brushed this aside, smiling and saying that he was the best judge of his future wife. In an agony of embarrassment I told him I did not truly know what my feelings for him were, and that perhaps I was not yet sufficiently grownup to think of marriage.

He seemed in no way put out. "You're eighteen, Lucy, and far more grownup for your age than most English girls. But I expect you need time to get used to the idea. I'll wait awhile, then ask again."

"Oh, thank you, Robert. I'm sorry if I've offended you."

"Not at all." He took me by the shoulders and kissed my cheek. "I'll ask again. Next week."

"Oh!"

He laughed, and left me to my confusion.

When I went to bed that night I could not sleep, and after lying for an hour with thoughts jostling in my head I lit the little lamp beside my bed, put on my dressing gown, and sat in bed hugging my knees and trying to sort out my tangled feelings. The germ of an idea came stealing into my mind, vague at first, but slowly taking form.

[246]

I was not sure of wanting to marry Robert, but I could truly say that I had no strong wish *not* to marry him. If I had not known that Mr. and Mrs. Falcon were against it, would I have accepted? I did not know. Would they still think me unsuitable for Robert if they knew that the marriage meant Moonrakers would be saved? This would surely make a big difference.

I believed I had found a way to save Moonrakers, and at the same time ensure that if the war lord's treasure could be found and brought home it would be shared between the Greshams and the Falcons. The answer, I thought in my stupidity, was simple. I would agree to marry Robert in return for his promise to share the fortune with the Greshams. And then I would tell him the wonderful discovery I had made in solving the riddle. He could go to China and come back with the emeralds. Perhaps I could even go with him. The thought made my heart beat faster with longing to see the Mission and the children again.

When we returned, when the fortune had been shared and the Moonrakers debt paid off, I would marry him. Surely this would be the best answer to all problems? And I would try with all my heart to be such a good wife to Robert that it would make up for my being unsuitable.

I took a writing pad and pencil from my chest of drawers, got back into bed and began to write carefully. First I set down the riddle.

> *Above the twisted giant's knife*
> *Where the wind-blown blossom flies*
> *Stands the temple where fortune lies.*
>
> *Beyond the golden world reversed*
> *Marked by the bear-cub of the skies*
> *Rest the sightless tiger's eyes.*

Then I began to write the solution.
The words GIANT'S KNIFE form an anagram. When the

letters are twisted round they make TSIN KAI-FENG. The Mission, which was once a temple, stands on a hill above Tsin Kai-feng.

This was the discovery which had come suddenly to me out of the blue, that evening when we had been playing Anagrams and I had toyed with the names of some Chinese towns. Until that moment I had thought it impossible for our Mission to be the temple of the riddle, because the maps showed the river taking a different course. But then it came to me, a memory of something I had once heard in the village of Tsin Kai-feng. Some thirty years ago the little river had been dammed, and made to change course, so that more land could be used for growing. The maps showed the terrain as it had once been, not as it was now. With this realization, and with the sure knowledge that our Mission was the right temple, the rest of the clues seemed almost to solve themselves.

I wrote: *There is an old plum tree a few yards from the north side of the Mission, and nearby are ancient stumps of dead plum trees. This would be "where the wind-blown blossom flies."*

I paused, remembering how I had often lain in bed of a summer's night, the window wide open, and watched the stars reflected in the slim bronze shield set in the far wall, the shield I used as a mirror. It had never occurred to me to wonder why the pattern of the stars did not change, but simply revolved around one constant star. I knew now, for during my early weeks at High Coppice, when I began to read the set of encyclopedias, I had studied a long article on astronomy.

My pencil moved again: *A bear-cub is a small bear, and "the bear-cub of the skies" means the constellation known as The Little Bear. The brightest star of this group is the Pole Star, and this shines through the window of a room on to a bronze shield which is set in the wall. When polished, this shield reflects like a mirror, and shows the world in reverse.*

[248]

"Beyond the golden world reversed" must mean behind this bronze shield.

I read through what I had written, then realized I had not quite completed the solution, for I had told the meaning of the last line only to the Greshams. I wrote: *Tiger's eyes is a phrase used for emeralds in this area of China.*

I scarcely knew why I had written out the solution in this way. Partly it was because I could not sleep and wanted to occupy my mind; but partly, perhaps, it was because I felt that the secret should be set down on paper and not just kept in my head.

I folded the sheet of paper, sealed it in an envelope, then sat in deep thought for a minute or two. At last I wrote Mr. Marsh's name and address on the envelope. He had visited me at Moonrakers twice since Christmas, and we had spent a few happy hours together each time, but I had not told him of my discovery or burdened him with my problems. Above the name and address I wrote in large block letters, PRIVATE AND CONFIDENTIAL, then went to the wardrobe, put the letter with my little collection of treasures in my old suitcase, and returned to bed feeling rather foolish and melodramatic. However, at least I had made sure that the secret would not be lost again, and if ever it came into Mr. Marsh's hands I was content for him to do with it whatever he thought best.

The following week Robert again asked me to marry him. When I muttered a rather feeble refusal he laughed, did not press me, and asked again exactly one week later. That morning I had come to a momentous decision. I would carry through the plan I had been thinking about over these past days. I would tell Robert everything, how I had married Nick Sabine in Chengfu prison, and why. If he still wished to marry me, I would tell him that I knew where the war lord's treasure lay, and ask if he would agree to share it with the Gresham family. And if he agreed, then I would accept his proposal of marriage.

That was my plan, and I felt foolishly proud of it, never dreaming that fate would make a mockery of my hopes. Robert and I were in the drawing room that afternoon when he asked for the third time if I would marry him. I said, "Robert, before I can answer there's something I have to tell you—"

At that moment the doorbell clanged loudly. I stopped. Robert said, "Well, go on, my little Lucy. Tell me."

"We'd better wait. I don't want to be interrupted in what I have to tell you, because it's very important."

He smiled. "All right, there's plenty of time. I didn't think we were expecting any visitors today, but I believe I heard a carriage. Do you know where my parents are?"

"I think they're in the studio."

The door opened. Nellie, one of the two maids, stood there with a startled look. "I'm sorry, Mr. Robert," she burst out anxiously, "but there's a gentleman to see Miss Lucy. He says . . ." Her voice faltered, and she glanced back over her shoulder. "He says—oh, I can't hardly tell you what he says, Miss Lucy!"

"Then I'll tell her myself," said a voice that brought me to my feet, white-faced and trembling with shock. A figure appeared behind Nellie. A hand moved her firmly aside. Nick Sabine walked into the room.

"I've come to collect my wife," he said.

He wore a short coat with a velvet collar and carried a hat in his hand, a cane tucked under his arm. Without the stubble of beard he had worn in prison, his jaw looked longer and leaner than ever. Apart from this he was exactly as I remembered him, except that there were no laughing devils in his dark eyes. They were cold and without emotion.

It was impossible, but true. This was Nicholas Sabine, alive. Through the whirling haze of shock which engulfed my mind I felt a piercing shaft of relief and gladness.

"Mr. Sabine . . . ?" My voice was barely a whisper. I

took a pace toward him. "Oh, Mr. Sabine . . . you're *alive!* I—I'm so glad."

"Are you, Lucy?" His eyes flickered over me. Something showed briefly in them. Sorrow? Bitterness? I could not tell. "Well, that's fine," he said coolly. "Go and pack a case, will you?"

He moved forward, passed me by, and stood facing Robert. I turned, a hand to my head and a sudden sharp fear beginning to grow amid the chaos of my thoughts. If Nick Sabine was alive, then surely I *had* seen him in the flesh that night of the fireworks, when somebody had carried me into the Chislehurst Caves. And that meant . . .

My mind flinched from what it meant. With an effort I focused my eyes on the two men who confronted one another. I saw that Robert's face was as white as I knew my own must be, his eyes wide and burning.

"Your *wife?*" he said in a frightful whisper.

"My wife." Nick Sabine's voice was flat. "She's been under the impression that I was dead. But I'm not. Go and pack a case please, Lucy." The last words were spoken without turning his head. The two men did not take their eyes from one another, and it was as if an unseen thunderbolt were forming in the air from the tension between them.

There came a clatter of hurrying feet from the hall, and the sound of Nellie's voice. "In there, sir!" Next moment Mr. and Mrs. Falcon came in together. Nellie had run to fetch them. Nick Sabine turned, saw them, and made a little bow to Mrs. Falcon. "Good day to you, ma'am. Forgive this intrusion."

Mrs. Falcon looked from one to the other of us, then came to me quickly and put her arm about my shoulders. Mr. Falcon said, "Good God, it's young Sabine, isn't it? I remember you from Bellwood. What's all this?"

I felt Mrs. Falcon draw a long breath as if to steady herself. She said, "We feared you had come to harm in China, Mr.

Sabine, after so long an absence. I'm glad to see you safely returned."

"I doubt that, ma'am."

Two spots of high color showed in Mrs. Falcon's cheeks. "As you please, Mr. Sabine. But I'm not a liar by nature, and I have never wished any man ill."

He eyed her broodingly for a long moment, then nodded. "I'm sure that's true. I've no quarrel with you, Mrs. Falcon, and I ask your pardon for my discourtesy. And now, if you please, I'd like Lucy to pack a few things so that we can leave at once."

"Rubbish!" Mr. Falcon moved forward. "What's all this nonsense Nellie tells us about claiming Lucy as your wife?"

Nick Sabine looked at me. "We were in Chengfu prison together. We married a few hours before I was due to be executed. It was all very legal. Ask Edmund Gresham. He's my lawyer, and he has all the papers." He shrugged. "Better still, ask Lucy."

Every eye was on me. I nodded my head slowly, and whispered, "Yes, it's true."

Mr. Falcon put both hands to his head. "But Lucy, child! *Why?*"

Long before I could find words to answer, Nick Sabine said, "The reason scarcely matters now. But if your wife will be so good as to go with Lucy and help her pack a case, sir, I'll give you a brief narrative while I'm waiting."

Mr. Falcon's jaw jutted. "Never mind. I'm not at all sure how the law stands, but I doubt if you can make her go with you against her will, Sabine."

"She's my legal wife." The tone was cold but polite. He looked at me. "Do you refuse to come with me, Lucy?"

I held Mrs. Falcon's hand tightly, and shook my head. I could not refuse. No matter how it had come about, I had made promises to Nick Sabine and become his wife in a filthy prison cell thousands of miles away. And besides, I had a growing fear of what might happen, here in this room, if I refused. Robert stood with splayed hands resting on his hips, leaning forward a little, eyes burning like sulphur in a candle flame, as if about to spring at his enemy.

Trying vainly to steady my voice I said, "I'll only be a few minutes, Mr. Sabine."

Idly he brushed his hat with his sleeve. "You'd better begin calling me Nick," he said.

« TEN »

As IF IN a dream I packed as many clothes as I could in my suitcase, and put on my best coat and hat. Mrs. Falcon helped me, her eyes swimming with tears. As we worked I told her in stumbling phrases of that strange night in Chengfu when I had married Nick Sabine.

"I've wanted to tell you, ever since I came here," I ended miserably. "I hate secrets. But everything was so difficult, I didn't know what to do. I was just about to tell Robert when . . . he came."

She asked no questions, but held me tightly for a moment or two and said, "Robert has always told us he was a wicked man. I don't know . . he's hard to judge. I just pray everything will be well for you, Lucy."

Three minutes later my husband was helping me step up into the carriage in which he had arrived. I could not say goodbye to Robert, for he had disappeared. Mr. and Mrs.

Falcon kissed me, and said with forced smiles that they hoped we would visit them soon. Just as Nick Sabine was about to mount beside me, Mrs. Falcon put a hand on his arm. "I beg that you will be kind to her, Mr. Sabine," she said in a low voice.

For a moment something of the old wicked amusement flickered in his eyes. "That makes us quits, ma'am. I was offensive to you, and you've just paid me back in kind."

"Then forgive me. If I offended, it was only from concern for Lucy. Tell me . . . why do you hate us so, Mr. Sabine?"

His eyebrows lifted. "Hate you, ma'am? I scarcely know you, and what little I've seen I admire. I've simply come to collect my wife, nothing more. And now I'll wish you good day." He bowed, and climbed up beside me. The coachman clicked his tongue and we began to move. As we reached the end of the drive I looked back and saw Mr. and Mrs. Falcon each with an arm lifted to wave. I put out my hand, and a moment later they had vanished from sight as we turned into the road.

My husband leaned back in his seat, his face expressionless, and did not speak. After we had gone half a mile I said timidly, "Mr. Sabine, are you——"

"You'd better call me Nick," he broke in, absently watching the road. "It's usual between man and wife."

"I'm sorry. Nick . . . are you angry with me?"

He looked at me gravely. "Why should I be angry with you?"

"I don't know, but you . . . well, you don't seem to want to speak to me, so I thought . . . oh, I'm so confused. Please try to understand. All this time I thought you were dead, so it was an enormous shock to see you walk into the room just now. But I'm so very glad, Mr.—I mean, Nick." I touched his arm. "It's wonderful that you're alive."

"Even though I've taken you away from Moonrakers?"

I stared, not understanding. "Yes, of course. I like the Falcons very much, but you being alive is more important."

I put a hand to my head, for it was throbbing. "I can still hardly believe you escaped. However did you do it . . . Nick?"

"Your Dr. Langdon managed it," he said quietly. "He came back to Chengfu prison early next morning, after he'd seen you off, and asked me if I'd care to risk being killed by him rather than have the certainty of being killed by the mandarin's soldiers."

"I—I don't understand."

"Neither did I, at first. There's a drug derived from opium. A large dose produces a state of coma so like death that even a doctor has great difficulty in telling the difference. Often it *is* death. All the doctor can do is wait forty-eight hours and see whether or not the patient comes out of the coma."

I shivered. "And you agreed?"

"Gladly. At worst it was a damn' sight better way to die than Huang Kung had in mind for me." He grinned almost wolfishly. I saw the devils in his eyes for a moment, and felt a throb of relief. "I added some trimmings of my own to the drama," he went on. "Dr. Langdon gave me the drug, and left. Half an hour later he came back. When the jailer brought him to my cell they found me lying on the floor. My belt was in two pieces. One end was looped around my neck, with a raw friction mark on the flesh to show how tight it had been. The other end was fixed to the lantern hook in the ceiling. It looked as if I'd hanged myself, and then the belt had broken under my weight. I'd arranged it to look that way before I took the drug."

Tears suddenly rolled down my cheeks. "Oh, Nick . . . it's like a miracle."

"Don't, Lucy!" he said sharply. "Don't do that!"

"It's only because I'm glad. I didn't mean to cry."

"For God's sake," he said in a harsh voice, and looked away. I could not think why he was angry with me, but I quickly stifled my tears, wiped my eyes, and said, "I'm sorry. Please go on."

[256]

"Well . . . it worked." His voice was flat again. "When the mandarin heard I'd hanged myself he had the jailer flogged and sent doctors to make sure I was dead. They said I was. Then Dr. Langdon asked if he could take my body away for burial in the English cemetery. That cost him a twenty-sovereign bribe, so it was lucky you'd left him your wedding-present money. I don't know how he arranged everything, but a coffin full of stones was buried later that day, and old Tattersall conducted a short funeral service. There can't be many clergymen who've married and buried the same man within twenty-four hours."

"He didn't know the truth?"

"No. He might have let it out. I was lying in a coma at the time, in a shed which used to be a chicken coop at the back of Dr. Langdon's house. It was rather more than forty-eight hours before I began to come round. Dr. Langdon told me he'd almost given me up for dead when I started showing signs of life."

I said, perplexed, "But he took me to your grave, and I put flowers there. Why didn't he tell me then?"

"Because I'd made him promise not to. I still had to get clear of the whole region without being caught, and after taking that death drug it was a month before I could even stand up, let alone travel. If I did get caught, I knew Dr. Langdon and anybody else in the plot were sure to lose their heads on the executioner's block." He smiled the lopsided smile I had first seen come to life in charcoal on the Mission wall, by Robert Falcon's skill. "After saving your hand, I didn't want to cost you your head, Lucy."

The coach came to a halt. We were at the station. He helped me down, and the coachman carried my case on to the platform. In that space of time Nick again relapsed into a bleak, somber mood, and I did not venture to speak until ten minutes later, when we were alone in a first class compartment of a train bound for London.

I said, "May I talk to you, Nick?"

He stared. "Do you feel you have to ask?"

"I don't know. You seem to be preoccupied, and I—I don't want to disturb you."

"You won't. Talk if you wish." His eyes were hard. "And never ask my permission like that again."

I felt more bewildered every moment. His words were at odds with his manner, and I could not begin to guess at his thoughts. For a moment I was unable to remember what I had been about to say, but then it came back to me. It was a very important question. I said, "When did you get back to England?"

He looked out of the window, narrowing his eyes, and it seemed to me that his thoughts were racing. At last he said, "A week ago. I was hiding in Chengfu, getting my strength back, for nearly three months, and when I left I walked most of the way to Tientsin wearing Chinese peasant clothes and living rough. Huang Kung has a long arm, and I couldn't risk being recognized, for Dr. Langdon's sake as well as my own."

I was sure it was a lie. He had been in England long ago, on the night of November the Fifth. I said, "Did you write that letter to me, telling me to wait six months before going to the solicitors, just before you took the drug?"

He nodded. "I thought that if I survived I'd be home before the time came for you to make your claim as my widow, but I hadn't reckoned on being ill for so long. I saw Edmund Gresham at his office yesterday, by the way." His grin came back. "He was more than a little startled. In fact he seemed to feel it was most thoughtless of me to be alive when he'd gone to such trouble in respect of my death." He lifted an eyebrow as he looked at me. "And the treasure is in emeralds, Edmund tells me. Was that all the help you were able to give old man Gresham?"

"Yes, it was." I hesitated. "Will you ever go back and try again?"

He shook his head. "That particular enterprise is a dead

duck, I think. Especially now, with the Boxers starting to make trouble."

"The Boxers?"

"That's what everyone calls them over there. It's one of these tongs, or secret societies. I think Dr. Langdon called it *I Ho Chuan* in Chinese."

"That means . . . The Fists of Righteous Harmony."

"Well, whatever they're called, they're dangerous. They've already killed some missionaries in Shantung."

"*Killed* them?" I was alarmed. "I haven't seen it in the newspapers."

"Perhaps missionaries are poor news. Foreigners living in China know there's big trouble coming, but they can't persuade our government to believe them. I admit these Boxers sound unreal. Dr. Langdon says their one aim is to destroy all foreigners, and they indulge in some sort of mumbo-jumbo magic which they think makes them immune to bullets or bayonets, fire or water."

"But the Empress would never let them attack the foreign devils in China!"

"You're out of touch, Lucy. Dr. Langdon told me that by winter's end she'd be encouraging her people to do so. And he's no fool."

It was only an hour since Nick Sabine had walked into Moonrakers, and the shock had left me so dazed and battered inwardly that I would have thought it impossible to feel any new emotion. But, perhaps because I had glimpsed him on the smoky valley side weeks before, whether in imagination or reality, the shock today was a little less than it might have been, and I was still able to feel a gnawing anxiety for my friends in China.

I said, "Do you think Dr. Langdon will be safe? And Mr. and Mrs. Fenshaw at the Mission?"

"I think the sensible ones will move into the legations in Peking before trouble really starts. The even more sensible

[259]

ones will make for Tientsin, or any big port. They'll have protection from the Navy there."

I sat lost in my scattered thoughts, gazing from the window but seeing nothing. It was only when the train began to slow down that I came to myself with a little start. Nick Sabine sat watching me. The curtain had come down again, and there was no laughter in his eyes, no half-smile twisting a corner of his mouth. I remembered how he had held my hands through the bars in Chengfu prison, how he had smiled and comforted me, and I wondered what he felt toward me now, but his face told me nothing. He was remote and withdrawn. Perhaps it was the armored look of a man who had set himself to do something he hated, yet would carry it through regardless.

As the train stopped at Charing Cross I said, "Where are we going now?"

He took my case from the rack. "I've a cottage in Chelsea, small but quite pleasant. There are no servants. I don't like servants. Will you be able to manage without?"

"Yes. Oh yes, of course, Nick. I always have, until a few months ago."

His words had brought a new thought to my mind, and when we were settled in a hansom cab, trundling westward along The Embankment, I said, "Did you know about Mr. Marsh—I mean, your father?"

"Being the Greshams' butler? Yes I've known for years, but I've never spoken of it. And I know why he's no longer their butler. Edmund told me about that night when you went out in the snow to find the Falcon boy, and how my father laid into old man Gresham with some barrack-room language." He gave a brief, humorless smile. "That rather pleased me, but I suppose my father will only go into service somewhere else."

I said, a little apologetically, "I know how you feel about him being a servant. He told me. But he's proud of his work, and surely it isn't anything to be ashamed of?"

He shrugged. "We won't argue about it."

[260]

"He thinks you're dead, Nick. I must write to him today. I have his address—"

"No need. Edmund has it too, and he's already written to say I'm alive and that I'm taking you home today." He frowned. "What I haven't yet fathomed is how you came to discover that he was my father."

"It was just by chance. He saw the ring you gave me. The ribbon broke, and one of the maids found it outside my room, and gave it to him. He recognized it."

"The ring?" Nick looked at me strangely. "My signet ring? What do you mean about the ribbon breaking?"

"I've always worn it round my neck on a piece of ribbon, ever since we . . . ever since we were married. But your father gave me a lovely chain for it. Look." I reached inside my collar with one finger, found the chain, and drew it up until the ring came clear. "It's a nice strong chain, and it was your mother's once, like the ring."

Slowly he turned his head away and looked out of the cab window. "Why do you wear it?"

"I—I don't know how to answer you, Nick. It never occurred to me not to wear it . . . I suppose because you were so kind to me, and I treasured the ring as a keepsake, and . . . well, I was your wife."

"My widow, surely. Or so you believed."

"Have I made you angry? Didn't you want me to wear it?"

He leaned back in his seat, folded his arms and closed his eyes. "No, you haven't made me angry." I waited for him to go on, but he said no more. After a few moments I took off my hat and leaned back myself. My head was still throbbing, and I settled it in the corner cushions, closing my eyes. For the moment I felt too weary even to wonder what the coming hours and and days would hold for me.

* * *

I woke from a doze when the cab halted outside a small, pretty house in a road leading north from the Chelsea Embankment. It was almost dusk now. The house stood on a corner with a tiny strip of garden all around. On two sides of it were rows of tall, terraced houses. I could understand why Nick had called it a cottage, for with its white walls and virginia creeper growing almost to the low roof it was more like a cottage in the country than a London house.

There were two very pleasant rooms and a kitchen and scullery downstairs, and above there were two bedrooms, a bathroom and a small box room. The house was not heavily furnished, and the furniture itself was on a much smaller scale than the great couches and chairs I had known at High Coppice and Moonrakers, but I could see at once that the furniture, the rugs and the curtain materials were expensive, and the whole impression was one of comfortable elegance.

A tiny flame burned constantly at each of the many gas mantles, so there was no need for matches. When the slender chain was drawn down, the mantle lit automatically. As Nick took me from room to room I exclaimed with pleasure. "It's beautiful," I said as we stood in the larger bedroom. "Just like a miniature palace, Nick."

"You're not hard to please, are you?" He set down my suitcase.

I stared at him, then looked about me again, at the two wardrobes, the small easy chairs, the quilted coverlet on the double bed, and the rugs scattered on the polished floor. Two beautifully made chests of drawers matched the elegant dressing table. Set in the wall was a gas fire, burning on a low flame, which made the room as warm and comfortable as a drawing room. I said, "I'd be very hard to please if I didn't think this was a lovely room, Nick."

"I'll leave you to unpack. The bathroom's on the right."

"Yes, I noticed as we passed it. I've never seen such a modern bathroom. Does hot water really come out of the tap?"

"Yes. There's an anthracite boiler in the kitchen, and it's easy to manage. I'll be in the drawing room."

The first wardrobe I opened was empty, and I realized that this must be meant for me, together with the empty chest of drawers beside it. As I took my clothes from the suitcase and hung them up I began to feel nervous. Everything had happened so quickly. It was almost impossible to believe that less than three hours ago, at Moonrakers, Robert Falcon had been asking me to marry him. Now I was here with Nick Sabine, my husband, a man I scarcely knew, except for those few hours we had spent together in Chengfu prison.

I wondered why he had come to claim me. He had married me only to make sure that the Falcons would lose Moonrakers, not because he wanted me for a wife. There must surely be many beautiful young women in London who would gladly have married such a man. And why did he pretend that he had only recently returned to England, when I knew I had seen him in Hawkfield on Guy Fawkes Day?

I was surprised to discover that I did not feel afraid now. Nervous, yes, and that was only natural, but not afraid. I reminded myself that he had found me unconscious in the valley, he had carried me deep into the black labyrinth of Chislehurst Caves, and left me there. It was hard to imagine a more wicked act, and I should have been in terror of him, but I was strangely unable to feel even the dawning of fear.

I went to the bathroom, washed my face and tidied my hair, then made my way down the short flight of stairs to the drawing room. Here a larger gas fire burned brightly. There was no coal to be carried, no grate to clean. In such a house it would have been difficult to find enough work for a servant to do.

There was a well-filled bookcase against one wall, and a small pile of newspapers and magazines lay on a side table. The curtains were drawn to. Nick sat in one of the armchairs, his legs stretched out toward the fire, smoking a thin black cigar. He got to his feet as I entered, and said, "Have you found everything you need?"

"Yes, thank you. I looked in the linen cupboard, and there are plenty of spare towels and sheets. Have you had this house long, Nick?"

"I rented it a year ago, but I have an option to buy. It's fairly well stocked, I think you'll find, but if there's anything we need, just tell me. That includes any clothes you may want."

"Clothes? But I've plenty, thank you."

He half-smiled. "I wouldn't call your wardrobe extensive." Reaching inside his jacket he took out a wallet and drew from it three five-pound notes. "Here, Lucy. Tell me when you need more."

"But that's enough to keep us for weeks!"

"It's not for keeping us. It's for your personal needs. You'll find the larder reasonably full, but you can go round to the shops tomorrow and make what arrangements you like for deliveries. I'll settle up weekly with the tradesmen, but you'd better have a little for incidentals." He added another five-pound note, and pushed them into my hand. I held a kitchen maid's wages for a year.

"You're . . . very generous," I stammered. "But I won't be extravagant, I promise. May I go and look in the kitchen for a few minutes? I want to see where everything is and find out how the stove works. Are you hungry now, Nick? I could make a sandwich if you are. And what time will you have dinner?"

He shook his head. "I'm going out," he said almost brusquely. "Just get whatever you want for yourself."

"Going out?" I stared in bewilderment. The clock above the mantelpiece stood at ten minutes past six. "Won't you be back for dinner?"

"No."

I hesitated, feeling hopelessly at a loss. "When will you— I mean, do you mind if I ask when you'll be back, Nick?"

[264]

"Don't ask my permission to ask me anything." He picked up his coat and hat from where they lay over a chair. "No special time. Probably before midnight. I have my key, so go to bed when you feel like it." He stubbed out the cigar in a big ashtray, and moved to the door. There he paused for a moment or two, looking back at me without expression, then gave a brief resigned smile. "Well, at least you're better off than in Chengfu prison."

He turned away, and seconds later I heard the front door close. Slowly I moved to an armchair and sat down, staring into the glowing radiants of the fire, and wondering what his last words meant. Five minutes later, still none the wiser, I got up and went into the kitchen. When I had seen what the larder held I would make a list of anything to be ordered from the shops next day, then I would spend some time making myself familiar with the kitchen and the gas stove before preparing a simple meal. Now that I looked more carefully, I saw that the house had not been dusted for a day or two, so there was plenty to keep me occupied.

By ten o'clock that evening I had eaten my dinner, washed up, cleaned through the kitchen and downstairs rooms, and was sitting by the fire in the drawing room, reading a book of verse called *The Rubaiyat of Omar Khayyam*. It was strangely haunting poetry, but although the words and their rhythm fascinated me I found it hard to concentrate. At half-past ten I turned out the gas fire and went upstairs to the bedroom.

When I had combed out my hair, I put on my best night-dress, turned out the fire, then stood wondering what to do about the lights. I had left the gas on in the hall for Nick's return, but I felt he should not have to grope his way into a dark bedroom, so after some thought I turned out the gas mantle over the bed, then turned down the one by the door to a dim glow.

Lying in bed in the near darkness, I waited for my husband to return, my mind slowly turning over questions to which I could find no answers. Why had Nick claimed me as his wife, brought me here to live with him, and then, on this first night, gone out for the evening on his own? Why did his mood change so? One moment I could begin to see the man I had known in Chengfu prison, wicked perhaps, but warm and alive, and amused by life's antics even though they had brought him to the brink of death. The next moment all this was gone, as if he had slammed down a barrier between us, so that I found myself with a remote, cold stranger.

An hour later I heard the front door open and close, then came the sound of his feet on the stairs, treading softly. I was holding my breath, listening, but I did not feel afraid or even nervous now. I felt only a strange and heady excitement, as if I had drunk too much wine.

I had left the door half open. Nick was on the landing now. I could hear the muffled sound of his feet on the rugs. He stopped at the door. There was complete silence for a moment or two, then the dim light from the mantle over the door faded away, and the room was in darkness. I heard the faint click of the latch as the door closed. Silence again. No movement in the room at all. I was about to speak when I heard, very faintly, the sound of the bedroom door on the far side of the hall being closed.

It was only then that I realized I was alone. He had reached in, turned out the light, closed the door, and gone to the other bedroom. I knelt up and groped for the chain of the gas point on the wall above me. The light came on with a faint pop. I got out of bed and went to the second wardrobe, the one I had thought was Nick's. It was empty. The chest of drawers I had thought held his belongings was also empty. Slowly I climbed back into bed and turned out the light.

This was not our bedroom. It was mine alone.

* * *

During the next two weeks I was sometimes happy and at other times almost in despair. I loved the little house, I enjoyed keeping it spotless and making nice meals. On the second day I spent eighteen pence on a cookery book, and with this and what Mrs. Cox had taught me I found that I was able to make a variety of tasty dishes. I enjoyed going to the shops, walking beside the river, and watching some of the artists who set up their easels on the bridge or on the pavement, to paint scenes of the river. The people of Chelsea were something of a mixture. Some were poor and some rich, but most of them were friendly, and the atmosphere was gay and exciting.

But Nick remained a stranger, and I saw little of him. I learned that on most days he spent several hours at the London Metal Exchange, which was something to do with buying and selling copper and tin and other metals. All transactions were on paper, and he never saw any metal. When I asked what it meant he simply said, with one of his rare smiles, that it was a respectable way of gambling, and very profitable if you guessed right.

The evenings he spent at his club, and once he came home the worse for drink. It was well after midnight. I heard him fall on the stairs, and went down to help him to bed, but he made me take him into the kitchen and keep pouring cold water over his head as he leaned over the sink, until at last he was able to stand, unsteadily but without help. He was in such a fury with himself that I found it impossible not to giggle at him as he stood there wet and scowling, swaying on his feet.

I began to make black coffee for him, which I had heard Mr. Falcon say was the best remedy for too much wine, but he told me to leave it and go to bed. When I ignored him, he shouted at me. And then, for the first time and to my great surprise, I raised my voice and shouted back, saying that he was my husband and I had a right to look after him; that I had been looking after children all my life, and it seemed the bigger they were the more stupid they were, and he was more stupid than any of them if he thought I *minded* him taking too much to drink just for once.

What I said was very muddled and confused, but he sat down on a kitchen chair, rested his head in his hands, and laughed until he almost choked. Then he was very quiet while I made the coffee, and obediently drank two cups, watching me in silence all the time. When he had finished he said, "Thank you, Lucy, I'll be all right now," and took himself off to bed.

Next morning he came down to breakfast grim-faced, and said, "I apologize for last night. I've not been the worse for liquor since I drank my first pint of ale as a boy. It won't happen again."

"You weren't any trouble, Nick. I'm just glad I was here to help. And I'm sorry I giggled, it was so unkind, but I couldn't help it. Suddenly it all seemed so funny, you standing there with your head soaked, trying to stand straight, and so cross because you couldn't—" I had to put my hand over my mouth to stifle new laughter at the recollection. Then immediately I was dismayed at having repeated my offense, and looked at him anxiously, expecting well-justified anger. To my surprise I saw the grimness fade from his face, and he gazed at me with a baffled air.

"Dear God," he said softly. "You're a very remarkable girl, Mrs. Sabine. But then I've known that for a long time."

He picked up a plate and began to serve himself from the chafing dishes I had set out on the sideboard. When he returned to the table he wore a curious, self-mocking smile, and said, "Would you like to go to the theatre tonight, Lucy?"

I felt my face go hot with excitement. "Can we really, Nick? Oh, I'd love to!"

"There's *She Stoops to Conquer* on at the Haymarket. I'll reserve seats on my way to the City, and we'll dine at the Café Royal afterward."

That was one of my happiest days. Nick arrived home unexpectedly at lunchtime, took me in a cab to Regent Street, and there bought me a beautiful evening dress in white and gold, and an evening cloak. While the dress was being altered slightly to fit me, he took me to other shops to buy shoes, gloves, a gold bracelet and a diamond-spray brooch. At first I kept protesting in genuine alarm at his spending so much money on me, but then I stopped, for it seemed that this was what he wanted to do. He looked more carefree, more himself, than since the day he had first brought me to Chelsea.

As well as being the happiest day I had known, it was also the most exciting. With my beautiful clothes, I felt quite pretty, even among all the elegant ladies and their escorts. I enjoyed the glitter and the thrill of the occasion as much as the play; and at the restaurant afterward, amid red plush, gilt moldings and sparkling mirrors, I felt as if I were in a glorious dream.

Nick was an amusing companion, and we talked more in those few hours than in the past two weeks. He said little about himself, but commented on all that went on about us, or encouraged me to talk. Stimulated by two glasses of champagne, I told him of the day I had arrived at High Coppice, and the awful moment when I had revealed that I thought Mr. Gresham had brought me to England as a concubine. It seemed funny to me now, and I giggled as I told the story, but Nick himself was almost helpless with laughter, and made me describe the scene again. I did so, and recounted how kind and understanding Mr. Marsh had been to me afterward, then made him laugh anew by telling of the day I had disgraced myself on my first morning at church.

We arrived home in a cab some time after midnight, and it was then, as Nick helped me down, that his manner changed completely. In the lamplight I saw all expression fade from his face, and a cold look come into his eyes. He turned to the cabbie and said, "Wait." Then, to me, "I'll just see you indoors. I'm going back to my club for an hour or so at the card table, and I'll sleep the night there."

The warmth and happiness that filled me was wiped away in the time it took me to absorb his words. Numb with sorrow, trying desperately to think what I had said or done to bring about so swift a change, I watched dully as he unlocked the door and stood back for me to enter. In the hall I turned, aching to speak but feeling I had no right to question him. I was his wife in name, but not in reality, and I could have no claims on a man I had married only to pay my debt to him before he died.

He had already turned away. I said, "Thank you . . . thank you for such a lovely evening, Nick."

Without looking back he said, "Good night, Lucy," and moved on toward the waiting cab.

This was the pattern of my life in the following days. Sometimes, for a few hours, he would be as I remembered him in Chengfu, intensely alive and with the reckless demons dancing in his eyes. Then he would perhaps spend an evening at home with me, or take me to a restaurant to dine. One Sunday when he was in such a mood, we took a trip on a river steamer, and though the weather was cold and rainy I enjoyed every moment. But then, abruptly, the barrier would come down, transforming him to a man who seemed to find my very presence unbearable. It was sometimes hard to hide the pain I felt when he turned away from me with what seemed such bleak dislike.

One day, when he had gone off to the City after breakfast, I suddenly had a great longing to see Mr. Marsh. Perhaps I even imagined that he might be able to explain Nick's strange behavior and tell me what I should do. I knew the address of his master, the officer he had attended during his Army service and who was now Lieutenant General the Lord Shipley. It was in Duke of York Street, a few minutes' walk from Whitehall.

I put on my old felt boots for the walk. They were more comfortable than any of my shoes, and scarcely showed under my long skirt, which almost swept the ground as I walked. In little more than an hour I found the house, which was tall but narrow, set in a terrace of similar houses.

I guessed that this was a small establishment which Lord Shipley used for convenience in London, and that he would have large estates somewhere in the country.

There was an alley which led to the rear of the terrace for tradesmen. The back door led directly into the kitchen, and was opened by a plump lady wearing an apron and a mob-cap.

Even as I inquired for Mr. Marsh I heard his voice exclaim, "Lucy!" and next moment he appeared behind the woman, his face alight with pleasure. "Lucy, what a wonderful surprise! Come in, come in, my dear. Mrs. Burke, this is my daughter-in-law, Lucy." He embraced me, took my hat and coat, and made me sit down at the kitchen table, where some crockery and a pot of tea stood ready. "We were just about to have a cup of tea before Mrs. Burke goes out to the shops. You'll join us, won't you?"

"I'd love to, Mr. Marsh. Is it all right for me to be here?"

"Quite all right, child. My duties are very light, and his lordship is at the War Office all day."

It was not until Mrs. Burke had left that we were able to talk properly. Then I told my story. Mr. Marsh listened with a frown of puzzlement.

"It's a beautiful little house," I ended, "and we have everything we could wish for. But Nick isn't happy. He . . . he sleeps in a separate bedroom, and he's never even kissed me. He spends most of his time in the City or at his club, except just occasionally when his mood changes, and then he's a wonderful companion for a few hours. But it never lasts. Sometimes it's as if he hates me, and can't bear the sight of me. I know there's no reason why he should like me, but if not, then I just don't understand why he claimed me as his wife."

Mr. Marsh sighed. "I know less of the boy than you do, Lucy. I can't even begin to understand why he acts so strangely." His voice shook a little. "It was a great joy to learn that he was alive. Has he told you how he managed to escape execution?"

I repeated the story Nick had told me, and then we talked of other things for a while, until Mrs. Burke returned. I was disappointed to have found no help from Mr. Marsh in understanding Nick, but realized that I had been foolishly optimistic even to hope for it.

Mrs. Burke was a kindly woman and a great chatterbox. I was invited to stay for lunch, shown around the small but very elegant house, then spent another hour in the kitchen copying down recipes and instructions for some dishes which Mrs. Burke assured me were great favorites with his lordship, and which I hoped to try myself at home.

I so much enjoyed my visit that the time ran on, and it was almost four when I left. By the time I reached home dusk had fallen, and as I entered the house I saw that the lights were on. Nick came from the drawing room, newspaper in one hand, a cigar in the other.

"Oh Nick, I'm sorry!" I cried in dismay. "I didn't know you'd be coming home early."

He waved a hand impatiently. "I didn't know myself. But you shouldn't be out so late, Lucy—" He broke off, staring as I took off my coat and hat. "In God's name, why are you wearing those boots?"

"I went to see your father, Nick. He's with his old master in a house near Whitehall, and—oh! I should have asked you, but I went on the spur of the moment. I'm so fond of him, Nick, and it made company for me today."

"I don't mind you going to see my father," he said slowly, "but what the devil has it got to do with wearing those boots?"

"They're more comfortable for walking."

"*Walking?*" His eyebrows shot up, then came down in two black hooks. "You walked there and back? Why?"

"I—I didn't want to spend your money on cabs, Nick,"

I stammered, bewildered by his anger. "It's only four miles each way."

"Good God, will you never learn?" he cried furiously. "You have rights, Lucy. Rights! You're not in China now, you're not *poor* now. You don't have to walk to Westminster as you used to walk to Chengfu, just to save a few spoonfuls of food. Never do it again—unless it's for your own pleasure. Never! And don't behave as if you had to account to me for what money you spend."

I was greatly upset, and wished that I could cry, but as usual it seemed I was to be denied the relief of tears when I was unhappy; they came only with gladness. "I'm sorry," I said, trying to keep my voice steady. "Nobody could be more generous than you, and you won't even look at my housekeeping accounts. It wasn't that I thought you'd be angry if I spent money on a cab, Nick. I know you wouldn't. It's just that I—I have bad habits, I suppose. Please forgive me."

"Bad habits?" He drew in a long breath, and the anger faded swiftly from his face. "There's nothing to forgive, Lucy," he said quietly. "If ever I shout at you again, shout back at me, as you did that night when I was drunk. Stop saying you're sorry, and remember that you're not a servant, not a possession, and not an inferior being—even if most men think of women that way. You're *not,* and mark that well, Lucy, or you'll spend your life kowtowing to some pompous, condescending husband who's full of his own self-importance."

I said dazedly, "But Nick . . . you *are* my husband."

He blinked, disconcerted for a moment, then said in an odd voice as he turned back into the room, "Why, yes. So I am, Lucy, so I am."

This was when I first wondered, with a sharp stab of alarm, if Nick's mind sometimes slipped across the border of normality. He had just spoken for all the world as if marriage lay in the future for me, and with another man.

[273]

My anxiety grew as I followed him into the drawing room, for if Nick suffered mental lapses from time to time it would explain so much that bewildered me. In part at least it would account for his abrupt changes of mood, such as I had seen on that night when we returned from the theater after a joyful evening, only for him to leave me and drive away in the cab.

It might well account for his telling me that he had returned to England in March, when I knew he had been here months before. Above all, it could answer the greatest and most frightening mystery, to which I had closed my mind over these past weeks; might it be that when he carried me unconscious into the caves that night, his reason had lapsed, and he had never afterward recalled the dreadful act?

After a moment or two I said hopefully, "Will you be at home for dinner tonight, Nick? I have some new recipes to try."

He did not look at me, but studied the glowing tip of his cigar, smiled a tired smile and said heavily, "No. I'll be going out soon. Don't wait up for me, Lucy."

* * *

In the days that followed there was little change in the pattern of our lives. I wavered between hoping that my fear of Nick being unbalanced was absurd, and dreading that it was true. I tried always to be cheerful and affectionate, and to look after him well, but was careful not to behave too meekly, for I had now learned that this angered him.

I wrote occasionally to Mrs. Falcon, who always replied with a chatty letter about happenings at Moonrakers, though she said nothing of Robert. Each week I wrote to Matthew, at his school, and sometimes sent him a box of cakes I had made, or some sweets. I visited Mr. Marsh about every ten days, and on these occasions Mrs. Burke always provided a special lunch. I had begun to read *The Times* carefully now, because I was growing ever more worried about my friends in China. The situation there seemed to be very confused, and one day's news would contradict what had been said a few days before, but it was clear that the Boxers were becoming more dangerous all the time.

It was in the last week of May that I returned from shopping one morning to find a cab outside the house and a lady and gentleman at the front door. As I quickened my pace I saw that the visitors were Mr. and Mrs. Falcon. I was overjoyed to see them, and we were soon settled comfortably in the drawing room with cups of coffee. I noticed that Mr. Falcon was subdued, and not his usual cheerful self. His wife's manner was as serene and gentle as ever, but it seemed to me that her thoughts wandered as we talked of everyday matters for a few minutes. I learned that they had been staying with friends in Cornwall for the past two weeks, and had returned only the day before.

"We had something of a shock when we got back to Moonrakers," Mrs. Falcon said, looking at her husband. "That's mainly why we came to see you without writing first, Lucy. I hope Nicholas won't be angry at our calling."

"Oh no, that's quite all right, Mrs. Falcon. He'd only be angry if I asked his permission for you to call. But what's happened at Moonrakers?"

"Robert's gone," Mr. Falcon said slowly. "He'd been gone three days when we arrived home, and he left no message. But we believe he's taken a ship for the Far East, and we wondered whether you could tell us anything about it, Lucy. You see, with the troubles in China, we're rather worried."

"He—he's gone to China again?" I said, astonished. "But that's a stupid thing to do now! What makes you think I might know about it, Mr. Falcon? I haven't heard from Robert since I left you."

"Well . . . there's a rather strange story that you may be able to throw some light on. You remember Peggy, the maid? She tells us that one day while we were down in Cornwall she was busy cleaning and trimming the bedside lamps, and while she was about it she attended to the one in your old room, Lucy. The wick was rather charred, and she scraped the sooty carbon on to a piece of paper—in fact, on to the top sheet of a writing pad she found in the drawer beside the bed. When she had finished trimming and cleaning the lamp, she found something very strange had happened. Well, not strange in itself, perhaps, but—"

"Oh, Harry dear, don't be so long-winded," his wife broke in, with the first hint of impatience I had ever heard from her. She turned to me. "The soot scattered on the paper made some written words stand out faintly, words which must have been written on the sheet above before it was torn off."

I gazed wide-eyed, and said, "Oh! You mean the soot picked out the little dents I'd made with the pencil on the sheet below?"

Mrs. Falcon nodded. "Yes, Peggy said she could only make out a few of the words, but they were something to do with a giant's knife and a bear-cub. She was rather intrigued, and was looking at the piece of paper as she went downstairs, when she met Robert. He asked what she found so interesting, and she showed him. He became very excited and took the paper, saying that he would brush fine carbon from pencil-lead scrapings over it, to make the whole message visible."

"And that was the last Peggy saw of the paper," Mr. Falcon said with a troubled frown. "Next day Robert went to London, presumably to find out how he could best take ship for China. Two days later he was gone. We've inquired of various shipping agencies, and nothing has left direct for China in the last two weeks, but of course he could have taken the first available passage to Bombay or Singapore, intending to pick up another ship there. We're assuming that he found something to throw new light on that damned riddle, of course."

Mrs. Falcon reached out to put a hand on mine, her beautiful eyes anxious. "Do you know what was on the pad, Lucy?"

"It was the answer to the riddle," I said, distressed. "I just happened to stumble on part of the answer one day, and then the rest was easy. I wrote it all down, and I have the sheet of paper from the pad in my case still. I've never told anybody about it, but that's what Robert found when he made the pencil marks show up—the answer to the riddle."

Mr. Falcon sighed. "We feared as much. And now the foolhardy boy has gone to China again to seek out the fortune—at a time when there may be war there soon."

I whispered, "I'm sorry. I wouldn't knowingly have done anything to put Robert in danger."

"Lucy, dear, you're not to blame at all," Mrs. Falcon said quickly. She sat up straight. "Well, at least we know for certain what's happened, Harry. Better that than being in doubt."

"True. We can only do what parents do the world over, one way or another. Worry and hope." He gave me a wry smile. "So you told nobody? I always knew you had good sense, child. That damned treasure has spawned nothing but hate and malice for over half a century. We'd gladly see it at the bottom of the ocean, Tina and I. But not Robert. For him it means saving Moonrakers, and he'd risk anything for that."

They left ten minutes later, promising to let me know if they had any news of Robert, and I spent the rest of the day in a very troubled state of mind. Nick came home a few minutes before midnight, and looked surprised to find that I had not gone to bed. Quickly I told him of the visit by Mr. and Mrs. Falcon, then gave him the sheet of paper I had taken from the envelope in my case addressed to Mr. Marsh.

"This is what the riddle means, Nick. I'm sorry if you feel I should have told you before. To be truthful I've scarcely thought about it since the day you brought me here. And besides, I didn't want anybody to go off to China at such a time. It's madness."

He looked at me curiously, then sat down and studied what I had written. Two minutes later he looked up. "It's simple when somebody does it for you, isn't it? How the devil did you hit on it, Lucy?"

"It started when we were playing Anagrams at High Coppice, and I suppose the rest fell into place because I know the Mission at Tsin Kai-feng so well."

"Ironic to think that all those years when you were scratching for a few bowls of millet porridge you were sleeping with a fortune in your room." For a moment his eyes were brooding, then he grinned suddenly. "And now the bold Robert has gone sailing off across the deep blue sea to seize the emeralds and save Moonrakers from my greedy clutches. Very interesting."

I was baffled by his manner, for he was in good humor when he might well have been angry with me. I said, "You don't mind that Robert knows the answer and might find the emeralds?"

"All part of the game, and you didn't tell him, he just had a piece of luck." Nick shrugged, and handed me the sheet of paper. "Off to bed with you now. It's late. Would you like to see a Gilbert and Sullivan opera tomorrow?"

"Oh, I'd love to! Which one is it?"

"The Mikado."

"With the Lord High Executioner!"

"That's right. Tell me about that idiot Gresham woman again, on the train, the day you arrived in England."

I giggled, and tried to imitate Mrs. Gresham's voice. "After all, China and Japan are much of a muchness, I'm sure."

Nick laughed, and the devils danced in his black eyes. "No, right from the beginning, Lucy. Go on. And then do the scene about eating cat."

It was one of the good times, and I hoped desperately that it would last. Next day Nick bought me another new dress, and in the evening we went to the Savoy Theatre. I believe we enjoyed the opera more than anyone else there, because we shared a private joke about it. We dined afterward at the Savoy Restaurant, and Nick introduced me to a married couple of his acquaintance who also happened to be dining there. They were very pleasant and complimentary to me, and the whole evening was quite wonderful. When the cab brought us home I felt my heart sink, wondering if Nick would go off to his club for the night, but still his mood held. I brought him a whisky and soda before going to bed, and he persuaded me to have a sip of it, though I found I disliked the taste.

"I'll sit and smoke a cigar before I go up," he said. "You run along. Good night, Lucy." He bent forward and kissed me on the cheek.

That night, very quietly, I cried myself to sleep with happiness.

The next three days were the best I had known since coming to Nick's house. His good moods had never lasted so long before, and I found myself daring to hope that whatever had afflicted him was now something past and done with; that he was healed, and that in the end we would come to a happy and normal life together, for over the past weeks I had found myself longing for our marriage to be complete, longing for my husband to want me. During my time in England I had gathered the impression that it was not proper for a young woman to feel as I did, but if so I was glad to be different.

On the fourth day, at breakfast, between my going to the kitchen and returning with more coffee, the change occurred. I came back to the dining room to find Nick staring down at his hands as they rested on the table. There was a grim tightness about his mouth, and his daily newspaper lay crumpled on the floor beside him as if he had thrown it down in anger.

Trying to keep anxiety from my voice, I said, "Is anything wrong, Nick?"

"Eh?" He looked up, seeming hardly to see me. "Oh, never mind about more coffee. I'll be off now." He got up and went into the hall. There was a pause as he took his hat from the rack, and next moment I heard the front door slam. Wearily I picked up the paper, straightened the pages and folded it neatly. My high hopes had been cruelly shattered, and I spent the rest of that day wondering how he could change so swiftly and without cause.

Nick did not come home that night. I sat up waiting for him until almost one o'clock, and in the morning I found his bed had not been slept in. At midday a young boy arrived, a messenger sent by Nick's club. He had a letter for me, the envelope addressed in Nick's careless hand.

The letter was dated on the day before, and read:

Dear Lucy,

Sorry for such short notice, but I'm catching the night packet across the Channel and going on to China. There's an old score I have to repay.

Go and see Edmund Gresham. He is authorized to provide whatever money you need, and will arrange a drawing account at the local bank for you.

Never change.

Love,
Nick.

The words danced and blurred before my eyes. Nick had gone to China to repay an old score. Fear prickled in my chest. He had followed his enemy, Robert Falcon. What score did Nick intend to repay? And how?

«ELEVEN»

Next day I took a cab to Grays Inn to see Edmund Gresham. He greeted me a little shyly, sent a boy to fetch some tea for us, then sat down behind his desk and put his fingertips together.

"Well, Lucy. Nick never ceases to surprise us, does he? First he returns from the dead, then he claims you as his wife, and now he's suddenly gone off abroad again."

"Did he tell you where he was going, and why?"

Edmund looked cautious, and shook his head. "No, in fact he did not, but even if he had it might be ethically improper for me to give you such information, Lucy."

I decided that if Nick had not told Edmund it was not for me to do so, and I said, "If you don't know anyway, the ethical part doesn't matter, Edmund, does it?"

"Quite so. I was simply making my position clear to you." He opened a drawer and took out a folder. "Now, Nick authorized me to arrange a drawing account at the bank for you. I asked him what the limit should be, and he told me, rather offensively I thought, not to be a bigger fool than I could help."

If I had not been so troubled I would have smiled. "I expect he just meant that he wasn't afraid I might waste his money, Edmund."

"I'm sure, I'm sure. But it's so imprudent in *principle*, Lucy. However, my task is simply to carry out his wishes, so if you would sign here, please. Thank you. And here."

I signed a paper, and a printed card of some kind, then asked politely after Edmund's family. When we had talked for a few minutes, he came out into Grays Inn with me and saw me safely into a cab for my journey home.

For the next few days I kept house and performed my daily tasks like an automaton. By night I slept poorly and had bad dreams. By day I felt overwhelmed by a feeling of helplessness. Nick Sabine and Robert Falcon were both on their way to China, a country torn by strife, where anything could happen. I had a powerful presentiment that they would meet at Tsin Kai-feng, if they survived the hostility all around them. And when they met . . .

The thought of that encounter frightened me, for I remembered the moment when they had faced one another in the drawing room at Moonrakers, with that almost ferocious enmity pulsing between them. But here in England I could do nothing to prevent what might happen when next they met. And then, as the days went by, a new feeling began to stir in me. Was I really helpless? If only I could go to Tsin Kai-feng, if only I could overtake them on the long journey, surely I could find some way to prevent their hatred ending in tragedy?

Eight days after Nick's departure I went to see Mr. Marsh. I chose a time when I knew Mrs. Burke would be out shopping for an hour or more, and told him all that had happened and all that I feared. "I'm going to China," I ended. "I know it sounds impossible, but it isn't really. Some ships are much faster than others, and perhaps I'll be lucky in getting a quick passage. I'll draw some money from the bank this afternoon, then go to see a shipping agent. I *have* to get there in time, Mr. Marsh."

He said gently, "I don't think you realize how bad things have suddenly become in China. It will be in all the papers tomorrow, but my master told me last night. He has been put in charge of the matter at the War Office. Peking is cut off, and the Foreign Embassies are besieged there. It's a state of war, Lucy."

I was shocked by his news, but it did not lessen my particular anxiety. I said, "That may be so, but do you really think Robert Falcon won't get there? Do you think Nick won't get there? They're not the kind to turn back."

He rubbed his brow. "Both of them are very purposeful, determined men. Yes, I suppose they'll reach China. But it would be different for a girl, Lucy."

I said with all the emphasis I could muster, "Once they get there they'll have to travel *through* China, probably from well south of Tientsin, and then it will be different for *them,* Mr. Marsh. I know I'm only a girl, but if you put the three of us down anywhere in China I'll travel twice as fast as either of them. I know I can. Please don't tell me all the difficulties, I know them and I don't care. Somehow I'm going to get there."

He studied me, and nodded slowly. "Yes. As you got to Matthew Falcon that night in the snow, and carried him home, even though it was impossible . . ." His voice trailed away and he sat up very straight, his eyes unfocused, as if he had suddenly been smitten by a new and startling thought.

I said, "What is it, Mr. Marsh?"

"Wait, Lucy, wait. I'm thinking. I wonder if . . . ? H'mm! There's a chance, a good chance. I know how to handle the old devil better than anyone." He reached out and took my hand, smiling in a way that made the face beneath his prematurely white hair seem almost youthful, and strangely like Nick's, though I had never seen the resemblance before. "If I could stop you going, I'd do it, Lucy. But I know you, child.

You won't be stopped. So the next best thing is to—" He broke off and sat thinking again, his eyes narrowed. Then, "Go home and pack whatever you'd planned to take for the journey. Come back here at six o'clock this evening, with your luggage. No, wait. Go to see Mr. Edmund first, on your way home. Tell him you're closing up the house and he must arrange for somebody to keep an eye on it. Then carry on as I've just said. Will you do that?"

* * *

For the next few hours I was so busy with hurried preparations and arrangements that I scarcely had time to puzzle over what Mr. Marsh could be planning. I realized that "the old devil" he had spoken of must be his master, Lord Shipley, but I could not see how his lordship came into the matter, unless Mr. Marsh hoped to accompany me on the voyage to China and needed to get his master's permission. But that would hardly account for the haste with which he wished me to be packed and ready to go this very day.

At six o'clock I presented myself at the back door of the house in Duke of York Street. Evidently Mrs. Burke was expecting me.

"Put your case down here, dear. My, my, such mysteries and goings on. Goodness knows what that Tom Marsh is up to now, but he's a close one and no mistake. Told me not to bother you with questions, and he'd tell me what was what when all's done, whatever that might mean. He's up with his lordship now. Give me your hat and coat, dear. There, now you'd better tidy your hair in the looking glass over there. You want to look your best, don't you? And I'm sure you will, you'll look very nice indeed."

She chattered on, made me a cup of tea and offered me some biscuits I felt too nervous to eat. After twenty minutes Mr. Marsh came downstairs. He was very calm, and stood straight as a ramrod in front of me, looking me over almost as if inspecting a soldier on parade. "Very good, Lucy," he said quietly. "Now we'll go up. Follow me, please, and don't be frightened. His bark is much worse than his bite."

Lieutenant General the Lord Shipley was not in uniform. He stood with his back to the mantelpiece, and I was surprised to see a small fire burning in the grate, even though it was a warm June evening. He was tall and very thin, with a bony face and deep-set eyes, the whites of them tinged with yellow. His thin hair, brushed straight back, had been black but was graying now. In his hand he held a brandy glass with a good measure of brandy in it.

I bobbed a curtsy and said, "Good evening, my lord."

The yellow eyes blinked once. "Evening, young lady." His voice was rather high-pitched. "Marsh, who's this gel?"

"This is the person I was discussing with you just now, my lord."

A dark red flush crept slowly into the thin brown cheeks. The eyes seemed to shrink to pinpoints, and the tight lips to disappear almost completely. For endless moments Lord Shipley glared across the room, at Marsh rather than at me. Then he spoke in a shrill, angry bark. "Damn your eyes, Marsh, she's a *female!*"

"Quite so, my lord." Mr. Marsh's face was inscrutable.

Lord Shipley lifted his glass and drained it. When he spoke his voice was quiet at first, but gradually grew louder and louder. "Thirty-two years I've known you, Marsh. Soldiered with you over half the world. Seen you handle sword, rifle, and machine gun. Roasted with you in the Sudan, damn near drowned with you in the Indian monsoons. Know you better than any man alive. But by God's Holy Teeth, this is the first time I've had *insolence* from you! Drunk or sober, wet or dry, in the mess or on the field, you've never yet been *impudent!*" His voice rose to a yelp of fury.

Mr. Marsh said coolly, "My lord, this young lady is Lucy Sabine, my daughter-in-law. Be so good as to refrain from bad language in her presence, or we shall withdraw."

Lord Shipley's face became empurpled. His astonished glare swung from Marsh to me and back again. I expected him to order us both out of the room, but suddenly a spark of mingled curiosity and humor appeared in his deep-set eyes, and after a long pause he bowed stiffly from the waist. "My apologies, young lady. I stand corrected by my servant, and properly so. Will you be seated? This chair is quite comfortable, I think. Marsh, get me another brandy."

I took the armchair he had indicated. Mr. Marsh received the glass from his master and moved to a decanter on the sideboard. As he did so he said, "May I explain myself, sir?"

"I think you'd damn' well—ah, sorry m'dear. I think you'd better, Marsh."

"Thank you, my lord. If I may first recapitulate. Last night you spoke to me at some length about the situation in China. The Empress has now swung her authority behind the Boxers. Hundreds of foreign refugees have gathered in Peking, and are besieged in the grounds of the British Legation with only a handful of marines to protect them. The German Minister has been murdered."

Mr. Marsh moved to hand the glass to his master. I was listening with horror, for although I knew that the troubles in China had come to a head, I had no idea until now that they were so bad.

"As I understand the situation, my lord," Mr. Marsh went on, "the only hope for the besieged in Peking, and indeed for other smaller groups under siege elsewhere in North China, is for an army to reach Peking and subdue the city, seizing the Empress and her Council."

Lord Shipley grunted. "You've always had a good head for situation reports. Go on, man."

"I have written to your dictation many times, my lord, and trust I have learned a little." Mr. Marsh moved to stand beside my chair. "You have told me that a mixed force of several nationalities, British, French, Russian, German and others, has been assembled to march on Peking. Two days ago destroyers stormed the Taku Forts which cover the port of Tientsin, and seized them. The mixed army is now marching on Tientsin, which is expected to fall quickly. They will then have to fight their way to Peking, a hundred miles distant. Have I summarized the situation correctly so far, my lord?"

His master sniffed, and sipped some brandy. "You've made a messy business sound simple, but carry on."

"There's little more to say, sir. Our forces in the Tientsin area have no communication with the people besieged in Peking. As you rightly pointed out, what the unfortunate people under siege in the British Legation need is hope. If they know help is on the way—"

"You don't have to give *me* a lecture, Marsh," his lordship said testily. "I know all about the values of morale."

"I was speaking now for Lucy's benefit, my lord."

"Ah! Quite right, too." Lord Shipley turned to me. "Classic situation. Those people in Peking don't know what's happening. Every day, every week, they'll be getting shorter of food, water, ammunition. Now, you can take it from me, m'dear, that a mainly civilian group in that situation can very quickly lose the will to resist. Then they're done for. But if they *know* help is on the way, if they can be sure that in another month, six weeks, *three* months if you like, rescue will arrive, then they'll hold on somehow, even on a thimbleful of food a day. Understand?"

"Yes, sir. I can understand that very well."

"Good. Well, according to the telegraph messages reaching me from the commander of the British troops out there, it's impossible to get any message through to our people in Peking except by hand. So you see the problem. Any foreigner trying to make that journey will get chopped up pretty quick by the first bunch of these Boxer fellows he meets. And we can't send a Chinese chap, because the ones who don't like the Boxers are frightened to death of them. Even if a Chinese agreed to go, we'd never be sure we could trust him. They're *foreign,* you see, and we simply don't understand them, quite apart from the strange lingo they speak."

He turned and fixed Mr. Marsh with a stern eye. "That's enough recapitulation, I fancy. You told me you had the very person, Marsh. Someone we could send out posthaste on *Crocodile,* and who could be relied on to get through to Peking. What the devil d'you mean by telling me a yarn like that and then producing this—ah—very charming gel?"

"My lord," Mr. Marsh said quietly, "Lucy is indeed the very person. Until a year ago she had lived all her life in China. She speaks the language as well as any native. You may remember some time ago, when you asked me to sit with you and gossip for a while, I spoke of a certain young lady who came to High Coppice—"

"Hey?" Lord Shipley's eyebrows rose in two bushy arches. "You mean this is the same one? Lucy? Little gel at the Mission, trying to feed those starving brats? The one who went out in the snow for the what's-his-name boy last Christmas?"

"The same, sir. She is as well-used to hardship and difficulty as any soldier. She thinks nothing of walking twenty miles in a day, in bitter weather and through a land infested with brigands. I would trust her with my life, sir." He smiled. "Indeed, I expect to do so, for it is my hope that you will allow me to accompany her."

Lord Shipley turned to face me squarely, looking down at me with great curiosity. "Marsh is a canny soldier, so when he speaks like that I'm vastly impressed, believe me. But I don't understand why he should expose his truly delightful daughter-in-law to such danger."

"It's only because he knows I'm determined to go to China anyway, sir. I have very important personal reasons. I may be too late for . . . what I hope to do, but I shall go just the same."

Without taking his eyes from my face he said, "She really means this, Marsh?"

"Very much so, my lord. She is a most stubborn young person."

"Good. I like that. She may be too late for what *I* want her to do, but we must still try." Lord Shipley chuckled, and a gleam came into his eyes. "A girl," he murmured. "Now who would suspect a girl of acting as courier for the Army? She'd have twice the chance of a man, even if we could find one. By God, we'll give it a try, Lucy! Now listen. *Crocodile* is a fast destroyer, waiting at Marseilles. You can be there by dusk tomorrow, and she'll make Tientsin in twenty-two days. But you'll have to attend to my business before you attend to your own, young lady!"

Twenty-two days! I had never dreamed of such speed. I could make the overland journey to Peking and still reach Tsin Kai-feng before Robert or Nick, even though Robert had left three weeks ago. I said, "I'm very grateful to you, my lord."

He stared down at me grimly. "I may well be sending you to your death, girl. But since you're set on running the risk anyway, I'll make the prize worthwhile. We can only guess at the situation in Peking, but I fancy there must be well over a thousand souls under attack. Without hope, they'll break long before the Army gets there. That means a massacre. But if you can reach them to say the Army is coming, they'll hang on. A thousand lives, Lucy. Perhaps more. So do your best, for there's no one else we can send with your particular knowledge and experience."

He turned to Mr. Marsh. "You will accompany her to Tientsin, but no farther. She makes the journey to Peking alone. You couldn't hope to pass as a Chinese, and you'd jeopardize the whole mission."

Something flickered for a moment in Mr. Marsh's eyes, and then was gone. "Very good, my lord," he said politely. "May I suggest that you write out the necessary authority for us to show the British commander when we reach Tientsin, and the appropriate travel documents? We must be off within an hour or so if we are to catch the night Channel steamer."

*   *   *

That night we crossed the Channel and took a train which carried us across France to the great port of Marseilles. We traveled first class, in sleeping compartments, and Mr. Marsh carried a paper of authority, countersigned by the French Ambassador in London, which was like a magic talisman in making every stage of our journey smooth and comfortable. At Marseilles we boarded a British destroyer called *Crocodile*, and sailed that same evening for the Suez Canal.

I was the only woman aboard, and was given the cabin usually occupied by the first officer. It was tiny, but I discovered that all cabins on a destroyer are very small, designed to save space rather than to offer comfort. The captain and his officers went out of their way to make our voyage as pleasant as possible, and treated us with marked respect. I noticed that Mr. Marsh no longer acted like a servant, but like a man of authority. Aboard ship he was called "Mr. Marsh," and I was always called "Miss Lucy." No questions were asked, and even the captain did not know why he was carrying us as passengers. He had simply received urgent orders by telegraph from London, and was obeying them.

To pass the time, Mr. Marsh taught me to play a card game called piquet, and then whist. We discovered that the captain had a great enthusiasm for whist, and sometimes of an evening we played with him and one of his officers. I had thought that I would spend the voyage worrying about all that lay ahead, but once again I found that being on a ship at sea is like being on a tiny world which is scarcely penetrated by anything from outside, so that there is a feeling of being suspended in time.

When we stopped to refuel at Colombo, Mr. Marsh went ashore and returned with a small parcel. Later I saw him deep in a pidgin-English conversation with a Chinese stoker from Hong Kong, and I wondered why he had not asked me to act as interpreter for him.

Next day there was a tap on the door of my cabin. When I opened it I stared in astonishment, for a Chinese coolie stood there. He wore roughly cobbled sandals, ragged trousers, a coarsely woven jacket, and a shapeless felt hat with a wide brim which flopped down over his eyes as he stood with head bowed in a humble attitude. A moment later I saw that this was no coolie, for his jet-black hair was too short, and he wore no queue. There were other small things amiss; something in his stance, in the stiff-wristed way he held his hands, and the way the cheap peasant clothes hung on him. This man was no Chinese.

I said in English, "Who are you?" He lifted his head, and only then did I recognize the face which had been half-hidden by the sagging brim of the hat. It was Mr. Marsh. With his white hair died black as a raven's feather he looked a good ten years younger, and for a moment I caught a wicked twinkle in his eye, reminding me of Nick.

"I know I've a lot to learn before I can really pass for a Chinese," he said. "But the sooner you start teaching me, the better, Lucy. These are just make-shift clothes, of course, but we can get some real Chinese clothes in Hong Kong."

I had begun to laugh before I realized what this meant. He planned to make the journey to Peking with me. I said, "But you can't, Mr. Marsh. Lord Shipley said—"

"I know. But I'm not a soldier now, so I can disobey orders if I think fit. And if I *can* pass as a Chinese, then you'll be safer on the journey, Lucy. Nobody will suspect you of being a courier, I know, but as a young girl alone, in a war-torn country . . . well, you'll be tempting prey for evil men, child."

"I know, but I'll be careful, and I can run very fast—"

"Wait, Lucy," he broke in quickly. "Just hear me out. I

want you to teach me how to be a Chinese peasant. You must give me a name, tell me what work I do and what my daily problems are. We have another ten or twelve days before we reach Tientsin. Then you can make the decision yourself. If I'm good enough, then take me with you. If not . . . well, I'll abide by your judgment. For your sake."

It was more to please him than because I felt it would be any use that I said, "Let's go on deck, where you can practise walking. I'm not sure I'll make a very good teacher, but we can try."

While some of the seamen looked on curiously, I made Mr. Marsh walk back and forth in his make-shift clothes, some of which he had borrowed from the Chinese stoker. *"Anyone* would know you were a foreign devil," I sighed. "A coolie doesn't walk like a soldier. Hunch forward a little, Mr. Marsh. Now let your wrists go limp, so your hands dangle. Your ankles are stiff, too. Ah, that's better. Try moving at a little trot, leaning forward, then gradually slow down to a walk. No, like this. It's a kind of shuffle. Oh dear, there's still something wrong, but I can't think what it is. Keep your elbows into your sides—ah, that's better."

At the end of an hour I shook my head doubtfully. "I don't know, Mr. Marsh. Apart from anything else, your hair gives you away because you haven't a queue. And it won't grow enough in ten days to give you one."

He grinned, and again I glimpsed Nick in him. "Lucy dear, you can surely lend me enough hair to make a queue. I shall have to keep my own dyed, of course, but the dye I bought in Colombo seems to work well, and I've plenty of it. What about the eyes? I thought if I wore a rough leather patch over one of them, with the string resting across the other eyebrow, it ought to do the trick. Anyway, you'll have to keep your own eyes pretty well hidden whenever other people are near."

"I know, but I can make them look longer and narrower by using pencil-black at the corners, Mr. Marsh. I sometimes did that at the Mission, because I thought my round eyes were so ugly. And when I'm near to anyone, I shall keep my head humbly bowed, as an unimportant female person should."

He laughed. "This insignificant peasant can do the same."

"There's something else. I know we're tanned from the sun and sea air, but we must buy some saffron to rub into our faces, to make them more yellow."

Every day we practised for at least two hours, and I found myself becoming ever more hopeful, for Mr. Marsh seemed to be really sinking into the skin of a Chinese peasant. As his walk improved, I made him loll his head to one side and hang his mouth open, so that he looked stupid. During the evenings I taught him to sing an old Chinese children's song in a high-pitched wavering voice. With much practice his performance became quite remarkable.

When we stopped at Hong Kong to refuel once more, I bought old clothes for both of us, including coolie hats, and some saffron. Later, when we were dressed for the part, I took Mr. Marsh ashore. He wore a queue of my hair attached to his own, and he was Lu Yen now, my father.

Holding his hand, I led him along the narrow streets and alleys. He shuffled aimlessly beside me, head wagging, and occasionally sang a few quavering lines of his little song. At several stalls and booths I stopped to talk, and not a single person realized that we were anything other than a young Chinese girl from the north with her afflicted father.

After such a test I knew that his presence with me on the journey would not add to the danger. In fact a girl with her simpleton father might attract less attention than a girl alone. The relief I felt brought me close to tears. It was wonderful to think that I would have his company on the journey to Peking, and in whatever lay in store for me after that.

Tientsin was full of soldiers, British and Russian, American and French, German and Japanese. The captain sent two of his officers to accompany us to the headquarters of the British command, and Mr. Marsh presented his papers to the Commanding Officer, Colonel Strake, a small stout man with a dour manner.

He read the letter from Lord Shipley, gazed at us with no enthusiasm, and said, "You're to carry a message to Peking? Well, I've often wondered if those johnnies at the War Office were out of their minds, and now I know. But these orders allow me no discretion. What do you need? Food? Supplies? Maps?"

"The young lady will make a requisition for our needs," Mr. Marsh said briskly and without deference. "I should like your appreciation of the situation north of Tientsin, if you please, Colonel."

"A damnable mess. These Boxer fellows are mad as hatters. They think they're immune to bullets, and they have the regular Chinese forces with them now. Badly organized, of course. With any luck you'll sneak through their lines north of Tientsin by night, if you can call them lines. Then all you have to do is follow the railway straight to Peking, but without being spotted as foreigners. Frankly I don't give you much hope. But let's assume a miracle, and you get through. What do you tell the poor blighters in Peking, if they're still alive?"

He turned and slapped his swagger stick against a map which hung on the wall. "We're almost as badly organized as the Chinese. What can you expect with half a dozen nationalities and no central command? Admiral Seymour underestimated the Chinese soldiers. He took a couple of thousand men north, in early June, got a bloody nose here, at Langfang, and had to fall back. Now everybody's *over*estimating the Chinese strength. We've nearly twenty thousand troops here, and we could strike through to Peking in a couple of weeks, in my view. But we won't, confound it."

He tugged at his mustache gloomily. "Seymour's telling Whitehall we need forty thousand men before we can start. The Americans are talking about sixty thousand, the Japs about seventy thousand. Damn rubbish."

He half closed an eye and lifted a finger. "But General Gaselee's arriving in eight days or so, as Commander-in-Chief. I know what *he'll* do. He'll just start north with our own lads, and the rest will follow for shame. So if you get to Peking, you tell Sir Claude MacDonald, the Minister there, that we'll be raising the siege . . . now let's see. By the middle of August. Yes. Tell him to hang on till then, and we'll be there."

Colonel Strake looked at me dubiously, then switched his gaze to Mr. Marsh. "Do you seriously intend to take this young woman on such a journey with you?"

Mr. Marsh smiled. "Not exactly, Colonel. She's taking me."

* * *

Long afterward, when I was home in England and had married again, people who knew something of my adventure during the Boxer Rebellion would sometimes ask about the journey from Tientsin to Peking, thinking that it must have been the most dangerous time of all. But the truth was that we never met with any serious danger.

We took with us a donkey, two panniers containing enough food and water for four days, and two blankets. A rifle and two bandoliers of ammunition were strapped along the donkey's back, and Mr. Marsh carried a pistol hidden under his tunic. Over the panniers and rifle we tied a large, loose bale of straw which hid everything else. I had my comfortable felt boots with me, and I found a pair in Tientsin to fit Mr. Marsh. He afterward said they were the best boots for marching he had ever known.

The Boxers wore no special uniform, but as a mark of their tong they tied up their hair in red cloth, wore red ribbons around their wrists and ankles, and a red girdle around their loose white tunics. To show that we supported them in their war against the foreign devils, Mr. Marsh and I tied cheap red scarves around our necks.

We left Tientsin by night, within eight hours of our arrival, and by dawn the next day we had passed through the Chinese lines and were several miles north, moving parallel with the railway. I had decided that we should cover thirty miles each day, and my main worry was that this might prove too much for Mr. Marsh, for he was a man past fifty. But my anxiety was needless, and no doubt his years of soldiering were to thank for this. Leaning forward, arms hanging loosely, knees always bent a little, he plodded tirelessly on with the trudging peasant stride I had taught him.

There were troops and Boxers in each town or village on the railway, but we made a wide circle around all such places, rejoining the railway line later. Sometimes we met people going about their everyday work, and sometimes we met soldiers or groups of Boxers. Then I would pick up the end of a short rope tied to Mr. Marsh's arm, so that I seemed to be leading him as well as the donkey. He would loll his head stupidly and whine a snatch of his childish song, while I would keep my head humbly bowed. By day we walked from dawn till dusk, resting for a quarter of an hour in every two hours. By night we slept in the open, for this was summer and the nights were not cold.

Once we passed a small Buddhist temple, and came upon a group of Boxers outside, who were chanting spells, bowing to the southeast, and making strange signs. I gathered from their chanting that this was a ritual which would give them the power to turn aside bullets with a wave of the hands. Some of them glared suspiciously as we passed. I patted my red scarf, waved my arm, and cried *"Sha! Sha!"* This was the war cry of the Boxers, and meant, "Kill! Kill!" They gave back the cry in a great shout, and we passed on without trouble.

At noon on the fourth day we came in sight of the great walled city of Peking, and when we were still a mile away we settled down in a hollow beside the road to study the map of the city which Colonel Strake had provided. Peking was divided in two main sections, the Chinese City forming the southern section and the Tartar City the northern, with a great crenelated wall between, forty feet high. In the center of the northern part was the Forbidden City, where no foreigner had ever been allowed to go, and where the great palace of the Empress stood.

We marked where the Legation Quarter lay, made our plans, and entered by the south gate of the Chinese City an hour before sunset. There were soldiers and Boxers everywhere, mingling with the people of Peking, and from beyond the high wall came the occasional sound of rifle fire. Nobody took any notice of us as we made our way through the gate called Ha Ta Men. Here we were close to the siege itself, and we made a slow circle around the streets which hemmed the Legation Quarter, noticing the positions from which the Chinese were firing on the defenders. Then we settled down in a narrow street near the Anglican Mission to wait.

It was not a continuous battle. Often there would be no sound of shooting for half an hour or more, then would come a fusillade from a group of attackers, answered by no more than two or three shots from beyond the walls. It was a great relief to have Mr. Marsh with me now, for all seemed confusion and I had no idea which was the best route by which to get into the Legation compound without being shot by defenders or attackers. But Mr. Marsh had grasped exactly what was happening all around the perimeter of the besieged compound.

Two hours after sunset, Mr. Marsh took the rifle and bandoliers, and we began to move through the streets toward the wall of the compound, keeping in the shadows. For the last fifty yards we crawled on hands and knees through a tangle of roughly made barricades, passing within thirty paces of some Chinese soldiers who were settling down for the night at their post.

At last we lay beside a low, crumbling wall with only a broad empty road between us and the high wall of the compound. Mr. Marsh must have detected a sentry position on the wall here earlier in the day, for now he cupped his hands about his mouth and spoke in a sharp, penetrating whisper. *"Sentry!"*

He waited several seconds, then repeated the fiercely whispered word. After the fourth time, a low voice sounded from somewhere on the wall. "Who goes there?"

"Friends. British. Two of us. Hang a ladder down. We're coming in."

"Stand fast!" the voice snapped. "Identify yourself or I fire!"

I could have screamed at the man in my mingled fear and anger, for this was the moment of greatest danger. Lying flat beside me, Mr. Marsh drew in a long slow breath. Then he spoke again in that same penetrating whisper, but into it he put more venom and menace that I would have thought possible.

What he said began: *"Speak soft, you kettle-mender's scut, and say 'Sir' when you address me or I'll . . ."* Then came a string of phrases which were so heavily larded with words I had never heard before that he might almost have been speaking a foreign language. But I could guess what he meant, and the soldier beyond the wall seemed to understand clearly, for when Mr. Marsh paused there came a ghostly chuckle from the darkness and the voice said, "'Old on, friend. We'll drop the ladder in a jiffy."

The jiffy lasted for three minutes. Then came faint scuffling sounds by the wall. The sentry's voice said, "Right. At the double."

We rose and darted across the road. A rope ladder with rough wooden rungs hung down the wall. I went up first, and tumbled over the top on to a platform built against the wall to form a firing position. Two figures stood waiting, one with a rifle pointed toward me. The other held a shielded lantern. The first said, "Cor, it's a girl, sir!"

Next moment Mr. Marsh came over the wall. I saw that the second man held a pistol in his free hand. He said, "Now then, who the devil are you?"

Mr. Marsh drew himself up. "Acting-Colonel Marsh, special emissary from the War Office under orders of Lieutenant

General the Lord Shipley," he said in a cool, haughty voice. "Who's in charge here?"

Even though I felt weak with relief, I had to suppress a splutter of shaky laughter as I wondered what Lord Shipley would have thought if he could have heard his manservant claiming to be an Acting-Colonel. The man with the lamp said uncertainly, "Sir Claude MacDonald is in charge, sir."

"Then take us to him at once, if you please."

"Yes, sir. May I ask, who is this Chinese girl?"

"She is English. Her name is Lucy Sabine, she is my guide and aide-de-camp, and she has brought me safely from Tientsin in four days. Now take us to Sir Claude, and look sharp about it, young man."

Sir Claude MacDonald was a tall, thin-faced man with a mustache so long that the ends could be seen protruding beyond his cheeks from behind. He must have been sleeping fully dressed, for he appeared within moments of our being taken into his quarters.

At first he could not believe that we had come from Tientsin, but when Mr. Marsh showed him our papers of authority his relief was evident. "Thank God," he said quietly. "Everyone is in very low spirits here. We feared the outside world believed us already massacred by the Boxers, and that there would be no urgent attempt to reach Peking."

"Another three weeks, sir," Mr. Marsh said. "That's what Colonel Strake instructed me to tell you. I've observed the forces and terrain between here and Tientsin, and I believe his estimate to be accurate."

"Three weeks." Sir Claude nodded and smiled a tired smile. "I've been wondering if we could last another seven days, but this makes all the difference, Marsh. We'll cut the food ration again, and make every bullet count. Be sure we'll hang on somehow, once everyone knows that rescue is certain." He looked at me, perplexed. "Was it really necessary to expose this young lady to such danger?"

"That's for you to judge, sir. She has lived all her life in

China, and in fact she is the authorized messenger. Without her, I would not be here."

"Then it was entirely necessary," Sir Claude said slowly. "I can only offer my profound gratitude."

It was not until the next day, after twelve hours of wonderful sound sleep, that I realized how much our coming had meant to the defenders. Everywhere we went, men and women of many different nationalities would stop us and ask anxiously for reassurance that help was certain. Our replies were translated from tongue to tongue, and a spirit of resolve seemed to sweep the community.

Within the walls of the Legation compound there were more than three thousand people to be housed, fed, and given medical attention when they fell sick or were wounded. Of these, only three hundred and fifty were soldiers. There had been more, but fifty had died on the walls already. The whole area had been turned into a fortress, with trenches, ramparts, and strong points. More than a thousand of those under siege were Chinese converts who had been brought in from far and wide by missionaries when the troubles in China first began. Although they were extra mouths to feed, they provided labor for digging trenches and building strong points. Without these defenses, the compound would have fallen long since.

I had planned to leave Peking and strike northeast for Chengfu and Tsin Kai-feng as soon as I was rested, but Mr. Marsh dissuaded me. "It's not only dangerous, Lucy, it's pointless. I don't know where Nick and Robert Falcon are, but do you really imagine that either of them can be moving freely about China? Robert may have reached Shanghai by now, but he'll get no farther. I doubt if Nick has even reached China yet. And we're of use here, Lucy. I'm needed on the wall, and you in the hospital. When the siege is raised, that will be time enough for us to make for Tsin Kai-feng."

I knew that what he said was true. No foreigner could travel through North China until the Forbidden City had fallen to the mixed army gathered in Tientsin. I began to work in the make-shift hospital which had been set up, and found more than enough to do. I asked if Mr. and Mrs. Fenshaw, together with the children at the Mission, had reached Peking before the siege began, and learned to my dismay that nothing had been heard of them.

Small detachments of soldiers had been sent from Peking much earlier, to bring in missionaries and converts from outlying parts. Many detachments had not returned. It was believed they had been cut off, and that throughout the area minor sieges were going on, with a handful of soldiers defending a Mission or church where foreigners had gathered for safety.

On the seventh day, Mr. Marsh sought me out in the hospital. His eyes were red-rimmed from lack of sleep, but he looked lean and hard as a wolf. "A Chinese came in last night through a dry sewer, Lucy. He's from Tsin Kai-feng. You'd better come and talk to him, his English isn't up to much and I can't make out what he says."

The man was squatting in one of the kitchens, greedily eating a bowl of thin soup. I recognized him at once. He was Chang Li, the convert Mr. and Mrs. Fenshaw had brought to the Mission with them, driving the ox-cart. He remembered me, and began to express his amazement at finding me here, but I cut him short. "What has happened at the Mission, Chang Li?"

"It is bad, Lu-tsi. I think they will die. Before the Boxers came, the Lady with Red Hair and her husband brought in much food, and there is the old well for water. But the *I Ho Chuan* are camped in Tsin Kai-feng. For three weeks they have attacked. Forty, fifty of them. They shout that they will kill all, the children too, as they are contaminated by the foreign devils."

"Three weeks? How have you stopped them?"

"Before the troubles, the American doctor came from Chengfu. He brought two rifles."

"Dr. Langdon! He's there now?"

"Yes. He shoots with one rifle, and the husband of the Lady with Red Hair shoots the other. The outer wall is strong. The Mission stands on a hill. Only once have the *I Ho Chuan* reached the walls. Then I, and the Lady with Red Hair, and Yu-lan, and two other big girls, we went to the wall with spears we had made, knives tied to long sticks. We drove back the *I Ho Chuan* at the wall."

I felt sick with horror. "But surely if the Boxers come from all sides, they must break through?"

"Ah! They do not come from the north side, which is the most difficult to hold. They have some fear of it, we do not know why. And then there is also the other one, who came ten days since. He too has a rifle. And when there were few bullets left, he went out by night to the camp of the *I Ho Chuan,* and stole bullets. He stole another rifle, also. Twice he has done this."

I said, "Who is this other one?"

"An English foreign devil. His name is Fal-con. He is very fierce and terrible."

I turned to Mr. Marsh, barely able to speak for shock. "Robert's there!" I whispered. "He—he says Robert reached the Mission ten days ago! They're holding it against a band of Boxers. Oh, those poor babies!"

"*Robert?* How in the world can he have got there so quickly? And what's this fellow doing here now, Lucy? Ask him!"

Chang Li shrugged when I put the question. "It was agreed. We cannot hold. Fal-con sent me out by night three days ago, to come to Peking and bring back help." Another shrug. "He did not know it was so bad here."

"How did Fal-con come to you without being killed?"

Chang Li grinned. "He came on a horse, dressed in the clothes of a Boxer he had killed, and with a red scarf wrapped about his head so that none could see he was a foreign devil."

Ten minutes later Mr. Marsh and I stood before Sir Claude MacDonald. His face was lined, and the long mustache seemed to droop with weariness. "It's out of the question, Marsh," he said curtly. "I can't send a detachment to some outlying Mission ninety miles away. You must know that."

"I do, sir. I'm asking permission for Lucy and myself to go. We can get through."

Sir Claude stared. "I don't doubt it. But what good can you do? In any case, you're needed here."

"One man, one girl and one rifle won't turn the scale here, sir. It might just do so at Tsin Kai-feng."

I said urgently, "Please, sir! They're my children—I mean, I looked after them for years."

The Minister tugged at his mustache, frowning.

Mr. Marsh said quietly, "Do you not think you owe it to this young lady?"

*　*　*

We left the compound by way of the dry sewer that night, when clouds hid the moon. Mr. Marsh had redyed his hair, and fixed his queue in place. He carried his rifle rolled in our two blankets. I carried the pistol myself, tied to my waist under my tunic, and we had a small sack with a little food and a bottle of water in it.

Once clear of the siege area we lay in a disused stable until dawn, when we were able to pass through one of the city gates without rousing any suspicion. Throughout the three-day journey to Tsin Kai-feng I felt in a daze, as if I did not belong in my own body. It was hard to believe that I was returning to the Mission which had been my home; even harder to believe that Robert Falcon was there, and that every life within those walls was threatened by men half crazed with the lust to kill.

We made a half circle around Chengfu shortly after midnight on the third night, and came to the Mission from the north some two hours later. Lights flickered in the village below, but there was no sign of an attack in progress. Together we crawled toward the north wall. As we did so, the moon showed briefly from behind a bank of cloud, and we hugged the ground, waiting for darkness before we moved again. I stared ahead, and almost gasped aloud. There, on the outer wall, faded but still clear in detail even by moonlight, was the portrait of Nick Sabine. It had not been washed away by weather. Instead the soft charcoal had been absorbed into the porous stones of the wall.

Clouds hid the moon again, and we moved on. At the wall, Mr. Marsh lifted me and I clambered over. Seconds later he dropped down beside me. Together we ran for the door which led into the kitchen. We were halfway there when a cry came from a window above, a girl's voice I recognized. It was Yu-lan. *"Doctor! They come from the north!"*

I called in a fierce whisper, in Chinese, "Yu-lan! Let nobody shoot. This is Lu-tsi! Let us in quickly."

There was silence. We hugged the wall beside the kitchen door, which was barred from inside. There came the faint murmur of voices from above, then Yu-lan called tremulously, "Lu-tsi! Is it truly you?"

"Yes! I am Lu-tsi. How else would I know your name, or the names of Mei-lin, Mai-chai, baby Kimi, and Miss Prothero, who was called the Donkey-Leg-Lady? I have come with a friend. Let us in, Yu-lan."

"Wait, Lu-tsi, wait!"

A minute later the kitchen door was unbarred. As it opened I saw that a lamp hung from the ceiling, and on the far side stood Dr. Langdon holding a rifle aimed at us. I went in first, taking off my hat to show my face, and saying, "Dr. Langdon, it really is me! Oh, I'm so glad you're safe."

He lowered the rifle, staring. His face was gaunt with strain and weariness. "Good God," he croaked. "How on earth . . . ?"

Mrs. Fenshaw appeared from behind the kitchen door. In her hand was a broom handle with a carving knife tied to one end. Her red hair was drawn back tightly, and her face was more bony than I remembered it, but the green eyes were as purposeful as ever.

"Lucy Waring!" she said as Mr. Marsh closed and barred the door behind us. "What in heaven's name are *you* doing here? And who's this Chinese with you?"

"We've come from Peking, Mrs. Fenshaw. Chang Li arrived four days ago, but they can't send you help. No soldiers can get through. But Mr. Marsh and I came. Oh, excuse me. This is Mr. Marsh." I turned to him. "Mr. Marsh, may I introduce Mrs. Fenshaw and Dr. Langdon?"

"Your servant, ma'am. Dr. Langdon. I've brought a rifle and sixty rounds with me, and a pistol. It's less than you hoped for, I'm sure, but better than nothing."

The next five minutes brought a confusion of questions and answers. I told briefly how we had come to China, how matters stood in Peking, and how we had carried the news that a relief army was coming to the rescue.

"How long, Lucy?" Dr. Langdon asked.

"About another ten days, if Colonel Strake was right."

He exchanged a glance with Mrs. Fenshaw. "Well, we'll just have to do our best. At least once the troops take Peking this business will end very quickly, for the Empress will be bound to turn her own troops against the Boxers."

I learned that Mr. Fenshaw was manning a lookout post on the south side of the Mission. Yu-lan and some of the older girls took turns to watch at other windows by day and night, to give warning of any attack. All windows were blocked by earth-filled sacks, with small loop holes left for keeping watch and shooting. The two Chinese nursing converts spent their time looking after the little children, dealing with the dwindling supply of food, and taking their turn on watch.

"I'll go and relieve Yu-lan for a wee while," Mrs. Fenshaw said. "We never leave a post till we're relieved, and she's like a cat on hot bricks to see you." She made for the door, then turned. "A brave girl, that one. She was beside me with one of these pikes we've made when yon devils were trying to get over the wall. We'd not have driven them off, but for her."

I still had not asked the question I wanted most to ask, but I understood now why Robert Falcon had not yet appeared. No doubt he was manning a lookout post at one of the windows, like Mr. Fenshaw. When Yu-lan came down to the kitchen she hugged me, and cried, and hugged me again. It was a joy to see her. She looked older than I had expected, but that was not surprising when I remembered that she had fought at the wall against shrieking Boxers, and I made myself curb my impatience to ask about Robert until I had spent a few minutes in greeting her.

As Yu-lan chattered, I heard Dr. Langdon and Mr. Marsh talking. "They've only twice attacked by night, thank God," Dr. Langdon was saying. "They don't seem to fancy it much. When they come by day, they have to climb the slope from the village, so we have them in our sights for about three hundred yards. In the main we've been able to drive them back with a few shots before they reached the wall, but we have to hoard our ammunition."

"Chang Li told Lucy that an Englishman arrived some two weeks ago now, Doctor. Is that correct?"

Dr. Langdon nodded, grim-faced. "We'd have been finished without him. He reorganized our defense and put fresh heart into us all, especially the children. We'd have no ammunition left if he hadn't made night sorties to steal from those devils in the valley." He looked at me strangely. "Lucy knows him."

Mr. Marsh said, "Yes, we both know him, Doctor. I take it he's on watch now. May we go to see him?"

"He's not on watch. He's lying with a bullet in his chest. It's not a fatal wound in itself, but the bullet's so placed that probing for it is going to be dangerous. But if I don't get it out, infection will kill him."

I felt my stomach shrink from shock. "Please . . . may we see him?"

"Yes, Lucy. But even if he's conscious I doubt if he'll know you." Dr. Langdon took the lamp from the hook in the low ceiling. "Yu-lan, go back to your post till Mei-lin relieves you, then get some sleep. You can talk to Lu-tsi again tomorrow."

Mr. Marsh and I followed him upstairs to the room which had been Miss Prothero's. It had been divided by a tarpaulin hung from the ceiling. Two mattresses lay on the floor. Miss Prothero's bed was screened by the tarpaulin. Dr. Langdon lifted one edge of the heavy canvas, and we passed through.

A man lay on the bed, a blanket covering him to the waist. His chest was bare, and with a thick, bloodstained dressing strapped over the left side. Dr. Langdon lifted the lantern, and I heard my own gasp of astonishment mingle with Mr. Marsh's as we stared at the man who lay with eyes closed on the bed.

It was not Robert Falcon. It was my husband, Nick Sabine.

«TWELVE»

THE MOMENT OF disbelief was engulfed by a surge of emotion. I felt fear, anxiety and pity, but above all there was an aching of the heart so intense that it was like physical pain.

I stood by the bed and gently grasped his limp hand. "Nick," I whispered. "Dear Nick."

His eyes flickered open. They were hot with fever, and he gave no sign of recognition, but the dry lips parted in a caricature of a smile. "Dreaming again," he croaked in a voice so faint I could scarcely hear. "Dreaming of Lucy . . . the best of them all, Doc. They broke the mold when they made her. Too good for me . . . don't ever tell . . . how I loved her, Doc. Promise . . ."

His eyes closed, and the ragged breathing sounded loudly in the room. Mr. Marsh looked at me from the far side of the bed with haggard eyes, then turned to Dr. Langdon beside him and said, "When did it happen?"

"Only a few hours ago." Dr. Langdon wiped sweat from his face with the back of his hand. "The Boxers brought up a small cannon from somewhere, an old muzzle-loading affair, but effective at short range. They fired six cannonballs into the Mission just before dusk. Smashed part of the chapel and breached one of the corner rooms. Three children and one of the nurses were wounded by rock splinters, but only superficially. They'll be all right."

"But Nick has a bullet wound, you say?"

"Yes. When it grew dark he went out. He was gone for more than an hour, then there was an explosion from just west of the village, where the gun was sited. He'd blown it up with their own powder. We heard some rifle and pistol fire, and he came over the wall half an hour later. He'd even brought a small cask of gunpowder back with him . . . God knows how he managed it with that wound. He mumbled something about making bombs with it."

Mr. Marsh looked down at Nick. "The bullet has to come out," he said tautly. "Do you have the equipment? And anesthetic?"

Dr. Langdon nodded. "I brought everything with me when I came here before the fighting started, but the bullet's awkwardly placed. I daren't probe for it by lamplight, my eyes aren't good enough, or my sense of touch."

"Does every hour count?"

"Yes. But I have to wait. I've had the sandbags taken down from the window, ready for daylight. Pray God there's no attack."

Mr. Marsh said, "My eyes and hands are no longer young, either. But Lucy's are. Can she get forceps on that bullet under your guidance, Doctor?"

"Lucy? Are you out of your mind, man?"

"No. I'm suggesting we give Nick his best chance. Only you can decide what that is, whether it's better for Lucy to act as your hands now, or to wait another three hours or more for daylight."

Dr. Langdon stared at me in the yellow light. "Can you do it, my dear?"

Stiff with fear, I was about to shake my head, for I could not speak, when Mr. Marsh said calmly, "Lucy can do whatever she has to do. She always has."

"Well, in that case . . ."

The next hour was to haunt my dreams for many a month to come. Under Dr. Langdon's instructions I scrubbed my hands in a solution of antiseptic until they were sore, while Mr. Marsh busied himself boiling surgical instruments in the kitchen. Dr. Langdon placed a gauze mask over Nick's nose and mouth, and put him to sleep with ether. When I had removed the rough dressing and cleansed the whole area with a liquid from Dr. Langdon's bag, I had to cut with a scalpel to make a path for the forceps. From that moment I stopped feeling terrified and simply felt numb. I kept hearing Miss Prothero's voice in my head, "Just do what comes next, Lucy dear." And I was never so thankful for the experience I had of simple doctoring in the village with Miss Prothero, of stitching wounds, splinting bones, and delivering babies.

Mr. Marsh held the lamp, with a hand mirror belonging to Mrs. Fenshaw reflecting the light on to the wound. I made myself forget that this was Nick, forget even that this was a human being. Dr. Langdon talked quietly, telling me what to look for, what to do, what to avoid, how to feel for the bullet with the forceps. Then came a moment when I drew the smeared instrument away and held up the ugly piece of lead.

My knees felt suddenly like jelly, but Mr. Marsh said harshly, "No nonsense, Lucy! There's more to be done."

I took a new grip on myself, and again followed Dr. Langdon's instructions, cleansing the wound and cleansing it yet again before putting in a little tube for drainage and making three or four stitches to draw the edges of the wound together. Then I put on a new pad of dressing and fastened it in place with court plaster.

[310]

Dr. Langdon exhaled a long breath. "Good girl, Lucy. Whether he lives or dies, nobody could have done better."

I stepped back from the bed. The room seemed to be lifting and swaying beneath my feet, and I could not see properly, for my eyes had been focused intently for so long. I heard myself give a silly giggle, and began to speak a random thought which had come into my mind. "Miss Prothero once told me it's called court plaster because ladies of the court used it for sticking patches on their faces . . ."

My knees gave beneath me. I turned to Mr. Marsh, and he caught me as I crumpled. Then all went dark.

*　*　*

I woke to find myself lying on a mattress in one of the upper rooms on the south side of the Mission. I could hear the sound of rifle fire, familiar to me from my days in Peking, and I sat up with a start. Mrs. Fenshaw was at the sandbagged window, peering through a square loop-hole from which a cone of bright sunlight streamed down into the room. I scrambled to my feet and ran to join her. "Are they attacking?"

"Aye. There's a bunch of them coming up the hill." She moved her head a little so that I could look through the loop-hole with her. Some twenty Boxers were running up the slope of the hill from the village, pausing sometimes to fire their rifles. I could see the red sashes and ribbons they wore. Mr. Fenshaw was crouched on a cart against the outer wall, waving a small Union Jack on a short pole.

"Why aren't we firing back?" I cried. "Why is he doing that with the flag? They'll come straight for him—!"

"Hush, child," she said briskly. "Your Mr. Marsh is in charge now, and he's at the next window." She lifted a white handkerchief, and stood ready to wave it through the loop-hole. "He's arranged a surprise for yon poor misguided devils."

The group of Boxers came on, shrieking and making straight for the waving flag. When they were only twenty paces from the wall, Mrs. Fenshaw thrust her arm through the loop-hole and waved the handkerchief. Below, her husband was watching. I saw his arm swing, and an object soared over the wall. It landed amid the Boxers, and there came a loud explosion. Several men went down, and the rest turned tail. As they ran, I heard the steady sound of a rifle being fired from the next window. One of the running men sprawled headlong, then another and another. Of the three, only one picked himself up and crawled on down the slope with one leg trailing.

"What was that?" I whispered.

"A bomb your Mr. Marsh made. Gunpowder and nails and pieces of flint rammed in a cocoa tin with a fuse stuck through the lid. They'll not come at us again today, I'm thinking." She straightened up and patted her tangled, unwashed hair into some sort of order. "As a good Christian woman, I'm much opposed to violence, Lucy. But I'm a wee bit more opposed to letting babies and bairns be butchered, so I'm hoping the good Lord will understand." She looked down to where her husband stood waving a hand before jumping down from the cart and running toward the Mission door. "Stanley there troubles me, though," she said dubiously. "I sometimes wonder if he's not taking more than a smidgen of pleasure in smiting the ungodly."

Mr. Marsh appeared in the doorway, rifle in hand. "We hit them hard that time, ma'am. Ah, Lucy, how are you?"

"Well, but I didn't mean to sleep so long. Is Nick . . . ?"

"Asleep and breathing comfortably. The fever's abating, Dr. Langdon says. Now child, don't cry." He put his arm about me. "You run along and sit with Nick. There won't be another attack for a long time, I fancy. Mrs. Fenshaw, will you take me around the defenses? I think there are some changes we could make to our advantage."

Mrs. Fenshaw's green eyes smiled from her gaunt face.

"I've never been overfond of the military, Mr. Marsh, but I confess it's a great comfort to have you here now. You're a formidable man."

"I've a fair knowledge of my old trade, ma'am. And this is a useful occasion for it."

They went off together, and I made my way to the bedroom. Yu-lan sat watching Nick, her makeshift pike beside her. She smiled a welcome, and we talked in whispers as I felt Nick's forehead and pulse. His brow was still hot and there was a sheen of sweat on his face, but he seemed to be in a deep, natural sleep now. Yu-lan went off, and I sat watching my husband.

If I could have seen into his mind, would I recoil, I wondered? Would I flinch from the hatred and malice which had brought him here in pursuit of Robert Falcon? Would I find that the answer to his strange behavior toward me lay in the darkness of an afflicted reason?

There was a stubble of beard on his chin, and except for the gauntness of his face he looked very much as I had first seen him in Chengfu prison, when he had held my hands, and spoken gently to me, driving away my fear.

Something stirred suddenly inside me, in an awakening so fierce and strong that my thoughts seemed to disintegrate. Tears began to run down my cheeks. Scarcely aware of what I was doing, I knelt beside the bed, took his hand carefully in my own, and pressed my lips to the back of it. My tears were wetting his hand, and I could not understand why I was crying until slowly it came to me that in this moment, despite all anxiety and mystery and doubt, I was filled with a kind of happiness I had not known before. I whispered, "Nick, dear Nick," and simply knelt there, not thinking, just feeling.

I do not know how much later it was when the canvas partition stirred, and Dr. Langdon came in. "Ah now, Lucy child, don't be afraid," he said softly. "That's a very strong and healthy young man, and I'm sure he'll make a good recovery now. Just to wake and find you beside him will be a wonderful tonic. He worships you, Lucy."

I rose from my knees and sat down. "Do you mean those things he said when I first saw him last night, and he didn't know it was really me?"

"Yes. I thought perhaps you'd been too distressed to take them in."

"No, I heard them. But they were just words spoken in delirium. He didn't mean them."

"I've heard him speak of you when he wasn't delirious, Lucy."

"Well . . . Nick's a strange person. You might think he felt a particular way, then suddenly he changes, and you know it wasn't real. I've lived under the same roof with him for weeks, so I know." I went on quickly, because I wanted to change the subject. "I still can't understand how he reached here from England so quickly. He left only eight or nine days before Mr. Marsh and I, and we came by a destroyer, much faster than any ordinary ship could sail."

Dr. Langdon smiled. He looked much less weary and haggard than when I had first seen him, only a few hours ago, and I began to realize that after the terrible blow of Nick being wounded, Mr. Marsh's arrival had put new hope into everybody.

"Nick didn't come by ship," Dr. Langdon said. "He came most of the way by rail."

I stared. "The Trans-Siberian Railway isn't complete yet, surely?"

"No. But it runs right across Russia as far as Sretensk, which is over five thousand miles, and then there are river steamers which connect with the railway line running down to Vladivostok. He came from there on a Russian troopship, by claiming he was a war correspondent for a newspaper, and paying a few bribes. The whole journey took him twenty-one days. He was lucky, of course, but I fancy a young fellow as determined as Nick makes his own luck."

I said, "Chang Li told us that the Englishman who had come to the Mission was called Fal-con. We didn't dream it was Nick."

"It was a precaution, Lucy. He used the name of some fellow he knows, who was out here before."

"But why?"

"Well . . . so far we've been lucky in one respect. Our old friend Huang Kung, the Mandarin of Chengfu, has sent most of his soldiers to help in the attack on Peking. He hasn't troubled much about this little Mission, except to send forty or fifty Boxers to destroy us. But think, Lucy. Suppose he heard that a foreign devil by the name of Sabine was here? We cheated Huang Kung of his victim last year. If he knew Nick was alive, and here in the Mission, he'd scrape together every soldier in the city and send them against us."

A shiver touched me. "Yes, I see that, Dr. Langdon. But how would Huang Kung find out?"

"From the time Nick first came, we knew we might have to send Chang Li to Peking for help. If he'd been caught on the way, he might have babbled Nick's name, or been persuaded to tell. So it was safer for Nick to use a false name from the beginning."

Dr. Langdon took an empty pipe from his pocket, looked at it wistfully, then put it away again. "Have you eaten breakfast yet, Lucy?"

"No, not yet."

"Run along down to the kitchen, then. You'll be swamped by children, of course. They're at breakfast now, and they're longing to see you."

Later that day I was allotted my particular duties by Mr. Marsh. For certain hours I would look after Nick. During other hours of the day and night, I would be on watch at one of the lookout windows. If an attack came, I was to go to the kitchen door with Mr. Marsh's pistol, and guard it as best I could. One problem had troubled the men in the Mission deeply. In an attack it was vital for them to remain at vantage points with their rifles, firing down on the wall and beyond from the upper rooms. But this left only Mrs. Fenshaw and the big girls to deal with Boxers who reached the wall. On the one occasion when this happened they had been ready with the ox-cart, stripped of its canopy and used as a platform which they had wheeled to the danger point at the wall. There, mounted on the cart, they had fought off the Boxers with their pikes.

This had been the most terrible moment of the siege, but with the bombs Mr. Marsh was now making we hoped there would never again be need for hand-to-hand fighting at the wall. This meant that I was unlikely to have to use Mr. Marsh's pistol at the kitchen door, for which I was truly thankful.

All that day Mr. Marsh himself seemed to be here, there, and everywhere, knowing exactly what he wanted to do, and giving his instructions with a brisk confidence which made us feel that we were safe in his charge. He had some of the windows blocked completely with sandbags, and others opened to provide loop-holes which gave a better field of fire. When dusk came, he went over the wall and set up strings the children had made by plaiting strands from an unraveled blanket. Anyone blundering into one of these strings, which were at knee height above the ground, would cause hanging tins to jangle together, and so give warning of any approach by night.

I was in the kitchen when he returned from his sortie. "Hallo, Lucy dear," he said. "How's Nick?"

"Still sleeping well. I'm going to relieve Dr. Langdon now. He's been sitting with Nick for the last couple of hours."

"Let me know when he wakes. I'd like to see him." Mr. Marsh rubbed his chin thoughtfully. "I didn't have enough string to set a trip-line on the north side. I know they never attack there, but it worries me that I don't know why."

"I think it's that portrait of Nick, Mr. Marsh. The one Robert Falcon drew on the wall. They take it as the picture of some foreign-devil demon, and it frightens them. The Boxers are very superstitious."

At that moment Dr. Langdon came into the kitchen, smiling. "He's awake, Lucy. I've told him you're here, and he's asking for you. Hurry along."

Mr. Marsh put a hand on my shoulder and squeezed gently. "You've saved him, Lucy. Give him my love. I'll come up in a minute or two."

The funny lopsided smile was on Nick's lips as I entered the bedroom. "So . . . it really was you last night," he whispered. "I thought I was dreaming again. Foolish little monkey, following me out here."

I went to him, and bent to kiss his cheek. "How are you feeling, Nick?"

"Not too badly."

I sat down and took his hand in mine. He looked at me, then turned his head away. "Don't be too kind to me, Lucy. It only makes things harder."

"Makes what harder, Nick dear?"

"Just . . . everything. Oh Lord, I'm so damn weak, I can't even hold my tongue."

"Why should you, Nick? Please say whatever you want to me."

With an effort he turned his head to look at me again. "Ah, Lucy . . . that would never do." A look of anxiety came into his eyes. "Is my father here? Doc Langdon said he was."

"Yes. We came together."

"I have to talk to him urgently, Lucy. There are things to be done, for when those Boxer madmen attack again."

"Don't worry, Nick. Your father—" I broke off. "Ah, here he is now."

Mr. Marsh came to stand by the bed. "Hallo, Nick. It seems Lucy did a good job of surgery on you."

"Yes . . . Doc Langdon told me. Listen, Father. I got some gunpowder last night, and you have to make some bombs with it. That's your only chance now, or they'll be over the wall. You'll need to compress the powder in tin cans, with bits of iron or stone to make shrapnel. And you'll need some sort of fuse. I haven't worked that out yet—"

"I mixed some powder with a little sand, to make it burn more slowly, then filled a straw and set it in a hole in the tin, Nick. It worked very well. They took heavy casualties in an attack today."

Nick stared from sunken eyes. "What else have you done, Father?" he said at last.

"Rearranged some firing points. Set trip wires. Mined the gate with a small charge." Quietly and without wasting words, Mr. Marsh explained all that he had done, and his reasons for it. As he ended his account, he smiled. "Don't look so surprised, Nick. I've fought in fourteen campaigns, you know."

Nick lay silent for a long minute, then said slowly, "I didn't know that anyone could be a servant and a man at the same time. It seems I've badly misjudged you all my life." His pale lips formed a wry smile. "But one of my few virtues is that I know when I've been a fool. I'm sorry, Father."

Mr. Marsh shook his head. "Don't apologize to me, Nick. I'll never feel shame at being a servant, but I'll always feel it for the way I failed your mother and you. Perhaps it's late to start being friends, but . . . could we try?"

I felt Nick's hand tighten feebly on my own. "We might even find it easy," he said, and tried to smile.

"I'm very glad," Mr. Marsh said simply. "You must rest, Nick. I'll leave you with Lucy now. Don't worry about the Boxers. Before I've finished with them they'll wish they'd never been born." He moved away, brisk and erect as a man half his age.

There was a long silence, and then Nick said, "Tell me about it, Lucy. About you and my father. How you came here, what you've done, everything."

[318]

"I don't want to tire you, Nick dear."

"It won't tire me. Please, Lucy."

And so I told my tale, perhaps not very well, for I kept forgetting the order of events, and had to go back and explain anew. Nick lay with eyes closed, and as I drew to the end of my story I thought he had fallen asleep, but when I stopped speaking he opened his eyes and whispered, "Poor Lucy. If it's not one trouble it's another. Never mind . . . everything will come right for you one day."

His eyes wandered as he spoke the last words, then the lids fell, and his breathing deepened. I sat holding his hand for two hours, until Mrs. Fenshaw came to relieve me. She and Mr. Fenshaw were not on watch-duty that night, and would be sleeping in the other part of the divided bedroom, so if Nick called they would hear him at once.

I did not see him again until the following afternoon, for I was on night duty, and Mr. Marsh insisted that those coming off duty must sleep for at least four hours before starting work again. In the morning the Boxers peppered the Mission with rifle fire from a distance, but this did no harm, and we were all pleased to hear them wasting ammunition.

In the afternoon I took a bowl of thin soup to Nick. With Dr. Langdon's help I managed to prop him up slightly on pillows, and then I fed him with spoonfuls of the warm soup. He took it obediently, rather like a child as he solemnly opened his mouth for the spoon while keeping his eyes on my face. His voice was a little stronger today, and his lips were less pallid.

As I set down the empty bowl I said, "Nick dear, will it tire you if I talk?"

"No." He smiled faintly. "I like listening to you. And I'm much better today."

"I want to ask you something. A favor, Nick. I know why you came here. You said in the note you left that you were going to pay off an old score. But please, please forget your enmity with Robert Falcon. It frightens me to think what might happen if the two of you met out here—"

"Wait, Lucy." Nick was staring at me. "Did you . . . did you think I followed Falcon out here? That I planned to do him some mischief?"

I pressed my fingers to my cheeks. "I knew you meant to stop him getting the emeralds somehow, even if you didn't care about them for yourself. And I was afraid of . . . how it might end."

He began to laugh feebly, then winced with pain, and stopped, but I saw that the devils were dancing in his sunken eyes. "Oh Lucy, is that what you thought? But I didn't care about Falcon and the emeralds. I've not even troubled to look behind that bronze shield yet. He can have them, and be damned to him." He reached out and took my hand. "I came to pay an old score that I owed to Dr. Langdon."

"Dr. Langdon?"

"Yes. Didn't you read the newspaper that morning I left? There was a small paragraph in a dispatch by *The Times* correspondent, on his way to Peking. He wrote that he'd spoken with an American doctor in Chengfu, who said that the troubles would come to a head any day now, and that the massacres would soon begin. The doctor was going to a nearby Mission, to help the people there, but he said that if the American and European governments didn't send relief quickly, it would be too late for foreigners all over North China. They'd be dead."

I felt lightheaded with relief. "You knew it was Dr. Langdon . . . and that's why you came?"

"I had to, Lucy," he said gently. "I owed him my life. I know how slow governments are to act, and I couldn't sit comfortably in England while he and everybody else here were slaughtered. So I came to give a hand."

I found myself laughing and crying at the same time. Clutching his hand I said, "Oh Nick, Nick, I've been such a fool."

He closed his eyes. "I'd never harm Robert Falcon. I know you love him, Lucy."

"Love him?" I caught my breath. "What do you mean, Nick?"

He opened his eyes, and gave a tired smile. "That's the first time you've ever pretended with me, Lucy. Please don't. I know you love him because I saw you with him one night in November, on the valley side, when the bonfires were burning and everywhere was thick with smoke. I saw you in his arms. And you're the Lucy I knew in Chengfu, without an ounce of guile or deceit in her whole body. You wouldn't put your arms around a man and kiss him if you didn't mean it."

My cheeks felt pinched with shock. I said, "Nick, please listen to me, and try to understand. I was alone, and unhappy, and with no friends. Robert began to pay calls on me. He was very patient and good-natured with a strange girl in a strange land. Then the Greshams forbade him to call any more. On the night of the bonfires, he came out of the darkness to where I was standing alone. He didn't speak. He looked at me strangely, and then he took me in his arms and kissed me. It was my first kiss, and from a man who had been very kind to me. Yes, I did kiss him back, and later I wondered if I loved him. When you don't really know what it feels like to be in love, Nick . . . you wonder, you're uncertain. After I moved to Moonrakers he began to court me again, but that was the only time we kissed."

My hands were locked so tightly together that they were trembling. "And that's all, Nick. I'm not ashamed, and I'm not making excuses. I'm just saying that you shouldn't think I love him just because you saw us in that moment on the valley side—" I broke off, startled. "Then it *was* you I saw just afterward—you were there!"

He lay staring at me in perplexity, as if still trying to take in what I had said. After a little while he nodded. "Yes. I'd just come back. I knew from Dr. Langdon that you'd gone to live with the Greshams, and I went straight to High Coppice to find you. The whole family was busy with fireworks in the valley. I went down, and I saw you with Robert." He stirred restlessly. "After that . . . I don't quite know what happened for a few minutes. I remember wandering about in the smoke, but I didn't see you again, Lucy. I don't think I saw anything much, so I didn't know you'd seen me there. It must have been very frightening for you. I'm sorry."

"It doesn't matter now. Go on, Nick."

"Well . . . then I went away. Nobody knew I'd come back from China. I went over to Normandy for a while, with some idea of buying a fishing boat and doing some cross-Channel smuggling." He smiled wryly. "But that sort of thing didn't seem entertaining any more. I just drifted for a while, and then I came back for you."

I wanted to ask why he had returned for me, but another question came suddenly to my mind, and I blurted it out. "Nick, do you know Chislehurst Caves?"

He looked at me blankly. "The caves? Yes, I know of them, but I've never been in them. Robert Falcon knows them well, so Edmund once told me. He obtained permission to explore them a few years ago for some pamphlet he wanted to publish about them. Why do you ask, Lucy?"

"I fell down a slope soon after I saw you that night, and banged my head on a rock. While I was unconscious somebody carried me deep into the caves and left me there. It was only by a miracle that I found my way out. Oh Nick, I—I've sometimes thought it was you. Please forgive me."

His face was white, and I had to restrain him as he tried to sit up. "God Almighty, that was Falcon!" he said savagely.

"No, it can't have been. Why would he do such a thing only a few minutes after kissing me?"

He lay back, angry with himself for his weakness. "Why? Because he's Robert Falcon. I can't explain how his mind works, Lucy. I can only tell you that at times he's capable of anything at all. When he came to you on the valley side, it might have been touch-and-go whether he kissed you or throttled you. And then, when he found you lying unconscious later . . ." Nick shook his head grimly. "When Falcon's in a particular mood, he'll do anything to get what he wants, and feel completely justified. And what matters to him most is Moonrakers. It's an obsession. Maybe he's getting worse, but he was never fully sound of mind, Lucy. Edmund Gresham and I know that, because we were at school with him. I fancy his parents must know it, too. I'd judge Mrs. Falcon to be honest—did she never warn you?"

"She said that she didn't want me to marry Robert, but I thought she meant I wasn't a suitable match."

Nick looked at me. "Does she really strike you as the kind who would care a damn about that?"

"No, I suppose not. Oh Nick, do you think she was worried for *me?*"

"I'm sure of it. Robert can play a part when it suits him, but I've always known he could be dangerous. I don't doubt his parents knew, too."

"But why would he want to . . . to do away with me?"

"Probably because he thought that with you dead, Moonrakers would be safe for a little longer."

"No, Nick. He didn't know I was your wife then, didn't know about the will."

"He certainly knew I'd married you, Lucy, even before he went back home from China. I know he was stunned that day when I arrived at Moonrakers to collect you, but he was only surprised to see me alive, not to learn I was your husband."

I was so startled that my voice sounded high and quavering as I said, "You mean he knew all the time? But how?"

"Simple enough. He came into Chengfu the day you said goodbye to Doc Langdon. You met him on the road that day, remember? If you're making inquiries in a foreign city, the best place to start is with one of your own countrymen who's lived there for many years. So Mr. Tattersall was an obvious choice, and he blabbed to Falcon that he'd married us. I know, because Tattersall spoke of it later to Doc Langdon."

Into my mind flashed a mental picture of those strands of golden hair I had found caught in my cuff button, after I had been attacked in my cabin by an intruder while *Formosa* lay at Hong Kong. So that was Robert Falcon. After talking with Mr. Tattersall in Chengfu he could easily have made the voyage to Hong Kong during the days I had spent at the Tientsin Mission, waiting to begin my journey home. And there he had come aboard secretly to steal my wedding papers and the will, so I would have great difficulty in proving my marriage. But no—I had only believed them to be stolen, for I had found them weeks later in the torn lining of my suitcase.

A new thought came to me. I remembered reading of the way Royalists had hidden or made their escape through the caves in Cromwell's time, and I said, "Nick, do you think there could be a way from Moonrakers to High Coppice through Chislehurst Caves?"

He frowned, his eyes still angry. "I couldn't say. But I know there's a disused door in the cellar of High Coppice which leads into the caves. Edmund told me about it when we were at school together. Do you have some reason to think Falcon used the caves to gain access to High Coppice?"

I told him quickly of the intruder on *Formosa,* and how I had believed my papers to be stolen. "I'm sure that was Robert. But one night at High Coppice I woke up because I heard somebody in my room, and I smelled the acetylene of a dark lantern. Perhaps Robert came into the house by way of the cellar, and put the papers back in the lining of my suitcase to make me think I'd overlooked them. But . . . I don't see *why* he should do so."

Nick lay with half-closed eyes, his brow creased in thought. At last he said, "It would make sense, Lucy, if he'd decided that the safest way to keep Moonrakers was to let you inherit it after all, but to make sure that you became his wife. Was it soon after you found the papers again that he began paying calls on you?"

I nodded, sick at heart to think that all the kindness and affection Robert had shown me during those weeks had been no more than a pretense. For as long as five minutes, Nick and I did not speak, for we were each busy with our own thoughts. I put Robert Falcon out of my mind, and sat remembering the mingled sorrow and happiness I had known during the weeks of living in the little Chelsea house with Nick. I knew now that I loved him, I had felt it come to glorious life within me in that moment when I knelt beside him and kissed his hand as he lay unconscious on the bed. I was sure, too, that what I felt for him now had been there before, sleeping, waiting, held back by doubts and fears, and by the knowledge that he did not want me.

I said, "Nick dear, would you like me to tell you truly what I feel?"

He roused from a brooding reverie, and forced a smile. "About me? Poor Lucy, I've given you a rotten time, haven't I? Yes, say what you want to. It can't be worse than I deserve, and you'll probably be far too easy on me, for you're a soft-hearted girl."

"No, don't close your eyes. Look at me, Nick, and listen. I love you. Oh, I know it's immodest for a girl to say that, but I'm not modest like English girls, I grew up in a different world. And I know I won't be able to hide what I feel, anyway. I'm not very good at it. You've often been unhappy with me since we've been together, but sometimes, when you could forget who I was, you were quite happy, and then everything was so wonderful. You don't have to love me back, Nick. Nobody can help how they feel, and it's not good to pretend. When this is all over you can—"

"Wait, Lucy, wait," he whispered. I saw that he was gazing at me with wondering eyes, and that there was a new film of sweat on his face. "Do you know what you're saying, Lucy?"

[325]

"Yes. Lie still, Nick, and don't worry." I wiped his face with a damp cloth.

"Worry?" He gave a strange little laugh, and flinched with pain for a moment. "It's your turn to listen now, Lucy, while I tell you a story. It's about a man who lived hard and enjoyed it, something of an adventurer, and like most of his kind he was a selfish man with little thought or tolerance for others. He'd known more than a few women, but they were just passing amusements for him. He just did whatever took his fancy, and be damned to everybody."

Nick took my hand and looked at it as if it were something precious. "And then," he said slowly, "there came a day when he was going to die. In a Chinese prison he met a girl, a young girl, different from anybody he'd ever known in his life before. Like Cinderella's slipper, she was made of glass, or crystal, for you could see all the way through her, and you saw nothing weak and nothing bad, only courage and love and unselfishness that took your breath away."

"No, Nick, please! I'm not like that, I'm not—"

"Hush now, and listen. This man married the girl for his own reasons, believing he was to die. But he didn't. A brave and good old doctor saved him. But he was very ill for a long time. In hiding, he lay abed for several weeks, slowly getting back his strength. And he had a lot of time in which to think about this little girl he'd married, to realize how rare she was, and to think about his own life. He fell in love with her, Lucy, very much so. But because he was a clever fool, he knew that he was really falling in love with a dream of his own creation, not a real person. In time he went home, and he found that he was wrong. He saw this girl, and in the moment of seeing her he knew that he'd made a great discovery. He knew at last what it was to love."

Nick touched my fingers to his lips. "But she was in love with another man now, or so he thought, because he saw her in his arms. So he went away rather than spoil her happiness. You see, he wasn't quite so selfish now, because he loved

[326]

her. But he began to worry, for he knew this other man well. Knew that behind whatever mask of friendship he might wear for his own reasons, there was a mind obsessed. So in the end this clever fool became so anxious about the girl he loved, that he decided to return from the dead and claim her as his wife, so that he could take her away from danger."

I started to speak, but Nick lifted a warning finger, smiling. "Truth to tell, he'd stopped being quite so foolish, and was a little more sensible than before, so he realized very clearly that he wasn't good enough for this wonderful girl he happened to have married, not by a thousand miles. He took her to his house in Chelsea, and they lived there together. But they didn't really live together, because he loved her too much and thought it would make her unhappy."

"Oh Nick, dearest Nick, why didn't you tell me? I was so sad that you didn't want me for your wife."

"Sad . . . ?" He closed his eyes for a moment, drew in a shaky breath, then opened them again. "Let me finish, Lucy. This fellow was so bemused that he scarcely knew what he was trying to do. Perhaps he thought that if he kept his wife away from the dangerous man she was in love with, she might forget, might even fall in love with somebody good enough for her. So he gave her every freedom, and kept away from her as much as he could, and tried to make her see that she was a person in her own right, who should be no man's creature in the way so many women are. But sometimes his resolution broke down, and then he'd be really selfish again, and take her out to dine or to the theater, and glory in having her beside him."

Though I made no sound I had begun to cry. Nick lifted his hand and put it gently to my cheek. "And then he'd panic, Lucy, because he knew he was in danger of taking her in his arms and kissing her and pouring out all that he felt for her. So he'd pull himself together, and leave her alone again, because he didn't dare to be with her. He never dreamed, never even began to dream, that she might ever come to love him."

[327]

His hand slid down to my neck. One finger felt beneath the collar of my tunic, found the slender chain and drew it out until the signet ring which hung on it came free. "You still wear it, Lucy?"

"Always, Nick. First I wore it in memory of you, and because I admired and respected you. Later because you were so good to me, even though you left me alone. That night when I came here, just after you'd been wounded, you said such loving words to me, Nick, and they made me happy even though I thought you were just delirious and didn't mean them. Perhaps I've loved you for quite a long time without knowing it. But I know it now."

"Then you must be out of your mind, foolish little monkey. I'm so glad. Never change, Lucy."

"You said that in your letters. The one in Chengfu, and again when you left to come here."

"I meant it with all my heart."

"I'm frightened, Nick. You speak as if I were so special, and I'm not, I know I'm not. I get angry and scared and unreasonable, oh and I tell lies and I've been a thief. You don't know what my page in the Recording Angel's book is like."

The old grin showed on his weary face, and the sparkle of wicked laughter was in his eyes. "That's good. I wouldn't want you too perfect. I loved it when you shouted at me that night when I was drunk. Will you marry me, Lucy Sabine? I mean, shall we be married again properly this time, meaning every word we say?"

"Yes. Yes, please, Nick. I'd like that so much."

"Then you'd better be immodest again, and kiss me. I don't seem able to lift myself."

I stood, bent over him, and rested my mouth on his dry lips. He put his good arm about me and held me. After a few seconds I felt his arm trembling, and gently straightened up. He lay back limply on the pillows, a little breathless, looking up at me with a tenderness I had never thought to see in those dark, wicked eyes. Then the laughter came into them again. "I'm as weak as a kitten, dammit," he said complainingly. "But I'll do better soon, Lucy."

"Everything will be better soon. Sleep now, dearest Nick."

*   *   *

The siege at the Mission continued for another eight days. During that time there were three serious attacks by the Boxers, two of them in one day, and four rather half-hearted ones. Even on the fifth and worst day, when the two big attacks were made, the Boxers were driven back by bombs and rifle fire before they reached the wall, and after this there was a tremendous feeling of optimism among us all, for we felt sure that the worst was over.

Throughout those eight days, except for the brief periods when we were under attack, I was only half aware of our situation, for Nick and I were living in a warm sunlit world of our own. I performed all my duties to the letter, and was careful not to spend time with Nick when I should have been busy elsewhere. For me it was enough to know that in another hour, or four hours, I would be with him again. Enough to know that he loved me.

His wound healed well, and each day he gained a little more strength. It was a joy to see the color returning to his lips and cheeks, to feel the passing of feebleness and growing of strength in him when he held my hand or put his arm about me. We talked of many things, of plans for the future and of small things remembered from the past, and often we laughed together at our memories, for now they were lined with gold for us, even those moments which had been harsh and dangerous at the time. I had never known such happiness, and I think this was true of Nick also.

"I know you loved Moonrakers," he said one day as I was changing the dressing on his chest after washing him, "but I've no wish to turn the Falcons out now, if they can't pay, and it's the last thing you'd want. Besides, we'd have the Greshams for neighbors if we lived there. What a sobering thought!"

I had to pause in my task to laugh, then said, "I did like Moonrakers, but a house isn't important in itself, Nick. Not to me. The people living in it make it what it is."

"That's right." He smiled up at me, the wicked eyes sparkling. "Besides, you have a moonraker of your own now, sweetheart."

"You?"

"Of course. Your idiot husband. Only a half-blind fool who didn't know the moon from a cheese could have failed to see how unhappy I was making you all the time we were in Chelsea. And I thought I was being unselfish for once, leaving you alone."

"I wasn't unhappy all the time, Nick dear. Only when I thought you didn't like me."

"Well, most of the time then. But that's over now, and for better or worse you're a moonraker's bride, Lucy. Where do you want to live?"

"Anywhere with you, Nick. I love our little house in Chelsea."

"Yes, that's fine for now, but it won't be big enough for a family when the time comes. Oh, and you'll need help then. I mean, a few servants." He made a comic grimace of self-mockery. "There go my old ideas, unlamented. Never mind. How many children do you want, Lucy?"

"I don't mind. No, do keep still, Nick, I can't kiss you while I'm doing this, you'll have to wait. Four would be nice."

"I'll make a note of it. Maybe we'll have a house in the country and a place in London, too. Would you like that?"

"It sounds lovely. Will we have enough money?"

"I'll make whatever we need, Lucy. I've a disgusting knack of making money in whatever I do. We could have a farm, perhaps. I'll quit the metal market. Maybe I'll go into Lloyds as a broker. Or if you like we could travel for a while before we settle down."

[330]

"Whatever you say, Nick dear. Now stop talking. Your dressing's done and it's time for kissing."

He smiled up at me and cupped his hand against my neck. "Brazen, immodest girl."

"I'm not really. Only with you."

"I love it. Come here, sweetheart."

On another day Mr. Marsh came into the room while I was with Nick, and dropped a limp black object on the bed. It was a small leather bag, like a scrip purse, almost black with age, and beginning to crack in the folds.

He said, "Since you've been too preoccupied to trouble about it, Lucy, I've just looked myself. That bronze shield in your old room wasn't plastered in place. It was held in by dried mud which had been whitewashed over several times."

Nick picked up the bag and stared from me to his father. "The emeralds? They were there, Father?"

"Look for yourself."

The bag held thirty-six large, uncut stones. In this state they looked like greenish pebbles, but Nick seemed to recognize them for the gems they were. He examined one of them closely, then gave a soft whistle. "By the naked eye, this one looks flawless, and that's rare for emeralds. Ten or fifteen carats at least, and this isn't the largest. There's no small fortune here, Lucy. I wonder where they came from, and how often they've changed hands? From an Arabian prince to an Indian Rajah to a Mongol Khan to a Chinese war lord, and perhaps passing through a dozen other hands between, over the centuries. Never cut or polished. Just a useless fortune, conveniently small enough for a man to carry in his pocket."

Mr. Marsh said, "What will you do with them, Nick?"

"Ask Lucy that. She found them, nobody else. But in my privileged position as her husband, I shall venture to advise that she retains a quarter of their value for herself, for you, for the Mission, and for Dr. Langdon—we never want to think of him scratching around for a few cash again. The other three-quarters to be shared equally between the Greshams and the Falcons."

Mr. Marsh said, "Leave me out, Nick. I have a job to go back to."

Nick grinned. "If that's what you want to do, fine. But as regards the emeralds, I'd advise you to accept whatever your daughter-in-law decides, and without argument. She has a terrible temper if she's crossed. One day I'll tell you how she shouted at me over a little thing like a cup of black coffee."

Mr. Marsh laughed. "Then I'd better surrender at once."

"You're a wise man, Father."

The siege of the Mission did not end dramatically. It simply petered out. One morning a young Chinese woman came walking up the hill, and called to us from beyond the wall. When I went out to speak to her through the stout wooden gates I found it was Liu, the woman whose baby I had delivered on the day that Robert Falcon first came to Tsin Kai-feng. She was astonished to hear my voice.

"Is it truly you, Lu-tsi? We thought you had gone to the land of the foreign devils."

"I came back. Why have the *I Ho Chuan* let you come, Liu?"

"They are no longer here. They went away in the night, Lu-tsi. A message came from Chengfu. The mandarin has been arrested by troops of the Empress. Foreign-devil soldiers have taken Peking, and the Empress has stopped the war. She has ordered all *I Ho Chuan* to disperse, under pain of death."

"Is this true?"

"I swear it by the baby you delivered of my womb, Lu-tsi. We of Tsin Kai-feng hate the *I Ho Chuan,* but we were too afraid to speak against them. Now they have gone, or I could not have come here to speak with you."

"Wait, Liu. I must tell my friends."

I ran back into the Mission to break the wonderful news. The Boxer terror was ended, and we had survived. In my joy

I thought that all troubles and danger were behind me now, and that only happiness remained. But I was a fool. I had forgotten the reason which first brought me back to China.

*　*　*

Next day a party of American soldiers arrived by way of Chengfu. Their orders were to collect all foreign survivors and take them to Tientsin, where they could remain until peace terms had been arranged and it was safe to carry on their work again. Mr. and Mrs. Fenshaw gathered the children together and set off with the soldiers a few hours later, riding in ox-carts which had been commandeered in Chengfu, Dr. Langdon said that Nick should not make such a journey for another week yet, and that he himself would not be going as he intended returning to his practice in Chengfu, now that the Mandarin Huang Kung had been deposed.

"I'm too old a dog to learn new tricks, Lieutenant," he said to the young officer in charge. "After thirty years in Chengfu, I'd rather die there when my time comes than any other place. So you go along, and don't worry about us."

I would not leave Nick, of course, and Mr. Marsh would not leave either of us. Yu-lan remained, because just before the Rising a poor farmer in the village had asked Mrs. Fenshaw if his son could have Yu-lan as a wife. Yu-lan was eager, and as she was at an age when she would have to leave the Mission soon anyway, Mrs. Fenshaw had agreed.

The American lieutenant said that he and his men would be returning in six or seven days, and that he would take us back to Tientsin then.

It seemed strangely quiet in the Mission, with just the five of us left. I made a huge dinner from supplies left us by the soldiers, and we ate our fill that night. Three days later Dr. Langdon left for Chengfu, riding in a mule cart belonging to one of the villagers. Both Nick and I begged him to come home to England with us, but he only smiled and shook his gray head.

"I'm old and tired, but I'm needed here, Lucy. And this is where I want to be. Write to me sometimes. I won't forget you and Nick, ever. He saved us all, you know. And then you came along with Tom Marsh, and carried on where Nick left off. No, I won't forget you, Lucy. After all, I gave you away at your wedding, didn't I? And that reminds me, I still haven't had a kiss from the bride. Come along, now."

The same afternoon, a few hours after Dr. Langdon had left, I went down to the village to find some material for repairing Nick's jacket, which had been badly torn during the exploit which had almost cost him his life. He had insisted on getting dressed today, and I had left him sitting on the edge of the bed, wearing trousers, boots, and shirt. He was still unsteady on his legs, but had walked slowly about the bedroom several times each day for the past three days under Dr. Langdon's eye, and had shown no sign of distress.

I was in the village for half an hour or more, for there were many who wanted me to stop and chat with them. As I climbed the hill to the Mission I saw a horse tethered at the gates. I found that it was lathered, as if it had been ridden hard, and wondered who the rider could be. The door of the Mission stood open, and as I entered my heart gave a great jump and my blood went chill.

Mr. Marsh lay sprawled on the floor, an ugly blue lump above one temple and a trickle of fresh blood running down the side of his face. I knelt over him, fear pounding within me, and found to my relief that he was breathing, but in the same instant new fear brought me to my feet and I ran for the stairs, crying, *"Nick! Nick!"*

As I raced along the passage to the bedroom I heard his voice lifted in a shout. "No, Lucy! Go back! Run!"

I burst into the room and stopped short. Robert Falcon said, "You didn't think she'd run, did you, Nick?"

He had pushed the hanging canvas back a little, and stood

against the wall where the room had been divided. There was a pistol in his hand. He looked much as he had looked at our first meeting, on the day when he had ridden into Tsin Kaifeng, except that he was smiling now, and there was something in his smile and in his eyes which made me feel sick with terror.

"This way, Lucy." He waved the pistol, and I passed in front of him into Nick's part of the bedroom. Nick was sitting on the bed, booted feet resting on the floor, the bulge of the dressing showing beneath his shirt, his face like stone. I ran to him, and he reached out an arm to draw me beside him, never taking his eyes from Robert Falcon, who moved from the wall and stood beyond the foot of the bed with his back to the hanging tarpaulin.

It was only now, dazedly, that I realized I had forgotten Robert Falcon for the past week or more, forgotten that my true reason for coming to China had been to prevent what might happen between him and Nick. And now he was here . . . with a pistol in his hand.

He grinned. "My luck's turned at last, hasn't it? After all these years when nothing went right. Two weeks I've been in Tientsin, fretting and waiting, desperate to get here as soon as the war ended. And then, on my way, I met those soldiers with the Mission people. So I knew you were here, and that Lucy was with you. Dear little Lucy, who found the answer to the riddle but didn't tell me. I thought you'd won again, Sabine, but you haven't. It's my turn at last."

I saw a vein begin to swell in his temple, beneath the golden hair. "My turn, Nick," he repeated. "Give me the emeralds."

Nick slid his free hand under the pillow behind him, and drew out the ancient leather bag. "They're all here." His voice was flat as he held out the bag.

"Throw it. I'll keep my distance." Robert's smile was brilliant and terrible. "Sick or not, you're a shade too quick to take chances with. I learned that long ago, at school. Remember?"

"I remember you venting your hate on Edmund Gresham until I stopped you." Nick threw the bag, and it fell at Robert's feet. "You're welcome, Falcon," he said in the same flat voice. "You were going to get your fair share anyway."

Robert shook his gold-haloed head, still smiling that eerie smile. "Winner takes all, Sabine."

"Then take them and go."

"Leaving you alive? I'd never feel safe, old friend. It's journey's end for you."

"So be it. Let Lucy go. Now."

"Leaving *her* alive to tell the tale? That would never do. And your father, he'll have to go too, if he isn't dead already. I hit him on the head. Didn't want to warn you with a shot." He looked at me, and his face twisted with sudden melancholy. "You betrayed me, Lucy, but I forgive you that. I don't want to kill you, but I have to. You understand, don't you?"

I said, my voice wavering, "No Robert, I don't understand. Please put down the pistol. You're overwrought—"

"Stop that," he snapped furiously. "Stop it! If you don't understand, it's because you're a fool. I should have done away with you in the caves that night, instead of leaving you alive, but I couldn't bring myself to do it. I don't know how you found your way out, but it taught me a lesson. I'm too softhearted. I won't make that kind of mistake again."

I felt that the longer he talked, the more chance there was that this fit of madness might pass, and I said, "Why did you leave me to die in the caves, Robert?"

He stared at me with angry impatience. "What else could I do? I was ready to *marry* you, by God! I'm a Falcon, yet I was ready to marry an orphanage girl, to save Moonrakers. That's why I put the papers back in your case. But then the Greshams forbade me to call on you, so I had to get rid of you, to gain time while the lawyers tried to find a next of kin— your next of kin, since you'd already inherited. For God's sake, can't you see that I couldn't help myself? Isn't it obvious why I left you in the caves? But you escaped. And when you came to live at Moonrakers I could think again of marrying you . . ."

I had no hope that Mr. Marsh might recover and come to our aid. The brutal blow on his head would hold him unconscious for far longer than I could expect to keep Robert talking. I could only pray that some word of mine might pierce the cloud of unreason about his mind. I said, "You were very kind to me, Robert. Didn't you feel anything for me at all?"

He looked irritated. "For you? What does that mean? The only thing I feel for is Moonrakers. Oh, you're pretty enough, and amusing sometimes. I never *wanted* to do away with you. I don't want to now." His eyes glittered suddenly. "But I'm going to settle the score with Sabine. He's a dead man. So you have to go too. Surely any fool can see that!"

The pistol came up to the aim. "You first, Sabine," he said.

I felt Nick's body tense, and knew that he was going to launch himself from the bed in a hopeless attempt to reach Robert before he fired. Suddenly my crippling fear was swamped by a fury I had never known before. I swung my arm, hitting Nick on the brow with my elbow so that he fell back, releasing me, and in the same moment I rushed at Robert Falcon. I could feel my lips drawing back from my teeth, the short hairs at the back of my neck bristling, and without volition my fingers were half curled like claws. *"No!"* I screamed.

I glimpsed the startled look on Robert's face, and then, as I reached him, his free hand moved quickly and his fist looped round to give me such a buffet that I went reeling sideways across the room, hit the wall, and slithered down to lie dazed on the floor.

I heard Robert exclaim, "Don't move, Sabine!" Slowly I lifted my singing head. Nick was sprawled helplessly on the bed. He had fallen on his bad side, and was struggling so hard to push himself upright that the sweat ran down his face. Robert recovered from his moment of surprise, and chuckled. "The tigress protecting her mate," he said. "So you've captured our little Chinese orphan's heart, Nick. How did you do that?"

Keeping my eyes on Robert, I struggled slowly to my hands and knees. "Nothing to say, Nick?" he inquired mockingly. He was smiling again, and a nerve in one cheek was twitching rapidly. "Have you run out of words as well as luck? Then we might as well get this finished with. I'm going to shoot you down like the dog you are. Now . . ."

He aimed carefully. I was still fighting to get to my feet when the shot came, and the sound of it struck into me with a force so terrible that it was as if I had taken the bullet in my own body.

I made a sound, a dreadful, retching sob, and looked to where Nick lay on the bed. He had not moved. His head was still lifted and he was staring toward Robert in unbelief. Incredibly, he seemed unhurt. The bullet must have missed him. I turned my gaze to Robert, a wild appeal on my lips, but I did not speak, for I saw that his hand had fallen to his side, and the pistol was slipping from his limp fingers. He swayed, staring at Nick with astonished blue eyes. Then his legs began to crumple. The light went out of his eyes, leaving them empty, and he fell back against the hanging tarpaulin.

His weight tore it free from the hooks which held it. He hit the floor full-length, the canvas beneath and around him as it fell. Then I saw Yu-lan, only a pace or two from where Robert's head now lay. She was clutching Mr. Marsh's pistol in both hands, beginning to lower it now. A wisp of smoke coiled from the barrel. She dragged her gaze from Robert Falcon and looked at me, her eyes wide, her face more gray than yellow. Her voice was trembling as she spoke. "I had to, Lu-tsi. This one has killed Mr. Marsh. I saw it happen, but he did not see me. Then I ran to get Mr. Marsh's pistol, and I heard you cry out, and when I found it I came up quietly. I heard him say he would kill you. I had to stop him, Lu-tsi."

Now I understood. Robert had been standing with his back against the hanging tarpaulin. Yu-lan had shot him through the canvas before he had time to fire. Hers was the pistol I had heard. From a dry throat I said, "You saved us all, Yu-lan. Don't be afraid. And Mr. Marsh is not dead. His breathing is regular." I turned to Nick as he rose painfully from the bed, his face colorless. "Nick, your wound? I'm sorry if I hurt you—"

He shook his head in impatient reassurance, and dragged a blanket from the bed with his sound arm. My head still pounding from the blow, I moved forward and helped him spread the blanket over Robert Falcon's body. "Poor devil," Nick said bleakly. "His mind was gone. He'd have killed us . . . and thought it right." Turning to Yu-lan, he gently took the pistol from her shaking hands, then said slowly and clearly, "We shall not forget, Yu-lan. As long as we live, you will never be in want."

"Nick . . ." I took his arm. "Please lie down, you look awful."

"I don't wonder." He gripped my hand tightly. "I've never been so scared in my life as when you rushed at him." He braced himself. "I can't lie down yet, Lucy. There's my father to see to . . ." He looked at the blanket-covered form on the floor. "And this. You girls can't manage alone."

"Yes, we can, Nick dear. We've managed a lot of things alone before, and I can bring a man from the village if need be. Don't worry."

He swayed, and I helped him to the bed. "Yes . . . you've managed too much alone." His voice was breathless, but his eyes were angry. "This is the last time. The last time you'll ever have to manage alone. I promise you that, Lucy."

*　*　*

We sailed from Tientsin a month later. By then Mr. Marsh was fully recovered from the concussion he had suffered after Robert Falcon's brutal and unexpected attack on him at the Mission, and Nick was almost himself again. That was a won-

[339]

derful voyage. Nick and I had a cabin with two bunks, but I slept in his arms. It was cramped and hot, but we did not care. To be together, and safe, was all that mattered.

We came home to England after the last leaves had fallen, and renewed our marriage vows to each other in a small church in Chelsea. Edmund Gresham came to the wedding, as did Mr. and Mrs. Falcon, bringing Matthew, who sulked a little when I kissed him, because he was jealous of Nick.

We told the Falcons a lie, for we said that Robert had been with us during the siege at Tsin Kai-feng, and that he had lost his life defending the gates against a Boxer attack. He lay buried now in the English cemetery of Chengfu. I believe Mrs. Falcon knew that our story of his death was untrue, for when she wanted to know more details I became confused and contradicted myself. She looked at me, her beautiful eyes heavy with grief, and said quietly, "Never mind, Lucy. I expect you want to forget. Robert was a strange boy, and we always feared he might . . . well, let's not speak of his defects now. It's kind of you to tell us that he died bravely. That's how we shall remember him."

The fortune from the emeralds we shared as Nick had first suggested in the Mission, and we received a rather stilted letter of thanks from Mr. Gresham. The Falcons were reluctant to take their share, for they had decided to leave Moonrakers now, and move to Cornwall, but I pleaded with them, and they accepted in the end. Nick sent money for Dr. Langdon and the Mission through a bank, and included five hundred pounds of his own money for Yu-lan, which in China would make her rich.

Another guest at our small wedding was Lord Shipley, who demanded of Mr. Marsh to be invited. He adopted a fiercely threatening manner toward Nick. "Make sure you're damn' good to that child, young Sabine, you hear me? Treat her like a queen, or by God I'll have you dropped in the Thames one dark night and marry her myself. She's worth ten of you, you young rip. Ten of you, hey?"

"More likely twenty, sir." The devils danced in Nick's eyes. "And if you were thirty years younger, I'd call you to account for daring to send her to Peking."

"Quite agree. But I couldn't stop her, boy. She was coming to find you anyway. And they damn' well saved the day at Peking, she and Marsh between them, hey? Marsh! More champagne! Oh, sorry man, you're the groom's father today, aren't you? A thousand apologies. I'll help myself."

It seems that when fortune smiles she brooks of no half measures. Throughout my life I had been desperately poor, but now all was changed. And there was more to come, for on a night two months after our wedding a letter came for me by the late post. We had been to the theatre and dined out that evening, so it was not until we returned to our Chelsea home at midnight that we found the letter, which bore the embossed stamp of the War Ministry.

I could scarcely wait to take off my evening cloak before reading the letter, and then I gasped.

Nick said, "What is it, sweetheart?"

"It—it's an official letter from Lord Shipley, and there's a draft on the Treasury for . . ." I gulped. "For a thousand pounds, Nick! He says it's for 'invaluable services rendered to Her Majesty's Armed Forces in bearing the message which sustained the defenders of Peking and thereby prevented their massacre—' oh, there's lots more like that. But then he says your father is being sent a similar sum! Oh Nick, what shall I do with it all?"

He laughed delightedly, caught me up in his arms and held me tightly. "It's a miserable sum. Less than a few salvos from a battleship would cost. Do with it, Lucy? I don't know. Buy yourself a hat. Or perhaps you could have your eyes altered so that they aren't all round and ugly, like foreign-devil eyes."

"Nick, stop teasing, and put me down."

"No. You're much too beautiful. If I put you down, somebody might steal you."

"Well lift me up a little higher, then. Your signet ring's

digging into me." It was set in a thick oval of beautiful jade now, so that I could wear it as a pendant with evening dress, when my shoulders were bare.

He reached down, put an arm under my knees and lifted me to hold me cradled. "Is that better? Good. Turn out the gas as we go." He kissed me, moved across the room, and began to carry me upstairs.

I said, "I'm so pleased about your father, Nick."

"Yes. He could have retired already, with his share of the fortune, but he won't. He'll go on being a servant."

"A good one."

"Oh yes, Lucy. A very good one."

"One to be proud of?"

"Yes, Lucy. And what will you go on being?"

"Me? I'll just go on being your immodest loving wife, please Nick." We were on the landing now. "What about you?"

He pushed open the bedroom door with his foot and carried me in. "That's easy, sweetheart." He kissed me again, very gently. "Just never change, and I'll go on being the luckiest man in the world."